The Maze

The Maze

Charles Wilson Thomas

Library of Congress Control Number:		2020901210
ISBN:	Hardcover	978-1-7960-8266-1
	Softcover	978-1-7960-8265-4
	eBook	978-1-7960-8264-7

Print information available on the last page.

Rev. date: 02/20/2020

To order additional copies of this book, contact:
Xlibris
1-888-795-4274
www.Xlibris.com
Orders@Xlibris.com
808182

CONTENTS

Philosophical View xiii

Introduction xv

Rank 1

Alvin and Debra..2

Terrance 3

Debra Thomas 5

Jean..6

Fort Houston 8

Fortunes of War 10

Preparation...11

Home..13

Newborn...14

Fruit...15

Poetry 17

Epiphany...18

Kidnapped 22

Love 25

Spoken 26

Video 27

Sight...29

Build...30

Decree...31

County Fair 33

Scary Monsters..34

Fear..35

Marijuana 36

Physical Training...39

Trust Issues 40

Planning...41

Care and Respect 42

Lesson 2 43

Set..44

Lesson 3 46

Guns 47

Site 48

Colorado 49

College 51

Eyes...61

Paper Targets..63

Knowing 65

Sense 67

Tests..68

Field Training 69

Stories 70

Surprises...72

Platitudes 74

Hesitations 75

Journe' Por Angel 77

Truths 80

Reflections 81

Fire Team 82

Face-Off..83

Rape...84

Obedience 86

Oaks 88

Situation Report..89

Captain W. Smith 90

Alert...92

Fair 94

Blessed 95

Trainee...97

Ambiance 103

Spiritual Guidance 104

Lessons Learned 105

Seizure 107

A Soldier's Prayer 109

Bombers 111

Commander's Intent 113

Man Down 114

Gains 116

Tactical 118

Winter 120

Destiny 122

Tyranny 124

Mary 126

Mary Terf 128

Alchemy 129

Danger 130

Prepared 132

Colonel 134

Gangland Shootings 141

Lieutenant Colonel D. Carne 142

Silver Hair 144

Thanksgiving 152

Wonder 153

Heritage 154

Christmas 155

Wedding 164

Honeymoon 180

Date 205

Flying 206

Timing 208

Training Days 210

Treasure 238

The Lonesome Blues 239

Bait 241

En Guard 243

Hoods 246

Terror 248

Alcohol, Tobacco, and Firearms 251

CID Convoy 253

ATF Assault 255

House..257

Sarita 259

Le Uhr 261

Compassion..263

ATF 264

Children..266

Poem 267

Rome 269

Witches 270

Growing Love 271

Terminal 272

Fire Starters 274

The Dance 275

Dreams 277

Desire..278

Cribbage 279

Lieutenant A. Carne 280

Passion 281

Picnic 282

Meteors 284

Fiction...285

Mark 286

Eulogy...287

Empathy 288

Team Lead 291

Time 293

The Night 302

Amanda 304

Heart 306

Attack 308

Doctrine...310

The Sea 311

Life..312

Amore' 314

West Point..315

Fictional 316

Maple Lake 317

Christopher 319

Virtuous...320

Lieutenant Stevens...321

Mastery..323

Technical Advisory Service (TAS) 324

Visitors...327

Grounds...329

Thirtieth 331

Johnny 333

Nemesis..335

Captain Stevens..337

Commitment 339

Lt. S. Williams 340

Eighteenth CEB 341

Curiosity 342

Aide de Camp 344

Amore Cai Vrai 345

Nightlife...346

Gifts...348

Ode to Joy..350

Lieutenant Nidden 351

Tactical Planning 352

Capt. Scott Williams..353

Major Stevens 354

Schema Design..355

Michael Gregory 356

Teams 357

Lovers 359

Captain Nidden 360

Generations 362

Caravans 363

Excellence 367

Hit and Run...369

War..372

Prayers...374

Jubilation 375

Lies Believed 376

Major Nidden 377

Lieutenant Colonel Stevens 378

Fleur due Vie...379

Shadows...380

The Mist..382

Forgiveness 383

Eli Brown 384

Review 385

Colonel A. Carne 386

Unison 388

Motivation 389

General A. Carne 390

Deliverance 392

Transit..394

Transmit 396

Enticement...398

Histoire in Vie..399

Judgements...401

Practiced Living 402

Lieutenant B. Carne 404

John Carne...405

Smiths..407

Recon...408

Missed... 410

Peace 411

Treasures 412
Crime Spree 437
Lieutenant D. Smith..438
Loves Beginning..439
Memories 440
Combat Engineering Battalion...441
Pause.. 442
Memorial 443

Philosophical View

Criminals, thugs known to be ick de' mons, abounded in the day. The process is malignant, and the intent is to do harm to God's children and to His plan in whatever way the ick de' mons can. This included bombings, kidnappings, assassinations, murder, riots, terrorism, et cetera.

Those who believed the Word strove to protect the people and the land for God's will, and they strove to do no harm. Their weapons were combat infantry divisions (CID), FBI, DEA, ATF, the local police, et cetera.

Joseph M. Due, October 13, 2016

Introduction

The long haul is only twenty, thirty, or forty years. The long haul at forty years is only 14,600 days of commitment where each soldier might be called upon to take a bullet for God and Country.

How you learn depends on whether you survive the day of battle or whether promotions come your way. The Army has a training manual for just about every skill a soldier needs. Based on time, the unit and special schools will teach the soldier what they need to know.

However, it is always the soldier's responsibility to train and study for themselves to prepare for that day of battle.

The introduction package contains pretty much the same lecture as the introduction briefs to the unit assigned.

The reality of combat if not taken seriously the soldier will probably not survive.

The gym was quiet upon the end of the lecture. Even when dismissed, the soldiers displayed a demeanor that was permeated by sober thinking for quite a while.

Joseph M. Due, November 4, 2016

Rank

The rank structure of the Fifty-Seventh CID is the same military rank you will find in any Army unit. However, the Captains coming in started out in Private, Corporal, Sergeant, or lieutenant positions. As you filled each position, that would be the rank you responded to when soldiers addressed you.

The military uniform for dress was actually civilian clothes because of the hazard of being identified as military while doing your job. The work uniform is issued blue jeans and black T-shirts tucked in and the vest and weapons carrier.

The soldiers thought of the pros and cons of working for the Fifty-Seventh CID and realized they might have to be more sober-minded in their thinking. The Captain's pay was nice, but being called a private when addressed would take some getting used to.

Joseph M. Due, November 4, 2016

Alvin and Debra

Alvin Thomas could see things in Debra Charles—that is what he told his dad. His dad thought it was doubtful and told him so. Alvin asked his dad if he could invite Debra in the house for dinner on Saturday. His dad and his mom agreed.

The great and notable day was upon the Thomas family, and Debra walked over to their house. She saw him sitting on the porch swing and thought about knocking on the door anyway. She thought about it and went to sit next to Alvin. He kissed her on the cheek nicely as she sat. The kiss startled her.

He said he did not mind discussions but did not like arguments in the process. He kicked off the floor and put his arm around her as she thought about what he said. She thought about what people might think of her, and she got embarrassed. The moments passed, and she decided to relax as he then pulled her closer.

The dinner was fried chicken with cream of chicken soup over rice and peas and carrots. They talked about school happenings and Alvin's plans, and some of them were about her. She admitted she argued some but was working on changing that in her life. Alvin's plans for him and her seemed nice enough though.

He walked in the moonlight with her, holding hands.

Joseph M. Due, October 12, 2016

Terrance

It was difficult at best. The little bullies mocked and scoffed sometimes three or four times a day. The more violent ones would gather before the buses and push and shove students around as the students came and went. Woe to those who were caught alone. A beating was preferred to being posted in the mortuary.

Terrance, like all the rest, prayed for relief from those that would distress oneself. Freedom was but a dream some served with their lips. Then it happened—the more violent ones were gone for a day. Even the mockers and scoffers were put out emotionally by arriving at school and finding the reception committees were gone.

Speculation ran wild through the school. A few found bravery to face those that would torment them. The mockers and scoffers brought the news that the violent ones were no longer alive. Some tried to bring back the pushing and shoving, and fights broke out at the bus stop in front of the school.

The parents heard the news and tuned in to the 6:00 p.m. news. A rash of deaths was reported, and it was blamed on violent youth gangs. The peace was noticeable and appreciated by many. Terrance ventured out to see Jean Nielty. She was a young thing compared to his seventeen years of age. He liked her a lot and wanted to tell her. He figured if she hung out still, he would tell her when she was sixteen.

For her part, she liked him well enough. It was a bonus he had a job of sorts at a production center that did wood crafting. He just cleaned the tools and reassembled them for other people's uses, the mockers said. She thought a job was a job. She was taking math and accounting principles, and she got mocked for that.

She wanted him to be more romantic and declare his intentions. She knew he sought her out when he could. Her parents thought he had promise. She wondered if she ought to say something herself.

She noted the diminishment of the mockers and scoffers at school, and now the bullies periodically disappeared. She thanked God for the relief. Everyone now knew what happened to the consistently violent. She thought they deserved what they got though she could not bring herself to be so outspoken and told no one so.

<u>In the spring of love, romance blooms.</u>
He talked to his parents about Jean. They sympathized with his plight and reminded him that sooner or later, he would have to announce his intentions in one way or another. He decided to write her a letter telling her how he felt.

He wanted to say what his heart felt, so he started with his intentions and then described how he felt when she was on his mind. Then he put down all the virtues he saw in her. He then signed it with love. She received the letter before homeroom class started at 0800 hours. She read the letter and sighed. He finally stated his intentions, and they were nice.

Some bullies saw the letter and took it from her. She told him in the hallway she liked the letter but someone stole it. She asked for another. The next day, the snickers and laughter started. By midday, they were talking about it in front of him.

Then the challenges came, and he answered the accusations the best he could. She sympathized but told him she did not know what to do. So he minded his temper and did his best. The next day, he dreaded. He knew he had to give her the next letter. Arriving at school, he thought the absence of those that were getting violent was nice, and she kissed and hugged him nicely.

<u>Joseph M. Due,</u> September 27, 2016

Debra Thomas

It was another great and notable day in the Thomas household. Their son was going to be married. Roger and Pamela Thomas were getting their eight children together when they realized the to-be-married son was nowhere in sight. They searched all the rooms and found he put two chairs together and fell asleep in the dining room.

She looked at her son and realized he was not presentable yet. She also realized he was just plain tired from the overtime he did on the Anderson farm picking peas. So Roger gently woke his son and reminded him it was his wedding day and they might be a little late.

Debra kept looking out her window for the Thomas family station wagon. They were half an hour late for the meet and greet Alvin was supposed to be doing while she got ready. Her mom told her that her anxiety would ruin the makeup if she did not calm down.

The seconds ticked by, and they heard a tumult of noise at the front door. Debra got up, and her mother told her to sit down; she would check to see if it was Alvin. When she heard it was Alvin, she visibly relaxed, and her mother put her back on schedule.

Joseph M. Due, October 11, 2016

Jean

Her wedding would be in the city gardens she planned. She would wear white, and he olive green. The bridesmaid would wear a nice yellow, sunny and bright. She loved the preaching at the First Baptist Church, and the elder pastor would preside. He would kiss her after the veil was removed, and everyone would get a glimpse of their love.

She just had to tell Terrance what she desired. He promised marriage, but she had not seen him bring up the subject—and she was now seventeen. He was working full-time production and cleaning tools on the weekend. She thought of the perfect wedding for her, and like the perfect letter she had from him, she wanted to see them married.

She decided to talk to her mom. She told her daughter there are times a woman has to state her desires and see where it leads. Jean thought about his letter and decided to write him one. She started with intentions and talked about commitment and how she loved him. She then started over as she panicked.

She did not mention work or children in her first attempt. Working through dinner, she finally finished and showed her mom. Her Mom said, "You might get a man's opinion. You could ask your dad to read the letter." Her dad said, "As much as I know Terrance, I am sure it is a fine contract you are presenting him with."

She put it on the table next to the swing and waited for Terrance to show up at 7:00 p.m. He saw the letter, coming up the porch. She handed it to him and visibly winced. He read the letter and asked if this was a proffer or an ultimatum. She said, "It's a deal." He said it was acceptable to him. She relaxed and tried to change the subject, and he said no. She looked at him as if he were a strange creature.

He said the deal did not include setting up the marriage or date. "Let's talk," he said to her. She said, "To whom?" He said, "My mom and yours." She asked when. He said, "I like July fifteenth this summer." She said "Deal." He said "Deal" and kissed her.

Joseph M. Due, September 29, 2016

Fort Houston

The day was nice and warm. The cavalry unit was doing demonstrations of historical processes, then a battle would be demonstrated. All the local families were there, and the place had a festive air. The Smiths were avid fans of the military, and their son Dennis liked to watch the horses and see the demonstrations.

The Scott family brought their daughters, and Dennis had a passing interest in Tammy. Once in a while, when Dennis remembered, they would walk around together. His preoccupation was how things fit together and, once in a while, would forget anyone was around.

Dennis's father asked him if he would like the military as a history. He said no; he was not interested in the military. Then Dennis's dad asked him what he would like to do. He said he liked putting production tools together, and when he gets married, that is what he would like to do.

Tammy, a little irritated, said she did not know how to put two people together, so how was he going to get married? Dennis blushed because he realized he had not been paying attention to Tammy though he liked her well. He told her sorry and then asked her if she was hungry. She said yes, and he determined to figure out marriage also.

After the live show, Dennis asked his mother what would be a nice thing to do for Tammy. She thought about it for a while and thought about how close to school the Scott family was. She suggested if he wanted to walk with Tammy he escort her to school. Maybe he could bring her a regard gift once in a while.

Fleur due vie's require water.

This practice continued for Dennis through his years.

Joseph M. Due, September 29, 2016

Fortunes of War

Dennis and Tammy were sitting on a swing on her mother's porch, talking about the weather, when Tammy asked him what he was thinking. Dennis said he was thinking about a movie called *The Fortunes of War*. He told her that he was trying to tell her he was looking for their fortunes in marriage and the arguing they were doing was getting to much.

He told Tammy he would like to learn to discuss issues and do less arguing. She thought about some of the comments she made to him and realized she was being difficult. She apologized and said she was sorry and she would learn to discuss issues instead of being ready to fight about them.

He kissed her on the lips and said "Deal." She kissed him back and said "Deal." Her dad coughed, and they both grew red in the face. He said, "Now that you two have reached a peace de accord, it is time for dinner."

The brave say what the timid think.

Joseph M. Due, October 6, 2016

Preparation

Jean prayed about Terrance's future, his job, his house, and the children she wanted to have. She thought about his long-term prospects and wanted him to do well. Then she decided that she would try to help him out, and she prayed for ideas that would help her do so.

She talked to her mom about what she could do to help Terrance out. Her mom asked her what she would like to do for herself. Would she like to work at home or have her own job? She said she would like to work at home.

Her mom said that she needed to learn more about things like cooking, canning, sewing, cleaning, laundry, grocery, and clothing purchasing and how to manage on a small budget as well as how to save for larger purchases.

Then her mom said to Jean that helping out at home would teach her the things she needed to know. She also said, "We need to talk about how determinant will affects the timing of having babies." Jean grew red in the face, and her mom laughed nicely and said it is a simple idea and is easy to learn.

So they talked about it for a while, and Jean made the evening meal and then prepared to meet Terrance because he wanted to go bowling.

He picked her up at 1800 hours and asked her what she had been doing in the day. She grew red in the face again and recounted her day. He said he appreciated her and her mother for helping them prepare for marriage. He said he could set aside 20 percent of his income with a little budgeting on the date side if she did not mind hanging out with him and his family.

She said "Deal." He said "Deal" as they pulled into the bowling alley parking lot. Hand in hand, they walked toward their future.

Joseph M. Due, October 6, 2016

Home

Eighty hours of tool production, moving time, and painting. That was just the beginning for Terrance Carne. His wife, who was handling two children and his administrative calls as well as the accompanying records, was also pushing eighty hours. Tired and stressed was he, and he had to admit Jean was almost as stressed as he was. He knew for God's blessing he needed to keep his cool.

His wife's nerves were frayed, and tired she was. She had to switch phones midweek. The children were tired and wanted the normal attention given, but they were holding up well. A week from now, life would be back to normal, and he would be able to relax a little.

Today, however, he was looking for three hours of sleep if he could get it. Hopefully, no one called in for a contract bid and there were no calls for equipment repairs. He thought about his wife, Jean, and his children, Nancy and Edward Carne. He prayed for them, and he prayed for rest.

Joseph M. Due, October 6, 2016

Newborn

The baby moved his hands and struggled to see them. Jean knew as she watched her baby. Her husband, Terrance, came into the nursery and asked her what is up. She told him Joseph was already trying to coordinate his hands with his eyes.

Terrance said, "You want to call him Joseph?" She said, "If you do not mind." He looked at the child as he hugged his wife. He said, "He looks like a Joseph to me." She smiled and hugged him back.

The colors above looked a little blurry to Joseph, so he returned to trying out his hands. Soon, he tired and fell asleep.

The day moves into the afternoon, and Terrance went out on a call. She heard a soft cry and looked at her watch. She realized that it was time to feed little Joseph. She smiled and turned on the radio. A little news would not hurt, and she liked the country music that was played.

Joseph M. Due, October 6, 2016

Fruit

The bitter vine was collecting again in the Houston area. The FBI had been looking at associations for six months when the formation of groups with intentions in kidnapping started to seriously form and organize. The connections and vans this group started in earnest to collect with the intent of making a huge splash in the papers.

They wanted to terrorize the citizenry and mass execute the children and have it aired live. The yearbooks were the keys that triggered the inquiry and then the investigation began when transit houses were set up and windowless vans became a commodity on the resale market for vehicles.

The ages they were looking for were from eight to ten. The children were easy to find and easy to track down and vulnerable to assault or suggestion. The crime spree the criminals imagined demanded a response from police investigations and the FBI. Then the Fifty-Seventh CID was tasked for a hundred agents.

Fort Houston was tasked to send a hundred Sergeants to Majors to the Fifty-Seventh to augment and back up the CID unit. The van purchases through the DMV and the list of yearbook purchasers compared to known netted associations gave the FBI the framework of the criminal network setup.

The next call-up was for walk-throughs at odd hours and drive-bys of known or suspected sites. This was to identify more associations through visits and was accomplished through license plate identification and composite sketches. The second set of barracks accommodations was filled up as teams 4 through 6 augmented the city-wide searches.

Three months into CID monitoring, the evidence for intent was proven at the Fifty-Seventh as well as the FBI, which had their own monitoring posts. The FBI was looking for the list of names to be kidnapped, the planning material, and operational date of the criminal enterprise.

The FBI's plan was simply to ensure there was no room for the criminals to talk themselves out of prison time.

Joseph M. Due, October 8, 2016

Poetry

Nom de jure, Donald thought. The day was just about right, and the feeling of normalcy encompassed him. He thought of his dad helping him learn basic tools and types of production. He thought of Uncle William teaching him the business. Then his mind wandered to his physical training and the military arts Uncle Joseph was teaching.

He realized all this teaching was not normal for some. He gave thanks to God for a beautiful life and then changed his focus to his mom. She also taught many things about taking care of people, especially him. He thought he would do something nice for her. Then he gave thanks to God for her.

Arising from his rest, he went into the kitchen and hugged her as she was mixing cookie dough. She asked him what the hug was for, and he told her he loved her very much for taking care of him. He then asked if she needed anything done. She asked him if he could peel the potatoes for the pot roast. "Done," he said.

He talked to his dad about his appreciation, and his dad told him that true, kind words mean a lot. Maybe he could write poetry about how he felt. He decided he would try.

Joseph M. Due, October 3, 2016

Epiphany

His epiphany began in the year of our Lord when he was two. A bright, quiet child, he realized that there were other people in life with needs other than him. He repented of his self-absorption and endeavored to see what he could do to help others get their needs met. He volunteered to help anybody around him and was a quick study.

Terrance Carne took it upon him to train his son Joseph on how to put things from Legos to desks together and showed him how his tools needed at times assembling just like many other things. Like picnics and dinners, assembly was required. The growth was phenomenal to the dad and mom. Joseph took to building things naturally and with great zeal. Finding contentment in putting things together enabled him to be a very content child who was willing to learn.

Kindergarten was a golden age for Joseph. Terrance and Jean prepared their children well to know the studies and to be kind and help others. Joseph's brothers and sisters had shown him the way or he got to practice on them in his days before kindergarten.

Practiced living is what Terrance called it as Joseph had to learn to adjust fire in new situations he was not familiar with. Some children wanted to still play on their own, some wanted to practice and pick things up on their own, and others still got downright hostile.

Jean would elicit from her children the day's events she knew about so they could practice memory and communication skills. The challenges got easier for all as the days of school went by, and Joseph began remembering his brother's and sister's stories.

Then he started to know things as he started to realize the importance of what was going on at the school, and some of the children began looking to him to explain the latest happenings. Some grew jealous as the days passed, and the pushing and bullying got worse for Joseph and his newfound friends. The teachers protected the students by interdicting the bullies as soon as intent was formed and some even got expelled.

When Joseph saw that some of the bullies got expelled, he took heart and redoubled his efforts to be of help to those who wanted help. He got many a fine star on his report card for his endeavors.

The kindergarten years were one of discovery for Joseph. His parents challenged his commitment to help others, and he grew a little wise in his years. His popularity was growing amongst the children of his age group and parents like the Carne's babysitting because little Joseph was such a good friend to their children.

One of the families even asked that William Smith be also trained because William shared the passion of Joseph in putting things together. The families became close friends. During these years, the miracle children came to the attention of governance, and they paid attention to the family group synergies for possible uses.

First grade came around, and both knew how to use basic tools to fix things and were glad to ply their skills wherever they were.

There was not much they did not learn. But Terrance only allowed the two boys to clean the basic components, and they also learned how to repack them under supervision. Those that saw the two boys were amazed they were so talented.

By third grade, they were saving their pay given for their help in Terrance's business. Governance then asked Terrance if he would learn to help in other ways being that both boys were so apt to serve and were bright and healthy growing children. He got the production contract for Fort Houston and the surrounding City.

Their improved posterity came to the notice of enemies of the state, and little Joseph was kidnapped in his tenth year. Joseph was used for criminal experiments in genetic manipulation with part of his hair turning silver on the right side of his forehead. He would be permanently marked for the rest of his days.

Because of Joseph's kidnapping, Terrance took a month with family for a visit to Sixth Army Advanced Infantry Training School as a technical consultant and returned with a mandate and the federal contract for Tool and Dye maintenance for the Houston area.

Some at school thought it cool that Joseph's hair turned silver and became admirers as well as friends. Some mocked him, so his dad asked his friends if he could be trained to defend himself. Instructors from Fort Houston did special duty to train both Joseph and William. Because of their friendship, he was also at risk. The resulting training helped both boys through several fights and led to their interest in hand-to-hand combat and knife fighting. AIT was on their horizon.

At seventeen, both boys joined Terrance's operations and command and received their AIT and then went off to College. Both boys took Production Management as a degree program out of a school in Los Angeles. Most of the class schedules were the same so they could take notes and study together.

Off time they spent on the beach learning how to swim in the ocean and how to surf. The ancillary training and insight into the criminal mind was studied with interest since both boys knew their education, though cash-free, was not free of obligations, with both to receive a Captain's commission formally when they were finished with school.

William met a nice young lady named Theresa Sullivan who said she could live with a combat soldier even in Texas. He explained Joseph's abduction and trauma and the idea behind urban assault. She was still determined to make William hers. Joseph dated Juanita La Tanya. She was determined that if Joseph was to get anywhere, he would have to relocate to Tijuana, California. Other dates were of a similar nature, and soon, the dates tapered off.

In the final semester of College, when Theresa knew William would graduate, she married him in a chapel in the student union. Her parents and brothers and sisters were in attendance at the wedding to wish them well. They spent their honeymoon finishing up their studies for finals. She saw her parents again for graduation.

Homecoming was a week of festivities for Joseph and William with his new bride. Then they had to reorientate to platoon life and switch to night work in the family's business. They were introduced to the corporate aspect of Smith Carne Industries and their brand-new two-year-old building. It was built for a thirteen-team rotating team structure with three teams up at a time. The alternate command post was a rebuilt old wood supply depot and sales area.

They were tasked to help build the command structure without changing the façade except the owner's sign. The schema was already put together by the parents, and the building materials were already ordered for the fall. There was plenty of time to study the schema and buildings. Their first priority was business OJT and platoon duties.

Working alongside the platoon members, they quickly figured out how things work together. In short order, they were sent out as team leads and picked up that portion of their studies as well.

By the fall, they were firmly in charge of their units and were building the alternate command structure. The construction took some learning in the form assembly stage, and all had a good time ensuring that the commander's intent was met in structure design. The years passed by, and both took more important positions in the Firm. William wanted his dad's job when he retired because he wanted the day job for him and his growing family. Joseph took the IDS interdiction job and helped out on the contracts with his teams.

Joseph M. Due, October 10, 2016

Kidnapped

The grief welled up, and Jean Carne started to cry. Terrance Carne decided to help her to the back of the church and out the door. The assembly watched in sympathy knowing, as friends, the pain of her loss. The preacher asked the members to pray for the family that so loved little Joseph.

Robert nodded to Dave, a member of the fighting Fifty-Seventh. Robert would lead for a while because the Fifty-Seventh Combat Infantry Division had suffered the loss of the leadership and their families recently. They needed focus and direction as well as the Carne family.

Robert walked up to Jean and Terrance, and they looked at him. Robert was a young man of twenty, knowing the prime of his life. What did he know? Yet he spoke of knowing their pain. The Carnes asked him if they could help him. He said he might be able to help them yet.

He knew of a few friends that were willing to help. The Carne family would just have to meet them though. Then they would have to bare their pain during more interviews so that the investigators Robert knew could help them. Jean and Terrance agreed and went to get their children out of Sunday school.

They followed Robert to a nice Southern-looking house in the suburbs of Houston. Robert told them to wait, and he went in to talk to his boss. The man at the door looked capable enough. A brief time later, cars started to arrive, and groups of men got out and formed up by the door next to the Carnes. This scared them a little.

Robert came back, and they were escorted into the living room through the kitchen. Two of the men were right behind them, and it scared them again. The rules were explained to Jean and Terrance. They would all be interviewed five feet apart together so they would feel safer. Investigations would compile the data and worked to see that Joseph was returned.

Some more men came into the living room from the kitchen and they were given seats as the investigators prepared. The review of Joseph's life took two hours, and then all the men disappeared. Disorientated, Jean started to cry, and the lady of the house took her into the kitchen while Terrance and the three children were fed sandwiches and milk.

Terrance worried about his wife but was told women talk to each other. Lilly would take good care of her. It was revealed that she did not trust some of the children Joseph knew. She then listed four that she thought was bad company. Robert, watching, called his friends and gave them the names of the children.

The records of each family were found and pulled, and the investigative teams went to work on the case while recon worked out ways to silently watch the suspect families. The process revealed a darker side to their associations, so they looked to see who gave the directions and took the lead.

The Carne family was told to stand by the phone come what may, and Terrance was to be escorted whenever he went to work. This would be until Joseph was returned and the criminals brought to justice. This made Jean fearful, and she asked why. Robert told her the kidnappers might try for another child.

The Smith family came over, and Jean greeted Thomas and Julie and beckoned them inside. They were over to console her and see how she and Terrance were getting along. She told them some people took an interest in their case and were seeking to help find Joseph. They asked questions, but she said it was secret and their new friends did not want to get into trouble.

The days passed, and Terrance consoled her anew. They prayed mightily that Joseph would be returned unharmed. The recon teams assembled. They were running out of leads. They had to procure the cell phones of the suspects so they could see who else they were talking to. They entered all four dwellings and retrieved three cell phones.

The phone numbers, names of the owners, and their addresses were looked up, and the names ran through CID investigations for their records. They came up with five possible people, and they put recon onto monitoring them. Team 1 noticed an extra-large group of people at one of the houses. They seemed to be a large family of medical practitioners.

CID knew the suspect himself had no medical qualifications, so they sent team 2 into the area to look over the house and put in audio and video surveillance. Three days later, they got a video of a young child blindfolded and bound being moved from one bedroom to the next.

That night, the interdiction teams went in and rescued Joseph and executed all the perpetrators.

Joseph M. Due, September 29, 2016

Love

"'The power of love sustains and bolsters the mortal soul.' Ze reason(s) por vie es excellent por vie por Angels et le hommes et ick de' mons. Reason(s) por vie es amore," Joseph said this to all who would listen, and hopefully, they would adopt this truth as a sustaining truth in their lives.

When the body, spirit, and soul are weak, the power of love sustains one in the worst midnight hour one can imagine. Joseph knew this from the time he was kidnapped. Recovering from that kidnapping, Joseph meditated on the truth of God's sustaining love and the love his parents had for him.

Surviving and healing both took a lot of love, and he took the time to know it and the time to reciprocate that love as well. God did not call him home because he had a purpose for Joseph to be there at that time in Houston.

The time was usefully spent as he recovered whether people thought he just sat there or not. He was looking for God's purpose for his life.

Joseph M. Due, October 20, 2016

Spoken

The hour cometh and all men draweth nigh for the Word speaketh anew. The Son speaks of the way, the truth, and the life. The people endeavored to understand the application(s) in their own individual lives. The people of Smith Carne Industry were no different to other believers in this regard.

Commitment and diligence are words that the Army knows well. They have given themselves to the word in dedication to master the art of war. Terrance was learning the meaning of commitment and diligence when he sought to do more of the work the Lord would have him do.

So Terrance and Dennis received a commission and a contract from the Army. Their duty was to build the Fifty-Seventh CID and Smith Carne Industry through the generations. Terrance and Jean and Dennis and his wife had a lot of work to do.

Their mentors, Robert and Samuel, were called almost daily for insight into building a corporate family life for their families. They needed to set a finer table and learn to teach their families how to safeguard and defend themselves.

The different things like taking time out for advance infantry training and college were demanding in the sense of time management. They began a new journe' in vie.

Joseph M. Due, October 13, 2016

Video

The firing teams were going through their unit issue for training when the call came from the command post. Brief time was in half an hour. The lieutenant thought about letting them fire but decided to signal the firearms instructor to cease fire. He then told his team to go to the armory and reequip. Assembly was at the tables.

The briefing was on gun running again. They were to recon the site and put the warehouse under audio/video monitoring. Suspects were armed and dangerous, and if seen, they might be fired upon. The sobering effect was nice, the Lieutenant noticed. The load out was already prepared, and they would hit their departure point at 0220 hours.

The warehouse was an older one with the lights off the building and none in the back of the parking lot. Recon had to have good vision to see through the lights. The journey was borne in reflection and meditation. Climbing in the lights would be dangerous, and the fire teams being less capable in the face of the lights, they knew they needed a few prayers.

The departure point on the south side of the warehouse was under another light two hundred feet away from the building. The southern exposure might even give the enemy a firm count of numbers. The entire team had received rifles from the armory while practicing their skills on the firing range.

He lined them up on both sides of the building knowing he was not actually going to attack. The Sergeants took the equipment and climbed the poles hoping mass fire would work in emergency. The time slowly crept by as they awaited the audio/video to come on line. Forty-five minutes later, the command post told the team audio/video was up and running as best it could.

The Lieutenant ordered the Sergeants back to the departure point. As they came off the poles, worry grew anew that their tired movements would attract attention. As they departed the mission point, he then said by the numbers to retreat in order.

The command post had known about the light problem, and one of their technicians had put up a second screen where the light was removed to a given degree and the picture rebuilt in almost real time. They waited for the troops to return, and they monitored the signal to see if anyone had actually noted their presence.

Joseph M. Due, October 8, 2016

Sight

In the morning, the bluebirds sang in the trees. The deer walked in the meadows, and life's energy was growing. The brewing coffee and the cooking eggs reminded one of God's love given to mankind.

The foulness and blight of some of the houses because of the sins of the people marred the landscape, and those that investigated saw it in the dawn for the most part.

Joseph saw it through fears and trepidations in the tenth year of his life as he struggled to live despite the horrors wrought by those who would be called ick de' mons. In his recovery period, God revealed to Joseph the beauty of the morning when, in patience, he would sit on the porch and await the arrival of the day.

The tentative first steps were important all the way through Joseph's life. He learned to work towards life and realized at times it did not come free. The sacrifice of the guards he noted as he greeted the dawn and he found in life what he would like to do.

He told his dad and mom despite his infirmities what he would like to do in life. They called Robert to see what could be done to prepare for the day. Robert said instructors under special circumstances for the well-being of the unit could be provided.

Joseph M. Due, October 3, 2016

Build

"Si vouse plait, monsieur, si vouse plait!" The consideration of discussion begins at times with such words. Dennis normally did not insist on his way, but he knew a little bit about construction and what would last under a high-use environment and what would not.

The Army Corps of Engineers that advised Dennis and Terrance frustrated him at times. He wanted a building that would not need new construction done every thirty to fifty years. He also wanted it built with the potential for upgrade to true Division size in case of need.

Terrance and Robert were on his side, which he admitted made the designing of the construct that much easier. For example, the Army Corps wanted six stairways with elevator access. He wanted four for security and building integrity.

The schema and schematic were worked out and ready for construction if approved because of Dennis Smith and his great endeavor. The next step was to bid the land it would take to build the building. He looked at the most expensive piece of land downtown he could find and made sure the funding would, if approved, cover any eventuality.

Joseph M. Due, October 16, 2016

Decree

The lists on the President's desk was from the FBI, ATF, DEA, CID, OSS, and Secret Service. The compendium depressed him as he slowly worked through the lists to get an idea of how much crime was going on in the States.

President Moses Anderson needed a break. The chief of staff recommended a staff proposal for the Fifty-Seventh CID that Robert proposed. He thought about the newly commissioned young man he met last year. He said, "As long as there is some good news in it." The Chief of Staff said, "There is hope in the report." He went on to say, "That is the best I can do today," as he handed him the recommendation.

The proposal talked about Dennis Smith and Terrance William, who had been given a federal production contract and why. It recorded the history of the kidnapping and the families requesting that they be allowed to help out in some way. It also annotated Robert asking them if they would take care of the Fifty-Seventh CID and its mission. Furthermore, it talked about their agreeing to the idea if approved and the list of resources they would need along with a breakdown of the proposed new Fifty-Seventh CID in manpower authorizations that needed the President's approval.

The President called the Army Chief of Staff and the head of the Secret Service in to talk about the idea, and they explained the pros and cons of the idea but urged the President to sign off on the proposal and the new law enforcement construct to be built.

The President liked the idea, and it would not hurt the yearly budgets at all. So he told the Chief of Staff to ensure it was on line as soon as possible. He also told him Robert needed a commendation. "Make Robert's commendation a nice one." He signed the authorizations, praying that it would be a signal for a new day.

Joseph M. Due, October 16, 2016

County Fair

Sprecken ze langage? The culture of the Fifty-Seventh CID needed to be kept secret for the family's sake. The members of the Fifty-Seventh had to speak the language of the parent culture, if not the language of the streets.

The county fair was coming around again. Terrance thought to help out, so he called the county and asked how much security augmentation the county fair people would appreciate. So he ordered 1,600 security T-shirts with County Fair on the front and Security on the back for his people.

Then he asked his people to provide two to three days' security on six-hour shifts to be signed their local by county fair personnel. The days were nice and warm, and fifty two-man teams relieved the fair personnel from hiring whomever might like the job.

They in turn got family admission as long as they wore their T-shirts. That confused troublemakers to no end to see another two hundred to three hundred families wandering around with security escort. The days went by, and he talked to those who volunteered daily at noon to reassure them this also was part of their mission endeavor.

The time his troops spent talking to those that attended the fair, the more it helped their language skills so they learned to speak even better.

The T-shirts were free for service rendered.

Joseph M. Due, October 13, 2016

Scary Monsters

The bus stop on Main Street was two blocks from Smith Carne Industry, and sometimes, the soldiers would use the transit system for when they were in between cars or needed a second car. One of the ladies got leered at, and she asked Investigations if the suspect was violent or not.

The description came with a nickname, so they looked it up for her. And they had a picture that she confirmed. He was talking to some of the others about defending his neighborhood, and she mentioned that to the investigators.

She identified three more juveniles as being a part of the group that scared her a little. The investigators said they would look into it, but so far, the persons in question scared people a little and skipped school.

The days went by, and the file on the juveniles in question grew. When they took over an abandoned house and posted their colors, they upgraded the case file and put two more investigators on the case and got permission from the commander for video and audio surveillance.

The activities of what was now considered a youth gang went to drug dealing, petty theft, and purchase of illegal firearms. The case was put in order and presented at the staff meeting, and Terrance asked for all the materials to be copied and for the copies sent to his desk.

He then called police investigations and asked if they would be interested in prosecuting a burgeoning youth group. The Captain said he would send a detective right over.

Joseph M. Due, October 14, 2016

34

Fear

The afternoon weather was just about right. The studies in school and the afternoon practices lent to a long-term feeling of being tired. He worried in moments like these when the conditions mirrored the hour of his abduction. The medical abuse and the chronic beatings then still became fresh in his mind.

Joseph looked around. The guard was still following him, and as a soldier un Imperium, he was alert and was paying attention. His panic subsided a little, and he felt better making his way home once again.

William's family would be there for dinner and then a trip to the gym for practice. Last week, it was his family that did the driving. The dinner was going to be hamburger, macaroni, and a tomato sauce made out of flowers as well as steamed broccoli and cauliflower. He liked the family dining hour, with each person sharing a story of the day especially when guests were present.

His dad once told him that when guests showed that much love, their really family discovered. Joseph asked his dad if that would make William a cousin or brother. His dad said that would make him a brother—there was no doubt.

Arriving home, he knew he had to get changed. His brother and his family would be over.

Joseph M. Due, October 13, 2016

Marijuana

At 1000 hours, the stand to command was given to the six teams. Their goal was a large combine of farms and barns south of the city limits by two miles. The adjacent roads would be occupied by the Sheriff's department at 0230 hours and 0300 hours east- and west-facing roads respectively.

The helicopter detachment from Fort Houston would drop off a blocking team north and south of the farm respectively. They would low crawl to two hundred feet and then move in with the attacking forces from the roads. The Sheriff's department would then close the road to the farm at two hundred feet to provide oversight with shotguns and rifles on the northwest side of the farm.

Two teams each would approach from the east and the west and be the primary fire support and attack teams. The process was designed to get the troops within a hundred feet before they came under fire and for the fire teams to eliminate resistance at two hundred feet.

First in would be the four fire teams on the north and south side respectively. If it was clear, they could low crawl as close as 150 feet.

The two two-man teams would low crawl to the edge of the outer buildings,

The approach of the fire teams on the west side would be by echelon from the road and would be protected by fire teams in overwatch position. Then the attack teams would low crawl to the front of each building in teams of two.

As oversight and weapon suppression is achieved, each building would be taken by the assigned east-west teams. The order for the rifle teams were after 0300 hours weapons released and before that if they or their teams are in danger fire at will.

The teams loaded up at 0130 hours and were in standby mode at the vans. Departure time for departure points was 0145 hours. Helicopter teams would load out starting at 0045 hours and circle the city until it was time to head for their departure points.

The timing was mainly contingent on the helicopters dropping the two teams off at their departure points at 0230 hours. Second was CID timing to site and third was the Sheriff's department timing for blocking roads and driveways. Then there was time to target low crawling and site location for the fire teams.

The movement had not been directly practiced before, and the Major knew as he sat with the sheriff's department cars that there might be some training mistakes made. She would have to remember them for ancillary training days.

When the helicopters were down, Maj. Janice Daniels received a sitrep from the east teams saying they were ready as well. She called the command post and informed Col. Terrance Carne that three teams had left their departure points at 0230 hours and the last team was standing by.

The waiting built tension as they hoped they would not be detected so soon. Everyone prayed the suspects would be deaf and blind until 0300 hours when the attack should commence.

The troops in the vans did not know whether a little low crawling or a lot was a good thing. They debated amongst themselves as to which position was the better one.

When 0300 hours came around, people were still working in the outbuildings. Major Daniels said, "Commence firing to the teams on one"—her mark. She quietly counted down as the vans moved up the road. The confusion as to who was firing at the suspects was paramount in the suspect's minds.

They saw the troops out front move into position, but they learned they were not the ones firing at the guards.

When the sheriff's cars blocked the drive, the sheriff announced over the loudspeaker that all those who wished to surrender should lie facedown with their hands laced over their head and neck. The vans were in place, and the fire teams rushed the ditch and then set up.

The return fire was emphatic at first, and the rifle teams hunted down the shooters quite efficiently. When the return fire died down a little, the assault teams were ordered to move in as quickly as they could.

Racing across the open lawn, they ran for the corners of the buildings so the rifle teams could keep firing at those that returned fire. Two by two, the assault teams assembled around the doors. Grenades were readied, and the doors were kicked in.

Joseph M. Due, October 14, 2016

Physical Training

For lunch, the meal was baked chicken breast au jus with potatoes and green beans. The boys and girls were introduced to unarmed combat by Sergeant Breen and Lieutenant Snow. The classes were all-day demonstrations, lectures, and practice on the mats. Judo, Boxing, and wrestling forms were taught to the children, and they were sorted out by twos so they had a partner to practice with.

Even though William was two years younger, he insisted that Joseph be his sparring partner. The days brought many children and many different levels of experience. The children were taught that if they paid attention to a problem on the horizon of their life, they could better mentally prepare for physical conflict.

The teachers taught that intent to commit to physical conflict resolution was to keep the person from harming you or anyone else. The bumps and bruises did not get so noticeable until the children advanced into open combat, and it was the use of boxing or fistfighting that produced the most noticeable bruises.

The teachers rated each person's skill level every three months by using the qualification standard in the army OJT manual for unarmed combat. Some of the parents worried about their children's attitudes and or safety while they were being taught to fight. The parents were invited to sit in the stands and watch if they wanted to.

Joseph M. Due, October 5, 2016

Trust Issues

All people know the past can come back to shame or embarrass. Ick de' mons use the past that we have not prepared an adequate answer for to tear down or destroy what they will. Lies, gossip, rumors, and even the truth are tools used by ick de' mons to bring hurt to people.

Terrance learned well as de facto head of the families that people go through grief and then others use that as a knife to hurt them again. He had no respect for those that did such things.

The day's greetings are to be blessings when possible, not insinuations that tear down families. He looked at the sitreps he received daily from the different offices. He thought even some of them in times past were little more than insinuations. He questioned what he could to see the truth daily as clearly as possible.

The questions were what to investigate, what to question, and what to act upon as well as what to leave alone. The morning briefs awaited after his breakfast, and today, he needed extra virtue to gird up his loins and return to the field of battle.

He thanked God that Jean knew him so well and trust was built on that knowing.

Joseph M. Due, October 17, 2016

Planning

To Joseph, the planning department had many purposes, like tactical planning to training exercises to ensuring food is purchased for when the post training ground is used to mobilization schedules, et cetera.

The long-term planning included yearly schedules to area schemas to new building spaces when approved. It was used in plotting out investigations and tracking manpower utilization. The great thing about planning was they had a tentative plan for every contingency imagined.

The officers, when they were not planning, could be cross-trained and could provide ancillary internal support to the unit before they had to ask for outside help.

The planning section could be also used for long-term upgrades to unit training and, when used properly, add to a unit's combat capability.

The stillness of the night in the evening heat gave the brave considerations to temper their activities and rest unto twilight, where the will of men is proven in the day. The movement seen was hard to perceive, and the cowardly did learn to fear the night.

Wrought iron from rock to the heat of conflict did give the brave a backbone of steel.

As the night passed away, the soldiers moved forward in time to face their destiny. The conflict visited upon them in their day was responded to by a judgement in the early morning hours. Peace they would have as they spoke together as one, and death did fall upon the ungodly.

Joseph M. Due, October 14, 2016

Care and Respect

The promises of the day are commitments that should be kept. When you keep enough promises, then good people give you the benefit of the doubt. This was an underlying requiem of Generals that the troops believed in. Trust is given when trust is proved.

For a soldier to follow wholeheartedly, they must have a basic trust of their commanders. To become a General, one must already have the trust of many, including the President. Promises also include family considerations like care and respect.

The avant-garde prima facie faced challenges every day, but the care and respect given should ensure the troops obey the lawful orders given by command.

Joseph thought about the Army and Family like Smith Carne Industry. The inculcation of family values are cornerstones in the foundation of both organizations. He thought of his dad doing God's will in his life. He knew he would follow in his dad's footsteps and someday lead the Fifty-Seventh CID. What he was looking for was the key to love.

He put away his training manual on command and leadership and went and asked his mom. She probably knew if anyone did. She told him care was knowing a friend and wanting to help while respecting the destiny and choices of that friend.

He talked to William about the ideas he had encountered, and they discussed how to grow care and respect one straightened thought at a time.

Joseph M. Due, October 21, 2016

Lesson 2

The lessons continued for Joseph, William, and the other students who attended the new community self-defense lessons. They also learned infantry skills like sitreps and recon. This allowed, with practice, the children to explain themselves better when they got in trouble. The skills they learned boosted their confidence that they could deal with life's conditions.

The mockers and scoffers, on realizing this, initially changed from verbally harassing the children to trying to upset their balance by bumping into them. The strength and balance learned in the taught forms of unarmed combat coupled with early detection led to a terrible surprise for the violent.

This did not discourage some of the violent, who would hit from behind. These type of violent offenders were expelled, and those that bullied others up front were met face up and fought off.

The days grew quiet as the teacher reasserted discipline in the school and the children gained the confidence to take care of themselves.

Joseph M. Due, October 6, 2016

Set

When the time arrived and the day dawned, the celebration anticipated would be enjoined. The birthday anticipated was his fourteenth birthday. Joseph was told that Terrance and Jean would allow him to have a gun set—a pistol and a rifle.

He wanted to protect himself and his friends. The requiem in vie then would be to learn the handgun and rifle as part of him being able to do so.

William wanted a set as well and had to petition his mom and dad with extreme fervor. The two families got together on a Saturday, and William and Joseph presented their need for protection and better equipment.

Both would be allowed to train on them, but they would otherwise be locked up until both turned sixteen years old. The compromise left both put out a little bit, but by the end of the day, they both accepted the necessity fully.

Thursday rolled around, and William and Joseph knew the families would gather at the outdoor shooting range on Fort Houston. The morning rolled by, and Joseph wanted to carry the entire family to the car though he waited patiently as he could for the picnic supplies to be packed.

The Sergeant watched him open the packages for safety, and a Sergeant watched William open his packages as well. The Sergeants then demonstrated loading and unloading the weapons safely. When

Joseph and William had done so three times, one of the Sergeants had them set the weapons down facing down range.

Then the Lieutenant called out the orders for using the firing range, and the Sergeants both demonstrated what Joseph and William should do. They then returned to the safety line, and the Lieutenant called out next and then took them through range safety while doing live fire with the Sergeants just a foot away.

The moments of firing went by as a dream for Joseph and William. Then the Sergeants secured their weaponry to take them back to the Fifty-Seventh CID's armory.

Joseph M. Due, October 10, 2016

Lesson 3

Journe por vie por Josef es ver gut. Joseph was learning that even in trauma, there were lessons in life to be learned. He learned God loves him. He learned God saved him. He learned He protected him in times of distress. He learned the kingdom was larger than he imagined and he learned God's children needed help from time to time.

He also learned amongst many other lessons that the kingdom is built on peace. His search in meditations and prayer garnered and reaped many a fine fruit. His parents were also teaching him it was important to set a good dinner table for one's friends.

Sometimes, his parents would take him and his brothers and sisters fishing, and they had to get used to his quieter nature. The negotiations proceeded apace.

Joseph M. Due, October 6, 2016

Guns

The firing started slowly and then increased as the grenade bounced across the floor. The denizens of darkness, as they called themselves, saw the grenade, and fear grew in their throats. It was too late to do anything but panic. The criminals saw the second one float in and then the first one exploded, killing three and wounding two.

The charge through the door came a second after the second grenade exploded and further wounded the injured. They both lived to complain about it to the judge they saw. The clearing of the house came first as the assault teams came through.

The cries of the injured they noted but ignored, just ensuring they could not reach a weapon until the building was clear. The assault team ordered the two survivors to turn over on their backs, and they were handcuffed in the front.

When the lieutenant came through, he commented on what a filthy house the gunrunners had. Then he called in the ATF and then the medics through the command post.

The ATF arrived in fifteen minutes, and then the medics were given permission to enter the crime scene five minutes later to pick up the two that were arrested.

The ATF carted off three pallets of handguns stolen from one of the arms manufacturing companies and looked for shipping documents and sales slips as well as papers or notes on points of contact.

Joseph M. Due, October 15, 2016

Site

The sighting on the rifle seemed a little off, so he asked permission to move to two hundred feet. He sighted the rifle for two hundred feet and pulled the trigger. He did so three times to check his spread pattern. The corporal checked the target and told Joseph he was off half an inch left and top of the target. His next three shots covered the paper target perfectly.

He then asked if he could move back to four hundred feet. When he was in position, the firing officer gave him permission to fire. He then did another three-round spread pattern. Then he laid down the rifle and stood up. The corporal said the spread pattern was right on the target. He smiled and certified the rifle had been sighted and adjusted and was now ready for use.

The officer in charge asked him if he wanted to go to sniper school. He said no; his unit needed him. He remembered to thank the Captain as he finished the ten rifles assigned to him. He knew the value of sites that were dialed in properly. He was seeing Diane Edward after for dinner. Then he was going to drop by William's house.

He was doing recon exercises during the day and knew he would be tired. AIT was coming up in two weeks, and each was preparing in his own way. They both needed night land navigation, so Thursday and Friday would be long days.

Joseph M. Due, October 3, 2016

Colorado

William talked to his parents, Dennis and Tammy, about being Joseph's friend, battle buddy, and partner. He used all his persuasive skills to move mountains of thought about what a young man can and cannot do. He believed he should be allowed to go to advance infantry training with Joseph so he could continue to help him out and back him up.

They thought about it for a week and then prayed and then had discussions with Terrance and Jean about what would happen if William did or did not go. They then called Colorado and talked to the Battalion Commander, and they faxed him a list of their deliberations.

The Commander of the school asked for a waiver from his command, who forwarded the request to Army command and then the President. He was suitably impressed by the young man's determination to help Joseph and the Army that he approved it forthwith.

It was a cold morning, and they were up before the sun. The enemy troops were 1,500 feet somewhere to the west, and recon was out looking for them. The topography was mixed in the hill country of Colorado. The enemy had a variety of environments to approach from, and they were watching diligently.

They could see William approach after a while, and they waited for him to arrive.

He said they captured Bob and they knew we were here. He gave his situation report (sitrep), and my friends waited for me to do something brilliant. I outlined the attack positions by order of two. Then I talked about approach and when, as William did, we should all low crawl.

Timing was set for when we should low crawl, when we cross the departure point, and when we should attack.

We left the rally point knowing they would reconfigure their posture if we were sighted. The approach took us some time, and I knew we were already watched. The hour passed by as we made our approach. I knew my commander would critique pace of movement.

The enemy was sighted, and we all wished ourselves silent as we deployed. The departure points were reached, and we had five minutes to sit. The seconds ticked by as the tension and stress built. At one minute, I told William to follow my lead.

I looked at those dug in and waited. The opportunity arose, and I fired at one, shifted fire, and shot the second and managed to hit the third, diving into the dirt. William followed suit and got two in the dirt. The team opened up and charged, and we got four more before the whistle sounded.

The trainers critiqued time for the Order of March and target identification. Then they talked about how even those areas would improve with training. Then they had us report to the next training area. William had trees in his area to deal with. This was a harder proposition because sight in the exercise area was only clear at fifty to one hundred feet.

This time, when the exercise was called, we had ten up to two. The critique was light, and we mounted up early on the trucks to return to post.

The days passed by with practice and critique the daily norm. The night exercises were more of a challenge because of land navigation and enemy positions being that much more difficult to see. We ended up with higher casualty rates but learned to use and trust our senses.

Graduation day came, and we took names and numbers. We wanted to remember our newfound friends.

Joseph M. Due, October 10, 2016

College

For Joseph and William, it began with the pickup at the airport. Their host had sent a serious-minded warrior to usher them to their destination. He had special ops written all over him. They learned they needed to be more sober-minded.

The scenery passed by as Brian introduced them to the protocols of the Eighty-Third CID. They started to pay attention as they realized the importance of what he was saying. Their orientation started with a briefing about paying respect to one's leaders in a civilian environment.

The next brief was a short one about not revealing anything to anyone about the unit, its mission or purpose. They were to say nothing in effect. Joseph asked, "How are we to know who is who if we do not ask?" They pulled into the drive as Joseph asked. As Brian exited the car, he said, "You will find out."

"Lieutenants," a person behind them said. They turned around and saw a guard standing before them. He did not salute. William said yes. He said, "Yes, sir." They both repeated, "Yes, sir." He said, "Your training continues, and if you do not mind, follow me." The day was nice, and Joseph and William were young and mentally adjusting.

"The dormitories are off the main campus," Austin said, and he added, "This place is a private dwelling that hosts the Eighty-Third CID. The last part is classified. The meeting rooms you two are going to are off the main corridor down the second hallway."

The walk across the lawn was fairly long. Joseph estimated the building to be about 350 to 400 feet in length. William commented on the art decor. He said it was very nice-looking. Austin opened the second set of double doors and said, "Of course, the art decor is very nice."

They entered and walked a few feet and realized Austin had not followed them in. They looked around for another guide and talked about the idea. Joseph said, "The meeting rooms are off the second corridor. I presume we have to find it." William agreed, and they counted the hallways and then William said, "I will take left. You take the right-hand doors."

They looked in each room until they came to a room where everyone waiting looked like them. That is, except the troop sitting behind an empty desk. Joseph introduced them and asked if this is where they were to report to. The person said sir. Joseph and William then said sir.

He said yes and "You may take a seat." They looked at what looked like boys and girls around them and realized there was a mantle of silence from the rest of the recruits. They both decided it might be wise to be silent also.

The left side door opened, and a young lady walked out and took a left at the door and disappeared. Then the next one was called. This took place about every ten minutes for both doors until it was Joseph's turn. He said he would see William when he got back.

William's turn came a minute later to enter the right side door. When it was their turn to exit, they obeyed orders to report to the bus without talking to anyone. Joseph waved to William as he boarded the bus. They could now talk to others again.

They reviewed their papers on the way into town to validate their experiences. William and Joseph's duty postings were the same. They would stay battle buddies, and college orientation was up next.

The city of Los Angeles could be seen clearly now, and it looked nice. The school could not be seen even though they knew it was two miles off Main Street. The vista was quickly gone, and they did not know the route well. They were assured bus 1 would drop them off right next to the gatehouse, so one of the things they needed to find was the closest stop to their dorm.

They thought about their luggage and realized it would be delivered soon. The campus was large for a school, and the dorms were many as they passed them by. There was a large building off to their left and up a block. It was one of the largest buildings in the area. It contained the College Amphitheatre, where they would receive their introduction to college life.

The bus drove around the front and dropped them off. They had half an hour to find their seat, so they looked at the map of the building they had and went to locate the student union to their right. The student union was on the first floor and was as large in the front as the Eighty-Third CID.

They looked around at all the offices off the far wall and saw in the distance, over the huge crowd, the bookstore. They then went for their orientation briefing.

The hour passed by as they were shown picture maps of the main buildings. The next subject was the welcome speech by one of the deans. They noted the theatre was packed with first year students. These were the students that did not know their way around.

Classroom requirements and job schedules were discussed next and then the academic grading and standard for attendance. Joseph and William noticed there were many nice-looking girls in the crowd. They both wondered if they would date a tool worker.

The question-and-answer session did not produce too many questioners; the students were probably a little scared of the crowd. Fifteen minutes after the end of the briefings, they were still in their seats as people slowly filtered out. They realized this was probably normal for the school.

The working day was passing, so they went to the back left of the student union in housekeeping to get their keys to their dorm rooms. The line for housekeeping was long, but they knew they had to wait.

The search for the right dorm took a half an hour, and by 1830 hours, they were looking for their rooms. As they inspected their rooms, they had noticed their luggage on the bed. They conferred and decided to find the dining room. William said he was sure he knew where it was.

The morrow brought an awakening of mind and body.

Joseph was a little stiff like William was. They decided at 0700 hours they would find the dining room again and, hopefully, admissions by 0900 hours. Setting out, they decided to carry the campus map, but they would try not to use it.

Arriving with only a mishap or two, they got in the extra-long line. William said it was part of the culture. Joseph said hot plates were part of the culture too. They knew they had to go to the bookstore after admissions anyway.

Looking at their class schedules, they looked at the map and marked out Monday's route so they would be prepared. They decided to get extra maps for Tuesday because the schedule was different.

They decided to buy a small pot set and a two-burner hot plate and find the nearest grocery store. This took most of the afternoon. They stocked up on rice and spaghetti.

At 1700 hours, they decided to stand at the dining facility again. On the way back, they picked up the necessary toasters and coffeepots. The walk back was easier as they had traveled the route several times. They met a few of the students on their floor and introduced themselves.

The meets and greets as more people came by lasted until 2200 hours. Then he realized he needed his sleep, so Joseph put out the sleeping sign provided.

At 0900 hours, William knocked on Joseph's door and said, "We need to follow route 1 to get used to taking the bus." They stopped at the local mini-mart and picked up some change and a few snacks for the day. Then they rode the bus twice to familiarize themselves with the bus stops.

That afternoon, they walked the routes they would take to get to their classes. They noted the places for sodas and the atriums for temporary shelter in the rain. Then they explored the Student Center and looked at the signs on the doors to figure out what services they provided, and they spent time guessing when they might need them.

Sunday services were full from the people from out of town and out of state. The preacher prayed for their souls and for good study habits. The sermon was on the judges of the land and the preparation that it took to become good judges.

William admitted that it was not like he was used to back home. Joseph said he wondered about how effective the sermon was in teaching the need for good study habits. They had met a few more people during the morning, but he had to call home. William returned to the privacy of his own room to also call his parents.

The preparation of the day required commitment. Joseph took the time to go through the forms he learned from the time he was twelve. The whole process took two hours, and he was glad he remembered to take the time. He told William, and he said he should do them also.

Joseph told him he would make up some rice pilaf and hamburgers when he got done. Joseph studied the readings, and he kept his door open so William could come by when he was done. Then he set up the burners on the counter next to the coffeepot and spent the time meditating about the pathway each was taking in their lives.

William brought over a book on tool production and care and started reading aloud the book while Joseph cooked. One of the ideas of tool production and care was enablement of the people by making in production products that would provide ease in their day.

Looking at items made by tool production in hospice, one could see that without tool production, there would be less capable and comfortable hospitals, especially regarding tools used in forms and fabrications.

The care of tools extends the capability of fabrication so that mass production can make products that are more affordable. Joseph asked him if he thought that would be in the subject material for the first class. He recommended phrasing the ideas as questions and writing them down on three-by-five-inch cards with the answers on the back for their studies.

Joseph gave him some three-by-five-inch cards his dad gave him for that idea. William took some rice pilaf in a bowl they bought and thought about the idea of figuring out the instructor's tests early. He asked Joseph if that was cheating. He said, "No, the notes from the classes come from the instruction. We can actually do the cards."

William thought about the idea and said he could help write the notes but Joseph had to take notes and produce cards as well. He said

"Deal." William said "Deal." He then read for half an hour and then said he would go write the cards up. Joseph pulled another pack of three-by-five-inch cards out of his backpack and said he would do the same.

As William stepped out into the hallway, he turned to say something about repetition of work producing the cards, and he walked right into Theresa, knocking her clothes out of her arms. He bent to grab the clothes as they fell and hit her in the head. She pushed him away and started to rub her head. He looked at her and said, "Ma'am, are you all right?"

She told him she was not. She was mighty upset he was not looking where he was going. He apologized and returned to picking up her clothes. As he did, she refolded them as best as she could. Then she told him, "Do not call me ma'am. My name is Theresa Sullivan. If you have to call me anything, you can call me Missus Sullivan."

He turned red and said, "I would rather call you Theresa." She looked at him and said, "You are almost not old enough." He turned red again and asked, "What am I not old enough for?" She turned red and said, "You are almost not old enough to be here. But if you would like to study or something, I am right across the hall in room 208."

Knowing his mother worried for him, he called her and told her all about Theresa Sullivan that he knew. He wondered what her degree program was. He then looked at the three-by-five-inch cards and sighed. He better get to work since he started the studying. He thought about four years of cards and sighed again.

Joseph's alarm sounded, and he dressed for the day and packed his book bag. He then went next door to see if William was ready. They walked to breakfast before class as Joseph wondered about whether the dining room would be packed.

Theresa came out and said to William, "You going to breakfast?" He said, "Yes, you want to come along?" Joseph let her walk next to William. He thought that was pretty quick. He asked Theresa what her degree program was and what kind of classes she was taking.

The dining room was half-full, for which Joseph was grateful. They bought their breakfasts and found an open table. Then she asked about where they came from and what degree programs they were doing. William then talked to her for a half hour over the intent and purpose of college for both of them.

Joseph was glad he did not mention the intent and purpose of the Eighty-Third. She might not understand.

She did find out he was on a military scholarship and his degree was Tool Production and Care. That did not seem to faze her much. She did ask him to describe what he did for Smith Carne Industry. Joseph knew he now had something to talk to his mom about.

The first bell rang, and they were sitting in the same row. The instructor said he was originally from Ohio and the class was the Introduction to tool production. As the day went by, they collected many a fine set of notes from tool production to Military Science 101.

When their last class was done, they went over to the student union. Joseph went to the student union to do more shopping and William to meet up with Theresa and then do some shopping of his own.

During the study hours, they all sat in Joseph's room and talked about their lectures to refresh their minds. Then they broke up to tend to personal considerations they needed to tend to at 2100 hours.

Joseph told his dad everything was starting out fine, especially their studies. He asked about William's new friend and asked him to look out for William's best interest.

Week 3 arrived, and at 0500 hours on Saturday, he woke William up to tend to military matters. Debts owed. They thought of their experience to date and tried to figure out what would be in the day. Assembly was the first thing they did at 0800 hours, and the commander greeted them and then the XO talked about the team training rotation.

At 0900 hours, they were issued a lock, locker, and exercise clothes for their needs. Then they had a few minutes before 1000 hours, when unit equipment with black duffel bags were issued. At 1100 hours, they were to be briefed as to the team training exercise for the afternoon. At lunchtime, they were served MREs.

They did recon of the obstacles set up in the backyard. Some of the other students had also decided to take a look at what was in the backyard. They talked for a little while, and then they saw the teams forming up. Returning to their units, they lined up at the end of each team.

Team 1 approached the side of the lawn on the left side of the fake trees. The instructor raised his voice so the boys could hear him. They would approach the fake house on the Lieutenant's command in teams of two from the front and side. The Lieutenant gave the signal for attention and one minute.

He then counted down the time. The teams pretended stealth, counted enemies, and did further recon by exaggeration. Then the squad leads were given orders to attack, and the teams pretended to attack the house using assigned equipment. Then the boys were up.

The day went by, and the boys practiced approaching all sides of the house several times. *Stressed* and *tired* were two good words to describe their state of being as they rode the bus back into town. They quietly talked about the training exercise, admitting what they were slow at doing.

The teams did not mind. The teams looked like they took it for granted that they would be as they were, just learning to work with the teams.

Situational awareness of the enemy was embarrassing. The instructors told them they always needed to know and not guess. The response maneuvers seemed to be good, and their recon of the target site at entry point was praised.

They missed the overview of the city as they talked about the day's endeavor, trying to recount every step so they could navigate the building better. They thought about the organizational structure of the Eighty-Third and still could not see it in the layout that they knew.

The next day was filled by classes and conversation on interpretive analysis and how to use information from situational awareness. Even the experienced teammates said they learned something new here and there. They also said the reminders were important for life and limb.

That night, Joseph decided to call home and rest. Theresa took William out to a diner, and they talked the night away about the necessity of the military in the modern age. They knocked on his door at 2100 hours and said they would like a group study until about 2230 hours.

The morning saw all three tired and moving slow. They would not have extra time before the first class. Theresa's first course was in bookkeeping and her degree in Accounting and Finance. She wanted to set up budgets for businesses.

William was tempted to see her between classes, but Joseph asked him where she would wait for him just in case she could see him. He reminded William that she had things to tend to as well.

By the afternoon, they were feeling better. Joseph went to the student union to sit for a while as William and Theresa walked home. He met another Accounting major, Susan Flir. They talked for an hour, and she agreed to visit him in his dorm.

Mealtime for the three was spaghetti. William made it while Joseph lounged. Theresa came over and brought the cheese and bread as they talked about the events of the day and what their studies were. Susan came over a half hour later and took post on the bed while they conversed about world events.

The alone time was new for Joseph, and Susan thought it was endearing. He had desire and passion but little skill. As he took her shirt and bra off, he tried to remove both at the same time. She let her desire carry him and her through the night.

At 0300 hours, she showered with him and realized she wanted more. After dressing at 0500 hours, she kissed him passionately, and their desire flared again. They showered each other and got dressed. She then decided to stay and talk for a while.

The dawn came, and she kissed him at the door and said it was nice but she did not agree with his politics. William was walking up the hall, and he thought of Theresa. She seemed to agree mostly with what he believed. He hoped she would come around.

Susan said hi to William and walked past William down the hallway and out of sight, probably for good. Joseph had stepped into the hallway to see her go. He said hi to William and said he was up. Joseph left the door open, and William entered and took a seat.

They talked of Susan for a while, and then Theresa came across the hall and sat in William's lap. Joseph noted they were even getting along better. Then they decided to go to Perkins for breakfast with Theresa driving.

The city was larger than Houston by far, and they worried about their first class. The ordering was quick and Perkins was half-empty. They paid the waitress what they owed and were only a couple minutes late.

Joseph said to William after the first class he was feeling better already and said he appreciated the thought but outings should be saved for after class.

Saturday morning came, and Theresa wanted to go to the beach for the morning and shop on the way back. They rented a surfboard on the way to the beach and took it into the waves. Theresa coached them on how to mount the surfboard, how to balance, and how to dismount. Practice took several hours until they got the hang of surfing. William liked it well enough, but Joseph decided to get a car and a surfboard.

All three talked about the idea on the way back. She thought sharing a board would be fun. She agreed to pay a third of the cost of a surfboard, and she would help pick it out. She said Joseph and William needed a car, and they might go half each.

The grocery shopping went well. All three got carts even though they knew they would share some of the food. They shopped the canned aisles first for long-term use. Then they calculated refrigerator space plus supper.

Dinner was chicken noodle soup and crackers with a really nice salad. The afternoon studies were on philosophies and management practices. The debate was superfluous but entertaining. Theresa kissed William right there and told him he was a nice debater. Joseph had papers to do, he said, which was true.

Theresa and William went over to her room to study.

Joseph M. Due, September 27, 2016

Eyes

The look at visual sight starts with a knowing of the optics one does have. A simple set of tests that are open books will do. Range capability is the first test. Second is the understanding of what you can properly define in the range of the distance you can see.

The third is memory retention in the use of the eye. The fourth is the thinking skill you apply to the use of your eyes. The fifth used by the Army is situation reports or sitreps. The more you practice all these, the better you can use your eyes.

Recon demands good use of the eyes for many reasons. The first need in Recon for good eyes is target identification. The second is enemy fortifications that need to be identified to neutralize or bypass. The third is navigation to and from targets with minimum exposure to being discovered by enemy forces.

The overnight camping expeditions and the use of Recon throughout helps a person assimilate in one thought process the sum of the individual skills a soldier needs to learn to survive on any battlefield. The skills looked at here are not the sum of skills necessary for combat or other required tasks the Army has for its troops.

The new Lieutenants had fifteen minutes to assimilate the data before the eye exams would be given. Joseph and William remembered their lessons through AIT and prayed they would do well. They did not realize how important normal body functions were to survival on a modern battlefield.

Dennis and Terrance said to them when they were at home that if they were sober-minded and determined, they would pass the courses. The two went to the gym with not a few trepidations. The process in the gym, because of all the students, took up the next hour. Getting an evaluation, they also got advice from the Sergeants and Officers on what to concentrate on as skills needed to utilize their eyes the best they could.

Joseph M. Due, October 16, 2016

Paper Targets

The instructor, Captain Brown, preached range safety for quite a while. Lieutenant Smith and Lieutenant Carne paid attention as best they could with the range fifteen feet away and it being a very nice day. Carefully the soldiers lined up at their station and unslung their rifles.

The command was given, and they could take their station. Lying prone, they pulled out the first clip they had filled with ammunition. They laid their clips beside their rifles. Waiting for the order to check their rifles, they looked downrange at the targets and figured out which one was theirs.

William told Joseph to remember intent. Joseph remembered that sighting the target was enabled by having the willingness to execute someone with said rifle. Joseph said he understood and looked downrange and said, "Remember to adjust your weapon because of ambient conditions like wind, air, and heat between you and the target."

William remembered that some adjustments in firing at targets comes from the mind rather than adjusting the mechanic of the sight. He said OK.

The order was given to check their rifle, and each soldier manually checked first visually then physically their weapons. Then the order to fire three rounds for sighting the weapon was given. Then the order was given to safety their weapon.

Both Joseph and William were a quarter inch off. They both agreed that it was wind gusts they noted as they fired. The next three rounds were for validation of the changes they made, if any, in sighting their weapons.

Being an eighth of an inch off, they decided they would fire for effect with what they had. The new paper targets were put up, and they were ordered to stand to approach their weapon and then load a ten-round clip.

Joseph M. Due, October 17, 2016

Knowing

To see or not to see is an internal struggle or angst over whether to behold anger or violence or not to see anger or violence. Each soldier has to commit to seeing, smelling, hearing, and emotionally knowing immediately when anger or violence is present in the nearby local of your influence.

Every day before this class, many soldiers sought not to see, hear, or smell anger or violence in its many forms. This is detrimental to your life and your calling. Practice dealing with the issue when in the community and know the form of anger and violence you come across for what it is.

This made sense to William, and he said so to Joseph. Joseph thought of all the angry people in Los Angeles and mentioned this to William. William said, "I only want to run two hundred feet, and I am not going to listen to all of Los Angeles."

On the way back to their dorms, they sat and listened to the passengers, many of which were angry about something or another. They talked about it for a while as they rested in Joseph's dorm room from the endeavor to perfect their ability to know danger as it is. Theresa said that it might be a rough going doing that until you learn to school your face to not give away what you know.

William said that that was a part of the guidance of the lesson. Then Joseph turned on the radio and pulled out his reading assignments to study. William and Theresa followed suit; they all wanted to do well in school.

Joseph M. Due, October 16, 2016

Sense

Hearing is an integral part of life for humans. For those who endeavor to own the night, it is absolutely essential to the life and endeavor that hearing be perfected. Definition as well as how well a soldier hears is a learned process that can be taught and practiced.

The first part of hearing better is knowing that you can hear better so you apply more energy to the process and, in the endeavor, learn to hear better. Practice during night exercises with limited ability hones the ability and should be done periodically.

The night fighter must also learn to feel and interpret that feeling. This can also be practiced.

The third idea that one can perfect is smell. The construct of smell can help define what one hears or feels.

The instructor said, "For the night exercises involved in honing our abilities, we will practice with the lights out in the gym first and introduce you to the sounds of the night from different locals. So to perfect your abilities, all you students will spend the next hour and two days in the gym. Report time is fifteen minutes. Class dismissed."

The Officer Candidate School was a little different than William thought. Joseph told him as they approached the smoke area, "It seems like we will learn to do better after all." William lit up his cigarette as he nodded in agreement.

The other students seemed to have the same sentiment.

Joseph M. Due, October 16, 2016

Tests

The tension was like a fine wire being pulled apart from both ends. The vibration of that fine wire filled the air with a heavy sound. The training days were now set on hold as the soldiers took their PFE and SKT tests before a proctor to be graded for the points garnered for promotion.

The hours slowly passed as the groups came and went and the test proctors administered the tests to Sergeants and Colonels alike. The stress could be felt as it built up as people concentrated to remember the lessons that had been taught.

Each soldier's endeavor was measured and weighed by the PFE and the SKT. The determination for the tests to be fair and impartial was a driving force of command and had been a standard the Army could be proud of.

When the tests had been put away and the results graded and posted, the troops knew that it was one of the fairest parts of their evaluation. The satisfaction each could garner came from studying and doing their best.

This was one way an Army soldier could be motivated to endeavor to persevere.

Joseph M. Due, October 20, 2016

Field Training

The midnight local had a few lights, but there were bright streetlights every hundred feet. The troops wended their way down the street because it was empty and they could be quieter. The passing cars were slow enough in their passage that many remained unobserved.

The soldier's destination was a house that sold drugs and guns to the local criminals. After a while, they could hear the sound of music coming from up the street. It was the house across the way. The lights were on, but the doors were closed at their target destination.

The Lieutenant gave last-minute instructions on surrounding the house from the backyard where nobody was visible. The soldiers faded into the landscape and slowly made their way to their posts. The minutes passed by as they took their time crossing open areas.

A half hour later, team 1 announced post, and the rest soon followed. Lieutenant Smith and Lieutenant Carne took point on the porch and waited for the signal. When the time was set for attack, they positioned themselves on either side of the front door.

They battered down the wooden door, which was fairly old, and attacked the house as team 5 entered from the back door. The occupants were up and watching television, and they met them in the living room. Both were taken down physically as the house was searched.

The all clear was given, and the Lieutenant in charge entered and used the house phone to call command. Undercover police agents from LA County would arrive in fifteen minutes.

Joseph M. Due, October 3, 2016

Stories

Theresa Sullivan knew a lot of things going to College, but she did not know William's heart, where it came to romance with a surety. Joseph had proclivities, and he even talked about them from time to time. William was even more a silent thinker than Joseph.

Getting a small mountain to move required a lot of prayer. She wanted him to be a little more proactive. She thought about ways to get him to express himself more and wandered around in frustration until her mom called.

She told her mom she loved William, but she could not see a proactive romantic bone in him. Her mom thought about it and said, "Maybe he is just that way." She sighed and said, "What do you think I should do?" Her mom said, "Ask him about family issues and how many babies he wants."

She talked to her mom about her second-year studies and told her she was posting As and Bs. The last semester's grades were in the mail. Then her mom told her that she and her dad wanted six grandchildren they could send gifts to if that helped.

She decided at the end of the day she would wear her nicest dress with light perfume and ask him out on a date.

She walked across the hall and knocked on his door. He was interested in her, she could tell. They talked for a while, and then she just blurted out she would like to take him out on a date that night. He thought about it and said, "Can we do a movie then dinner?" She agreed and they walked to school with Joseph.

William dressed up in his finest black T-shirt and blue jeans. She wore a yellow dress that was "quite becoming," Joseph said when he saw them. The movie he selected was *The Quiet Man*. She wondered how quiet William really was.

He talked about his family and their contributing to his college funds and then admitted he wanted to know what she thought about him being avant-garde army. Frustrated, she thought about it and realized he was serious. She said that if he turned into the hangman, she would still love him. Seeing her belief, he thought about it and said that he would like to have six to eight children.

Joseph M. Due, October 5, 2016

Surprises

Oh my, my. Surprise on the battlefield can often lead to death. The idea is to be the best soldier you can be, gain the best information that you can have, position your troops to encapsulate the enemy, and by being prepared, offset any surprises the enemy might bring about.

The tactical maps of the area were the latest that could be had. Recon had perused the perimeter the day before and would report in again with anything new before the assault team hit the departure point. First Lieutenant Carne and First Lieutenant Smith had done the battle planning under the supervision of the Captain in charge of both teams.

The ideal was written and briefed. The night fighters would endeavor to ensure the ideal was kept. The assault team would be led by Lieutenant Carne and the rifle team by Lieutenant Smith. The move to the departure point was by civilian vehicles parked two or three streets down. The local had been looked at by Recon as a viable place to park cars.

The teams listened to the night and then deployed with lights out in the cars. This meant no lights whatsoever. The rifle teams went first walking down the sidewalks and working at not attracting notice. Two teams went up the alley, and two went up the street. When they were between lights, they low crawled to their firing points and tried to disappear.

The cordon tightened in the early morning hours as some slumbered and others fretted. The seconds ticked off until the radio checks came in. Lieutenant Smith reported in ready status. Then Lieutenant Carne reported in when all four teams were up and ready. The Captain said, "Go on three." Then he counted down slowly.

The two by the door grabbed the screen doors and pulled them back. The Sergeants kicked the doors in, and the corporal and private on the second set of teams entered the domicile first. The snipers picked off two one in the living room and one in the bedroom then had to check fire.

The assault teams were looking for three more hostiles. One was in the living room and, when down, the corporal ran to the first bedroom and entered. The woman had a pistol, and he shot her and swept the room to the closet.

The third was found in the second bedroom and was turned over and handcuffed. The remaining rooms had to be searched and the first teams took point. When Lieutenant Carne said the all clear, the post was notified, and they were told to wait for four undercover detectives. They were then ordered to search for the car keys and drive the cars back if they could.

Joseph M. Due, October 16, 2016

Platitudes

Beware the platitudes of the damned; error and sin await. The Chief Instructor at the Eighty-Third warned the students to keep their thoughts and actions clean. They should ensure to avoid hypocrisies, which God does not appreciate. If you want a blessing, you have to be in a place to receive one.

The intro class was let out, and there was time for review. The soldiers were reminded once again amongst themselves to keep their honor clean. William said to Joseph that he should be careful around some of the women he dated. Joseph agreed wholeheartedly.

The wiles of cunning women have led to many a downfall. Joseph prayed about finding one. He even told God he would take one he could get along with to go the distance. He knew he should not; the thought did not feel right to him. He prayed again.

The bus ride back to town was filled with the quiet of the working crowd as they left another workday behind. It was as close to peace as could be managed. Joseph and William thought over the idea about platitudes as well as the other lessons they needed to learn.

The discussion was lively, and many came down to Joseph's room to talk about the virtue, energy, and strength lost at times to the wiles of those that would destroy.

Joseph M. Due, October 21, 2016

Hesitations

His third year and fifth date left him wondering about women. The ardor and desire was there, but he could not get a straight answer on commitment issues of many sorts. He prayed about finding the right one for him. He even talked over his dates and conversations with his mom and dad.

He thought about giving up on dating. His parents encouraged him to continue negotiating, and sooner or later, the right one would come along. He thought about taking each date through steps to see if they would support his endeavors and decided he would just be himself.

Linda Patricia Roberts, as his dad knew, was a business major out of Phoenix. She was nice enough and liked him so far. He figured he would ask her what type of family she would like. He also put it on his list of things what kind of future she imagined as a business major on Tuesday.

They sat on the steps of the dorm and ate Doritos and drank Mountain Dews. He asked her the first question, and she said she did not want any children until late in life. He told her he wanted three but was not sure when.

They talked for another half hour, and he asked her the second question and she thought about it for a while and then admitted she wanted an open relationship with little or no jealousy. He thought about it for a while and said he was a conservative person in a family that went back three or four generations.

They both thought about the basic incompatibilities, and the talk diminished to an uncomfortable silence. After a few minutes, she said she had to study and kissed him on the cheek before she left. Joseph knew she would not be back and sat there and prayed. He greeted William and Theresa as they walked up to the rooms.

He hesitated before he joined them.

<u>Joseph M. Due,</u> October 5, 2016

Journe' Por Angel

The consideration for Theresa Sullivan was her love, William Smith. To be and do were motivators that drove her to take her Accounting certification tests early. She wanted him and to leave college with him. The school gave the waivers, and she was scheduled to take the tests a week before graduation.

Ms. Theresa Sullivan did not exist anymore except at the college. Married two weeks before, Theresa was now Mrs. Theresa Smith. She told William one hot July night she had no sympathy for him because he had his love. She had some sympathy for Joseph Carne but would not tell him so.

The month began with the turning in of term papers as usual. Life in school did go on. However, the three were already planning on what they would take with them when they left. Joseph was busy deciding what accessories in his room he would ship to Houston when William and Theresa came by.

They planned to hang ten one last time on Saturday morning after the thunderstorm that would be coming in the day before. It would be a cold day but a memory of the coast to remember. They reminisced for a while then talked about shipping nonessentials by Friday so they could be there in Houston when they arrived.

They decided they could eat in the school diner until they left so all the packaged food and pots and pans would be shipped by Wednesday. Theresa knew she would be living with William at his parents' house and Joseph would be staying at his.

It would not be easy transitioning houses twice, but they were willing to do so for the idea. William and Joseph both did not have their own residences. On Wednesday night, they found UPS was busy with the commerce the college students were bringing them. They knew some of the students as they chatted to drop off some of their belongings.

The line moved slowly, and the clock seemed to tick faster than they expected. Then it was their turn, and they still had armfuls of wedding gifts given to William and Theresa. At 2330 hours, they finally finished shipping the last they wanted to ship.

Perkins was open late, and they went there to relax. The crowd was mainly students trying to relax off campus. They ordered the eggs over easy meal with orange juice instead of coffee. After supper, they returned to the dorm to now-mostly-empty rooms. It was a sobering thought that college life would soon be a thing of the past.

The surf was up, and it was still raining when they went out. Winter would be on them soon. They could tell by the cooling of the water. They endeavored for their memories' sake as they worked the waves. The afternoon was over by the time they stopped by UPS to ship the surfboard.

The cars would go to salvage after they took flight. There were many memories in the old cars, but they were on their last legs. Sunday was the last day they would attend service on campus.

The preacher was preaching on diligence again. It was a nice sermon, and they understood it better than the first one. They decided to join in the recommittal for their life's endeavor.

William remembered the first time he could be honest with her about his life's endeavor. He remembered the fear he had she might reject him. She looked at him truthfully and said, "I figured out what you two do for a living." She said that it took a while to truthfully be able to fully support William for better or worse.

Joseph thought over all his courses and the many hours of study to prepare him and William for their jobs and their lifework. He prayed that he could labor long and even see William's grandchildren grow. He knew William felt the same way.

Joseph M. Due, September 27, 2016

Truths

The wounds across the hand and leg were not that serious. What Joseph was to say to his classmates, however, was serious indeed. The bandages fit well, and the leg bandage could not be seen. But the reason for the level of hurt had to be explainable.

While the medic bandaged Joseph up, the Lieutenant and Sergeant were there and paid attention just in case the injuries became more serious than anticipated. They told Joseph to tell the truth insofar as he could, and they told William to follow Joseph's lead in how he explained his injuries.

On the bus back to the dorm, some of the riders asked how he got injured so badly. Joseph replied that he was up on Maple Drive going to a party and someone from a house up the street opened up with a handgun and managed to tag him twice before the shooting stopped. They asked him what happened to the shooter. He said he did not know what happened to the person.

Furthermore, from all the people at the party, he was not sure totally which one did the shooting. He was asked who bandaged him up. He then said some Medic he was introduced to on Elm Road two streets over. That seemed to answer the undue questions, so William and Joseph mentally rehearsed their lines especially for Theresa.

Joseph M. Due, October 7, 2016

Reflections

Destiny's call comes in life to the love in the heart. It builds an interest in the person so the person can find his/her way in life. Joseph liked fixing and maintaining tools, but he knew from the heart that he would work out better in interdiction.

William liked interdiction and the truth that it helps people to be free when they make their life's decisions. But his true interest was the fixing and maintaining of tools. He knew his wife, Theresa, liked him as he was. He was a simple man of simple pleasures.

For the time one has, there are times of reflections. While they waited for their briefings after they submitted their reports, they took the time to reflect on what was done, how well it was done, and the possibility they find what they needed to improve themselves.

The critique went well. Both did commendable in their posts. The teacher told them they were learning well enough and then bid them a good Sunday night. On the bus, they discussed their classes and watched the city of Los Angeles appear to approach them.

Joseph M. Due, October 7, 2016

Fire Team

Two by two, he was taught. The room where the terrorists were pacing back and forth had three he thought he could get. The Lieutenant told everyone to stand too. On his mark, he would fire his rifle. The distance to the targets was only 120 feet.

The seconds ticked down, and he readied his rifle. The Lieutenant said go, and Joseph opened fire on one, then two, and finally hit the third. There was no one in his sight area, so he checked his rifle. Then he scanned the area. The Lieutenant said something about three shots fired, and when the last all clear was sounded, he went to see for himself.

The team secured the building, and Investigations took a look-see at the cell phones recovered and any notes left behind. Then the order came to return to the rally point. The Lieutenant said he was officially going to cite him for not obeying orders. When he attended the debrief, the commander commended him for his shooting skill.

Joseph M. Due, October 3, 2016

Face-Off

Another moment went by, and ten thoughts flitted through his head. Meanwhile, his hands were moving upward, and he saw his handgun fire. He felt the bullets pass him by. He turned and there are two others. He fired at the second and took two steps backward as he looked for the third.

He heard noise from the kitchen and heard a chair scrape in the corner. The sound of gunfire marked the passage of time as he rounded the kitchen door. He brought his pistol up as he scanned the kitchen. It was William standing by a body as he checked to see if it was alive.

Satisfied, Joseph turned to the living room and rechecked the living room and then the hallway. Satisfied all were down, he took up post on the door and waited for the next signal, which was all clear or a go to command as others entered the building.

The silence thundered through the house as the seconds ticked by. The rooms were finally all cleared, and that signaled the Lieutenant was coming through for an inspection. He turned the bodies faceup so the Lieutenant could see their faces.

Joseph M. Due, October 11, 2016

Rape

The phone rang in the living room, and Lieutenant Carne went to answer it. The command post wanted him to report to Investigations in the gym. He told them ETA would be in about twenty minutes. He changed into his work clothes just in case and drove over to Smith Carne Industry. It was a proper building for professional people.

The guard said he would be in the dining room as they decided to take the elevator. He wondered what it could be since his last shift had been through training. He walked into the gym and saw two teams were up and being briefed. He went over to the table marked Investigations and waited his turn to talk to them.

A lieutenant came up to him and told him the table on the far south wall was where he was supposed to be. Walking on over to the table, he tried to imagine what Investigations wanted from him. He reported as ordered, and they told him to sit down. He looked at the photos arrayed around the table, and he recognized three from the night before at Perkins.

They wanted to know if he overheard them talking in the booth behind him. He said, "Yes, they were talking about a high school football game the Vikings against the Bears or something and two girls Valerie and Tonya."

He recounted his steps into Perkins with William and Theresa. They asked him if he heard anything at each step he took. He remembered some things and told them the words that he heard. They asked again about those sitting on the other side of the table where William sat. He drew a complete blank where it came to those.

They told him William was being interviewed in the dining room with Theresa because the police had noticed them sitting near the suspects in a rape case that Friday night.

The dining room was full, and he waved to the guard to tell him he would be eating there, and as he looked around, he saw William and Theresa. They were still being interviewed, so he got his plate and sat next to the guard. It was rice pilaf, lamb, and mixed vegetables.

Joseph M. Due, October 10, 2016

Obedience

The times remembered contain the original ideas that become truths we use as guides we live by. As we use those truths properly, we find God gives virtue to those that do well. As we learn the truths within us, we find growth inevitable and we develop uniquely.

The training officers at Fort Houston watched as those they had trained with virtue assaulted the kidnapper's house. They knew success depended on good training and the earning of virtue. Lieutenant Smith's teams were going in while Lieutenant Carne's team was doing the sniper/overwatch positions.

The shots fired resulted in two criminals down as the Captain waited for the teams to get into position. The swift, sure movements in obedience to timed commands ensured a minimum of casualties for the interdiction teams. Lieutenant Smith's teams indicated they were ready to assault the doors, and the go command was given by the Captain.

The fire teams now sought out targets on purpose and fired on the criminals as they were seen in the windows. The doors were broken down, and the teams entered the front and back door. Lieutenant Carne ordered the rifle teams to now check fire.

The firing moved from room to room as Lieutenant Smith's teams cleared each room. Then the return fire diminished, and the all clear was sounded from each room and the criminal bodies were checked for life. Those that were still alive were then handcuffed.

Lieutenant Smith told the Captain the kidnapped babies were alive and well. The Captain called the command post and told them the

FBI could now take the house. The command post asked for a casualty report, and the Captain said two were injured and gave their names. The command post then said the FBI had an ETA of thirty-five minutes.

The two injured were to report to the rally site to have their injuries attended to.

Joseph M. Due, October 11, 2016

Oaks

The oaks were flowering, and the seed harvest looked like it would be a good harvest. The ten trees were going to give to the cause joy and pleasure as a luxury crop. Dennis Smith thought about the tentative early years and knew the stress and tension of the day was a good thing to motivate people to learn.

The children were scheduled in at 1000 hours to pick up the seeds that dropped and the older ones to climb the trees to pick the ripened acorns. The working picnic was nice as people enjoyed themselves and went away with shares.

The ladies would do the cooking, and the gentlemen would organize and supervise the toddlers to the teens. The dinner would be baked cod and potatoes with green beans. Coffee and juice would be taken care of by the older children.

Once the lawn was air-sprayed to chase the acorns to the back drive, softball and horseshoes would be the events of the day for the teenagers and adults. The women and children would play croquet.

The acorns set to baking would be cooked in teams throughout the get-together.

Joseph M. Due, October 20, 2016

Situation Report

Words paint pictures when the definitions are known by all. The opening statement of an instructor from the Eighty-Third CID pointed out that the choice of words used on a sitrep has its own meaning and can be easily misconstrued. The preference is the soldier's language, which you pick up in schools like basic training or AIT.

Lt. Donald Carne and Lt. Paul Litz nodded when they thought about preparing their earlier versions of a sitrep in practice and at AIT. They knew the opening statement was so true when they were asked a few times to redo the sitreps to be more understandable.

The two talked about the issue during lunch. In their 1300 hours class, they had to draw maps of where they had been and write out a sitrep for each step of their travels. The practice would stand them in good stead when they would do live fire exercise/mission events.

The thirteenth rolled around, and they were there by 1800 hours. They rested in the alert bunks until 2400 hours, they were then on alert status and they were rested and ready. The mission was to be an easy one for thirteen people. They would get a taste of their chosen job.

Joseph M. Due, October 20, 2016

Captain W. Smith

The rain fell like heavy sheets. The early dawn mist was rising. The attack on the munitions warehouse was scheduled for 0900 hours, and the rain did not seem like it would abate. Captain William Smith was perplexed. He had a mission and the need. He prayed mightily and decided he would use the vans.

There were six teams, with two on recon and two on perimeter security. He placed a reserve at the primary entrance and a reserve to cover the loading docks. Recon would fall back fifty feet as the teams went in and provided fire support. The vans would drive to the parking lot lights and provide a further distraction with the drivers moving back and forth on the west side under the lights.

He prayed now for the morning mist and rain to continue. The staff thought it a dubious plan, but command approved as long as the Captain was willing to adjust fire.

The doors were manned, so Captain Smith ordered two teams for each door to knock and see if they could gain entry. At that point, they would disarm or shoot the guards. The remaining teams would then follow them in. If that did not work, they were to use explosives to blow the doors and use grenades to gain entry.

The departure points were reached on both sides of the building. Captain Smith got six ready reports and told them to proceed to the next step. The rain was hindering sight something fierce, so it took two minutes for the last security team to report in.

The teams were ready, so he ordered them to attack the building. The fire teams had nothing to report except they could see the attack teams on the walls. The quiet was deafening, and there was no audio except on the radio transmitters the soldiers wore.

Time dragged on past five minutes to eleven minutes, and then the team reports came in. The building was secure. He ordered team 1 in to help out and called up Investigations as team 2 reorientated to cover the whole building.

The body count was seven, and the administrative section looked like it could still be used. He cleared the four wounded and had the bodies carried outside for van pickup.

Joseph M. Due, October 3, 2016

Alert

The Fifty-Seventh had packing down to a science. The duffel bags were stored in individual equipment (IE) for mobilization. The list they carried for each person listed the items they might be short of at any time. They even made space for your favorite books if you were deployed.

On alert, you would draw your individual equipment and have it stored for immediate use. The next step right next door was the armory for pickup of weaponry and ammunition. Behind the line and opposite IE and the armory, you would don the gear and weapons and prepare for inspection.

Capt. Joseph Carne stood waiting for his troops to don and inspect their gear. He would take them to their briefings and supervise the alert teams while they were on alert. This time, they would wear their vests and turn in their weapons and do recon duties.

The process of urban recon had to be experienced and practiced. They were not to get into a gun battle; they were to do their recon and report without detection. The vans took them by half squads and dropped them off at their departure points, and one at a time, every five minutes, they were released to recon the departure point, the facility they were to look at, and their egress point.

The exercise took all of an hour on-site, and on the way back, each was to compose a separate sitrep to review against the staff sitrep of the same facility. That took another hour and a half. Then they turned in their equipment and were released from night training.

It was 0500 hours, and Joseph went down to the dining room. At 0800 hours, he had a date to attend to.

<u>Joseph M. Due,</u> October 3, 2016

Fair

The new rides were stomach-wrenching, and all the cotton candy was making them a little sick. They decided to drink some water and sit down at the picnic benches that littered the county fairground. Janice Quille and Theresa Sullivan sat between Joseph and William. Conversation changed from tool usage and repair to marriage and babies.

William thought it was funny. Joseph thought it was embarrassing. He already knew Janice did not want to have any babies in the near future. He knew his mom wanted him to move on, and Janice sensed it, he was sure. Why they were talking about babies, he did not know. That is, until Theresa asked Janice if she knew Joseph wanted three children.

She said she knew he wanted children but not how many. That quieted the conversation down to everybody going home. They dropped Janice off at her apartment, and she turned to Joseph and Janice said, looking him in the eye, "I will see you later," and then she walked off.

William said he needed pancakes, so all three went out to eat. They talked about the weather for a while until Theresa said she was sorry to Joseph, but she was occasionally giving her bad vibes. Joseph said, "Apology accepted. There was not much harm done."

Joseph M. Due, October 7, 2016

94

Blessed

William told Joseph that today, Theresa would, for the first time, see what he did for a living. Joseph asked if he could do anything to help William and Theresa out. He said, "No, just be kind to her as she adjusts her sight picture of life."

Love-Amore' can, at times, have no boundaries.

Theresa knew William was on call, and she was just a visitor that had been cleared for a tour of the Fifty-Seventh CID. She cleaned the house and took another shower just to be ready. She then selected her finest to represent their union the best she could. She did not want to embarrass William.

Her thoughts were on the reality of what he did for a living. He told her a couple times, but she had to see the reality to actually know what he did with a clear view. She prayed she could take the adjustment well. William told her some of the Ladies did not.

She thought of the women that found fault with Joseph, who was a gentleman as much as anyone can be. She thought of the different things that turn some women off to men in uniform. She remembered William told her she had come a long way and she was doing fine. She believed him.

The minutes ticked down to 1045 hours, and she got in her car in anticipation. She knew William trusted her, and that is part of what love is. She rethought Joseph and William's injuries, and she knew they were from armed combat as she thought it through. Acceptance of the risks William takes is part and parcel of accepting him as he is.

She thought about death and swerved on the road. Righting the car, she followed that thought out to what it meant to her. She thought, *No wonder many of Joseph's girlfriends freak when they realize what the guard is there for.* She decided that if she recommended a date for Joseph again, they would have to be a sturdier sort.

The meal was fried chicken, small potatoes, beans, and baked Alaskan pie. The introduction to the workers in the dining room intermingled with those dressed for alert duty was reassuring that she was not alone in her belief of what her friends and family did.

The tour started in the alert quarters and then moved to the sixth floor, where she saw where William and Joseph's dad worked. There was a team in the gym going through the alert briefs for tactical urban assault, and they spent an hour seeing what William and Joseph prepared to do every day.

The next stop was the firing line, and team 1 was up firing rifles. She saw Joseph and asked him how well he did. He asked the instructor if he could show her. The instructor briefed her on qualification standards for the rifle. She watched how quickly Joseph shot up the target, and she asked William how well he did with a rifle. He said equitable to Joseph since both surpassed the training standard.

The command post was next, where she saw the dispatch and monitoring of the troops. She had a few questions for William, but that could wait. She surrendered her visitor's badge, and then he escorted her to the car. He kissed her, and she said, "Friday night." He knew she had other questions to ask, but they could wait.

Joseph M. Due, October 9, 2016

Trainee

The night was dark and warm. He had his gear and his pistol. He could barely see. An hour had passed, and he had yet fifteen minutes left to go, he hoped. The seconds ticked by as he listened to the night for the passage of the sound of man. The waiting was building up stress and tension. He knew from those before that this was so.

He reached out his senses to see if he could feel the presence of the other members of his team. He knew where they were both in physical topography and on a site map. He knew their vigil was a righteous one, so he prayed.

The warehouse was supposed to be abandoned, but earlier recon showed it was a place for people to cook drugs and sell firearms. The Lieutenant who assigned the teams their position said he would signal in five minutes, and they would interdict the now-mainly-sleeping enemy.

He reviewed in his mind the steps, the pathway to the building that he would take. Then he checked his watch again to be ready. He wondered why the criminals shut off all the lights with a full parking lot anyone could see.

The minutes passed away, and the radio sounded for all team members to stand to post. He pulled his pistol and ensured the safety was off. He heard the word *execute*, and dim flares lit the building as they approached. He approached the side of a window and checked to see what was on the inside of the building.

He backed up off the window he was to guard, and then he heard the Lieutenant say go. The door was unlocked, and the teams fanned out before the warning was given. Team 1 said, "Two with weapons." Team 2 cleared the workers and took post between the sleeping criminals and the weapons storage area.

Teams 3 and 4 then took post at the hallway junctions to provide backup. Then each team said, "Ready," in turn quietly. The Lieutenant had entered the building, and he then, at the last ready, flipped the lights on full. Team 1 ordered the criminals to lay down their weapons. When they resisted, both were shot posthaste.

Team 2 ordered the workers to lie down on the ground and put their hands over their heads. When the Lieutenant finished checking on the teams and the building, he then said aloud, "Command post, we have secured the building." The answering reply said police vans were inbound, ETA ten minutes.

The fears and trepidations were not over yet, not until the prisoners were secure and they could return to their rally point. The police sirens grew in the distance as the criminals pondered their fate. The wondering about riot was a stress on the body's central nervous system and would not abate until the mission was concluded.

The vans pulled up initially on the road, and a team member went up to the first van and asked them to pull into the parking lot. They were reassured the criminals were secure. Ten minutes later, they were each handcuffed and put in the back of one of the vans.

During this time, police investigations arrived and said DEA and ATF were half an hour and an hour behind. The last criminal was taken outside with the two bodies. Team 1 was relieved by the police and exited the area returning to their rally point.

The sight of Smith Carne Industry was a welcome sight by the team. The Lieutenant reminded everyone they had a sitrep to accomplish and equipment to turn in. The hours passed by as the weapons were cleaned and turned in. Finally, they had their mission review and were released to normal standby.

As they moved to the dayrooms or the beds, they saw team 2 prepare to go to full alert and response. The quiet of the city assured the teams full eight hours of sleep. They went through their prework activities at 1500 hours. Then they would be on full standby after team 3.

The week's alert leaves a person a little tired, so Joseph slept ten hours before his first normal shift. Training would be investigations in the morning and practice in the afternoon. The next day was Tuesday, and urban assault principles would be trained again in the morning with map practice in the afternoon.

The soldier's life, Joseph thought, *was pretty fine.* Practice, Preparation, Principles, and Alert Posture. Then one was off to visit Mom and Dad or brothers and sisters. The sociopolitical considerations were there. One felt good about helping God out so people had more peace in the day with violent criminals either executed or jailed.

His OJT records were signed off quite quickly as he rotated through alert status. It was nice that his training was progressing so well. The combat fighting training gave him and William practice that left both bruised but confident they could do close fighting when called upon.

Then he thought about Brenda. She was a fine woman, and he could mostly relate to her. Her ideas of criminal justice though needed a dose of practicality. He wondered when or if she would come around to his way of thinking.

The months passed by, and Brenda turned into Elizabeth, then Julie. Some did not agree with him about criminal justice and some had ideas about the marriage relationship that he was not comfortable with.

The team assignments had rotated enough for him to make assistant squad leader and first Lieutenant. William was just a month behind him and was then transferred to second team. He was with Theresa, working on their first child. He had decided to wait to see if it was a boy or girl before buying a gift. His mom said he was growing up.

Joseph lived with his mom and dad until he could afford a down payment on a nice one-level ranch-style house. It had a two-car garage and plenty of room to invite friends over. He did so about every two weeks. The mortgage was a little heavy, but when he made team lead, Captain position, his budget would not be so strained.

The activities of the gunrunners was under investigation just like kidnapping or bombers. The amount of thefts of production and distribution and home-owned weapons was rising throughout the States. The need for people like him and William was growing.

It began with a car accident and a beating on the north side of Houston. The victim had gotten in the way of a driver in a cherry-red convertible. The police were quick to apprehend the criminal because he was driving such a noticeable car. They also found three stolen rifles and an address for delivery taped to the boxes they were in.

Police investigations asked the Fifty-Seventh CID if they had any information on the house or occupants. It turned out that its occupants were suspected of light drug use and it was a possible address used for criminal transit. The joint investigation began, and the ATF was notified. The ATF said they were working too many cases and asked the Fifty-Seventh CID and the Houston police to keep up the investigation.

The neighborhood recon by the Fifty-Seventh revealed the casual connections to fifteen other houses and two warehouses. The only thing was, for a month, there was nothing going on at the sites. The police told the Fifty-Seventh they could monitor the warehouses.

Teams 1 and 2 were up on alert again and did the sight recon by drive-bys through the day and sent the teams in to plant audio and video devices so Investigations could keep an eye on the place and the teams could have some recon experience.

A week later, the warehouses started posting guards, and two weeks after that, a shipment of arms was received at both sites. The audio pickup heard of plans to use the weapons to murder local authorities. ATF was notified, and they said interdiction could seize the weapons.

Six teams were put on alert. Two teams were tasked to do outer security of each warehouse site and two each to do the raids. Return fire was expected at each site because they hosted many guards apiece. Investigations was working on following the criminals to track down any nodes that grew, like conspiratorial planning, recruiting, or fundraising.

The night grew heavy with expectations. The sites were looked at once in a while in the day as the warehouse parking lot filled up. The video feed was transferred over to the command post, and the teams prepared for their departure points. Ingress would come from adjacent warehouses for the fire teams to approach without being detected.

The security teams doing overwatch would approach by road when they heard shots were fired. The departure point at Smith Carne

Industry was the gym on the sixth floor. ETA to departure points was at twenty minutes. At 0300 hours, the teams would cross the departure point and set up and engage the enemy.

The teams set to charge, and the firing teams engaged long distance. The lights were shot out, but you could still see fairly well from the well-lit facilities. The people in the warehouse responded fairly quickly by rushing to the windows. The firing teams then moved up to the next rank of cars and set up again with two drawing pistols as the door was forced with charges.

The teams covering the back now had troops in position to cover the sides of the buildings. The forced entry was affected with troops converging from all sides. The firing grew heavier as the enemy reorientated for the forced entry.

Before the firing of the criminals could be suppressed, three were down at site 1, and two were down at site 2. When it was validated that the crime scenes were controlled, the Captain told command post they could now send in Investigations. The Captain ordered the teams to retrieve the dead soldiers and to have them bring up the vans.

The next step was for Investigations to find out the complexity of the sales or potential sales of the stolen weapons. Then command would determine whether to call ATF again or not. The assault teams returned to post and sent the bodies on to Fort Houston for processing.

The transit houses were looked at for any activity. The teams were ordered down for two hours and ordered to stand by for further orders. Investigations followed up on addresses they picked up from the site and any cell phones they found on the bodies.

The drive-bys of the transit houses did not show signs of activity, but the investigations found two houses that were doing fundraising activities to buy the weapons. Command called the DEA and sent a courier to the local representative with copies of evidence garnered to date.

The DEA said they would send in fifty agents to process the evidence. They wanted the houses themselves. The ETA of the DEA was to be 1600 hours local the next day.

The rest of the bodies were to be processed by the police and mortuary affairs. The ETA was one hour for mortuary affairs and the police. The security teams loaded the weapons on the vans and sent them to Fort Houston for disposal.

The security team would be picked up at 0900 hours if all went well.

The commendations and promotions were many. Joseph and William became team leads. The change in positions meant that Joseph and William now supervised training of their teams and got to plan some of their own missions under the tutelage of their Captain.

Two years passed by and William took a position in the tool and dye section and Joseph took a position as a Tactical team Captain.

Joseph M. Due, September 27, 2016

Ambiance

The ambiance was light with the feeling of work rather than sweat. The odors of virtuous people endeavoring was a light perfume/cologne that permeated the building even into the locker rooms of the gym. The delight of the feeling brought many nice emotions to the fore of each person's thought like peace or happiness.

Smith Carne Industry was a model building that was classified and the model persona found in the unique synergy of family life. Colonel Smith appreciated the confluence of needs and desires that brought the building into existence.

He toured the building daily because it was his responsibility. The building was one of his babies, and he cared about his babies a great deal. The troops knew how to do a light cleaning without an excess of chemicals, and the natural odors with the state-of-the-art filtration system took care of the building quite nicely.

The tour was relaxing, and he brought his other babies on a tour to see this baby of his frequently. The tour was not long if you put a good pace on the inspection. He brought his children to the dining halls last for rest and food. To him, it was a nice touch to end the tour rested and well fed.

The day brought paperwork and phone calls to return. He put on a good attitude and returned to his office.

Joseph M. Due, October 15, 2016

Spiritual Guidance

"<u>Behold Heaven before you and weep for the days that are not.</u>" This is a favorite saying of Samuel Brown, the local preacher. Each application was another spiritual principle his flock would work on week by week.

The families and the generations of their families attended because of the enablement in daily living that was spiritually provided indeed. Robert, Alvin, Dennis, and Terrance as well as many others brought their children for instruction in righteousness to the family church.

The evening meals on Sundays were great get-togethers, and the families enjoyed them immensely. Preacher Brown and his family would rotate between the families over the months and years of his life, attending their dinners and their needs.

The sad news was the attacks on the families that used to attend like the Mathews and Michaels families and the continuing attacks on the families like the Smith and Carne families. Under the pressures of the day, the congregation as a group withheld the evil and their demands and, in unity, prayed for peace.

<u>Joseph M. Due,</u> October 13, 2016

Lessons Learned

The next wave of students poured onto the field and looked for their place markings. The students all in all were given a map that specified where they should stand. The fifteen-minute shuffle was a little too much for soldiers that should know where they are going.

The lieutenants were then told to validate each person on their list by squad assignment. This took another ten minutes before the lieutenants were ready to report. The chief instructor, Lieutenant Colonel Walters, made the points clear as to his expectations. If a soldier did not know where they were going or how to find it, the delays and errors could be the death of the squad or platoon itself.

Colonel Walters let the lesson sink in, then welcomed the student body to advance infantry training school. Lt. Donald Carne thought about the lesson and realized his errors in judgement in not getting to post on time. He prayed about it and decided he would give extra energy to the directions given from Command.

The equipment and supply issue were up first thing in the morning. Billeting was the last order of the day to impress on the soldiers that the mission comes first, rest second. This was another expectation of Command's, and one to remember. Command expected soldiers to prioritize properly and know the mission comes first.

The meals were full, and they were encouraged to eat. They also said when you get tired, you should eat the same or more because your body needs the extra fuel. The soldiers dug in and realized they were already a little tired and it was only the end of the first day.

The morning was coming, the instructors said, and they needed to tend to business and get their sleep. It was 1900 hours when the last sewing kit was put away. By 2000 hours, the night instructor turned out the lights even though lights out was not until 2200 hours.

<u>Joseph M. Due,</u> October 18, 2016

Seizure

The investigation was continuing, and the associations at the bomb facility were being tracked. Joseph was tasked to take in six teams to seize the production facility. He tasked one team for fire support and security during the raid. He then tasked another team for recon and attack. They were to be first in the building.

Then the other three teams would enter in succession half in the front and half in the back. The criminals were armed and facing twenty years plus in prison. There was to be no hesitation. The teams were to approach from neighboring buildings on the east and west side.

The fire teams were to set up right behind recon and before they were ready to enter. Next would come the successive teams by twos. The raid would be conducted at 0300 hours. The departure point to attack formation was less than thirty seconds. Then the fire teams would open up on the armed criminals. At the same time, the doors would be blown.

The vans were loaded up at 0200 hours and departed at 0215 hours. They would wait in the neighboring production parking lots until 0300 hours, the departure time. The surveillance van and command site would be across the street parked in view of the production parking lot.

The command post surveillance said occupants were still not noticing encroachment as the teams lined up on the walls. When they all reported in, he gave the order to commence. The fire teams took care of the armed security as team 1 entered the building.

The occupants picked up weapons and ran to the doors, so the firing teams kept firing until the first team was seen. Then the order for the fire teams to check fire was given. Team 2 reached the offices and knocked out the occupants because they were destroying evidence.

There were six casualties all told as the area was cleared. The next group inbound was Investigations. Then security for the site as the teams returned to their rally point. The six bodies with them had the sobering effect on the soldiers that command would like.

Joseph M. Due, October 3, 2016

A Soldier's Prayer

Tomorrow's dinner. Does tomorrow offer a dinner? Maj. Joseph Carne wondered about the expression as he looked over the tactical map with Capt. Donna Charles. She was looking at two houses and eight cars in the lot at any one time. The fields of fire were going to be more than difficult. The assault teams would be more exposed, and the number of gunrunners with Army-issued basic rifles was an unknown quantity with an unknown net capability.

Grenades were mandatory, as well as flak vests. The situation called for a lot of prayer, and not guessing right on the unknowns could be fatal for her teams. She wanted two rifle teams front, four in the middle to cover both houses, and two rifle teams to cover the back of the second house.

For the assault teams, she wanted four teams for each house and the front side teams to assault the first house first and then, when the second house was shut down, to assault the back door. Lights would be blown on a go for the front door and the second house fired into. This would help her assault both houses almost one at a time.

The midnight hour would be the darkest and allow her troops approach time, except it was a clear, warm Friday night. The assault would be under the lights for both houses at 0200 hours as they moved into position. Distance was fifty feet to cover the windows. The only good news was the cover for the rifle teams was the neighbor's trees.

The Captain said approach would be from the alley, the darkest part of that area from both sides, and then they would cut through the neighbor's yards, abutting the property. A distraction was needed if there were people out and about. A Smith Carne Industry accident 150 feet down the front of the block would do just nicely.

She wanted the van to rear-end one of the cars down the block and lock the horn so that it would distract the people that were up. The idea amused Joseph to no end. He asked her if she wanted to drive out there with her car. She said she would not be able to carry any weapons if the people responded to the accident.

The soldiers thought of the exposure and decided to say two prayers.

Joseph M. Due, October 17, 2016

Bombers

The Super Bowl was to be anticipated and, hopefully, when it came around, to be greatly enjoyed. The chips and pop were purchased, and William and Theresa invited both teams to show up for a potluck dinner the ladies were hosting.

The Minnesota Vikings and the Houston Oilers were going to be the contenders of the day, and a big crowd was planned for the house. The deranged had other ideas though, and as for the teams, they would be working through the festivities.

The explosion took out half the classrooms on the west side of the school. The police and fire departments responded right away. The EOD sent in a team from Washington to determine what kind of explosive device was used as well as what type of explosive. The federal agencies were tasked under the auspices of the FBI to send their latest data to the FBI on Second Street in Houston, where the FBI officer in charge would be located.

The agents spent twenty-four hours sifting through the hot rubble and figured out the bombs were placed in backpacks left in the school cloakrooms. They surmised that students might have placed them there for the adults who collected or made the bombs.

The group responsible for the bombing threatened to bomb every school facility until fellow bombers were released from federal custody.

The President would not have them released and gave the order to his agencies that nobody was to be released under any condition except time served. The news reporters asked the President if this denied parole to convicted bombers. He simply said yes and would not elaborate.

The Fifty-Seventh CID was to provide full support to the FBI for the endeavor to arrest said bombers. The alternate command post was brought on line and Fort Houston donated an extra two hundred troops for the endeavor. Investigations and the teams went to twelve hours on and twelve hours off for the duration.

The augmentees were tasked to post at schools and governance facilities throughout the Houston area to check every package they could see that was brought in. Two teams were tasked to help out investigations, and the rest were on call for SWAT support for the FBI when they were needed.

Joseph M. Due, October 10, 2016

Commander's Intent

If you have already said it once, there is no reason to say it again. The two exceptions to this truth are if the person did not hear and or they did not understand. This truth directly stems from stating the commander's intent.

Those truths in repete' that are for training might need to be said more than once. Joseph learned his dad's intent at an early age with good discipline. His dad also taught him line upon line, precept upon precept with his tutoring so that Joseph might be enabled to find his destiny.

Joseph, as a young lieutenant, learned to practice teaching commander's intent to his newly formed squad and training in repete' as they practiced obeying his orders to perfect their skills and tasks, which would keep them alive.

This is a platform to build team synergy and cohesion just like the principle that everyone on a team should know what they are doing and be responsible for what they do.

The meditations and prayers over advanced concepts help one think the ideas through and find the person's life applications. Joseph learned these principles through practiced living.

Joseph M. Due, October 8, 2016

Man Down

The hit-and-miss approach was hurting a little bit. His battle buddy was hitting him twice for every hit he was given. He thought about it for a while and decided he was aiming too far beyond the body, so he changed his swing to a shorter jab and stepped back.

William was then out of position and missed him by a bare inch. Joseph smiled at William, and for the next five minutes, he had the timing down until William adjusted again.

They took a break and both agreed judo and karate were better forms for interdiction to use for unarmed combat. They finished their third round dead even and decided that was enough boxing practice.

William was going out on a date with Theresa and hurried through his shower and dressing. Joseph was just getting off the bench when William said, "Karate next week." Joseph said, "With Judo." William said "Deal." Joseph said "Deal," and then William left.

Joseph decided he would go over to his mom's house. There was always something cooking, and he could have someone to talk to. The drive on a Saturday night was warm and dry. It felt refreshing and relaxing in the sparse, cooler wind that he felt.

He saw the police sirens going by one at a time and decided to tune in to the police band radio receiver he had. The man down call was for a fellow officer, and Joseph signaled and turned around. The investigation would start out slow, but he still needed to see the police reports as they came in.

The tempo of the command post was professional relaxed. The officers knew the drill, and the chief of investigations was already there. A board was cleared as a starter, and the suspect's house was on the list for monitoring, which he approved of as XO.

He asked when police investigations anticipated filing their initial reports. They said four hours or 2000 hours. He said he would be up in his office, and they were to wake him if there was anything else that happened.

The time slipped away in the night, and the ringing of the phone aroused him from his slumber. The watch officer reported the known suspect could not be found and an APB was put out for his arrest.

He asked if investigations would quarter the city for the suspect's car. They agreed they would do so, and with the investigators up, it would take three hours. He said to the watch officer, "Have team 3 report to Investigations so they can take their time."

Law enforcement needed to know where that bird would land and what kind of company he was now keeping. Joseph went down to the dining room and had steak au jus with sautéed onions and baby potatoes boiled just right.

Joseph M. Due, October 21, 2016

Gains

Joseph smiled in sadness as Kathy Welky told him the top ten things she thought was wrong with him. She glared at him as he said, "I guess you have ten reasons as to why our dating relationship is over." She asked him if he had any reason to stop dating. He told her he was set in his ways and he liked peace in his days. "That must be two good reasons," he said.

She glared at him one last time before she got in her car and pulled out of the drive. He watched until she turned the corner to go to her house. He turned and walked into the house humming a Travis Tritt song about love lost. Making coffee, he nodded as the guard took a seat in the kitchen. He thought about it and said to himself, "At least Mums loves me."

He read the latest spy novel waiting for Mums to give him a call. He knew Kathy would call her when she got home. He was determined to live in peace, and if that meant living alone, well then, he needed to get used to the idea.

The call came at 1800 hours. He was now listening to his favorite country music CDs. He turned the music down as he answered the phone. Mums was wanting to talk about the summer picnic in July a month away. She asked him if he would prefer to bring ten pounds of baked or fried chicken. He told her he would bake the chicken. It was less a mess than fried chicken.

She then asked about Kathy and how she was doing. He said he had a "deal or no deal" argument with her and she gave him ten reasons why it was a no-deal argument. She said, "Oh, that is kind of sad." He knew Mums meant it. She said, "On the other hand, Theresa said she knows a teacher named Brenda Dione, and she seemed available."

Joseph M. Due, October 17, 2016

Tactical

William did not think it a bright idea. Even Joseph thought it was a dubious endeavor dating a blonde visiting her mother in Houston, and she was a die-hard liberal. But on the other hand, she seemed to like him and had invited him to date her.

She was avant-garde in liberal politics while Joseph was a true believing conservative. His dad was alarmed and had her investigated for casual associations, but she had no known ties. She was just the way she was.

Joseph and she debated every date the merits of the criminal justice system. At first, it was polite social repartee. As the weeks passed by, as well as the dates, Joseph fully realized his mistake, and she became more angry and bitter.

There was no consolation. There was no solution to each being determined in their ways. William asked him after he broke up with Donna Lyre if that was a lousy tactical choice. He said, "Yes, but I learned so many tactical things not to do."

As they attended command school they revisited Joseph's romances, of which there were a few. They both decided that until he found his love, who would not be jealous of his first love, he should tactically stick to dating and short-term romances.

The school was part of Joseph's first love, and he noticed things William did not. They both loved the people and the Army, just in different degrees. The command and leadership principles were at times business philosophies, but their applications were unique to the Army.

At home, they both realized their OJT records and personnel records were updated, and then they studied staff planning, operations, training, et cetera. More and more, they had a greater hand in their own training. Tactically navigating military sections to chart out their own destinies, they found commitment and self-responsibility as the pathway to command.

Joseph M. Due, September 27, 2016

Winter

The moon was not out in the winter sky, but the ambient light from the poles lit up the area as the light was reflected off the snow. Whites were used over the garb they normally wore. The roads were slick, and they looked like they would be clearing during the assault.

The senior Lieutenant asked for and got another team, though the house was small. It had a wide field of approach in the ambient light that was just right for return fire.

He also asked for four sandbags to be added to the load list. They could be taken from the stock of items the garage had.

The approaches would be from the alley. East and west would take up their posts first. This way, they could provide some suppressive fire in the side yards to the house. The front road approaches would be by van, dropping the assault troops off in plain sight of the house. Fire support would be the first van through and then the assault teams second.

The vans would then block the roads to the left and right of the house.

Sniping at the fire teams began in the rear of the house and happened as the vans were dropping off the fire teams in the front of the house. The situation demanded the fire teams return fire. This lasted until return fire died out.

The assault teams were now ready, and they were ordered in. Two by two, the teams entered the house as the fire teams looked for targets. Two minutes later, the teams started checking in and giving an all clear and a report on injuries or dead.

The lieutenant then reviewed the scene, ordered the three dead removed to the shot-up vans, and then called the command post to inform them the DEA could have the house.

Joseph M. Due, October 8, 2016

Destiny

Captain Donald Carne believed in a man's destiny before God and in His Holy will. He remembered the Tinkertoys he put together with such determination. He remembered the cowboy days when he was six and Uncle Joseph would stop by and he would ask questions like "Did He love the people enough to protect them when life got difficult?"

He remembered as a teen the understanding that Joseph was looking for a woman with that love. He remembered his dad's training to prepare him for AIT and OCS. His trip to California taught him many things, one being the reality that he was not a born surfer. He knew he just did not have a passion for surfing as some people did.

As a Lieutenant team lead though, he had found his desire and passion. He had found that great love Joseph had. He thought about the wait for the other great love in his life and sighed.

He looked at his gear and realized from the last fight with a wounded prisoner not yet handcuffed that he had another cut he had to repair. He sat on his bunk and decided now was as good a time as any to do repairs. The Sergeant came in, and Captain Carne looked up. He saw that the Sergeant was smiling and had all the unit sitreps with him.

He looks at his watch. A half hour to review and another half hour before team debriefing in the gym. The assault was filled with action. There were many of the criminals smoking grass and carrying knives and guns. The assault teams had to sneak around the front and back and jump the gunrunning criminals before they could take the house.

It turned out all right though. There was only one injury and some broken equipment.

<u>Joseph M. Due,</u> October 17, 2016

Tyranny

It was a beautiful fall afternoon when security alerted the watch officer that there were crowds gathering outside the building. They were told to lock the doors and lower the gates and escort people in and out the side doors as needed. It took less than five minutes to do so, and the people on the streets then crowded up to the doors and fences.

Teams 1 and 2 were up and were ordered to the first floor. Team 3 would monitor the stairs and then the watch locked the elevators off on the first floor. The alert sounded, and personnel put away their tools and centrally located for protection.

The signs came out first when the rioters thought they had a big enough crowd to ring the building. The Armory was busy issuing extra ammunition, which was taken to the first floor. All personnel wanting to be issued a hand weapon had to wait ten minutes outside the armory.

Meanwhile, the shouting and chanting began as the sixth floor personnel could see rocks and other assorted weapons distributed. The volume got louder as the extra ammunition clips were passed out to the soldiers protecting the core of Smith Carne Industry, who steeled themselves to fire into the crowd to resist tyranny.

Capt. Donald Carne was the overall team lead for teams one and two. He and the lieutenants took center point around the elevators. The exposed position by sight line from the doors was a vulnerability he decided he had to endure to talk to all the troops at station on the first floor.

The banging on the glass doors turned to the mob moving back so they could throw rocks at the windows. As the rocks were thrown, some would pick them up and throw them again. The glass chipped then splintered then finally started to break.

When the crowd rushed the wall of windows and doors, the order by Captain Carne was given to fire until the soldiers ran out of ammunition. The wall of windows held for a second then caved in, and the first of the rioters were trampled under. The sound of gunfire muted the screams of built-up rage, and the time seemed to be suspended in rapid fire as the wall of the rioters came to look like a building wave as the death toll mounted.

The wave came within two feet of the soldiers and then stopped. The sixth floor saw the crowd surge and then dissipate. They waited for the streets to clear, and then called Capt. Donald Carne for a sitrep.

Joseph M. Due, October 18, 2016

Mary

Thirty-two and lonely, he perused the vegetables and wondered what he would buy for the week's groceries. The moment's indecision passed by, and he decided to make hamburger soup and get some crackers. As he picked out the carrots, he needed he heard a young lady say, "Excuse me."

He looked around until he found the voice. He realized his cart was in the middle of the row, so he colored a little and apologized. She started to pick cabbage, which was where he was headed next. They started to converse about dinner and recipes then he asked her name.

She said her name was Mary Daniels, and she lived two blocks behind the store. He said he lived on Maple Corners. She said there were some nice houses on Maple Corners. He said she would be welcome to come visit, say, at 1800 hours. She thought about it for a while. Then she said "Date" and put out her right hand. He said "Date" and took her hand and shook it.

She seemed forthright and honest. The guard called her name in as Joseph hurried through his shopping. The morning passed by as Joseph made the soup and let it simmer. He thought a nice, firm base would please Mary.

The hour appointed arrived, and the guard stood outside in expectation. She was five minutes early and seemed to be familiar with the surroundings. The guard decided to run her plates and ask for a picture identification.

The investigators cued in on the guard's concerns and rushed identification. They sent four investigators over with the picture identification they had received from DMV. The guard said that the woman in the house was not that of the photo identification, so they went in by twos to ask her who she was.

Joseph M. Due, October 8, 2016

Mary Terf

Mums guaranteed that Mary Terf was true-blue. She was a person you could count on, and the background investigation came up clean. He thought about it for a while. The last date seemed so nice until they arrested her and checked her purse and her cell phone.

The four-inch knife might have been for safety, but the list of bad boys on her cell phone with the knife was indicative of intent to commit when a person knew she was using a stolen car and fake identification.

The time she served for carrying a concealed weapon without a permit did not seem enough time. Neither did the time she had added to her sentence for the stolen car or fake ID seem enough.

He knew his Mums loved him and wanted to see grandchildren by him. He thought of being a tad bit lonely and asked to hear her name again. He called the Terfs and asked for permission to date their daughter. He then called her up, but she was not at home. He decided he would try again later.

The return call was nice enough, and he invited her to church and Sunday brunch. She agreed that that would be a nice enough way to get to know him. The preaching service was on timely repentance and used the flood as an example that time does run out for people.

She talked over ideas like children. She wanted ten. Her favorite colors were red and green. They even had a few dates together, but Joseph got the idea that she had decided she wanted someone younger.

Joseph M. Due, October 8, 2016

128

Alchemy

The reality of the creation of guns and gunpowder proves a type of alchemy is real. The usages for modern weaponry demonstrate that alchemy, in a given way, is beneficial to humanity and deserves respect unto the word.

The tactical use of philosophical truths means that by knowing the art of war, we understand the truths around us and respect them. Clear sight of the truths extant means we see the applications that much better.

That means the tactical considerations need a base of knowledge to draw upon for proper decision-making. Sometimes, that is alchemy.

Army Command School for Joseph and William was exacting and demanding. The tactical courses were not too bad, but the philosophy they had to debate so they could understand it enough to pass the tests. The management philosophies they remembered from their College days.

The recompilation of old and new thought needed time for the synergy of the essence to utilize properly. They both adopted habits after new information of such an extent to make way for a day of rest and a day with their friends. The drive back was a relief from the challenging course. William had placed first, and Joseph had come in second place. The celebration when they got home would be nice.

Joseph M. Due, October 23, 2016

Danger

The smell of her perfume was wearing off, and the odor from her sweat was rising in the air. The smell mirrored her attitude as she showered and prepared to leave. He noticed the smell was muted by the shower soap but was still worsening.

He called his guard in and told him he could stay in the kitchen but be prepared for inbound. He then called Investigations and gave them Sarah Strong's name and address as well as the license plate number he memorized from dropping her car off at his house.

The weekend was moving slow, and the investigations unit was busy. So he had to wait to find out what she was up to.

There are zillions of flavors of ice cream. Some people like their favorites, and some people like to try the new flavors.

He looked out the window and saw a strange car slowly passing by. The people stared at the lawn as they passed by, checking out the landscape. The guard said, "Is that the trouble you saw coming?" Joseph said probably. The guard called the watch and gave a description of the car and the people in the car and explained the driver and the passenger's activities.

He decided to get a cup of coffee and watch the alleyway. He told the guard to sound out if he saw anything suspicious. The day was clear, and he could see quite well. He periodically scanned the backyard and alleyway for any unwelcome visitors.

The car parked in the back, and they sat there and waited. He could now see weapons in the car. He asked the guard if he had anything out front. He said, "Six people so far." Joseph said, "Close the kitchen door and meet me in the hallway." He called the watch and said he needed a team at his house and be prepared to come in hot.

He then put the cell phone on the coffee table and returned to the hall to await the break-in. The minutes passed by as the tension mounted. There was noise at the front door first and then the back. They kicked in the front door, and as it swung open, the guard and Joseph opened fire.

Then Joseph turned and started firing at the intruders as they entered from the back door. The rooms kept filling up, and when they emptied their pistols, they backed into the hallway and switched clips. Then there were none up and shooting anymore, so they took turns covering each other as they reloaded again.

Joseph M. Due, October 4, 2016

Prepared

En garde monsieur. To be vigilant without being told is for the ready to be alive and live. The wiles of Femme fatales, Joseph's parents did know. Until and even after he had an angelic guardian, they provided a human guardian to protect his interest—to protect his life.

The morning briefings brought Joseph the tidings of the health of the city of Houston as his people. God's children could perceive it, and their perceptions were usually accurate. As Joseph was an up-and-coming Captain of the watch, his dad told him many things about command and leadership.

He told Joseph to be prepared and vigilant always because it could be fatal for him if he were not. He told Joseph furthermore that the people needed him alive and healthy to protect the people that desired to live in peace. He even admitted man-to-man that Jean and he loved Joseph very much.

Joseph returned the comment of love because he knew there was a bond of love between him and his parents. His Majority was filled with the new thoughts many people were teaching him. He also knew this was a form of love.

Returning home, Betty Terf met him at his door. She was dutiful and a very nice help. Both knew she was practicing for another. As nice as she was, they both knew where her heart fell. The idea unfolding was both a happy and sad thing as both worked out their destinies.

They talked on the couch of the advice Terrance had given Joseph and how important he saw the morning briefs. They talked of his shift work, and in the nuances of her listening, he could read that she was almost done helping him.

He told her she had to follow her destiny, and when the time came, he would understand.

Joseph M. Due, October 10, 2016

Colonel

Colonel Carne, newly frocked, stood by his parent's door and greeted all the well-wishers good day. The promotion and party they thought were well deserved. His post as executive officer waited for him. He thought about current operations and worked on the constructs of the cases in his mind.

His current girlfriend actually was avant-garde for God and Country, but he felt she did not think of him as husband material. Nicole Smith was a distant aunt to William and came with high recommendations—for the good of the corps and all. She awaited the end of the party, and he thought a little sadly about the end of their relationship.

She liked him well enough and desire and passion did arise a time or two, but she did not like his house colors. As the last of the well-wishers left, he thought of her kisses with great fondness. He shut the door and went into the kitchen. He was sure his old coffee cup had been picked up a while ago.

Mums was there with a remnant of a tear in her eye. She was proud of her boy. He was proud of her. They loved each other dearly. He walked over and kissed her on the forehead. She blushed and hugged him.

The Folgers was as good as always, and Mums had plenty of extra-large coffee cups for her men. He thanked the ladies for their help as they cleaned up. He then went into the living room, where some of the senior ranking officers were still talking to the General, his dad.

Training, he heard, was the key to reducing the deaths experienced in combat. Troop loss was to be avoided. They made room for him and kindly asked him what he thought. He paused for a moment in prayer and said, "Ladies and gentlemen, I believe we officers should motivate the troops to self-train at times by showing them we train and aspire to meet the standard before us."

The General said he wholeheartedly agreed. The troops knew that it was the new commander's intent and would be enforced by the old commander. They thought about it a while and asked for applications. He said Lieutenants should be on the firing range and post with their troops. The trainers should at least live fire demonstrate the intent of the drill.

The Captains and Majors should practice their form and continue self-training in the gym when the men are up. Tactics should teach the formulation of the plans by drawing up, as demonstration, their own plan and showing the teams. Senior staff should participate in unit issue considerations when they have five or ten minutes to do so.

The General gauged the unit's consideration of commitment to his son's ideas. He knew it would take time and practice to perfect. It would take sacrifice to perfect. He knew it could be done and let his support stand with his son's. The officers now knew what new changes were in store for the Fifty-Seventh.

Late that night, he and Nicole talked about the plans for the future they had. He touched her skirt, and she sighed with longing. He caressed her and then gently undressed her. He then carried her to the bed and turned out the light. The desire grew, and the passion flared as the night disappeared in the longing.

In the morning, he awoke to the alarm and knew she would not be back. She had said her goodbye. It was a nice breakup—truthful, honest, sincere, and said in love. As he showered, he knew he would think of her now and then.

Fishing was on the horizon for a nearby lake. William and he liked bass fishing just fine. He made some coffee and waited for William to arrive. The fishing gear was already by the door.

The noon hour passed as they chose another fishing spot. Fishing took patience, and so he practiced patience as William asked him questions he thought Theresa, his wife, would. The day was looking up. The new fishing spot held promise as William dropped anchor. William told him he was actually improving in his date selection as his line went under.

That evening, Theresa asked him if Laura Brown would interest him. He knew the women were talking as he ate his roast beef and potatoes. He asked who the dad was and how old she was. He told her he liked emotionally mature women. They left a person better, he continued.

He turned on the light in the living room and went into the kitchen for a bottle of venos. Then he turned on the CD and sat in his chair, reflecting on both Nicole in the past and wondering about Laura in the future. After an hour, he called Laura and asked if she was interested in a date.

The first shift he took as XO, he decided after the briefings to tour the building. The sixth floor was the easiest, being only three teams were up. Some were in the gym playing basketball. It was fairly empty otherwise. The fifth floor he asked for a brief about the numerous empty bins he saw. The briefing told him the order and stocking status was inordnung.

The fourth was a collection of odds and ends like offices for the Team Captains. The third was Armory, equipment, and supply issue as well as the firing range. The obstacles were set up, and the soldiers were lined up to fire in their turn. He asked the soldiers if he could take the next turn. He walked through the course quickly, not wasting motion. The trainer had said that despite walking, he course-qualified.

He then went to the armory to reload. One of the privates asked, "When do we get our own weapon?" His Lieutenant said, "When you buy the weapon and rigging." He then motioned for the next one to proceed. Joseph smiled. He knew they would take to heart the lessons they picked up while critiquing his firing run.

The next stop was investigations. He wanted to know what they were looking at from intent to suspect's house maps. They had five different ideas from planning, recruiting, operations, transit sites, and funding of the criminal's activities.

The current obsession with the local criminals was firearms and bombs. One of the investigators reminded him that the criminal interest changes frequently. He nodded and made a mental note to remember the lesson. He then asked about the status of current investigations. They showed him what they had on the more numerous IDS houses and what their past preferences were.

The next stop was the training area. He wanted to know about the scheduling and doing more in-depth demonstrations. They talked to him about more complete demonstrations and agreed to work on improving the training.

The officers agreed the troops could be motivated better by the staff, and they were working out a schedule through training. This pleased Joseph very much. He hoped to see other people walk the unit and keep an eye out for the opportunity to help out.

Dinner was at 2000 hours, and he decided to eat in the dining room. Some of the staff would be there. He got his plate and ordered a tater tot hotdish. The command post watch officer was already there, so he joined her. The room filled up with troops as he ate. He told some of them about what he would like to do.

The watch officer invited him into the command post to watch another staff exercise. He decided he would stop by and watch. The scenario was one of a series of kidnappings in the area. The inputs covered the search for the missing children. The teams were called up and augmented by Fort Houston. They determined to augment investigations with coordinated searches by the police and FBI.

In reality, the alert teams walked through equipment issue and investigations set up in the gym to brief the teams and have them do recon by map grid coordinates. The exercise proceeded to strike teams being sent out to interdict the kidnappers and bring the children out safely as possible.

The command center seemed to know what they were doing, and there was only a slight delay in briefing the troops. The exercise was logged two hours later with the executive officer's comments, and then they cleared the boards and returned to normal operations.

He noted how efficiently they turned around and waited for the last to say they were fully on line in operational mode. He told them they were the finest he had seen. The captain of the command post thanked him and said he would enter it in the log.

The day closed out, and Laura Brown awaited him. They would go to Perkins for breakfast. She told him she thought he was a nice, considerate person that anticipated people's needs. She then told him that she worked at Pennies, in the clothing department. He told her that Theresa gave her high marks for caring and helping people out really well.

She did ask if he could talk about Nicole. He said a little. He told her Nicole was a very nice person who cared and was highly organized and she communicated really well. She was just not walking down the same road he was, and she finally realized she was looking for someone who had different color preferences.

She thought about likes and dislikes in life, and they chatted the hours away. He then took her home and turned to see if she would kiss him. She turned and leaned forward, and he kissed her with desire. Five minutes later, she asked him to come in. She opened the door and stepped in two steps and stopped.

He hugged her from behind and kissed her again for a while, and when she moved forward, he removed her blouse. He then closed the door and put his hands on her lower back, gently caressing her. When he got to the bra, he gently twisted it open, and she let it fall to the floor. She turned around and hugged him as he gently picked her up and followed the light to her bedroom.

The next morning, he cooked her two egg sandwiches with cheese and a large cup of coffee. She said they were delicious and inhaled them. They then talked on the couch for a while before she had to go to work. He told her he worked from 1600 hours to 2400 hours and would like to see her again. As they left to go their ways, she promised she would call.

William was at work and they needed to schedule their next fishing vacation and he could stop in and see his dad. He looked out his window and slowed. There were two people arguing off the street. As he passed by, he saw one knife the other. Now he had to stop in investigations.

The neighborhood gangs were becoming more active, and investigations said they would look into it after taking his report. On the way out, he heard them call the police to request any information they had. He hoped it was only a personal dispute.

His dad was doing supply requisitions when he checked in. They talked for a while, and he mentioned Laura Brown's name. His dad said he knew her dad from way back. He worked as a shift lead in a production center in the industrial area of town. He told his son what he knew about Mr. Brown.

William was making paper airplanes and sailing them across the room. He said that everyone was functionally working him into boredom. Joseph commiserated with him for a little while and then asked him if Saturday, the sixteenth of September, would be nice for another try at the bass. William agreed and then asked about Laura. He said the information was for his wife.

Joseph told him of his impression and the date and then went silent. William then asked him if there was anything wrong, and Joseph said no. Joseph turned the topic to what he had seen that morning. William thought it was sad that people could not get along at times.

The days went by, and the years passed. What was said was not forgotten.

The midnight hour had come, and Joseph was headed for his car when his cell phone went off. It was the Watch Officer saying he might want to come back up to the command post. He pressed the elevator button and turned the key to allow him access to the floor the command post was on. He wondered what it could be.

Robert was there, and he said, "Colonel Carne, I have a visitor from the FBI with me. The warning order we decided to deliver in person."

"The FBI station was bombed in Washington as well as the interdiction unit assigned there. You know of the Fifteenth CID. Some of your people were stationed there." "Who?" Joseph asked. "The trail leads to Arizona, but the distribution net leads here." He wondered about the applications and started asking the agent twenty questions. The Watch Officer and shift supervisor for the command post were taking notes.

He thanked the agent for the briefing and sent for investigations. He wanted to know if there were any transit sites that were more active of late. Investigations said they were checking suspect names and license plates. They also said some were, but they needed more manpower. He told the post to get teams 3 and 4 up and briefed. Time was a luxury they did not have. He then told investigations to brief the reception team and response force.

He decided to call teams 6, 7, and 8 back to work and put them in the gym. Joseph decided to wait to call up the Fort for augmentation. The soldiers would all be at work at 0800 hours if they were needed.

Joseph M. Due, September 27, 2016

Gangland Shootings

The whine from the jail cell was in several parts, with part A saying the burden they would now bear in the way of prison term earned, and part B saying they were betrayed by their buddies and did not know what their buddies were actually up to. There were so many categories that the sheriffs wished the police had not brought them in.

Across town, police donned civilian garb and took to five houses. They would do twelve on and twelve hours off for the duration. As long as one was up, they could rest in turn. They took their lunch breaks outside for sight time to let the people know they were still open.

For three days, they waited for criminals who had not known to come on by. The police got about another twenty criminals all told before they put up the yellow crime scene tape on the houses.

The ATF were conducting full interviews for those that would accept an interview.

As the newly caught came in, they were double billeted with the other criminals. The net was spreading its manpower to get as many of the criminals as it could. The Fifty-Seventh picked up monitoring the seized houses, and thirty-five investigators were tasked with the interviews.

The net yield was potentially five houses in Kansas City and some transit houses along the way. The teams were on twelve and twelve hours off. The teams were tasked with setting up surveillance locally. The ATF decided they would send the majority of their agents to Kansas City.

Joseph M. Due, October 8, 2016

Lieutenant Colonel D. Carne

The storm passed over Houston, and the people were glad before God that the refuse of the storm was gone with the storm. The nom de jure at times was idyllic peace, and they prayed about the criminal refuse that it, too, be washed away in the storms. Contentious people bring in the violence of their days.

Major Carne typified his training as peace won by war. He believed that prior preparation prevents poor performance—the five P's of life. He was determined him and his people would learn to live by it. His daily regimen in the gym on third shift set the example for others to follow. The morning briefs for General Terrance and Colonel Joseph Carne set a tradition that went back decades.

The interest of the day was kidnappers again. They seemed to just come out of the woodwork at times, and they caused a lot of problems for the family and the larger community. Vans had been stolen, hospital baby records breached, and school yearbooks were on an upswing in interest to the criminal mind.

A citywide search might be an idea that has come again. He put that on the briefing slides along with a recommendation to query the FBI to see what they might have that affects the Houston area. The day dawned, and from his office, he could see a sliver of yellow to the east as the sun broached the trees on the horizon.

He waited for an answer before he headed home. His parents appreciated it when he showed up a little late so they could have a little time together instead of worrying about one of their children in the house. The day shift briefing team returned the slides to each office. He saw the Captain bringing him his slides back.

The Captain greeted Colonel Carne and said, "Colonel Carne approves the suggestions and you are to take point." Donald asked the Captain why he was called Colonel. The General said, "Sir, he said that approval was received to have you frocked to Lieutenant Colonel as of the first. That was ten hours ago, sir."

Joseph M. Due, October 18, 2016

Silver Hair

The silver of his hair highlighted him in any crowd. He thought about the torments that incurred the coloring of his hair and sighed. He still wished he could have learned without it being so marked in his body. He remembered the times he tried regrowing his hair, and then he tried a variety of hair dyes. Neither the cutting of his hair nor the dyes did anything but embarrass him.

The light of the elevator flashed by him, and he refocused his thoughts. His team awaited his arrival, and he prepared to give his speech and then the orders and directions that would follow. The elevator opened up on the sixth floor, and he stepped out to go to the meeting room when the building was rocked by an explosion under his feet. The energy from the blast almost made him stumble.

The alarms sounded high and long. *The response force downstairs must be busy*, he thought. He walked over to the reception desk and paged the first floor. His team poured out of the meeting room and surrounded him at the desk. The answer was grim. The elevators were damaged and two of the stairways were opened, so there were bad guys penetrating to the floors above.

He pressed the intercom button and spoke to the people in the building, telling them help was on the way but response should be with care and each person team up and control and patrol their respective areas two by two. Response would be from the inside out. His managers nodded and awaited further orders as he disconnected the intercom.

The control system was guarded and held, he knew. It would take a second bomb to penetrate the area. He sent four down the back stairwell, telling them to take care. They were to interdict any bombing teams sent that way. The other seven would take the staircases and clean out levels 4 and 5. He looked at them with confidence. So far, they had been through worse disasters.

The day progressed as the villains were hunted down one by one, and in the afternoon, the building was searched again. He thought about governance. They would be worried about the scope of villainy. The criminals were lined up or laid out in the first floor lobby. Questions were asked, and identification of the criminals got underway.

Their purpose was to delay operations, damage the group, or exterminate his people. There was no surprise to their affiliation or purpose, and they were verbose in their commentary about the so-called glories of their purpose. They knew where he and his people lived and worked, and that gave him a chill. Relocation would have to be resurveyed and expedited. He knew his teams had to hurry up the tempo of planned operations and yet spend more time thinking through each problem to see if there were any inherent traps.

As the building was cleared, the families came in to the parking deck and were given bunks in the mission planning rooms. The idea was for team 2 to take them to Fort Houston and use the available officer's quarters to house them securely. Gen. Mavis Tims would approve the use of light infantry guarding the housing area for the duration.

The next move was to ascertain the cell's locations to see if they were up and running and if their teams could be located. This was highly dangerous but necessary for planned operations. They would strike the cells they found at dawn if possible. The team augmentation was just hours away, so he called governance house to gain necessary approval to use the troops tasked for later operations.

It would be a long day, so he headed to the briefing room to bring his teams up to speed. Team 3 would augment the building for the duration, and he knew they were good troops. Team 4 would patrol the city grid for large movements of armed people and infiltrators spying on the comings and goings of his teams. Team 5 would set up an alternate command post just in case the spies could not be identified.

The other teams knew the planned operational areas and went to work organizing the squads so the Sergeants knew the plan as well. The secretaries were doing well. The kitchens were up and running, and food was prepared for all. The building still had concrete dust going through the ventilation system, he noticed as he looked at his suit coat. He called down to the second floor, and they told him the filters had been changed and it would be another hour before the dust would be cleared from the air.

Thinking of Robert Young, he headed for operations to see how well the teams were moving. At 1700 hours, all was going well. Team 5 had even picked up some more perpetrators, and things looked hopeful. By 1900 hours, the ladies would be moving, and the team protecting them was very good. The inbound were already filtering in and being briefed as they showed up with their duffel bags. It was a good sign that the troops came prepared for just about anything.

Sylvia from team 1 called and asked what he wanted to do with the Smith Carne Industry sign that was shot down. He told her to break it down and asked ops to call Cynthia and have her order another sign for putting up about the first of May. That should give the construction crews enough time to fix the façade on the outer door structure.

Supper was roast beef and cheese sandwiches and milk courtesy of the secretaries, and he decided to take a nap in his office. He told ops where he was headed, and Tim Reger was tasked to clear the atrium and secure the floor just in case there were any further problems. When 2000 hours rolled around, planning did a final brief for Teams 6 through 11 before they were to disperse.

At 9:00 p.m., the convoys dispersed into the city grid. Bearing his business logo, he knew the vans were easy to see. Did the enemies of state know he used the vans for dispersal? They did not brag about that knowledge, so he wondered.

The interviews would start on Monday when the Feds arrived in town in sufficient numbers. What nonsense would the criminals spout? He knew the tapes were continuous and clear. Their actions speaking for them as truths they would face. Destroyers of hope they were, and his people stood in their way.

The last van pulled out of sight in the distance. He said a prayer for the soldier's souls that they would find good hunting and for their safety in God's hands and in their training. Donald was standing beside him, a young prince of the land and heir apparent. He knew Donald since he was two, growing up in his younger brother's house.

Dedicated and diligent, he showed the troops he cared for them and the individuality of their lives. When it was his time, he would do the job well. He turned and asked Donald what was up. Donald said, "The Post Commander sends his regards. The first families are already bedding down in sleeping bags from supply."

He asked him, "And the rest?" "Within the hour, sir," he replied. He said he was getting reports from the observers at the checkpoints that there was not much traffic and they did not see anyone following yet. They would make their final reports at 2100 hours.

He told Donald to brief him about the alternate command post. He said they could not see any long-term stragglers, but they were prepared. "Departure hour is still 0600," he said. He said, "It looks good to me. Remember to pray for good success always."

The families that chose to stay were rearranging the bunking as Silver Hair walked into the community room. He stopped in for an hour to see them and check on their needs. *The children are the hopes of the future*, he thought. *How precious they are.* They seemed to have settled in just fine, and the secretaries were taking turns looking in on them.

The business was more than a front. It was part of the lifeblood of his people and provided revenue for the extra things in life. That being so, he returned to his office to catch up on the paperwork. Tooling was a slow but steady business he had to keep on top of. Donald as XO was very adept at system design and regularly posted good ingenious designs for tool/space usage.

Robert Young was another good asset in a business of good assets. He was just pulling himself off a cot when he walked in. Both sides of planning, scheduling, and operations he coordinated with flair. The communication nets were up, and normal traffic was flowing. His people did him proud.

He said, "Bob, I hope I am not disturbing you too much." Robert said, "No, sir, just getting up." "Dan will have to brief us both on current operations." He walked over to station 1, which was technical services, as Bob joined him and Dan. They continued to special services, and he realized he only lost twenty, all told and all of them in the building.

Special services were on air and reported everyone was well. They said that with the General providing area support, they could release ten primary operatives to other duties. Dan said Donald was notified, and he wanted them to report to team 6's local. Silver Hair agreed, and the orders were transmitted. Team 2 was augmenting the building security with team 3. Some would be released later in the day to run errands for the children. During times of distress, they did not go back to the homes, but command picked up the tab for purchases through AAFEs.

Looking at the Alternate Command Post, they reported all systems in a go status for 0630 hours. He then reviewed the team's sitreps (situation reports). They were in better shape than expected. Bob said, "We could offer infantry straight-up commissions as well, as things were going, if Silver Hair did not mind." He said, "What does Donald think about group augmentation?" He said, "If the General and you did not mind, it would add thirty qualified operatives to our list."

"If it could be done, sir. Donald wanted to talk to the infantry soldiers about the idea during the after-action report scheduled for 1500 hours." He said, "When the General calls to say he is up, page me and I will broach the subject then. The General may have qualifications as to whom he can afford to release. Let Donald know what I said, Bob. We may have to delay the idea until Tuesday."

He then told Dan he would be in Ops next door when Donald started giving orders for movement at 0630 hours. He then had the Team 2 section call up to have his wife meet him in his office. They ordered coffee and eggs for two from the kitchen as he was leaving Operations.

The city planning maps were the same as the team's maps they studied in the pre-dawn morning at their rally sites. This was the best governance could provide, so they rarely had few surprises on that score. The team's ingress points were plotted, and ops was going to follow along via radio/telephone communications. Coffee and doughnuts were provided on a side board. Anticipated wait time was one hour from departure to rally. When they were counted at the rally point after egress, the sitreps would be compiled and reviewed. At 1400 hours, Training would look at the mission and give the troops an overall evaluation at 1500 hours.

At 0630 hours on the dot, the teams left their rally points in the growing dawn. Latest ETA was 1650 hours with a minimum time frame for approach and attack. The routes were plotted again the day before for obstructions like road construction. The growing traffic could be heard even in the buttressed Operations center.

The tension was palpable. You could almost cut it with a knife. Delays or obstructions could damage the synergy and endanger the mission. As the teams started pulling into position, the tension was seen in every shoulder. They worried about the mission and the lives of their children. The teams cleared the departure point plus or minus one minute of the ETA.

They could not hear the explosions or gunfire, but they could imagine what the troops were facing. The time slowed down to a crawl. The nets started chattering with sitreps of "troops down" and, gratefully, "area cleared" calls. Time sped up as the action was recorded for posterity.

The timing of clearance in the heaviest units was nominal, and all they could collect was minimal. What was collected did indicate their targets and objectives. The other four who had a surfeit of data, command could study and send off to governance. Governance would be interested in the data so they could get a feel for what the enemy knew about their operations.

The bodies were collected on orders to egress the soldier's mission area. The way back was made sober by the bodies they carried. Reflections kept the troops on the lookout and on mistakes and errors they would have to be men about and admit for future operations.

Happy were the troops. Mission accomplishment was high and the overall critique light.

Expected resistance was high, indicating something command would be interested in. They did not anticipate commands recovery after their attack on command. They would now think twice about anticipating command's response capability.

Rest after sitrep and body bag detail was in order. By 0900 hours, they were heavily asleep knowing the facility was guarded. Cleanup would be at 1400 hours for individuals. Area cleanup would be from 1430 to 1445 hours and then setup for mission sitrep briefing.

Meanwhile, the count was relayed to Fort Houston, and the negotiations began for transfers if the soldiers were willing. The morning went by as people plied themselves to the endeavor of recovery. Of interest was the knowing if the enemy knew of the troop's home addresses. Other interests took a backstage to the knowing if their troops needed new names and addresses.

At 1000 hours, they had their list. Sixty-five soldiers could transfer in. Donald received the news with relief. He could hire full and partially trained infantry instead of picking inexperienced troops from Advanced Infantry Training School. These troops were committed and blooded in combat, and they did very well.

He ordered the infantry team leads awake at 1330 hours so they could be briefed. They would inform their soldiers of their choice so that they could report to command their choice. The cleanup and determination of body assets started, and the morgue was called to pick up those bodies that were cleared for release.

By 1100 hours, the majority of equipment had been cleaned and returned to supply. The effort was a miracle accomplished in part by the civil side of operations, which chipped in their two mites. The people had reviewed the sitreps, and those with known addresses were notified to stay on station for new housing assignments. They could not go back to their houses on a permanent basis.

Dinner was a festive affair, with people knowing they were going to be taken care of. All they had to do was stand to; they were used to the idea, so some put in for long-term care purchases and games for their children. Dinner for the sleeping troops would be at 1700 hours.

At 1300 hours, the women were ferried over to mate up with their spouses. They were free to attend the briefings, and that gave purpose to the day's mission. The children were babysat by the young women, and the secretaries not on duty checked in on them.

Donald briefed the infantry team leads to spread the word for those who could sign up right away and discussed policy and procedures for those that would. At the end of the briefing, he fielded questions about his command and why some soldiers were needed at their parent command.

At 1400 hours, there were showers for the soldiers and plenty of towels to go around. A half-hour shower was a luxury to the single men. The details were light—bedding was placed in laundry, cots put away, and chairs brought out for all to have seats in the gym. Donald's team set up the podium and viewgraphs. The after-action briefs were underway from contact briefs and conclusions to policy, dinner, and release time for the units.

When the primary teams had a day's rest, the covering teams would then receive the same briefing. Meanwhile, there was a watch to keep and a mission to perform.

Joseph M. Due, September 17, 2016

Thanksgiving

Amidst the problems of the days before, Joseph there was the motif of life itself. There were also moments and days of peace sprinkled throughout his life, providing the peace and happiness that those that seek His righteousness earn. Also, amidst what at times looked like a sea of trouble were all his faithful friends to enable and provide comfort.

The blessings of peace could be seen in the health and well-being of all the people and the conditions set to include roads and buildings.

The days included the advent of the mornings he appreciated to the friendship of warriors trained and born.

Thanksgiving Day was one of Joseph's favorite days. He found out what new and old friends were truly grateful for, and the celebration was spiritual to him.

The phone rang, and he looked at the alarm clock. It was 0500 hours. He thought he would be called in, so he reached for his bedside phone. Straightening his mind out and focusing, he said, "Carne residence."

His Mums called for a favor and thought he might need the time to purchase the ingredients and cook the food. He reached for a pen and paper on the nightstand and said, "Go ahead, Mums." She gave him the recipe for deviled eggs and ordered two hundred of the deviled eggs.

He showered and then went shopping at the local grocery store for a hundred eggs for the morning snack at Mums's house. He had to be quick; guests would be arriving by 1000 hours.

Joseph M. Due, October 15, 2016

Wonder

Touché Monsieur. The touch of a truth not lived has a strength all its own that has to be adjusted to in order to live well and fight effectively.

William cast in his line and hoped the ripples he had seen would produce a bass. Maybe he would be able to net a nice-size five-pounder. Joseph looked for ripples on his side of the boat and said to Theresa, "How many truths did you face before your orientation? You took it very well."

Theresa replied, "Five or six major truths. On the big truth that affected me about you and William's activities, I swerved and almost drove off the road."

The boat rocked as Joseph cast out. William said to Theresa, "I'm glad you righted the car and took it so well." She then went on to talk about her decision to look for better dates for him, and she knew a young Lady in the cooking department that might come around.

William asked her who it was. She said Sarita Thomas. William said, "I know her parents. He works on third shift in tool maintenance." She said, "He's her father, but she has some hesitations about marrying a soldier that might take a bullet."

Joseph said, "If she comes around to accepting the idea, let me know."

Joseph M. Due, October 8, 2016

Heritage

The morning smells were fresh at 0700 hours, and the day beckoned in welcome greetings telling people of the newness of the day. The wind moved gently through the farms and gardens and brought to the city folk a smell to tease the senses and refresh the mind.

The promotion of Joseph to the general's rank did not go unnoticed. The house party was a three-day affair with the troops scheduled so that there was plenty of room for drop-in visitors. The party for Colonel Donald Carne had left the Carne household no choice because of the overcrowding at Donald Carne's earlier promotion.

The Chief training position was held by the Carne family as well as the division commander position. Auspices of good fortune were felt all around. The representation was saluted far and wide.

The process of training was revamped under Gen. Terrance Carne, Gen. Joseph Carne, and now again under Col. Donald Carne. It would be revamped again.

The soldiers that were there for the long haul knew, in regards to training, it was going to get better yet again. They also knew they would be challenged to become even better soldiers, and in the endeavor, the percentages of deaths per combat event would drop even more.

Meanwhile, glad tidings of such a magnitude did not go unnoticed by those who would be jealous and hateful. One plan after another was looked at and discarded. They finally figured out they could get at least one teen in the garage if a distraction were provided.

Joseph M. Due, October 17, 2016

Christmas

The Christmas tree was bright and cheerful. The lights gave each color an ambient glow that lit up the room just right. The smell of red pine needles permeated the room. Joseph thought the ambiance was sort of what heaven must be like.

That is he thought. He could use some company. Everything was right except he did not find anyone that could put with his lifestyle. Friends were fine, but he did get a bit lonely. The living room was twenty by twenty by twelve feet. He could tell. The others were out and about, and he was a little tired. A young lady came into the room. *Sarita Thomas was her name*, he thought.

Sarita looked at Joseph and apologized for interrupting his rest. William had told her he was here. He looked at her, and she blushed, taking another chair overlooking the tree. He said yes. She said she wanted to know if he was interested in her. He said, "You look like a very nice lady that I would like to get to know." She blushed again and said, "At first, I did not know if I could live with a soldier, but I came to realize I might be able to."

He asked her if Alvin were her dad. She nodded and said, "I cook second shift in the kitchens. This is my fourth year." He asked her what her specialties were, and she told him she specialized in American casseroles and things like tater tot hot dish. He nodded and said, "My favorite is omelets and over easy egg sandwiches." He asked her if she was hungry. She said yes, so he invited her to attend him in the kitchen.

Thinking of the change in his life that might be taking place, he said an emotional short prayer and then asked Theresa if he could use the fry pan and some eggs. Theresa said, "No problem." He then asked Sarita if she preferred over easy sandwich or an omelet with toast. As the time passed by, the party guests started arriving in ones and twos. He was then told he had to surrender the kitchen and Sarita for a while as they got the cooking underway.

He promised to sit by her at dinner, and she nodded as she put on her apron. She wondered where what she started would take her in the future.

The holidays were pleasant, and IDS/IDC sites were at a low ebb in membership. The horizon was clear of conflict for a while though the watch kept up to date with even the rumors of violence that might become real.

He was grateful that weapons were hard to find and harder to resecure once seized. He called Alvin and asked permission to continue dating his daughter. Alvin said he was pleased at her choice, and of course he could date his twenty-three-year-old daughter.

He waited until 0800 hours to call her and asked if she would like to go out shopping. He said he needed new clothes because his wardrobe was getting bare. She agreed to see him at 1000 hours and spend the day with him. He knew women liked to take their time.

At 1000 hours, he picked her up at her apartment, and they drove to the mall. There was a nice men's store that sold suits. He talked to her about growing up with her parents and then told her a little about what it was like to live with his parents. He found she had a good attitude, great manners, and sincerity. And she knew a little about his story.

The One Potato Two was a great stop for a nice brunch. She then recommended the Arizona Jean Company for nice shirts and jeans. He was impressed by her choice of shops. Her particular selections he could live with. Then he asked her about late Christmas shopping, so they headed for Dayton's on the mall.

He asked her if she liked skating and whether she would like dinner before or afterward. She told him she liked Dinner first, but she needed to change into jeans for the skating. At 1800 hours, they were finished with the shopping part of the date, and then he waited in the living room while she changed.

"Denny's or Perkins?" he asked. She said she preferred Perkins, and so they went to Perkins for Supper and then went skating afterward. The dinner this time was three pigs in a blanket. That is, the dinner was pancakes and sausage. He let her pick the entrée. The diner was filled with what looked like shoppers.

After looking around, she whispered, "Isn't that Tim Becket in team 5?" He replied calmly, "No, that is Tim Becket in the protection detail looking out for us." She stared at him for a while and readjusted to the idea that she now needed protection. She said, "Me?" He said quietly, "When you became important to me, you became important to my enemies."

The news was sobering. When they were finished, she leaned into him as they left Perkins. He put his arms around her until she felt comforted. The skating took her mind off the new reality. The music was country, and they held hands and danced.

She talked about her job and wondered if she would lose it. That is, being a house Frau and all. He reassured her that she could even take a more prominent position like secretarial and help organize the Firm and Unit if she wanted to. She asked if babies would interfere with her job. He said, "Only during illness or the last month."

"Company policy," he said, "is job security." She then asked him how many babies he wanted. He said, "Four of either sex." She thought about wanting three. After a minute of silence, she said, "Four sounds nice. I can deal with that." He noticed the pause and asked her how many she wanted. She said three. He thanked her for her consideration, and if three worked out, he would be just as happy. She blinked and thought about her dream of children. She was finally getting close to realizing her dream.

She then asked him if he wanted coffee. He replied, "It would be nice, but I cannot stay long because of work commitments I have to see to." While she was brewing, he called work, and they connected him to his dad. His dad said he was covering his shift for him so he could enjoy his date.

The blues were nice to listen to, and the conversation, though sporadic, talked of hope. Falling asleep on the couch with her, he finally felt at home.

At 0400 hours, he gently awoke, and he realized they had been entangled. He kissed her on the forehead and decided he could shower and change at work. He knew his dad and, later, his mom would want to know all about the date.

At 0500 hours, he was fully awake, and coffee and his dad were waiting. His dad had been waiting a long time for him to bring forth children. They briefed him as he ate doughnuts and drank the coffee. His dad waited for him to speak. He asked his dad who ordered the security on Sarita. His dad said he did after he heard how seriously his son was taking the date. "Your tracking pin let us know where you were, and we assigned a team to Sarita."

He talked his dad through Christmas Eve to the present. His dad asked a few questions about dealing with the reality of his son's position but seemed satisfied. He then asked if both were committed to marrying. Joseph said yes.

Sunday was upon him, and he decided to write her a poem and call her at 1000 hours since she was so tired. At 1000 hours, she said she was going to attend church at 1100 hours. Then she would make him a 1400 hours dinner if he did not mind. He said he would be there.

There was rumblings in some of the IDS centers that were on the hot list, so he went down to Planning and asked to see the history of the center and asked about proposed intent and preparation. The history of the centers was pretty bloody, but they did not have a goal and had access so far to a limited amount of weapons.

Some of the fundraisers were house parties for liquor and drugs. He asked if they had been sporting parties to raise funds for weapons. Planning told him two had active parties once or twice a month. He thought about it and told planning to keep after them they might surprise us.

He checked out at 1300 hours to buy Sarita a flower. He guessed a Lily might be a nice gesture. He presented the flower and the poem, and she hugged and kissed him.

The dinner was relaxed, and they chatted about her cooking. She said she talked to her mom about the meals he might actually like. She said she did not mention she already slept with him. He told her his dad took most of his shift and was waiting for him when he arrived at work. She blushed when she realized security would already know that he was here until 0400 hours.

The day saw both of them tired, so they relaxed and listened to some more rhythm and blues. She murmured that she liked country music well enough and would buy some tapes he liked listening to. He thanked her for her consideration as she fell asleep in his arms.

Monday saw the advent of another round of meetings with the firm and his unit. The holiday schedule was fully in place though each had to call in once a day to verify they were still safe. He still had enough to field three teams if necessary.

In the afternoon, he took Sarita to Music World, and they listened to some country music selections that he liked. She picked out ten that would go in his/her collection. He insisted on paying for the music. Then they stopped by Wendy's for carryout before work. He dropped her off at the firm's garage door and went to park the car while she hurried to work.

Mom called Joseph at 1600 hours with a bunch of busy questions until he said, "Oh, Mom." She then said, "OK, tell me about Sarita." He answered another half hour's worth of questions before he went down to the command center to check on the status boards.

As he perused the status boards, he noticed a new one was set up in the ops area. Initially, he wondered what was up until he remembered Sarita had security assigned to her now on what appeared to be a permanent basis. He asked John Turch, the Command Center Supervisor, if they had yet taken bets on when he would get married.

John said the predominant pool of thought was New Year's Day considering how serious he was about Sarita. He smiled and told John he was on his way to planning, then he would spend two hours talking to training. He could see Marisa update his board as he spoke. He knew when he left, security would be apprised of his local.

He thought about New Year's Day and wondered if she would go for it and if he could arrange for the wedding in time. He thought about Sarita and realized she would like a fairly nice wedding with parents and all. He thought about his parents and made a note to see if Mums wouldn't mind him using her house for the wedding.

Date 3 had to be different. *Sports, music concert, or theatre?* he wondered. He knew a good dinner theatre he could get tickets to but probably not so soon. He decided to order tickets anyway. He talked to his secretary about local and regional bands. There was nothing in the works that she knew about.

She knew that her world was going to be different today. She was now invested in someone else's life. The workers there knew she had a shadow that they were obligated to help do their job. The family interest was what she expected to see in the questions of the day. Her coworkers had questions, and she prepared in her mind to give a good answer.

So as she prepared the macaroni for cooking, she was asked by her fellow cook if she could talk about what she daydreamed about. She described his virtues and told the cooking staff about the long serious dates and how she was attracted to him. She even admitted she asked him first if he would be interested.

She found that they accepted her and found no harm in what she was doing, and that bound her closer to those in the kitchen. By the time the sauce and beef for the macaroni were ready, she had found a peace that had been missing.

Turning to her break, her boss told her she was going the wrong way. He said, "You do want to take care of Romeo, do you not? He is waiting at table 5." She blushed and went to look. Sure enough, he was there waiting for dinner. She prepared him a plate gladly and took one for herself.

He rose as she set the plates down and greeted her with a kiss on her cheek. She was very happy that he showed his affection and was not trying to hide his interest. She asked him how business was going, and he gave her a short synopsis of the day's events so far. She then heard him ask about the next date. She wondered how far he would go before he kissed her earnestly.

She thought about movies and said, "How about we check out two movies and some popcorn and stuff from a video store and have dinner at my place?" He thought about the latest movies and the classics. He thought of which movies to pick so that both would be satisfied. So he suggested *Brave Heart* and asked her to pick out one at the cinema store they would go to in the morning.

She had to return to work, so he watched her go. She was a fine woman and nice-looking too, he thought. He put the plates in the cleanup area and returned to work. His desires were at conflict inside him, for she was a very attractive woman. He thought about a ring and decided she must be a size 4 or 5 hand. He could arrange for her to pick one out on the next date.

Thinking about her stated intention. He wondered if it would do any long-term harm. *Would she have regrets?* he thought. As he pushed the elevator door to go to floor 3, he thought about his teams and what kind of message that would give.

The teams were practicing sniper emplacements as he entered the prep area for his teams. They were taught to think of the place as theirs. Making it their own and owning up to the responsibility to be the best trained they could be added a margin of safety to urban assault and the troop's overall training.

He pulled his handgun and checked the load. Working the forms with his troops inspired them to work at the forms themselves and do better. He relaxed into the task as the time passed by. The troops did not mind when leadership got in line and demonstrated. He knew it built confidence and trust as well as respect.

He was at peace with the cosmos, and it showed in the scores he received. He took the critique the officers gave at the end of the task. He made a mental note to practice more often and maybe bring Sarita through the confidence course they had.

The pickup was humorous as some tried to hide in plain sight, and some tried to be present to see if she would kiss him or he would kiss her. They laughed about it on the way to the cinema/video store. They picked up a John Wayne film about his wife and his command and

Brave Heart as well as popcorn, candy, and some Mountain Dew. She said she could drink the soda but mostly drank coffee.

The snow was lightly falling on the ground, and it was fairly warm, so they agreed to plan on going for a walk on one of the dates. They both talked through the movies; the angst of the movies, they both knew a little about. The candy was hardly touched, so she made sandwiches instead. The Mountain Dew was left in the refrigerator. Both opted for no more popcorn though she could have made some more.

The night started turning into the dawn as they fell asleep again. The couch was becoming habitual. Christmas night was that night. Both would need to visit parents as they thought about it at 1000 hours when they awoke. She let him use the shower first, and he put his day clothes back on, feeling refreshed but kind of grungy.

He commented on the idea, and she said he smelled just fine. Being it was Christmas, she asked him if it were too forward to ask him to marry her. He said he did not think so. So she asked him to say "I do wed thee." She repeated the words to him and kissed him heartily. Then she said that tonight, they could use the bedroom if he did not mind.

They first stopped in at her parents' house and asked them for the blessing. They asked to see the ring, and she blushed. He said it was Christmas but tomorrow he would have rings on her finger. They looked at her questioningly but went on with questions about the details of the wedding.

The morning turned into 1500 hours, and he said they must report in to his parents as well. So they gave their blessing as they returned to his car. She said, "They know, do they not?" He looked at her and said, "They presumed we already committed, so they gave us their blessing." "They did give us their blessing," she said, and she smiled warmly as she wrapped her arm in his.

His parents were just as happy, and it did not take long for the long times they spent together to tell on them. His dad smiled and said, "When can we expect grandchildren?" His mom said, "Oh, I did not think of that. I hope you have two boys and two girls." The day turned to planning as the women ensconced themselves in the kitchen to talk about details. The men went into the living room to talk about childhood, schools, inherent dangers, and fishing. He might not get much fishing in as he worked through the early years of their marriage.

Joseph M. Due, Sep 18, 2016

Wedding

The consecration of their vows began with a little tense light chatter in her apartment. The reality of their choice as she put their coats up struck home. The day was upon them, and both were a little nervous. She saw his arms were held out for her, and she hesitantly came to him across the room. Their desire was a palpable thing that grew, so he kissed and hugged her.

She wanted him in the worst way. This was the man of her dreams, and her desire was rising within her. She held him in her arms and rubbed his shoulders. He in turn rubbed her lower backside as they kissed. For a while, the room warmed, and the perfect moment continued.

Then he picked her up and held her by the legs and looked with desire into her eyes, and she kissed him again as he walked to the bedroom. The clothes, a little ripped and crumpled, littered the floor as they consummated their vows, a distant sight forgotten in the moments of passion.

The day broke over the horizon and peered in the window at the newlywed couple. The stirrings of the day brought them awake, together for the first time. He patted her behind as he got out of bed. She turned over to look in his eyes. She saw the care and was reassured that he loved her. "Coffee?" he asked. She sighed and looked at the clock. It was 0700 hours and this was a little much for her.

She looked at him and realized this time was part of his life, so she said cream and two sugars. He nodded and walked to the kitchen as she struggled to get up. The little things one gets used to, his mom had told her, could be quite the surprise.

Gathering up her clothes, she headed for the shower. *All in all, a great experience*, she thought as she realized their being together would now be permanent. Showering, she touched her lower abdomen and wondered if she was already working on number 1. *Hopefully a boy*, she thought. This would please Grandpa to no end. *A girl*, she thought, *might please Grandma*. Someone for her to teach how to cook would be about right.

As she toweled dry, she thought she smelled eggs. A nice thought. She hoped he had put some on. She realized she was hungry. Walking into the kitchen, she realized he cut tomatoes and cucumbers as well. She sat, and he poured her some orange juice. She looked at the coffee and picked up the orange juice first.

The egg and cheese sandwich was a tasty dream, and the meal was just right for the occasion. She told him that everything seemed to be perfect to her. She asked him how he felt, and he kissed her with feeling so she would understand.

He told her this was one of the best days in his life. She smiled and touched his cheek. The moments were to be cherished and remembered during the tough times, her mom told her. She now thought she knew what her mom meant.

The morning whiled away as they cleaned up, and they began planning when she would fully move into now their house and maybe their child's. Her body felt like it was changing, so she hoped for the best. He mentioned rings, which she forgot about for a while, and she admitted it. She told him she usually went to the mall jewelers for jewelry because they seemed so reasonable.

That afternoon, they spent reviewing rings and trying them on. The selection pleased him mightily. So she reported to work wearing her rings, and the news spread throughout the building. His dad heard about the rings while he was making last-minute rounds and decided to head to the kitchens before heading home.

His son was in briefings, so he decided to talk to him later. His mother would probably ask him about the rings anyway. He liked the diamond and the size of the ring. He thought her selection was very tasteful.

His mother called him at 1830 hours and asked if he already said his vows. He affirmed he did. She asked if he still wanted the formal ceremony. He told her yes, with all the bells and whistles. So she started crying, and he asked her if she would be all right. She said yes, it was just that her baby boy was finally getting married, so she saved tears for the occasion.

He told her that made him feel kind of sad that an age in their life had passed into history. She told him he should feel a little sad that now he was on his own with his new wife. The luggage wasn't much, he thought. She needed a house budget, so he wrote a note in his planner to attend to the matter.

He went to the gym to attend the hand-to-hand combat practice scheduled for the in-house response teams. They were broken into eight groups and mats. He joined a semi-circle and picked up the hand-to-hand combat training lesson for the evening. He watched the privates and corporals square off and remembered his officer training.

The lessons he saw were practiced with diligence and the lessons necessary to be taught. He nodded to the instructors as he checked out as many groups as he could before the three-hour session was over. He appreciated his Sergeant's and Lieutenant's diligence. It boded well for survival during operations being conducted.

The day passed as he thought about the bet, so he called down to the command post. He inquired if anyone had bet on Christmas. The operator told him two people had bet a couple bucks on Christmas. When they asked him why, he said never no mind.

The operator called over the watch supervisor and told her what the commander had asked. She looked at the security board operator, who smiled and said, "We might have to pay out on Christmas anyway because that is when he believes he is getting married."

On the ride home, she asked him about her car, so they drove to the apartment to pick it up. The reality of the venture was bringing up another set of awkward moments. This was the first time he had anyone move in with him, so he told her that when they parked in his double driveway.

She carried the two smaller suitcases to the door and waited for him to open the door. He blushed and apologized for not having another set of keys made. She then waited for him to pick her up and carry her through the door. She believed in some traditions.

They carried her suitcases to the bedroom, and he told her she could have half the dresser and he would get a dresser for her that she picked out. She told him she had a nice dresser and vanity; they just had to have it moved. He blushed again, and she smiled and hugged him.

Dinner was spaghetti and creamed beans flavored with sweet onions from his garden. She asked him how often he cooked since he cooked so well. He said that once in a while, he feels like making something. Then he asked her if he had lost his cooking privileges. She told him as long as the kitchen is hers, he just had to tell her when he wanted to cook so she did not make a double meal.

He thought about it and said it might take a little practice and a few reminders if that was ok with her. She said "Deal" and put out her hand. He said "Deal" and shook her hand and then kissed it. She smiled and blushed at the same time. This many "peace de accord" agreements she had never negotiated before, and she told him so.

He thought about her words and said to her that as far as he could tell, she was doing a really good job for a first-time negotiator. They both smiled, and she said, "Your mom has some definite ideas about the formal ceremony." She explained for twenty minutes what her ideas were and what his mother would like to see. He told her he would like to be married in the living room of his parent's house, and she knew his favorite colors.

After discussing the wedding, she said she would like to spend more time with his mother and then she asked, "What date can we be married on?" He told her he could pick up the license on the way to work. The Preacher she should call to find out what dates were good for him. His preference was New Year's Day, but he could wait if necessary.

She then headed over to his mom's house, promising to call the preacher. He decided that he would start the process of procuring the marriage license early so if there were delays, he would have time to deal with any unexpected issues. She had asked him if he would meet her for lunch.

Governance was congenial and helped him fill out the request form. They even told him that normally the preacher picked it up, but since he was trusted, they could release it to him. They also told him Robert wanted to talk to him, so he went up to the third floor for coffee.

Mums was delighted that Sarita came by, and they both headed to the kitchen to make lists of things they would need. The tailor had already been called so Sarita could be fitted the next day and the dress delivered Saturday afternoon. No need to worry about the bridesmaids if the color is white. Invitations could be done by the command post. They would be happy to do so.

The time went by, and the issues were resolved one by one. She told her mother-in-law that she had noticed some changes in her body chemistry but was not sure. Her mother-in-law looked at her and gave her a hug, and she said she hoped so but she would not tell her husband until it was confirmed. Sarita agreed.

The band was the hardest part to get in place at such short notice. The caterers were more than happy to schedule another date. Sarita wondered how well a high school country band would do. The teacher said they were pretty good at country selections but could not promise they would sing bridal songs. She thought Joseph would appreciate the country music and not miss the bridal songs. She thought about it and realized that with full-scale decorations, it would be a fine wedding.

Her evening shift started with talks about New Year's Day. That was just as her mother-in-law promised. The invitations had already gone out. She greeted her coworkers, and they congratulated her for getting married. Well wishes abounded through the first evening meal. The schedule was discussed, and she was asked what the commander would like served that day since it was so special.

She thought about all the dishes he liked and surveyed the team as to the unit on duties concurring likes. She then wrote down a tentative menu and recommended to her supervisor that it be approved by his mom. The supervisor agreed that it would be a very good idea and then thanked her for her input.

She mentioned the idea to Joseph at dinnertime and asked her what the proposed menu was. She gave him a verbal list that she remembered, and he thought it would be a fine celebratory meal. He then asked her about career aspirations, and she said she would like extra OJT for training into management so she could do more.

He said that it would be approved when she asked. He would talk to William about the additional training, and it would be provided. She then told him about the updates to the wedding plan. He asked her if she wanted to hear bridal songs anyway. She looked at him honestly and said she was happy with the formal ceremony.

The dinner was hamburger, macaroni and cheese with baby carrots, and a muffin. He told her he appreciated the quality food the kitchens put out. The silence of the day pleased him. He knew she could appreciate a quiet time.

His dad called him to get the latest updates he could communicate over the phone lines. He said he was just down in communications, which was down, but he had some news he could only convey in person. The reforming of an IDS/C center in a different local with a baseline objective to attack the governance center directly was an important bit of information that he had conveyed to the watch.

The walk-ins at city governance were overheard talking about walking off the rooms and preparing to bomb the place. The bomb-making process had to be located, assets seized, and the IDS center shut down.

The holidays were seeing a lot less violence than usual. It was a welcome respite. *A calm before a storm*, Joseph wondered. His outlook on life had changed a little since Sarita. He decided to write her a short note of appreciation.

Day 1 in the house began with a quick turning down of the sheets to catch up on sleep. At 0400 hours, Sarita woke him to show her appreciation. After a while, he turned on the CD player on low, and they talked until dawn.

The breaking dawn brought a slow and fairly warm snowfall, so Sarita asked him if he would show her the neighborhood. So they walked around the blocks, and he told her about the neighbors. Drinking coffee, she told him a little about her neighborhoods in the past.

The twenty-eighth brought warm sunshine and a light melting of the snow. It was a good day to move furniture. Some of the workers volunteered to help Sarita move her furnishings, so she spent the morning packing as he attended briefings. The hours whizzed by as they packed and then unpacked Sarita's furnishings.

Work went well, and his dad came in to see if he could offer suggestions on tracking down the renewed IDS and figure out where they would get the bombs from. They did not have an idea of what type of explosive they were looking for, so they looked into old fabrication sites and had the troops inquire into wiring purchases at electronic stores.

As the twenty-ninth day was winding down, Sarita took a home pregnancy test that was supposed to be 95 percent accurate. The test came out 100 percent positive, so she told Joseph she was 95 percent sure that he was going to be a dad. He took the news with much happiness and joy. She asked him what he wanted, and he said either a girl or a boy. She saw his sincerity, and her worries abated quite a bit.

He told his parents she might be pregnant and he would inform the watch. They asked if she was going to slow down, and he said in front of her when she knows she needs to slow down, she will decide to.

The counting of days was very stressful for both. Anxiety even when tempered with the knowledge it was only a formal ceremony to the reality was rising in fears and trepidations. Only three days to go to wonder how their wedding at noon would turn out.

Her dress fitting went well, and the alterations would be complete and the dress delivered to his parents' house on the morrow. In the meantime, plans for the honeymoon would have to be discussed, so more coffee was in order for the night, and dad would take the morning briefs for him. The anticipated activities were ideas they both worked on for the first to the fourteenth.

Mikael Dirk from Fort Houston would be filling in for him. He was Fort Houston's training officer and was familiar with urban assault protocols. He was said to have overseas and combat experience to help him get through the experience. The idea was that he would bunk with the troops and live at the facility for two weeks to facilitate his working there.

On Saturday, the dress arrived by post, and she tried it on to see how well it fit. She could breathe comfortably and looked stylishly sharp. The caterers arrived at 1500 hours and practiced setting up in the formal dining room.

Both had Saturday and Sunday off this week and enjoyed the company as the arrangements were organized and set out. The walkthroughs were not complicated, and the women used a downstairs bedroom to prepare and present.

The ladies were in their element and enjoyed the walkthroughs. The men, on the other hand, bore with them a tad bit impatiently. It was the preacher that reminded the ladies that good is good and he had a family to attend to and it was getting late.

She apologized for taking the preparation so late, and he apologized for the men being impatient. He said he wanted the day to be as perfect a memory as possible since they were only getting married once. She agreed and laid her head on his shoulder. "Tired?" he asked. She replied, "Yes, a little." So he stopped at a drive-through Wendy's so she did not have to cook.

Lights out was at 2200 hours, and both fell asleep hugging each other. The night passed away, and the morning broke fair as could be to see both still slumbering until 0900 hours. She woke and kissed him on the cheek. He moved a little but remained asleep. She decided to get breakfast ready and make some coffee. She put on her favorite country album and decided to pray and meditate for a while. The smell of coffee and the music gradually awoke Joseph, and he thought he imagined a kiss.

Dressing in his robe, he walked into the living room. She looked up and greeted him. She asked if he was ready for breakfast and coffee. He said yes, and they both repaired to the kitchen for coffee, bacon, and eggs with a cup of milk each.

Her frame entranced him as she cooked the bacon and eggs. He could almost see the changes coming over her due to her pregnancy. He told her what he was thinking. She said, "You like?" He said, "Yes, I like. I wonder how much sleep the preacher got last night with a full house." She replied, "At 1100 hours, you will see him preach on Noah and the flood. That is what he announced last week."

She then kissed him again and said, "Continue eating. I will take the shower first." He kissed her back and said OK. As she rinsed, she thanked God in her heart that their relationship was working out. He was washing the dishes when she came out to tell him it was his turn.

The preacher must have been revitalized by the word because he preached a great message of hope and salvation. The offertory was compelling, and many responded.

It was the nicest of days, and they decided to take a short afternoon walk in the park. They met along the way well-wishers from church and work and were glad to see them, and they stopped and chatted for a while.

She told him they needed to go shopping, so they stopped at the local grocery store. She pulled out a list, and he asked her about it. "Well, I was loading up my groceries. I remembered what I brought over. When I was stocking the milk and stuff, I made a mental list. When I was meditating this morning, I took a gander at what I would like to make for you and compiled this list."

He actually enjoyed chatting and shopping. She told him what her recipes were, and she shopped accordingly. It was $580 worth of groceries she said he had room for once they got rid of the pans they were not using. She had chef supplies she saved up for but told him his favorites were nice also.

He remembered thinking she had nice cookware. He said it would make a fine addition to family assets. She said the groceries would also last a month or two. She did not know about his entertaining yet but assumed he did some.

The reorganizing of the kitchen did not take long. He realized it had been awhile since he bought and most of it was low budget. He did not mind the improvement at all and told her he was grateful enough to bag the pots and pans and take out the garbage.

When he came back in, he had brought a bottle of Chateau le Blanc. He told her there was a wine room in the back of the garage. She pulled down two glasses and joined him in the living room. They sipped the wine while they listened to some of her more emotional favorites as she told him what they meant and what they meant to her.

After an hour, they danced the night away and fell asleep on the couch. Neither was wanting to leave the moment behind.

Monday saw her up at 0600 hours, and she slipped into the shower. She realized as she washed that she was living her dream. She started to cry and decided to let the emotion continue to finish the experience so she would not have to repeat it. Her mom told her people sometimes quit crying too soon and others cried to long. She thanked God for her family again and proceeded to the kitchen, where she turned on the coffee and put the hash browns and sausages in their pans.

She then wrote a note to Joseph explaining what happened in the shower. When he awoke and read the note, he hugged her gently and held her until she wanted to return to cooking.

She decided she would listen to the music while Joseph was at work. She had to ask him about a household budget. She pulled her budget out and wrote next to it an estimate for two living in a five-bedroom ranch with a formal dining room. The dining room was a little smaller than her mother-in-law's but sufficient for three or four children. She would talk to Joseph after she knew what the entertainment budget was.

Mikael Dirk was a very pleasant person and seemed very knowledgeable about urban assault. He talked Joseph through unit actions he saw overseas. He asked very astute questions about training and operations. He also seemed to appreciate the facility and had already picked a bunk in a room of one of the teams on call.

Joseph took him on a tour and headed home at 1000 hours. The drive was littered with snow-cleaning trucks and realized he needed to slow down because of the loose snow. The planned itinerary was honeymoon and budget. He figured that, as a couple, they would need to adjust things.

Pulling into the drive, he surveyed the neighborhood to check to see if there was anything out of the ordinary. Locking his car door, he admired his wife's taste in cars. The day looked very fine to him. As he entered the door, he heard country music being played. He figured they would gradually work through all the CDs and rank order them. She might have already started on the idea.

Sarita was working on paperwork, he saw. She looked up as he went over to kiss her. "How was your morning?" he asked as he sat down beside her. She smiled and said, "I was wondering about house funding—budgeting, I mean." He looked at her and said, "It is a new idea for me too. I have an idea." He said the house was on a fifteen-year mortgage and was paid for, so there was only maintenance and upkeep. "I will pay for those."

"The entertainment cost is $600 a month. I went over a couple months of my bills, and I will pay for that. Joint savings for new cars we can both contribute to. That is the same thing with food, clothing, gas, and Insurance. What does your budget look like?" he asked She showed him her tentative suggestions, and he showed her his budget idea. She looked at the two numbers as he did, and he noticed the budget he had.

He saw her own personal budget and said, "Fifty-fifty would actually make these numbers larger than we need. Insurance goes down significantly, and my contribution can be 15 percent higher because I make a little more than you do." He said it very nicely. She drew out another piece of paper and started with the ideas he mentioned since her budget seemed sound enough. She liked the idea that she had enough for a daily operating budget and her investments in Folgers's stock.

He realized a 10 percent savings on his budget if it worked out, and she did the math on that. She was traditional enough to see why he volunteered to pay the 15 percent more on the budget and realized he was man enough that he wanted to contribute more but sensitive enough to let her pay her share. She told him the house budget looked sound enough. "But when should we review ancillary costs?" He said, "How about the twenty-fifth of each month?" She agreed and kissed him.

She asked him if a joint account could be set up at his bank on the second to get things rolling. He said that was good for him. He liked the idea that she bought consistently stock in Folgers Coffee. He told her to pick out baby names, and when the baby's sex was known, he would also buy stock in the child's name. Her eyes glistened as she kissed him and rested on him now that the tentative budget was agreed upon.

The weekly activities could wait for a moment as they drank coffee and rested. The budget was a big worry for both of them and now that they both agreed in principle, they could rest from the stress a budget incurs. She asked him what he would like to do after fifteen minutes. He said he looked up some ideas in the surrounding area and down at the shore.

She pulled out her list of ideas, and he smiled. He prayed for peace de accord and read her list. On the list were half-day visits to his brother's house and her sister's house. She had tentatively scheduled both. She had asked each for times to visit. He liked how she was fitting into his life.

She had put down two days for skating and shopping, which, with her, he did not mind. She had left both Saturdays with a question mark and fishing annotated by the question mark. He appreciated the gesture and erased the question mark and put in high school football for the second date and then looked at her.

She nodded approval as he continued to peruse the list. She had put R. C. Morrow rhythm and blues on Fifth Street for Friday night, and the next Friday she left blank. He pulled out the concert ticket seats for a regional favorite she recognized, and she smiled so he put it down on the list. She put the tickets in her purse.

His mom called and asked for Sarita. The flower arrangements had been delivered, and she wondered if she would come over to take a look at them. She looked at him, and he said yes. Dad and Joseph could talk shop if she wanted to go over at 1700 hours. She mentioned the time to her mother-in-law and she agreed. She wondered if all the bridesmaids had procured white dresses and if the men would show up in navy blue.

He asked her what she was thinking as she hung up the phone. She told him she worried about the colors the wedding party would wear.

"Oh, that's Mums's surprise," he said. "She has dressed the unit before for short-notice weddings," he said. She looked at him, and he crossed his chest and said, "Truth." "Truth," she said. "Truth," he said as she relaxed. He kissed her forehead and asked her if she wanted more coffee. He did.

She hummed the song "Oh My, My" and smiled. She appreciated his mom even more. The coffee started meaning more to him as he realized her long-term investment in the company. She had bought two shares each month since she was seventeen. It made for a nice investment, and he could invest some of his funds in coffee too.

The songs from her heart he did not know yet, so he asked her if she would share some of them with him. They spent the afternoon singing songs and drinking coffee as the time slid quickly by. She asked him about his favorites, and he shared a couple with her on the way to Mums's house. He told her the band was given his favorite dance song, and they were practicing it for tomorrow.

She asked him if he could tell her the story about his hair. He told her the vague outline, and he said when they had more time, he would tell her more. She made a note to ask him next Monday or Tuesday as they pulled into his parents' driveway.

The evening passed in good humor for the men who were exiled to the den. The ladies present were trying out arrangements and were not to be bothered. The goings-on of the community and what ideas they could find was the subject matter for the evening. In attendance was William and his parents and her dad and mom as well.

At 0600 hours, two alarm clocks rang, and Joseph helped Sarita to the shower. He made a light breakfast of toast, juice, and cornflakes as well as the required coffee. He heard her come alive in the shower as she sang, and he liked that she did.

His use of her waffle mix prepared the day, and she smiled in delight as she took over making breakfast. He hurried through his shower routine to get them back on schedule. The waffles were a delight, and both were happy that they took the time to make the time. Coffee was a morning blend of Folgers coffee as he cleaned up and she prepared to meet her day.

The morning signs were there for her to feel, and she praised God's Holy name as she finished her makeup. He kissed her tenderly on her forehead, and she hugged him quite firmly. Then he quickly dressed in the Navy blue suit she helped him buy. She smiled and collected her purse, and he collected his wallet and keys.

She told him she felt her body changing again, and he hugged her lightly while he looked in her eyes. They looked at their watches and went out to the kitchen. They were now early, so they discussed what his entertainments were like and how long they lasted. He told her that with a new wife, some of the ladies would now want to attend more often.

As 0745 hours rolled around, she looked at him earnestly. He smiled, getting up and helping her out of the chair. He said tenderly, "Showtime." They decided to take his car. Though it was older, it was a much larger car and would be more comfortable.

At 0801 hours, they were in the driveway, and she worried a little about being a tad bit late. He reminded her the wedding was not until 1000 hours, and it was fashionable to be a minute late once in a while. So he ushered her into the house, and she noticed the photographer and smiled. He smiled back and waved for her to stand there with Joseph. He snapped a couple pictures and then indicated he was done for now.

She then looked around and headed to the ladies' prep room to drop off her coat and purse. She saw that the area where the photographer set up was cleared of flowers, and she frowned as she passed by. He sighed, and Joseph smiled at him and said she noticed the flowers. He agreed, knowing one of the ladies would ask why there were no flowers behind him.

Joseph began his two-hour wait, knowing from past weddings he attended that grooms can get mighty impatient. He headed for the coffee service for something to do. William and his dad had already been exiled from the kitchen and the ladies' presence until called upon. Sarita's dad was running last-minute errands, so he would be in at around 0900 hours. His wife had already been dropped off a half hour ago.

The well-wishers came by to drop off gifts for the couple, and the men, once in a while, got to do a meet and greet, relieving the tension of the moment. The gradual gathering of the Captains increased the stress amongst the men, but it was the ladies' day, and they were bereft of an outlet for their considerable talent, so they all tried to relax and figure out something to say.

Doing something like playing baseball as they were wont would earn them censure from the ladies' aid society. The hour passed slowly for the men where time was on fast speed for the ladies. They talked through the wedding one minute at a time, and Sarita remembered the flowers. She asked Mums if she could do something about the plants and the photographer.

Joseph's mom made an appearance at 0845 hours and talked to the photographer. He pointed out he needed the space, and he moved them nicely. She frowned and turned to the men and took out the flowers he moved and spent twenty minutes rearranging the flowers as they were before he came.

Sarita came out and checked on the flower arrangements herself and stood there lost in thought. Joseph asked her if she was all right. She smiled and Mums escorted her back into the ladies' prep room as she frowned at her son.

The guests and their gifts started showing up in numbers, and the tension went up another notch. Some of the ladies started serving the snacks as people milled around. Some of the men went outside to smoke, and the ambient temperature radiating from the house was warm enough for them to do so.

The preacher arrived at ten minutes to 1000 hours. He went immediately to the pulpit brought out for the occasion and placed his notes and the Bible so he would not forget them. He asked Joseph's brother if he had his ring. He inquired about Amy Smith. Her husband said she had Joseph's ring. He inquired if any needed to use the restroom because of too much coffee consumption.

Two of the Captains took advantage of the opportunity. Then the preacher headed over to the coffee service himself. He was magically greeted by Mums, who had come out to check at the last minute the preacher, ushers, et cetera. She smiled at him. She knew she would bring back a good report.

At 1001 hours, the preacher started the service by nodding to the head usher to let the ladies know the wedding had been convened. Then the pianist started the music repertoire, and he started to speak.

Joseph M. Due, September 18, 2016

Honeymoon

"Do you, Joseph Carne, take Sarita Thomas as your lawfully wedded wife?" He said, "I do." Then the preacher turned to Sarita and said, "Do you, Sarita Thomas, take Joseph Carne as your lawfully wedded husband?" She said, "I do."

The preacher then said to both rings. Joseph placed the ring on her finger and said, "With this ring, I wed thee." She placed his ring on his finger and said, "With this ring, I wed thee."

The preacher said to the couple, "I now pronounce you man and wife." He then said to Joseph, "You may kiss the bride."

The women of the community then cried with joy over the union and the wedding was fait accompli.

The pianist played the anthem march as they walked down the aisle together. As they made their way to the back of the chairs, the people congratulated them and stood as the ceremony was ending. They stood by the door to greet well-wishers as they left the house. After the last one left, he drew her to him and kissed her again.

She then returned to the ladies' prep area to remove the lovely wedding dress and pack it away as a keepsake. The ladies greeted her with hugs and kisses and congratulated her on getting married. Mums told her it was one of the finer weddings she had helped put together.

Sarita asked how she got the white dresses for the ladies and the navy-blue suits for the men. She said, "Some actually had theirs. Others we hooked up with the men's clothing store, and Macy's had a sale on white dresses." She said, "I called around several stores to find the right sizes."

She then asked her new daughter-in-law what was planned for the honeymoon. She said, "A little visiting of family, shopping, skating, and I know Joseph likes to fish." Her mom hugged her and wished her well on her honeymoon.

Sarita rejoined Joseph as they talked with family about upcoming events. The itinerary was given to security, and they called the list of events in. The caterers were setting up, and the women retired to the kitchen and the men to the living room. As they made their entrée, the band arrived and was shown to their place, and they began setting up.

Joseph went into the dining room and asked if they were good at the song he picked out. They assured him it would work out just fine. The caterers indicated they were ready and the band nodded, so one of the ushers went to the kitchen to get the ladies. Joseph waited for Sarita in the middle of the dining room for the first dance.

The song "The Blues" started playing, and Sarita missed a step. Joseph waited for her to regain her composure as they returned to the dance. She looked into his eyes, and this was one of the reasons she loved him. They danced to the song and then the next country song as the guests entered the dance area. She looked at him and said thank you. He drew her closer, and she decided she could go country after all.

She opined that the wedding being the prelude to the honeymoon he had scored almost a 100 percent in her being satisfied category. He said the moments were almost heaven to him. They decided to sit and talk for a while.

The hour passed quickly as they discussed with friends their schedule for the honeymoon. Mums announced it was time to open the gifts. Sarita took a chair in the middle of the dining room with her husband. The gifts were brought out first for those that were still there so the rest could be opened later.

The drive home left them tired, so they carried in the dress and the plants and the cards. The rest would be picked up later. Then he tended the plants, and she called him into the bedroom. She wanted to make love to him in her wedding dress. Her passion arose as she saw the desire in his eyes. As he kissed her, she wondered if she could get the dress retailored.

The afternoon passed in happiness and joy as each heard the other's likes and endeavored to please. They slept until midnight and realized everything was closing by the time they showered and dressed. So they dropped in on the unit's kitchens for a place to go and talk and visit with friends.

The hour they spent was profitable for both as Mikael had questions and so did the kitchen staff. Then they decided together that they would check out Netflix and watch *Captain America*. Both knew the story line very well, and Joseph could talk about the units overall mission in comparison to the Fifty-Seventh CID mission.

The time passed by, and they both fell asleep watching a Green Lantern movie. She woke up at 0600 hours and decided the first order of the day would be to gather gifts. She watered the plants, turned on the coffee, and went for her shower.

Joseph heard the shower turn on and gradually awoke. He smelled the coffee and decided to water the plants. He noticed they already had enough water and decided to put the pitcher back in the kitchen on the table. He sat down and waited for her to finish her shower.

The time passed by, and he heard the water shut off. He went to get new clothes as she appeared. She asked him if at eight they could pick up the gifts from Mums's house. He nodded and kissed her. She followed him in the bedroom to repack her wedding dress, and she put it on a shelf in the closet and went to get some coffee.

She heard him singing the blues and smiled. She had another reason to treasure the song. The coffee was still warm and the creamer mixed in nicely, and she thought of Mums and the lessons she was learning about herself and others. She decided to write herself a note to get a louder alarm clock especially if she was going to sleep in the living room periodically.

The morning was a little on the gray side with a hint of snow. She noted the neighborhood as she passed through it. Her husband noticed all the time. It was part of his training, and she had to make it part of hers. She asked him what type of production makes bombs.

He talked about the cooking of the explosive, the forms used for molds, and the type of electronics necessary for wiring and detonators. She asked him what was similar in the industry. He said all the components are common across the spectrum of industry—it is the collection together that makes the process unique.

She asked him how far back in the unit's history did William have to research to find where the missing tools might have come from. "Five to ten years," he replied, "for the assembling together and thirty years for the overall tool loss that would make it possible. The problem is that the tools or bombs might be imported from a neighboring city."

After they reached Mums's house, they packed up the gifts and stayed for some coffee. She then blurted out she needed the name, address, and phone number for the tailor that did her dress. Mums looked at her and asked why. Joseph turned beet red. She looked at him and smiled. "OK," she said and went to get the information. She handed Sarita a copy of the address and looked at Joseph again.

The afternoon at her sister's house was a getting-to-know type of meeting. The two couples talked about family issues and future plans. The girls hugged when her sister found out Sarita was definitely pregnant. Then they talked about babies for a while, and Sarita admitted Joseph's mom wanted to help decorate the nursery.

The local ice rink was lightly filled, and the music being played was varied. They were both good skaters, so they skated in and out of the others that were there. The dancing was sporadic, so after three hours, they returned home and Sarita made Joseph Texas chili. As they waited for the mix to cook together, they took Joseph's planner and scheduled out the next couple parties they planned.

Then Joseph called it in to the watch center. It only took a few minutes, and the Lieutenants and Captains would be notified through the watch. The merged chili was par excellence. They both ate up because they were hungry from skating.

The review of the CD library began in earnest. Joseph said since she picked out her favorites already, how about starting on his. The hours passed by as they listened to songs and made a list together for their joint favorites. At 0200 hours, she said, "Enough talk. Can we go to bed?" She wanted to show him a different collection and get his input on it.

The next day was Thursday, and they spent the morning unpacking gifts except the two extra toasters. She had picked the four-piece toaster with bagel selection to replace the existing toaster. She thought anything fancier would be too much for little children. The old model still worked, so they packed it up after Joseph cleaned it, and they mailed it to the Good Will kitchen. The other two would be saved for future gifts for weddings or Christmas.

The letter writing they both did. Mums had given her a gift of thank-you cards and envelopes as well as a bath set from Macy's. The eight towels would come in handy as well as wash cloths, et cetera. The cards were nice and came with money or store credit cards. Most were for Macy's or Dayton's.

Her mom gave her five robes from Macy's all the same navy blue but in adult and children's sizes. Her dad had paid for the catering, and his dad for the band and the plants. The hosting by his parents was also noted. He suggested, and they picked up a $500 gift card for the preacher's endeavor to Macy's, her favorite upright store.

The additions to her kitchen were very welcome. They ranged from specialty bread pans to different types of pie and cake pans. She also received a coffee and tea set to upgrade the commander's old coffee set. The other assorted gifts they also wrote thank-you cards for like the fishing gear security bought for the commander.

She cried a few times in happiness as she considered the love in each gift. Joseph held her hand as she expressed herself. The day finished out as they dropped the letters in the mail. Invitations she ordered online and would be mailed within two weeks.

Dinner was roast beef au jus et potato with stewed carrots. He found her cooking refreshing. The day finished out by an after-dinner walk that tired both out. She remembered some of the neighbors and realized that some had teenagers. She had not seen that before.

The dance was important to them, and they committed to keeping it up periodically each week to reconnect. They spent the night by firelight listening to their newly made playlist. They made one for reflections and three for easy listening.

Friday morning was errands and light shopping. The afternoon was spent with William and his family. William was glad to host, and his wife made meatloaf for ten with mashed potatoes. Their children's favorite, they reassured. The day was spent playing rummy. Rummy is a good pastime to be appreciated.

The skating rink was full of regulars that she recognized or knew. She mentioned this to Joseph and introduced him around. He in turn talked to security about the unknown ones that were new. The music was now half dance favorites, and both appreciated the selections. She said she felt like she could fly when she was skating, and dancing on skates took her to another world.

The night darkened, and they decided to leave by 2200 hours. She said that kept her in her comfort zone. He told security to check out some of the late arrivals and the new ones after he left. Synergy, he told them. Sarita lost her comfort zone. He said next. They called the watch for more people.

The watch center sent team 2. Team 2 looked at the group interactions as the children got more rambunctious. Some of the team members pretended to videotape their friend skating, and they got some names to go with the faces. Violence peeked its head out when two groups got into a minor argument, and the video recorder recorded the whole argument. Team 9 would have something to investigate.

The night was young, and Sarita perked up as they entered the house. She challenged Joseph to cribbage and cheese on crackers. He found the board and set up in the kitchen. She was cutting the cheese when he was done. He admired her beauty and told her so. She blushed and asked him how she was beautiful.

He told her she had a fetching look and a fine face. But he had to admit her spirit and attitude were the truly beautiful things about her. She kissed him and sat down. He asked her what kind of vino she would like as he walked to the garage. "Red!" she called, treasuring this moment like many others.

On Saturday, they loaded up the fishing gear and started out to Galveston Bay. The ride was nice and serene, and she drove his car with the fishing gear in the back. He navigated taking this road many times before. The cooler was full of sandwiches, and he had two thermoses filled with coffee for the boat.

The sky was clear and warming, so he knew it would be fairly warm on the water. They rented a sixteen-footer with a full tank of gas and a spare tank. They loaded the boat up with their supplies, including a short blanket, which Sarita surmised was for her. The fishing she said she could do. It was the saltwater fish she was unfamiliar with.

He asked her about her experiences and threaded his fishing rod as she watched. She talked for a little bit about river fishing, and he knew where she had been. She threaded her fishing rod with a fair degree of expertise. He told her so. They then talked about his childhood while they were fishing.

He told her about how he was surprised and kidnapped, how a little boy had distracted him while his dad hit Joseph in the back of the head and knocked him out. She commiserated with him and learned it took five weeks for friends to find him while he was beat up every day and experimented on.

It took him a month for his visual orientation to return. His hair never grew back in right since then. He then talked about the interviews and his dad putting an end to them. Then there was the guards and advanced hand-to-hand combat as well as surveillance techniques he was taught so when out and about, he could take care of himself.

Then he talked about his dad's newfound mission of IDS interdiction and then his army training and college. He even told her about some of his surfing experiences he had received while in college. He then said questions, and they spent the last hour with her asking him questions about this and that.

They turned to shore with four fish between them. The boat yard bought them and gave them a deduction on the rental. It was a good way to conduct business. Returning the live bait to the water, they cleaned up and headed back for Houston. He drove while she laid her head on his shoulder and listened to their playlist.

Returning the gear to the garage, they decided to take a bath together and do some more talking. The evening was free, so they drank coffee and talked about the little things they would like to accomplish while on their honeymoon.

The day was running on the warm side. The sun was bright rays on the couple at 0900 hours. They both woke to the awareness of each other and the held each other as they awoke. They had time, so they dressed slowly, talking of the day. Sarita wanted chicken for dinner. Joseph asked, "Fried or baked?" She said, "I think fried, like my mom does." He then asked if he could have rice pilaf to cut the grease of the chicken. She agreed that that would be a nice dinner. She asked him then, "Peas or beans?" He thought about it while he buttoned his shirt. "I think beans will do," he replied.

Coffee was fine, and Joseph and Sarita balanced the house budget because of all the little expenses that were ancillary to their honeymoon. So far, they had a few bucks to spare. Then they switched to orange juice for their health and listened to the morning radio broadcast. The night's news was repeated on the hour.

The 1000 hours service was on John the Baptist and faith versus sight. Sometimes, you have to have faith, and once in a while, you are directly shown. The 1100 hours service was about service to others for salvation and other needs. The life of Jesus Christ was illustrated.

The preacher waxed eloquent and did an inspiring job. The people were grateful and hung around to thank him. Joseph told Sarita she and he needed to stop by operations on the way home. They had some pictures she might be able to identify.

She asked him what it was about when they got in the car. He told her she intuitively saw something he initially did not. She thought about how she started losing her comfort zone while on the ice and followed for the first time the pathway she should have seen more fully. The tension around the rink was rising to the point she was getting tired and confused.

She looked at him, and he asked her what she was thinking. So she told him her surmising. He told her a fight broke out after they left, and later, some hoodlums showed up selling drugs. She knew that she was emotionally open when she skated. She had told him so. She thought about the danger and realized other regulars had left before she wanted to. She wondered if they saw emotionally or knew the people that would cause the problems.

The pictures were legible, and she could tell them some of the names of those that showed up once in a while. The shortened clip showed her the gathering her other senses had picked up. She said she did not want to give up ice skating. Joseph reassured she did not have to. She would now have a chaperone. They would go earlier and leave by 2100 hours, and with security, she should be just fine.

She nodded her head, and Joseph held her until she was more composed. They went back to the house and talked about the process of investigations that had started. She decided he could help cook, so she asked him to prepare the chicken while she worked on setting the stove up.

They worked without saying a word, and he could see in her energy she had gotten over the problem and put it aside as she prepared the beans, and he got out the rice. Then she said, "Sit and talk to me while I finish up."

She asked him what her new duties-to-be would entail. He told her she would learn more about Smith Carne Industry and help in the moral welfare and readiness department. "That means you will learn what Mums knows and help out in that regards in your own way."

The meal was par excellence. He told her he appreciated her, so he started doing the dishes and she joined him. He asked her to tell him about how she learned to cook so well. She started talking about her desire as a child and her mom teaching her how to cook for the family. She then erudiated him about some of the lessons as the time passed away.

He poured her some Chateau le Rouge, and they danced until the passion flared, and he carried her off to bed.

Monday was another shopping endeavor for house needs and this time she had a large list of necessities. They started with Dayton's as she checked quality on her list of sundries. They talked about the necessities and their usage and he told her he admired her organizational ability. They worked through the departments from table clothes to a new cheese grater. The hours passed to the humor of both and the exasperation of sales clerks.

The trip to Macy's and the other stores saw him getting a firsthand education in quality purchasing. He told her the orientation in purchasing is fine enough for her. He said after that he would sign off on that portion of her OJT record. She smiled at him because she knew the compliment was sincere and all her years of endeavor had earned her that comment.

They stopped at One Potato Two in the mall for a light dinner. She said she was almost done and then she would be done for a little while. He laughed and smiled at her, and she thought again of how fine he looked to her.

At 1500 hours, they put away the last of the supplies and went and sat down on the couch. Then they rested up for another visit to her parent's house. She then said she had to invite Mums to help her organize the party materials they had bought. She would be familiar with party composition, structure, and purpose. He thought that was a great idea.

He thought of his dinner table and realized he had needed the supplies for quite some time. He told her he should have dated her when she was fourteen. Then he would have had the job done way back then. She thought the idea was a nice one. He had needed her for a while. She told him it took a few years to learn. She called Mums and said she was reorganizing her son's dinner table and she wondered if she would come by tomorrow to help out.

The time would be 0900 hours for three hours. They would do a practice setup at 1200 hours with a cooking of appetizers to see how long that took. They then headed out for a couple hours at her parents' house. They were happy to see their grandchild-bearing daughter, as they put it. They were busy, she noted, renovating one of the bedrooms. It would be a nursery for a boy. She hugged her mom. She was going to have another brother.

The conversation started with the topic of child-raising and continued in that venue for most of the evening. He got an idea of how she was raised by the topics covered. She asked him if he were bored, and he thought about it and said, "Once in a while, I need to hear new things." The dad asked him to attend him in the living room to hear his daughter's life experiences, and she said, "What might those be?"

He talked about some of the mishaps she encountered for a while, and then it was time to go. She asked him on the way out if she still liked him, and he said, "Everyone has those moments in life. Mums could tell you of a few moments in my life that I am not exactly proud of. I like you even more."

She thought about what he said and realized it was a good thing he knew her history.

They picked up ice cream on the way home, and she said it was for the birthday he had forgotten about. Mums had told her, not knowing if she knew. She asked him if he knew hers, and he said July 21. He had looked it up when his mom had reminded him his birthday was January 5.

He said he did not want his birthday distracting the process of the wedding or honeymoon. She put her hand in his and thanked him for the thought. She would bake him a nice cake made from scratch to celebrate tomorrow afternoon. It would not be much of a surprise, but it would be a nice gesture.

She liked the idea. He thought it was important to know hers, and in knowing hers, he had to have thought about his. She found that endearing.

The process of the personal comes with trust. So she told him what really turns her on and what she does just to enable the relationship. He was quite startled by the revelation. He thought about it for a moment and told her what really turned him on and what did not. He wanted to consider it during their personal time and she agreed.

Practice makes perfect, so they trained their desire to be more pleasing. As they practiced, it came more naturally and was more enjoyable. Tired, they drifted off to sleep, feeling even better with the knowing.

The ringing of the doorbell awoke them. Mums had the patience and knew they were home. Joseph put on his robe and opened the door while she scurried to the shower. She looked at him and asked if he was awake yet. The cold, he said, would do the job just fine. She walked into the kitchen to make coffee while Joseph remembered to shut the door.

He arrived a few seconds later and took a seat as she put on some eggs to cook for sandwiches. Coming around, he colored and told her the cheese was on the second shelf behind the milk. The smell of the eggs ushered in his wife, who took his seat so he could shower.

She greeted Mums with the taste of straight brewed coffee, and then she reached for the cream and sugar. She asked her daughter if she was still tired. Sarita said, "A little. It was a quick shower." Mums sympathized and handed her an egg and cheese sandwich, which she liked very much.

Mums then asked her about her reorganization, so she told her where everything had been put away. She looked through the cupboards and asked her, "Your dishes?" "Yes, Mums. We picked through all the stuff that was here, and we kept the better of the two." She said the frying pan is first-rate. Sarita said, "I saved my money and bought it from a store for chefs."

The tour only lasted a minute or two, and Mums said, "I am impressed." She sat down and sipped at her coffee while Joseph's eggs cooked. Joseph came in the kitchen, and Sarita went to kiss him and told Mums while she was up, she would get his eggs.

They waited while Joseph ate his sandwich. He looked at both of them and said the sandwich was nice. He sipped his coffee and said, "Where do all of us begin?" His wife unfolded the paper on which she wrote her ideas, and Mums wrote down the estimated number of guests he would now be hosting. He looked at the menu and the picture of the service and said, "I will get the extra tables."

The tables were set up in no time at all, and with a kiss from his wife, he retired to his den to read a book. The ladies were revamping his social life, and he let them do it. The novel was about Saint Thomas in California. It was an interesting read of wine country.

The setup took an hour the first time. The second time only took fifteen minutes because they figured the basic setup. On the list of light snacks, Mums added some recipes to flesh out the now-to-be full dinner. Sarita looked at the list and asked for recipe cards for the recipes she did not know. The rest of the recipes were made in the kitchens.

The snacks spent another hour on making so Sarita could see how they turned out. At the same time, she put in the cake early to provide at least a little surprise. When the cake was done, they iced the cake and put it in a glass cover she got for the wedding. She then put it in the large cupboard since the dishes were left out so Joseph could see the basic serving configuration.

When the snacks were done, they placed them in baskets on the table. They then called Joseph so he could see what the design looked like. They then asked him to take his seat, and Sarita sat with him holding hands. Mums said, "One minute," and retrieved the cake and put it on the table before him and sang "Happy Birthday." There were no candles, but he preferred none. So they cut the cake to celebrate the social upgrade.

Then Mums looked at her watch and said she had an appointment to attend to, so she let herself out. "The ideal serving set," he said as he ate his cake. She blushed and thanked him. They sat there for a while, and he said, "We could put the settings away after a brief nap." She remembered she was still tired from the night before, so he led her to the couch and settled in with her.

They quickly settled in and, without another word, fell asleep. The ringing of the phone brought them awake again. She looked at her watch. It was 1600 hours. His brother was on the line, wanting to know if he could bring over when he came twenty fresh tomatoes. She wrote that down on her notepad so they would not forget.

They decided to stay in for the rest of the day and worked on playlists, et cetera, to finish up odds and ends around the house. Putting the tableware away took forty-five minutes alone. The time passed quietly as they worked on squaring away the house. They talked of the nursery and what they might need, like baby bottles and baby food, when the baby is weaned.

The midnight movie attracted their attention, and they decided to watch a Seventh Cavalry movie. He asked her if action movies were too much. She said, "Quite rightly that they're all love stories." He was grateful she liked love stories. She was grateful she was accepted as she was.

She decided to set the alarm clock for 0600 hours. The day with his brother was an important one. The children were models of the expected outcome of family training. She asked him if he wanted to order another movie. He said they could set the alarm for 1000 hours if she wanted. She said 0600 hours would be fine. She wanted to practice the morning routine for when he started doing 0800 hours briefs again.

He agreed that getting up early was important, so they prepared for bed. She had a nice surprise for him. They drifted off to sleep hugging each other. She decided to get larger blankets as she fell asleep. The early morning light could be seen in the lightening of the predawn sky when she looked out the window. He was already in the shower, and she had a mission to practice for.

The pans came out one by one as she decided on a breakfast omelet and hash browns as well as sausage patties and orange juice. He believed in orange juice for breakfast and she agreed. At least one glass apiece. Their children might grow to dislike the drink, but it was for good health.

The smell of eggs and sausage greeted him as he exited the shower. He thanked God for her because he appreciated her spirit's endeavor. *Mums is probably quite proud of her,* he thought. She ate breakfast with him and realized she had the night's odor about her and grimaced. She did not know how to keep the schedule and be clean without getting up at 0530 hours.

He asked her what was wrong. She told him she smelled a little. He knew that and decided 0530 hours was a little too much after a 1600 to 2400 hours shift. He could get used to the disparity for fifteen minutes so they could eat together. She asked him if he was sure. He replied he was very sure. She sighed in relief and kissed him.

She asked him what he did at 0700 hours. He said turn the radio on and forget at 0730 hours to turn it off. "I listen to the top of the news to see if it has any bearing on what we do." She turned the radio on and went to take her shower. He smiled because he enjoyed her presence, and she provided for some things he was missing.

The shower went on a ways as she struggled for the energy of the day. She was determined and knew she could adjust. He noticed and decided to be patient and apply patience in the days to come. Her appearance was a little late in coming but fresh she was. She hugged him and said, "Brief me at 0800 hours like you get your briefs so I know what it is like."

So they went into the kitchen, and he pulled a pad out of the kitchen drawer and grabbed a pen so he could show her. His business briefings were after the post briefings, he said, but he outlined them first so she could get an idea of the corporate picture. Then he walked her through the major ones.

The Operations brief was first. Then the Planning brief was second, and the Watch brief was third. Then there were briefs from equipment, supply, administration, and finally, training. Slides were provided by research, et cetera, when they had a reminder or a change to what was in the wind.

He provided examples of each type of brief. She took the notepad and said, "Now that the briefs are over and so is the morning practice, how about you and I draw a nice warm bath." He thought she had great ideas.

The shopping was done at Wal-Mart so they could be assured of getting twenty ripe tomatoes. The ride over to his brother's house was relaxed but a little tired. They arrived a half hour early, and James was still inbound. The family had stayed home to greet their new aunt, and the air was slightly festive. Robin took the bag into the kitchen for them as they entered the living room. The children were in different stages of activities for each and were quite well-mannered and studious. The baby crawled over to Sarita, and she dutifully picked the baby up and started rocking her. She knew this from babysitting.

Then Hope introduced her five children, starting with the returning Robin and Donald. He nodded and returned to assembling an erector set. The adults went into the kitchen. Joseph went into the kitchen for coffee, and Sarita to help prepare the stewed tomatoes and talk to Hope about parenting. He listened in for twenty minutes then James arrived home. He got a much more active greeting from his children, and they could hear him from the kitchen.

As he entered the kitchen, his wife gave him a kiss and a hug. He brought a passel of cucumbers Sarita took from him and he smiled. He said their sisters were inbound, but Dave had to go out on an emergency call. He then asked his brother if he wanted to sit in the living room. He then gave a short synopsis of each child's life since he last visited.

The ladies came into the living room soon enough to hear about Donald's latest encounter with life. Hope then gave a list of each child's accomplishments to date. Then the topic turned to training and about the good schools in the area. While the men were babysitting, Robin was invited into the kitchen to help cook. She helped finish up prep and cleanup and then helped to set the table. There would be two more in attendance. One was married, and she had two teenagers that were at school. The other was nineteen and had not gotten married yet.

The women then talked about women things and drank coffee. Even Robin was allowed to have some coffee, and she realized she was being trained to carry on tradition. The ladies came into the kitchen and asked if they could help. The pots were prepped and boiling, and the smell permeated the house.

He cared about his brother a great deal. After all, they were direct family. The choices one makes in life define who you are. His working for William was a good thing. The job he did was very demanding. His training was a standard for the family to follow. Sarita would learn these truths in good time, and his children would be raised just fine.

She thought of the differences in training between her mom and Hope and realized she could see the good side of both. She made notes of those things Hope told her that were different but demonstrably worked out just fine. Robin asked her what she was writing and she said, "The lessons you are learning. I want to learn to be the best mom I can be."

Hope smiled. That would encourage her daughter to listen more diligently. The boiling pots were near done, and the serving platters were prepared. The men were informed dinner was ready. As the family prayed together, the family unity was palpably almost visible. James said grace, and the children looked forward to the blessing and a fine meal. Sarita sat beside her husband on one side and got to talk to Donald on the other.

She thought he was a sweet boy and very endearing. As they talked that night, he indicated that Donald had similar interests in the business as he did, and he was being groomed to help out the business. She asked him in what way. He said, "Everyone in James's family has a destiny that they're being trained for. Just like our children will be helped to find their destiny. He might one day take over my position though it is hard to tell because children sometimes change their interests."

She thought and said that one day, her children might or might not want the business. He said, "That is true and only God knows each child's destiny." She thought about it for a couple minutes and realized they did not actually choose—the child does. She was told her children would be enabled to find their destiny. She heard his sincerity and saw the truths of it in her own life. She held out her hand and said "Deal." He quickly took her hand and said "Deal."

They looked at the ice rink as they passed, and he knew she liked ice skating. So he told her they could go skating Sunday at 1600 or 1700 hours. She smiled and said "Deal." He smiled because he was learning to love her a great deal. The snow started falling as they entered the house, so she set the fire and he got out blankets and pillows. She was opening the curtains on the living room windows when he returned.

He pulled out the vino and checked how full it was. There was enough for one and a half glasses apiece. He asked her if that would be enough. She said, "Maybe another bottle would do." He walked through the kitchen to the garage to procure another bottle of Chateau le Rouge. By the time the wine was poured, the soft music of rhythm and blues could be heard in the kitchen.

She had put on her and his favorite nightclothes, he saw. The fire was still growing, but he saw enough that his desire stirred within him. She was very lovely indeed. He let her see the passion in his eyes and in his kiss but tempered it with patience.

They lay closely together and drank and talked of this and that until their passion got the better of him and her.

At 0600 hours, they were awake to a cold fire and a slight chill in the air. They hurried to adjust the heater, and both decided to take a shower together.

The drive would be a short one, and only the indoor exhibits would be open for view. So they took their time. They arrived around 1100 hours and paid the fee. There was about an hour's worth of exhibits and a food court. The museum was something to talk about, and he always liked coming out and spending the time.

There were some of the carnivorous wild animals with pens and gates, but they seemed to be outside, possibly sleeping. They decided to come back later to see if they would come inside to be viewed. The tamer wild animals were out and about from their refuge and making noises, so the trip did have some sights to see.

The zoo's air system was working just fine. You could still get a hint of what they smelled like if you breathed deeply. Some animals had feed for sale, and you could attempt to feed the animals. They decided not to feed the bears, but the goats seemed fine. The morning passed in small chitchat, and the diner served burgers and hotdogs. She chose a burger and he ordered two.

After dinner, they studied the history of animal life in the Houston and Greater Texas area. The plethora of animals even today in the area surprised them both. The museum said the plethora was found on private farms and preserves for the most part. As they exited the museum, they heard the sounds of lions.

Taking another walk through, they got to see lions, tigers, and panthers as well as a quick walk through rest of the building. They walked hand in hand and talked together like it was their first date in high school. The other patrons thought it was quite endearing.

He asked her if she wanted to go skating, and she said no; she had other ideas. She wanted to pick up the book *Robin Hood* at the library. They made a quick stop, and sure enough, a copy of the book was in. She wanted to read with him the script for Robin Hood and Maid Marian. He thought he could improvise and told her so. She said she hoped it would turn out.

Showtime saw them in the living room with the rest of the vinos, a single light, and the night falling.

At 1000 hours, they both called it a night and set the alarm clock. Her goal was to be up to greet him in the morning, so they retired early. They kissed and hugged and held each other until they fell asleep. She awoke feeling grungy but refreshed. She figured she would take a quick one-minute shower and then she would get him up.

Feeling great, she looked at her tummy and then the alarm clock. She thought of some of the meals she could prep the night before and save time on the cooking. She woke him with a kiss and whispered, "Practice." He understood and went for the morning shower. He found his clothes on a hanger in the bathroom and thought that might save a little time.

The morning breakfast consisted of blueberries, oatmeal, and toast. The food was enough to get him up and going. He kissed her as she sat down to eat with him. The morning radio station was on, and they ate quietly. When he posted for the door, he was five minutes early. She smile and thought again she could enable his mission.

They cleaned up and retired to the living room. A little rest, a little conversation about Robin Hood and role-playing, and the day had already started out fine. Then they decided to read for a while, so she perused his library, and she asked him about the book on St. Thomas. He told her he had read it once, but she could read it so she picked the book. And they both retired to the living room. He decided to read up on St. Daniel from Illinois.

At dinnertime, she made tuna sandwiches with cheese and tomatoes. The drink was 2 percent milk from the grocery store. He liked the lighter dinner and how she considered what he needed. They took time to discuss what they were reading, and he found out she had very good comprehension, material retention, and a little different insight spiritually than he did. He went over her review and promised himself he would remember her commentary.

She asked him what was on his mind, and he talked of her insight, which was a little different than his, and he made a mental note to try to remember her review of St. Thomas. She told him, "With practice, it will come in time—all good things do. That is what my dad told me." They both agreed and returned to the afternoon readings.

At 1500 hours, she put her book down and told him she wanted to cuddle with him. She said she was a little tired. He put his book on the carpet and stretched out on the couch, and she put her book down and turned into him. Soon they were asleep.

The shower soon saw business as they prepared to attend the concerto in a minor way. She hoped the band was as good as its reputation. Scrubbing up, she realized she needed cowboy shirts and jeans. All she had was blouses and slacks. He wore a plain shirt and jeans instead and forewent the boots in the closet. He said, "These would do for this time but your idea is realistic."

He looked at her as she prepared herself at her vanity table. She talked about her mom teaching her how to use makeup more effectively. She appreciated her mom showing her how to use makeup and said a prayer for her mom. He patiently waited while she talked about what she was applying. When she presented herself, he told her she looked nice.

They held hands as they worked their way out of the bathroom. She picked up her purse as he looked for his keys.

The local cowboys looked at her ring and at him and left her alone with her husband. Being more a theatre than a bar, most took their seats right away. The Houston-based band was introduced, and they said their greetings. Then they got down to business. They hardly missed a beat all night, she noted, and the songs were sung strongly and clearly. She did get antsy at the end because she normally did not sit in one place too long.

He said he was satisfied if she wanted to go. She apologized but got up to leave, and they went out to Perkins for a late-night pancake breakfast. She made excellent eggs, and he was full of them, he said. She smiled and decided to wait on making him pancakes since he picked those up when they went to Perkins.

They talked about the band and she mentioned what she liked about the presentation. She told him she did not usually sit in one place for four hours, so she apologized again. He said not to worry; he usually got distracted by hour four so it was a good thing to do. "Besides," he said, "it was easier getting out and to Perkins leaving early."

She said, "You sure?" He looked sincerely in her blue eyes and said, "Totally sure."

The hour passed by as they talked about entertainments and how often each would actually go out. They both found out neither really went out as much as they were doing. They both thought going out less was a good deal for both.

The pancakes were especially good, so he recommended that they leave a two-dollar tip instead of the dollar they usually left. Sarita agreed and told him she would pay for tips. He told her he thought that was equitable. She pulled out two ones and left them by the salt and pepper shakers.

She and Joseph made the bed for the night and then she set the alarm clock he moved over to her side of the bed. They talked about the stray nice thoughts they had in the day and decided sleep would be best. She and he hugged as they drifted off to sleep.

On Saturday, she decided they would ice skate in the morning instead of Sunday night. After her practice, they set out for the rink. They paid their fee and donned their skates, and they had their music selection, so she chose country.

The air started warming, and she asked him if they could go cowboy shirt hunting. He said he knew an outfitter off the mall. She purchased three shirts, three pairs of jeans, and a set of cowboy boots for her. He bought her a hat and belt buckle in case she got brave, he said.

They returned to the house so she could change into the jeans and flannel shirt. She made Spanish Rice, peas, and a custard for dinner. He told her he knew he could not have married a finer cook. She kissed him soundly, and they set off for the school. When they arrived, he dug the fishing blanket out of the trunk for her and gave it to her to carry.

The game started on time, and it was Lions against the Eagles. She saw some of his and her friends and told him, and they both set off to sit with their friends as the Lions kicked off. She waved high to their friends, and they climbed the bleachers while room was made for them.

The parents were supportive, and they embarrassed their children by calling encouragements out to them. It did not matter to the crowd nominally who won. They just wanted their children to do well. The talking was nonstop through the evening hours. The men talked but not as much; they just smiled at the ladies' enthusiasm.

The game was called at twilight; the Eagles had won. The parents walked the field to say hi to their children. Sarita told him she understood why, but she thought it was kind of silly. He reminded her they might have children playing football, and then she would be encouraging. She said, "Yes, but you have to admit it is still silly." He agreed as they walked back to the car.

When they got back, William was on the line for her. William called and told her her extra OJT was approved and she could start 0800 to 1000 hours on Monday. She thanked him and then thanked Joseph. He said, "It is a good thing."

She decided to celebrate by making Baked Alaskan Pie. So Joseph turned on the coffeepot as she started to assemble the ingredients. She then asked him what the training entailed. He said, "Each department in turn does a hands-on familiarization of their section. The orientation lasts one to two hours. Administrative Management and Job Skills lasts up to twenty hours each. For the job skills, you have to pick a management post to study." "Any recommendations?" she asked. He said, "I recommend that you take the orientations first. Decide on a job that you would prefer last."

She thought about it while she assembled the pie for baking. She asked again, "No job preference?" "None," he said. That satisfied her as she put the crust in the freezer. She then mixed the topping and asked what shift he would prefer her on. He told her if she can get her desired job on second shift, that would be nice.

She did some more thinking as she poured the mix on the ice cream, and it soon was in the stove. She sat down next to him and looked in his brown eyes and said, "I like you a lot." He kissed her and said, "I like you too."

The alarm went off on the stove, and she prepared to serve the pie. He had gotten a spatula and two plates, so she put the pie in the refrigerator. The pie was very good, and they enjoyed the tastes. They talked for a while, and she got second helpings. After they talked some more, both cleaned up, and they went into the living room. He played some rhythm and blues CDs that he liked, and as they rested, she leaned on him and cried again.

He hugged her and kissed her light brown/yellow hair and let her cry and celebrated their new life together. The songs passed by as the crying abated, and she sought out a kiss with rising desire. They made love right there.

The night moved them to the bedroom, and she set the alarm clock and he smiled. He told her he was living in almost heaven. She agreed and turned out the lights.

Sunday came around with a feeling of peace for her and him. They took their showers and ate eggs, sausages, and hash browns. They both decided Sunday school service would be nice again. The preacher was teaching conflict resolution skills to the adult class. The preaching service would again be on salvation.

Robert was there at the church and invited both of them to his house. They agreed to come over after the service. When they pulled up to his drive, she noted he must be someone important. He replied, "He works for governance."

Cecelia waited for them at the door and ushered them to the living room. Sarita complimented her on the art decor. She said that pleased her. She urged them to sit and said her husband, Robert, would be right down. She then sat down and asked Sarita to give a biography of her life, say, since she was three or five.

She composed herself and decided. "I remember when I was six." Then she talked about the things she remembered. Joseph held her hand while she talked. The end of the first story brought Robert from his study. He asked her to repeat it again. Then she started over and talked for about a half hour. Drinks and snacks were served.

Robert talked about it being important we remember who we are. Sarita got the idea. Her heritage was her, and she was her heritage. She realized she should keep a diary for her children's sake. Cecelia agreed with her wholeheartedly.

They then talked about what they did to support the good Lord's mission in life. This took another half hour. She realized she had just become part of the privileged few to see how a part of everything really worked. She listened more intently, trying to remember it all. She had a feeling it would not be readily repeated.

Then they had light chicken salad sandwiches and potato chips with sweet tea served up by their kitchen. When she hit too much information (TMI) overload, they decided to talk about the local High School football teams so she could relax. They promised that in a month, they would get together again.

Being dismissed, Joseph arose and helped his wife to her feet. He shook Robert's hand and thanked both of them for their hospitality. Cecelia hugged Sarita and told her she wished her well. They were ushered to the door. When they got to the car, Sarita said, "How many people know what they told me?" He told her, "At a guess, about twenty all told out of 3.2 million."

She thought about it and realized she needed to know to enable her husband in his endeavor. She then asked Joseph, "How bad was I?" He said, "For all the new ideas you picked up, I reckon you did pretty well." Then he smiled at her.

She started humming again the blues song. He was working on learning to understand her better. He knew this time she was basically happy just compiling new thoughts. The trip home only took ten minutes, and he asked her if she wanted some coffee. She said yes, so he fixed two cups and carried them to the couch.

She started singing the song "The Blues" a capella and looked at him. He joined in and followed along the best he could. She laughed a little and then kissed him for his endeavor. The day was for relaxing, he said. She said she could take a sad movie, so he asked her about the movie *Of Mice and Men*.

She had read the book, she believed, in tenth grade, and it was a sad story. So he ordered the movie from Netflix, and since he had fifteen minutes, he went to the kitchen and got out some chips and peanuts.

As the movie started to play on the television, they settled in together to watch a family favorite.

The next movie was a remake of *The Karate Kid*. They decided movie night was a nice thing to have. She wondered if a child could do that. He said, "You do a lot of amazing things that you learned in childhood." She then decided it was really possible to be down and out and come from nowhere and then be successful. She learned how to cook as a child. She could have been hired at seventeen to be a diner or restaurant chef.

She thought about the morrow and training. Was a blouse and slacks good enough? She went to her closet and brought out a pale blue blouse and a pair of pale yellow slacks. She put them on a hanger to show Joseph. He said they were appropriate but might get a little dirty doing OJT orientation.

She decided that that was what she wanted to wear. She then changed into her nightclothes and brought two blankets with her. They got a little cold the last time. She then set the alarm and turned the signal up just in case.

He noticed right away and asked if she wanted more coffee or wine. She said the wine was good. She told him she had some ideas about cuddling he might like. He thought they were just fine. The night passed away, and the alarm clock found them sleeping on the living room couch.

She shut the alarm clock off, took a shower, and then dressed. She woke him at 0600 hours to prepare for his day. The shower awaited, and breakfast was being prepared—two egg sandwiches, juice, and hash browns.

Joseph M. Due, September 18, 2016

Date

The harmonics were off a little, and the music was a little too loud. The band was singing favorites of the last one hundred years. The crowd was a little country, and you could say, according to some, a little like hillbillies. The dance selection was one of "request and see if the band knew the song."

Sarita said she had not been to many country bars in her life. Joseph said he liked country music and the band was about normal for the local scene. She learned to dance country by watching the crowd as they moved around the floor.

The hamburgers and fries she rated as being done well, and the cover charge was reasonable. The night proceeded to pass by as the experiences mounted. By the time the last song was played, she could comfortably dance a few country dances as long as they were not going too fast.

They then went down to the riverside park and fed popcorn to the birds that lived on the edge of the river. They listened to rhythm and blues and talked some more.

Joseph M. Due, October 14, 2016

Flying

The hair was fine. He bent to kiss her neck and ears. She smelled like roses in midbloom. He felt her desire as she turned her face to kiss him back. He touched her soft face, and desire flared as their mouths met. Her soft, inviting lips opened, and he felt her mouth draw him in. He could hardly contain himself.

Her inviting shoulders felt soft and pliable as his hands moved downward across her back, which bent inward as he held her gently from the waist. She placed her hands on his chest to feel the rising warmth of his desire. Her hands drifted to his back as her passion drove her onward.

She moved her right leg between his legs as he bent her backwards with the energy of passion and desire. His excitement rose another notch as he caressed her back in passion. Their desire flared together and became one as he picked her up and carried her down the hall to their bedroom of desire.

The morning brought them gently back to the land of the living, with fond memories of the unity they achieved in love. The soft aches as they moved to the shower reminded them of their passion and desire when it became one.

The skating rink was a fine way to learn how to skate in tandem and fly. Joseph thought about the night before and asked Sarita if they could do that again sometime. She said when she recovered from the emotional storm of the first time, of course she would like a second time.

They watched *Old Yeller* and *The Magnificent Seven*. He asked her what kind of son she thought they would have. They talked about children and the raising of them until 0100 hours. They then drifted off to sleep in the eddy of their love.

Joseph M. Due, October 17, 2016

Timing

La diaz et diaz et diaz. Time being of the essence, being that man's time is limited in the mortal coil. God has numbered man's day in his judgement, so man has to pick and choose what he will do each day and what he will try to accomplish.

So all of God's children look at the reality of the truth and also know they will have to give an accounting for what they actually do. Sarita mentioned this to Joseph after Preacher Brown's sermon on Ein Judgement.

The discussion was on Joseph's mission, purpose, and home. She wanted to know what she should be doing. He discussed her work OJT and how, being familiar with the offices, she can then counsel the other wives and spouses on the expectations of debts, duties, and obligations of family members that work for the mission.

"Where," she said, "would she do that?" He said, "Mums does it from the kitchen, and sometimes, during the dinings-in, you will also." He also said, "Some will be done on the phone as people learn your number and call to ask questions. And the rest will be done in whatever office you're actually working out of."

She asked about her promotions. He said William was her supervisor, and when she was ready, she would get her next promotion. She then turned the discussion to timing and when it would be required. He told her the daily endeavor in love would be sufficient unto the day, and people would call her as they thought she might be able to help them.

She got some more coffee from the kitchen for both of them. She sat in his lap, and they talked a while more. She asked him if he thought she was getting heavy. He kissed her and said, "Delightfully so."

Joseph M. Due, October 16, 2016

Training Days

She shut the alarm clock off, took a shower, and then dressed. She woke him at 0600 hours to prepare for his day. The shower awaited, and breakfast was being prepared—two egg sandwiches, juice, and hash browns.

He emerged from his shower bright and refreshed. He was happy to be, and he hugged her firmly but tenderly. She told him, "OK, Romeo, work awaits. Breakfast is ready, and right now, that is what you get." He kissed her insistently, and her passion began to rise and she thought of giving way when he kissed her so tenderly on the forehead she thought she would cry.

He told her, "Later is agreed."

He appreciated the breakfast fresh and refreshing then both grabbed their keys and headed off to work. She drove sedately, knowing she was extra early while he commonly reported for his morning meeting at 0745 hours.

She wondered where he got his kisses because that one was a new one. Pulling into the garage, she saw he waited for her. It was a nice gesture. They entered the elevator together, but she was due in at the third floor training area, and he was due in the sixth floor briefing room.

As he emerged from the elevator, he saw Mikael had stopped in to say goodbye and the watch Captain was with him. He said good morning, and they told him that investigations came up with a potential site for the bomb makers and they found potentially two more IDS sites because of the fight at the skating rink.

He thanked Mikael for filling in for him while he was on his honeymoon. The briefing was to cover fourteen days, so he grabbed two coffees and settled in to hear what had happened while he was on leave.

The big news was accompanied by the reality that they needed extra training in investigations and in bomb making. The classes Mikael came up with seemed to handle the need really well. He thought about it and opened up his planner. The briefing stopped, and he asked for the next class dates. He would check out the classes himself.

The briefing resumed, and he realized Captain Dirk had done a fine job and he would have to commend him. He wrote another note.

At 1000 hours, he presumed his wife had gone home. The briefings were over at 1100 hours and he arrived home at 1200 hours after he talked to his dad. The rest he got with his wife was nice, and the sleep was greatly appreciated.

She had told him her first orientation was in business production, and the demonstration had been superior cleaning and packaging of production parts. Her blouse suffered a little from the cleaning chemicals. He recommended she wear the same thing each morning so only one set of garments got so marred.

They planned out their day at the table. Both enjoyed good coffee. Then they listened to the second playlist for their afternoon rest before their regular shift. The pace with a new wife Joseph would have to get used to. He told Sarita he needed to adjust fire too.

She thought about it and told him she would add that to her prayers for him. She then asked him about the morning kisses. He said he wanted to show her he really loved her, and the new kiss was more things he learned to appreciate about her.

The afternoon was busy with walkthroughs of all the departments, and he realized it was getting him tired. So he scheduled himself an extra fifteen minutes for lunch. He realized the wedding and honeymoon were hard work.

Praying, he recommitted to continue doing a good thing. It was his dream, and he knew it was God's will for his life. He thought of it as continued training. Besides, it would make a great story and set an example for his troops. He sequestered himself in his office and called his dad to get his opinion. He respected his dad a great deal and knew he could trust him with his thoughts.

His dad agreed with him and told him he was doing good and Mom was praying for him. He called her dad and said he appreciated the fact they raised her so well. He then told him she was also in training by choice and asked that they pray for her. They thanked him for the information. She had not yet said she was in management training and pregnant to boot.

Lunch was anticipated because he would get to see her for a while. She looked at the clock and knew he would be there in five minutes. She ordered her thoughts and cleaned her work station. Cleaning up, she pulled off her apron and looked for him in the diner. He was drinking coffee, so she went and got him a plate and one for her.

They ate quietly until he said, "You know, I jotted a few notes down for what I think the nursery might need." He passed her his notes, which looked quite comprehensive. She looked through them and was touched he thought so much about the necessity. She noticed though he did not touch on the art decor. He said, "Missy or Junior might notice the art decor, and that was a good thing." He knew Mom would like to help remodel, but the design was totally up to her. The accoutrements he figured were standard, and he would buy. She would furnish the decorations.

She looked up from the notes and said "Deal." He said "Deal." She put the notes in her planner to add to the schema that was developing. He said he would pay for the crib, but the style of crib was up to her feminine intuition.

She told him the morrow would put her in design setup, and she would take his advice. They chatted about designs that she had been thinking about. She had ideas for both a boy and a girl. The meal was chicken cordon bleu with fried baby potatoes and squash.

The chicken cordon bleu was her recipe of peppered cheddar cheese. She asked him if he wanted another, so she got him another plate.

She had to return to the kitchen, so she left him with the second plate and took the others to the kitchen. The remainder of the day would be doing paperwork for the orders for the next set of meals. The shift supervisor was handling that part of her OJT. He said he wanted to go to first shift to be home at 1700 hours for his children.

He looked at the unit mission brief and decided he would look at equipment checks and participate in the gear inspection for half an hour, so he went up to the firing range area where the gear was laid out by lot on the tables. The day passed quickly for both of them as they endeavored in life mightily.

They met at the house door and decided they would talk for a while. She had thought about an upscale store that carried baby supplies and she assured him they were quite conservative and he asked her to price the equipment so he could transfer the funds into the house budget.

He turned off the CD player when they were done, and she took the blankets back into the bedroom as he turned down the sheets. He said, "I love you," and she kissed him and she asked him to undress her. The night turned quickly silent as they drifted off to sleep.

She awoke in the semidarkness and saw the alarm read 0550 hours. She untangled herself and kissed him as she made her way to the shower. He awoke to the alarm, her kiss still on his mind. He could hear that she was in the shower, so he turned on the light and prepared for his turn.

The morning was transited with ease, and both were at the door early. The internal stress he knew was there, so he kissed her and he blew air in her mouth to remind her she should relax and breathe. Startled, she listened to him and now knew another reason to love him even more.

The day in system design started with an overview of purpose and then a look at some paper designs. The next step was setting up some production tools for safe use. Her hands were lightly covered with the oil used to store the equipment. The morrow would bring about resources for packaging and handling for storage. She cleaned up and headed over to Mums's house. They were going to do price shopping on the nursery.

The necessity for investigations upgraded their procedures for said investigations to the commander's briefs. He had to approve policy and approach. He also went to the command post to see how they were handling the information that would come in.

He had a few moments before Sarita would show up with the shopping list and maybe even a picture or two, so he decided he would spend the time in meditation and prayer. When he heard the car door slam, he put on the third playlist for review. Then he headed for the door to see if she needed any help.

Dinner was rice pilaf and baked chicken. They talked about supply, equipment, budgeting, accounting and finance, payroll, and scheduling as well as sales contracts for equipment or services and long- and short-term storage and tracking of equipment.

The naps were humorous at times. Setting the bedroom alarm clock, they cuddled on the couch until 1500 hours. Then they drove in together, and he talked about planning and investigations and where they were at in the process of validating culprits and determining level of charges that might be imposed.

She asked about enablement—Donald, for example. Joseph said, "Donald, for example, is mentored like I mentor you in talking through the issues of the day, and then his dad supervises over the weekend when necessary. His mom brings him to his dad's workplace, and his dad demonstrates what the operational considerations are." She noted that he did that for her, and she kissed him to show her love and appreciation.

She looked at the menu and set to work. She was taking a look at supply orders for the kitchens, especially glasses and silverware that got damaged or disappeared. The chili-mac she was making was a new recipe for her, and she appreciated the challenge.

The discussion at dinnertime revolved around the style of crib she was thinking about purchasing. He asked a few questions and then told her he had an opinion. She asked him why, and he explained his reasoning and showed her he cared by his insight into her choices. She thought about the pros and cons and decided for her use she would like to choose the heavy-duty crib with a half fold-down side. He said he could get used to using one since he did not have much experience using either. Then the talk centered around how William found the contracts that the company worked on.

The planning section had some ideas on how to proceed on the bomb threat, so he went up to see the raw data and how they wanted investigations to proceed. He then decided he had enough energy to do a light workout in the gym doing the forms for Judo. Team 6 was playing volleyball on one end of the gym, so he dressed and put out a mat to stretch out. The privates watched how he refreshed his training and kept sharp.

They were inspired and motivated to help their own training out by his setting the example. Later, some would put down mats and work through the forms, remembering to make it a subconscious part of their response capability and helping them become better teachers and demonstrators. He lived the five Ps of military life: "Prior preparation prevents poor performance."

The next day was Thursday, and he wanted to see the physical combat demonstrations to see how they were coming along. So he wrote a note down in his notebook to schedule the time to watch the trainers demonstrate.

He prayed as he showered for his people, including his new wife and baby. To complete the night, he attended to the day's worth of paperwork, thanking God for the job he loved. He then turned on his work stereo and put in a country CD to relax to as he rested and meditated.

The drive home he talked about the martial arts and how it helped combat soldiers survive battle. She asked if she had to learn Judo. He said, "Orientation will include necessity, purpose, and use. Then you will see a class with class personnel practicing after demonstrators show the forms." While pregnant, he recommended that she not take up martial arts training. She thought about his desire to see her effectively prepared and knew that after pregnancy he would like her to learn.

She told him that was a great idea then went on to talk more about what would be in the nursery. He appreciated her diligence and her organizing her life inordnung. The conversation turned to decorations she and Mums had discussed. He asked her if she decided what she was going to decorate the nursery with. She outlined her idea, and he gently squeezed her hand to show his approval. He made a note to transfer funds in the morning after the day's briefs while she hugged his shoulder to show her love.

The esprit de corps was growing slowly but surely. Considerations were going to base instincts as they worked on their love. They sometimes now thought in sync, and both were just doing things to help each other out without thinking about them. Their training was proceeding at a good pace. She said she was hungry, and he knew which type of consideration she was asking for.

He picked her up and carried her to their bed. He kissed her tenderly as the passion and desire mounted. He could see her and her love from the hallway light. An hour later, she reached over and set the alarm clock and then moved back into his arms, snuggling in for a good night's sleep.

On Thursday, he remembered to transfer the funds, and he put an extra $100 for her to purchase more Folgers stock for their baby. He picked up some four o'clock plants for growing around the house. When they were developed, she would pick a local. The flowers' colors reminded him of their wedding colors.

She was in the nursery, washing down the walls, when he arrived home. She asked him if, on Saturday, they could shop for paint. He said that they had the time, and it would be a good idea. He told her of the plants on the kitchen table, and she thinks about "reason por vie." She hugged and kissed him as he thought of their baby's arrival.

Dinner was chicken and rice in the form of a hot dish with sautéed green beans with butter and onions. The topic was myopia and delusion. She considered what "ick de mons" were prone to go through in relation to IDS interdiction. They talked over dinner, cleanup, and into the afternoon in the living room. She thought of all the questions she had and then decided to ask how it began.

He told her that it began in childhood rebellion against God and the Word until the ick de' mon demonstrated the myopic viewpoint to a delusional one, usually by violence and often ending in their death unless they repented. She said she would consider the truth and its applications she saw in life and ask more questions later.

Leaning against him and sipping her coffee, she said now she needed rest. They leaned on each other until 1530 hours, and he said to her, "Time for work, up." So they prepare to drive to work together. She had a review of the cooking budget to do, and he had a team to brief on their recon mission of a suspected sight for bomb making.

He felt good about the day and reviewed the operational considerations noted. There was light security at the facility, but setting up audio and video monitoring should not be too hazardous. It was a step to finding the facility and terminating its operation.

The command center noted the departure time of team 6. Radio monitoring was up, and the teams were inbound. The estimated time of arrival ETA was twenty-two minutes. The unit that did the drive-by timed the inbound and outbound routes.

The assembly points were to the north of the building at another facility shut down. They checked out abandonment of the facility and assembled in the darkened parking lot. The team split into two groups with equipment. The darkened side was covered by Team Alpha. Two soldiers would post up by the road for observation of any approach, two would cover the north side to warn of security's passage, and the other two, when able, would set up the monitoring system and visually scan the interior site.

The second group would try to stay unobserved beyond the lights in the parking lot and emplace audio and video on the light poles. The individuals had the same system configuration but were more readily seen from the windows and doors. They were also more likely to be interrupted.

The command post notified the Captain of the watch when the rally point was reached. She was also notified when the rally point was secured and then when team 6 went operational. The seconds ticked by as communications listened in to what the team was doing. Many prayed for the team's safety. When Team Bravo said "Bingo," the Captain called Joseph, William, and Joseph's dad in to work.

The ringing of the phone was a disturbing noise that brought both Joseph and Sarita awake. He told the Captain he was inbound ETA thirty minutes. He hurried to the bathroom for a quick wash while

Sarita got his clothes. He told her to take a quick wash with him and then dress.

The Captain got on the radio to tell team 7 to mount up and be prepared to move to the rally point. She then returned to the direct monitoring and thought about calling in operations itself but decided at this point it was not necessary.

Joseph's dad walked in, and the assistant watch officer updated him as the crisis unfolded. Joseph and Sarita were followed in by William, who was used to such events because of his experience and expertise in production facilities.

The first video came online and then two, three, and four. The teams withdrew to the rally point and mounted up. The order to return to the staging area was given instead of a return to post. They knew they might be sent back in and started to mentally reorientate their thinking.

The minutes went by as they drank the coffee provided in the command post. Joseph was thinking of waking Robert but was not sure yet he should do so. The second bingo was said by the watch, and the person announced that the bomb-making equipment was now identified. The forms could be seen on camera.

They noted there were no workers yet working production, so they waited to see when production would start up. Joseph reached for a phone and invited Robert to the watch. Robert knew what he was saying and said he would be inbound in twenty minutes.

Team 6 reached the departure point and reoriented before Robert arrived upstairs. The photo department was on call, and the stills had been made of the equipment and forms so Robert could peruse them. He was in time to see security change. It was a good thing team 6 departed the area before shift change.

Robert thought of waiting as well as did William and Joseph, but seizure of the tools, forms, and any bombs was paramount in his thinking. Interdiction teams were ordered in. He then borrowed the phone to call the shift Captain and authorized search and seizure of all vehicles and the owner's domiciles. The shift Captain gave the police the necessary information.

Then he told the shift Captain of the police to put out an APB for the search of the location of all the vehicles at 0600 hours. Robert called the SWAT team and told them to respond to the production site at 0600 hours and they would be met by Federal Agents.

Then he told Joseph, "No seizure of assets is to be done by your troops, but they can look for addresses and phone numbers of other suspected sites."

Joseph nodded to the Captain, and she relayed the order to the controller to pass to team 6. Then the controller said aloud, "Order is received, ma'am, they will do what was ordered."

The attack point or departure point was on the blind side of the production facility off the road. That point was reached by Team 6 at 0520 hours. Then a minute later, they moved into position and waited for the guard to come out and make his half-hour round. The observers confirmed he was on his way around the back side of the building, and Alpha Team indicated they were ready.

A private hit him hard in the face as he rounded the corner, then as he backed up to gain room, the corporal knocked him out with a blow to his head. "Man down!" they heard on the radio. Bravo Team then took a better look at the door to see if it was unlocked. Setting a small charge on the door where the bolt was, they backed up and detonated the charge.

They opened the door and entered one by one. Overwatch said one left and they proceeded to look for the now-warned security guard and the other team member went left to clear the building. Team 2 entered and followed suit. Team 3 posted by the door just in case they were needed. Twenty seconds later, they found and secured the remaining security guard. Five minutes later, they cleared the building. Then Alpha Team delivered their prisoner and searched the building for evidence.

The APB went out on time as assigned police checked out the houses of the security guards. The process was in motion, and the watch knew what they needed, awaiting discovery of the IDS/IDC local ratcheted up the level of stress and tension. The time ticked on, and the waiting continued. Team 6 had a video recorder with them as they inspected the bomb production site. The feed played out in the command center as they went from office to office. The information had to be garnered from another source.

The investigators were waiting a response from units sent to the houses, the APB, and receipt of the guards that were arrested. The command center was awaiting the arrival of the police SWAT on-site, and Robert was awaiting further development as well before full authority was transferred to the police awaiting the arrival of the FBI.

The police called in one by one. They caught one security guard off-site, and the other was still at large. At 0700 hours, SWAT took over the bomb production site and transferred both prisoners to the police jail, awaiting prosecution. They would be interviewed by investigations upon arrival and offered a deal at 0900 hours.

Robert thanked Joseph for him and his team, and he said hi to Sarita as he bid them a good day at 0830 hours. William said goodbye and left. Joseph told the Captain of the Watch, "Good day, and if something comes up, I will be at home." And then he and Sarita left the watch to continue their monitoring of the case. He told his dad on the way out, "Your shift," and then bid him a good day.

The drive home brought a dozen questions to Sarita about long-term planning, further involvement, team responsibilities, and further involvement in the case. He was very pleased to answer each question. As they arrived, she said to him, "Are you tired? I could use some more sleep." He concurred, and they headed to the bedroom to resume their slumber.

They slept from 1000 hours to 1400 hours and awoke with the ringing of the alarm. The showers were long, and the preparation for work slow as they energized for the day. He thought about orientations and said to her, "We could cut your orientations down some. If you know enough about a given sections mission, purpose, and job, you can have that certified without the actual class." She said, "What do I do?" "I ask you about our training section, for example, and you describe what they do and what their purpose and mission are." She talked about what she thought the training unit actually did for about five minutes. Then he asked her about the watch and command post as well as planning and operations. She could describe them well. So he called William.

William agreed and said he would qualify her on those sections and reschedule her training. He asked if she should be paid for observing the operations of the day. He said, "That is where she picked up some of her knowledge." William said he would write up the authorization.

She was pleased to get paid for the day and, at the same time, see what her husband did with the unit. She knew she was privileged, and she got to know the truth versus the story she saw in print. She asked him about funding and how it worked. He said, "I have to tell you at the office. Can you come up for an hour at lunch? Bring two large plates." She said she would work on it.

The day passed as he did his paperwork. The commendations and leave requests were almost equal in number. He almost took the time to see the planning people to encourage them to have ideas. He remembered his lunch date and turned the CD player on as she brought the cart into his office. He pointed to the couch, and she pulled up the cart.

She pulled out the napkins and handed him one. "Chicken Alfredo in a creamy white sauce—my own making, creamed beans with a slight flavor of onion, and rolls," she announced. She said, "It is accompanied by a pitcher of milk and one of coffee. The dining room staff wishes you well."

He thanked her and the kitchen staff for the endeavor. He then told her he was glad to see she could make it. They ate for a while then she asked about the unit funding. He began to talk as he described the source of their funds and how they used them. He went on to give some examples of fund sites as they finished eating. She asked him who had the contract this generation. He looked at her and said me.

She then asked if Donald would have the contract for the next generation. He told her, "If he is entrusted with the money." She then asked, "How much does the monthly operations budget use?" He gave her an approximate average. She then asked if she could have a raise in her operational budget to be commensurate with what she knew. He looked at her wryly and she then said quickly, "Just joking."

She then asked if her knowledge filled out an OJT requirement. He looked at her, and she said, "That's a no." He said yes. They then moved the cart out of the way, and they talked about games in relation to helping find a child find its destiny through its interest. He admitted Mums and his brother's wife were the experts in that understanding. He did say he knew what games they chose as a starter to that idea and named a few games he knew.

He recommended that she call and ask for a starter list for two- to six-year-olds. He said they could put up a storage shelf in the nursery or something. She said she would call. She then talked about the employee schedule in the dining room. Her training would encapsulate a monthly schedule with leave and overtime. He asked her how long that would take. She said she might need two months practice to get the whole idea down for certification.

He said that seemed to be a fast overview, but he knew she was a quick study. So he asked her if she seen any jobs on the list in supervision that she might like to do. She said no and hoped administration would bear more fruit.

She returned to her scheduling and prep work for the next meal while he worked on the daily report to include the areas of governance they were working with on the mission of the day.

The time flew by, and he thought about the weekend and plans. He hoped he remembered them. He called down to the kitchen and asked Sarita if she wanted to go skating Saturday at 1000 hours and then shopping for incidental baby supplies. She thought the ideas were nice, but she asked if they could sleep in. He agreed.

The drive home was filled by idle chitchat about various and sundry things. She told him her back was sore from carrying all the pans because of the larger group of people eating dinner in the dining room. He said, "Baby oil." "Why baby oil?" she asked. "It will help your sore muscles." He also said, "I will give you a complete family back rub in the living room like when I babysat my sisters when they were babies."

She appreciated how he actually explained what he did because if not explained right, it may seem improper. She moved a little and realized she might actually need the help, so she said OK. The living room beckoned as he looked for the baby oil. It had been a while since he last used it.

He came into the living room with towels and asked her to strip. She did so as he laid out the towels on the couch. He then had her lay facedown on the towels with her head facing the stereo. He then undressed to his underwear and got astride her. He said, "This will be a little cold." And then, like he used to do with his sisters, he gently massaged oil into her back and to her legs one section at a time until the back dried out a little bit.

She said she was feeling better when he was working on the lower back and spine area. He continued to apply oil to her legs to her knees. She was feeling better and sleepier as he proceeded. When he noticed, she totally relaxed he put the baby oil up and carried her to the bed with the sheets pulled down. He then set the alarm for her and crawled in the other side of the bed and turned out the light. A couple minutes later, she turned to hug him and fell asleep.

He woke with a start because she had touched him personally. The hour, he noticed, was 0500 hours. She was up and rested, and he turned back to her ministrations. The giving of love in a touch was a wondrous thing, he thought. They turned off the alarm clock ten minutes to the hour and decided to take a bath together.

Breakfast saw them alert, relaxed, and happy. Oatmeal and blueberries with orange juice were on the menu, and both of them ate well. They decided to go ice skating at 0700 hours. The music this time was rock and roll songs, but they were feeling better and did not mind.

At 1000 hours, she asked him about shopping for the baby. He told her he thought about generic clothes and diapers and such so they could stock up each month on different items to fill the closets and cabinets. She asked him, "About how much each month?" He said they should start with $100 each month and make a list of all the necessities. She hugged him and said that was fine.

The quiet of the moment was upon them. They had in a small way achieved "peace de accord." The drove to Target and perused the children's section for baby items they might need. He pulled out a notepad, and he asked her to tell him the items they would need. They went down each aisle and priced what might be needed.

She decided to buy a few items, and he checked them off their list. He gave her the whole list as he paid for the items. She put the list in her purse and picked up the bags. He knew she wanted an equal relationship, so he let her.

The afternoon dinner was ham and turkey with gravy, mashed potatoes, and corn as well as drinking water and coffee for liquids. After dinner, they decided to continue reading their book selections together. The critique was light, and they decided to watch football on television. For supper, they ordered pizza.

After the football game, they talked about the unit and the upcoming party. He asked her if people had given her an idea as to how many to serve. She said twelve would be available with wives. He remembered the table count and wondered how they were going to fit them all in. She said she had a plan and borrowed extra chairs from the kitchen. Some of the workers would drop them off, if he did not mind, at 1400 hours.

They turned the CD player on and decided to rest. They fell asleep on the couch again and woke up at 0700 hours. Security was knocking at the door at 0800 hours. They found out that there were four IDS/IDC sites active. She decided to ride in with him and be there in the background for him during the day.

Investigations had a brief they wanted him to see. A half hour later, they were on the sixth floor, and the briefers were lined up through the door. The police caught the fourth guard entering a domicile on Elm Street and followed him in and secured the twenty residents. In the process, they looked for weapons and found several bombs, handguns, and rifles with approximately five hundred rounds of ammunition and plans to bomb the city center complex.

Police investigations found a LAN setup in one of the rooms, and a Sergeant recognized three more addresses by the house directions and descriptions of services provided. Two were known drug sites for money-making operations, and the third was a fraternity that provided troops for the criminal activities that were planned.

Coupled with that, the investigators got the names off the cell phones and cross-checked them with the site's participants known to date. They put out arrest warrants for ten people—so far, two of them married. They believed they would get them by later this afternoon.

The police requested extra help and teams 8 and 9 were dispatched to SWAT headquarters for planning and operations. Captain Johnson received Robert's request for support and sent the troops over at 0600 hours. Additional support for securing the houses was requested, and the Fifty-Seventh wanted to send over four more teams.

Joseph thought about the federal troops coming in and realized they might not have enough troops for a couple days. He told Captain Anderson, the watch supervisor, to activate the secondary command post under his dad's leadership and bring up four teams for dispatch and two for standby. Captain Nancy Johnson was still there, and he said to her to get with Fort Houston and ask for two hundred more troops on standby here.

He would call Robert himself and inform him of the troops he would proffer to the FBI for their use when they needed them. He then asked for the name and number of the FBI liaison and called him and invited him to meet him in the command center.

The briefing continued with the investigation's list of suspects and their addresses on slides 4 through 10. He perused the slides and realized there were already five hundred additional suspects from planners and cell phones seized.

Operations then briefed which sections were fully up like supply, but the armory was still three shy of being fully operational. They also procured housing plans from the city engineers for the three houses, and they were on slides 12 through 14. The process was changing as their investigations compared the lists from the police against other known sites of criminal activity. He nodded, and the briefing continued to in-house preparedness based on a count at 0800 hours.

The briefing ended with the request for further orders. He told the people to carry on and that he would be in the dining room and then the command center if they needed him. Then he ordered them to continue to monitor police needs and call him if needed.

He knew his dad was inbound and would probably decide to meet him in the briefing room, so he caught the eye of one of the watch officers and told him to keep his dad posted as to his whereabouts and to secure a pass for his wife and the FBI agent.

He asked his wife to attend him, and he left for the dining room. As they were entering the elevator, she said, "Tuna sandwiches with cheese, pickles and chips—that is what you need." He had been wondering about handling the grease from the sausages. He agreed and she said when they get to the dining room, she would prepare them for him.

His dad was entering the dining room from one of the forward stairs, so he invited him to sit with him and Sarita. She told him she would get a plate for him too. He thanked her and shook his son's hand and then pulled up a chair. He briefed his dad and told him he was tasked to set up the alternate command post. He said, "Troops?" His son said, "On the way as we speak."

Sarita came back with the breakfasts/dinners and heard her father-in-law say what he intended to do with the alternate command post. He wrote the FBI control center number down on a card and put it in his wallet. He actually liked helping out, and this one might be a challenge.

The time passed as they ate, and Joseph's dad asked her how the baby was holding up. She told him the child was doing very well and quite happy to be. He asked her if he knew yet if it were a girl or boy. She said she thought it might be a girl.

The meal was over, and Joseph called the command post and told them to post the General as responding to post/inbound. He himself would be inbound to the command post. His dad bid them good day, and then they decided to take the stairs.

She said, "I did not know there was a door to the command post." He said, "Do not tell anyone." She nodded as they took the steps. She asked, "Why the steps?" He said he liked to watch her walk. She blushed and turned around on the stairs and hugged and kissed him. She liked the idea that he found her attractive.

He then smiled and patted her backside and said, "We need to be about the King's business," so she walked to the second floor. He pulled his keys and opened the door. Security greeted them and glanced at her badge.

Teams 8 and 9 were in attack posture, waiting to pass through their deployment site. The two hundred infantry tasked for the various teams were in various stages of transit, and fifty were briefed and ready for team augmentation. "Tell the police we have a platoon we could lend them and ask where they should be sent. Notify the General when you find out so he can mate them up and monitor their activities."

"The full alternate command post will be up and running when the General arrives. Our units will be at 100 percent within the hour. It is noted that it is 1115 hours." Joseph concurred and then pointed out the appropriate status boards to review to his wife. The controllers explained their station missions one by one, and then they gave a mini update brief. The commander appreciated the controllers for helping train his wife to be a better mum.

Team 8 and 9 took one of the houses that did fundraising for the making of bombs and went in. In ingress, team 8 suffered an injury, and team 9 one casualty when the shooting started. They were holding the facility until the police with augmentation could fully relieve them.

The general mated up the platoon and sent them out to augment security so team 8 could return to SWAT status. The appropriate boards were updated, and the shift log was updated. She noted how well the controllers interfaced and worked together. They had a good director and trainer.

An hour later, teams 8 and 9 were relieved of security duties and returned to their primary tasking as an augmented SWAT team. The second platoon was forming up, and estimated dispatch time was half an hour. Robert called to see if they could hurry the second and third platoons. Both SWAT and investigations needed the help.

The process of organizing though, Joseph told him for safety, could only be rushed so much, but he would try to expedite the process. Robert thanked him and bid him a good day.

Joseph called Fort Houston to see if they could move more quickly. He then told them to send the teams directly to the alternate command post. The lieutenants could brief the troops in on their mission almost as well as operations. He then called the General and updated him on what Robert wanted and that the next two platoons would be sent to the departure points when they were integrated with his teams.

Investigations were now required to conduct the interviews of the bomb makers that were caught. This further hampered their endeavor for their respective agency's push to organize each new set of data they collected. Joseph told his investigators he sympathized. Then he took fifteen minutes in planning to rest between information streams.

He bought Mountain Dews from the vending machine for him and his wife and kissed her gently on the forehead before he sat down. She said to breathe. He laughed and said, "You're right." She asked him, "How long will it be?" He said, "The process should crest within the next three hours. At 1600 hours, we will take a rest on the couch in his office." She said that would be OK.

Joseph called Robert and asked him if he could talk the FBI into sending a team of ten investigators to supervise both his and the police's investigations and maybe take over interviews sooner for prosecution. Robert thought about the request and then laughed. "That takes some nerve," he told Joseph, "but I see the need." He said he would do what he could.

She asked him what Robert said. "He said I have nerve suggesting operational protocol to the FBI." He also said he would talk to them. She said she admired his nerve, and his command persona was one of the reasons she approached him to begin with. He smiled and kissed her gently, and she remembered being carried as a treasured baby. She blushed, and they returned to the command post.

The troops for police support had hit the operation's points and were now assuming their duties. The SWAT time would be down for three hours and then hit the third site, which was monitored by detectives. The arrest teams would be departing for their targets local by 1500 hours. That was estimated organization, assignment, and brief time.

The investigators were still making connections, and team 12 was sent out to investigate two possible additional sites. "Do the recon as best as possible and get license plate numbers of the cars in the nearby local." The additional calls in were resting on the third floor and in the firing range. Shift changeover would take place at 1400 hours, and they would have two hours on and two hours off until the FBI was up and running.

The hard-core sites identified were staffed with armed gunmen, and they would fire upon the response teams. The reminder to the teams was broadcast at 1300 hours. He ordered it repeated to each team, especially the teams designated for SWAT team duties.

"The couch or the small bed in the other room," he said. She looked in the other room and said to him, "Can we lock the door?" He turned the knob and said no. She asked him if being discreet would work. He said yes and he shut the door. The enjoyment of love was quick, and they were soon asleep.

The second set of houses were about to be interdicted, and Sunday night was about them. He asked her if she wanted to go home. She thought about it for a minute and told him she could hang for a little while. He thought of his surfing days and Hang Ten as a motto and a challenge. Meeting that challenge, he had to learn a lot of things about the surf and spent a lot of time swimming.

He chuckled about the expression she used, and he told her why. He said, "People nowadays use *hang* as a general expression, but when I was younger, it was used for surfing." They decided to wait to go to the command post for when the teams crossed the line of departure. The command center would call him, and he didn't want to be there all the time as they were stressed out enough.

The teams came under fire as they approached the house. "The first team had two wounded, and the second team cleared the area with just a scare," the lieutenant said. Team 1 found plans and two bombs. Team 2 interdicted an IDS center, and they said there were three places that people were sent to. The first was known. The other two addresses, team 12 could investigate.

Teams 3, 4, and 5 were now tasked for SWAT support as they arrived for duty. They were going to be used to spell the command structure so more people could get a rest. The command post updated their boards, and the assembly area had to be moved to the Gym.

The armory and supply teams were augmented by the soldiers who could not sleep yet. The command post was working overtime with overtasked boards, but that would change with incoming Smith Carne Communication Controllers. The operation was stretched to its limit, but within twelve hours, that would be alleviated across the board.

Joseph and Sarita told the command post they were mobile, and he carried a radio. They started with looking at the briefs for the teams posted to the gym and then toured the meeting rooms used for the FBI investigators. They then toured the fourth, third, and second floors to see how things were working. They stopped in the dining room for macaroni and cheese and hamburgers.

They then went to the command post to see when the next group of FBI agents would be assigned. Containment meant the county jail, and the interviewers were working overtime to piece together the disparate pieces of conspiracy that the investigators had already uncovered. There were many perpetrators assigned to each cell and more being arrested every hour.

He did not know where the next group of agents would be assigned, but they probably would like the idea of interdicting their own fair share of houses. He told the Captain of the watch to spread the idea to each Captain verbally. When they were ready to do their own interdiction, they were to be aided in the endeavor.

At 0800 hours on Monday, the FBI now had two SWAT teams and four hundred agents combing the Houston area. It seemed to some that in every other house, there was a perpetrator. Joseph's people could now go to six hours on and six hours off. The police were equally relieved that the FBI took over their investigation endeavor and the housing of the criminals.

The newspeople caught on to the case when the FBI started using the county jail. Joseph and Sarita picked up a newspaper screaming "Read all about it!" They found the FBI control center and besieged the building before the agent in charge gave a press release. He said many citizens and local authorities were working on arresting the conspirators that had built bombs to attack government facilities. He said the Drug

Enforcement Agency might send agents of its own because it appeared to be that drug sales in the area funded the bomb making.

Sarita said, "Were many citizens criminals and drug users?" He smiled and said, "It appears to be so." As he opened the door to their house, he said, "Are you going to keep that newspaper?" She said, "There are many children readers that might want to know how Mom and Dad worked together in the good old days." He smiled and turned on the lights imagining what his grandchildren might think.

The house now reminded him of them, and he appreciated the change in thinking. He knew they were growing together. He said, "This house now has different types of memories. It speaks to me of us instead of just me." He kissed her and said, "I pray for a million more memories of us." She folded into him, and they spent a few minutes discovering each other again.

The phone rang, and he picked it up. It was the command center saying another two hundred agents had arrived and were now working arrest. The need for team 12 was to help the unit return to normal shifts. They wanted permission to go to 12 and 12 early. He said, "If you can arrange it." The watch officer said they had a plan and it could be accomplished at the next six-hour-on, six-hour-off shift change.

Sarita said, "Good news." He said, "Most assuredly. The watch will change to twelve hours after our next six-hour shift." She pulled open the refrigerator door and looked for the hamburger. She said to him, "We need something hearty. How about tater tot hotdish for supper and fried tater tot hotdish for breakfast?" He thought about how much cream that entailed and he said, "That sounds wonderful."

He pulled out the baking pan and reached for the cream of chicken. She put the hamburger on to cook. He then pulled the tater tots out of the freezer and started layering them in a pan. She put the coffee on and got out their cups. She remembered she saw the load out of one of the teams. She looked at him and asked him if the armory had that many employees. He said no.

They only had ten. The armory personnel got some of those that could not sleep to help them. She said, "Oh, I understand. That was nice of the sleepers." He said, "Family helps each other out when we need help. The kitchen staff didn't. They had to feed five hundred extra each meal. That was extra, so they got to keep their shift schedule." She nodded and sautéed the cream of chicken, mixing it in with the beef and a little fat she did not strain off.

The dinner was baked at 350 degrees for forty-five minutes. In the meantime, she told him to chop up some lettuce, and she got pepper, onion, three tomatoes, cucumber, and shredded cheese for a salad. When he was done, he looked in the refrigerator for the French dressing they both liked. She chopped a little of the pepper, grated a little of the onion, and chopped up a couple radishes. Meanwhile, he cut the tomatoes and cucumber.

A meal fit for a king and queen, he thought. They talked about cooking for a while and discussed likes and dislikes. "She was very particular," he noted and said. "My mom—bless her soul—told me that some people only see heaven through a meal. Since then, I endeavor to provide the best I can."

She told him she would serve; it was what she liked to do. He knew that was true and touched her hand as she sat down. She looked him in the eye and took his hand and said, "I do."

The evening was short, so she set the alarm clock for him and got out two blankets. They lay down on the couch, and he held her as they both fell asleep. They had enough time for a shower, and they were refreshed enough. They would nap in his office if necessary.

When they got in, they saw the workers had cleaned up the facility for the unit and had done stocking throughout the facility so all the vending machines were full. They even washed and prepped all the vehicles that were in. It was a commendable effort of William's workers. Then they went home for a few hours to see their families.

Joseph told operations he needed to see the ops officer and the briefing slides for team status. He did not want everyone waiting around when they could be resting. Things like that endeared him to the troops. *And they love him*, she thought. He shared the slides with her and explained what was going on.

He was told William was in doing labor reports and such. He called William to thank him and his teams. He asked if Sarita had more orientations over the weekend. He told him he could definitely sign off on both supply and equipment units and the armory as well as investigations. William laughed and said she was learning fast. Joseph agreed.

They decided to meet to talk over unit issues at 1530 hours that day. She knew the extra OJT training in operational mode were rescheduled. She also knew, standing by her man, she was getting trained anyway. She knew God was providing.

The casualties were light; they only lost four since he was in. The teams were adjusting well mentally and emotionally. They knew capturing the bombs was worth the sacrifice. The equipment expenditure was slight since they were keeping the houses that were taken. That meant equipment dropped or left so they could fight could be recovered.

The firing range had been shut down since the troops were firing live for real. That meant bullet expenditure was not significantly higher. So far, the manpower extra hours had been necessary. The cost would be borne and was justified to date. William would write up a report for him, and Robert was reasonable.

The command post told him the police sent the SWAT teams back to the alternate command post, and now they could return the teams that were used for physical arrests. He said, "Keep the troops on standby for interdiction. We may still need them on call. Send the other troops back to Fort Houston."

They then told him that the controllers called in. "We have enough fill-ins to see the controllers go back to regular shifts at 0800 hours." He said to the Captain of the watch, "See it done."

He was grateful the operations were ramping down. There were other sites that might need interdiction. Sarita asked about command staff. He said that when they move to twelve-hour shifts, they still need to run two command posts and the troops are still needed. "OK," she said. She was learning how the unit adjusted in times of stress. Command and Staff set the example for sacrifice.

They had an hour before he was scheduled to walk the unit again. And the command post was seeing relief in sight, so they went back to his office. They talked again of the need for manpower for each section and how, at times, some were on different shifts. He poured her some coffee, and he talked of the need for the unit and need for the unit to sacrifice at times. He even talked about the wounded and dead and their value in life and death.

She folded into him for a kiss and a hug. She let her emotions ambiate, and he could see them. Once in a while, he recognized what the emotion meant. He was getting better at seeing things like radiant or ambient emotions. His interpretive ability was getting much better.

He held her for quiet moments and let his love flow. She hugged him even more, and he knew she could read him as well. Her healing he noticed when she made love to him.

The clock indicated it was time for his walk. He looked in all the offices with her as he let the unit know he was there and that he cared. His review was an accounting in the armory. While he was there, they showed her how they did their counting to make it easier and take less time. They then showed the bookkeeping to both, compared issue used within the last month, and filled out the sitrep form they turned into the supply officer who had their briefing slide updated.

The response force for the building was cleaning the foyer, so he talked to them about their volunteering, and then he asked a private to describe his duties, his domain, and his mission. He did very well, hitting all the high points of what a response force did.

They saw the sun rising on the horizon and thanked God their shift would be over soon and they could get more rest. Before he left, the FBI called to thank him for being a silent partner in crime prevention. The President authorized another five hundred troops for long-term investigations, and most would be in by Thursday.

He was also told they were getting to the end of their paper leads to a degree except the out-of-state connections. He thanked the officer in charge and said he was praying they would find any extraneous bombs that might be out there. He was bid good day, and then he told Sarita they had to go to the command post before going home.

She said in the car on Thursday, "Do we need a bigger building?" He said, "We can be back to regular shifts by Friday and then people can go home if it works out that way. The need for a bigger building is based on events like these." She said that would be nice and hugged his arm. He said, "You feel like another nap? I'm more tired than hungry." She said, "That would be good."

The alarm was set for 1430 hours because she knew he needed to be there early. He said, "Since we have not done much and had a little sleep, why don't you set the alarm for 1300 hours?" She thought about her body's needs and decided he was right, so she said OK.

At 1300 hours, she was fresh and awake. He said, "Did you hear the song about the midnight hour?" She said yes. "The person used the midnight hour to do conflict resolution with his wife so they could enjoy each other's company better. I would like to hear ideas from you on conflict resolution just in case we get close to arguing." She said, "Can I sleep on it?" He said, "We can talk about it Friday night at midnight if you want." She said "Deal." He replied "Deal."

At 1600 hours, she was at her station. Cooking was a joy to her. She read the recipe and went to get the supplies. Western Chili with a touch of red peppers was on the menu. She liked the plethora of recipes on chili and liked to cook a variety of recipes. She asked if anyone had the song about the midnight hour, and her prep worker said she did. She asked her if she could borrow the CD. She wanted to meditate on the song and think about his interest in conflict resolution.

Christy Siaka asked if she got the Monday morning blues yet because of her pregnancy. She thought, *This is the day for difficult questions.* She thought about her emotional state especially when tired and realized she did get a little sad when she overextended herself. When Christy was done putting out the crackers, she admitted she got a little sad when she was tired, but that was not when she experienced the blues.

She then asked when the baby was due. Sarita missed her step and realized if she told the exact date, every woman in the family would know for sure about Christmas. This one she did not answer until she spent time praying about the right answer. The meat was browning and the peppers were being sautéed before she answered the baby question.

She told Christy she expected the baby to be born around September 25. She said that she said her vows in consecration and got pregnant about an hour later. She confessed to her it was mightily embarrassing.

Christy thought about it and said, "I probably won't get pregnant that quick," and then went to get the cheese to grate.

Dinner with Joseph was always good, and he had nice things to say. He thought of his love and told her he enjoyed being with her. They talked about when the baby would be born and schedules—his and hers. He told her that, in times past, he did day shift but got called in so much at night he just switched to the night shift. She told him she liked the evening shift she was on but that it would require a babysitter full time to maintain and then there would be the pickup of the baby at 0100 hours.

He said, "We both need to be on second shift. We will just have to find an understanding babysitter for now." She thanked him and asked if he needed a second bowl of chili. He said it was nice, but no. He would rather have her company. So they talked about colors and painting, and she asked him if he liked white.

He said he was used to it but would consider another color for the bedroom. She asked him light blue would be possible. He said that would be nice.

The command post was doing routine activities for the night, and most of the teams were getting well-needed rest. Some were even scheduled for regular training on Tuesday.

The ride was a quite one, and both enjoyed the time to be together and gather their thoughts. As they entered the house, he took her coat and asked, "Le Rouge or le Blanc?" She said le Blanc would be fine. She kissed him tenderly, and they stood there for a while, sharing their love. They moved into the kitchen, and she decided corn chips would be nice. He asked for potato chips, so she got two bowls. He went to the wine cooler and got out a good bottle of Chateau le Blanc. When he returned, she had put on their song on repeat. He noticed the placement of the chips and went to her. They danced through the song, letting their emotions run.

As the music was turned to the playlist selected, he touched her hair and then took her hand. They talked of ideas for the family and Christy's questions. He told her it was embarrassing to him that everyone would know, but he had peace over the choices they made. She then told him where in management she wanted to work, and he said he thought her decision was right for her and he would help when he could.

They talked of this and that, holding hands. She realized she was getting hungry, and she told him so. He arose and turned off the music and carried her to the bedroom. His desire grew with each step as she held onto him. The hour beckoned with desire, and passion reigned supreme in the lover's hearts.

Joseph M. Due, September 22, 2016

Treasure

Treasures are those things that build good, long-lasting memories like a good woman or a wedding ring or even obedient children to secure your generations. Other ideas of treasures pale in comparison and do not bring satisfaction in the day or comfort through the years.

He sat there and thought about all the treasures God had brought into his life. He reflected on the children he had trained over the years. Joseph remembered with delight the times God chose to show him the children that took the lessons to heart, and you could see they had grown.

He picked up his coffee cup and decided to go talk to one of his treasures in the kitchen. Joseph walked in the kitchen, and she was talking on the phone with Dana about the Christmas party planned for the twenty-fourth.

He kissed her on the forehead with his love. She still blushed after all these years. He poured himself some coffee and sat in the chair next to her as they worked out the party coordination process. She asked him what brought him into the kitchen so soon. He said he wanted another good memory with one of his chief treasures.

She kissed him and said, "Meet me in the bedroom in ten minutes."

Joseph M. Due, October 13, 2016

The Lonesome Blues

The lonesome blues are difficult to get over for some. For others, the lonesome blues come and go fairly quickly. It is all a matter of internal conflict resolution and self-control. Donald learned how to separate himself from those women that chose not to walk in his way after the eighth or ninth time. He understood Joseph better with each failed enterprise.

He remembered Joseph told him that each endeavor was a lesson from God. Once he learned those lessons, he was free to signal separate from the women when the women chose not to negotiate fairly or they just plain walked out.

He put on some rock and roll and decided to do some command staff reading and get some coffee. The hours passed by as he thought through the manuals he was reading. At 2000 hours, Mums called him. She was out shopping and ran into Cynthia Richards. She was about his age and did not know a thing about surfing.

Donald thought that was funny and decided to write her name and phone number down. He talked to Mums for a while and decided he might take her to an early dinner tomorrow. He called her up and asked her for a date. She asked him what he listened to, and he said, "Rock and roll at the moment." She agreed to meet him at his mother's house at 1600 hours.

The night shift was usually quiet except the command post and investigations. Most of the training was done between 0800 and 2300 hours, though there might be a few on the range. He decided a personal workout in the gym was in order. Then he might try the firing range as it was so quiet throughout the Houston area.

Joseph M. Due, October 18, 2016

Bait

The sun crept over the horizon as the wind picked up speed. The waves were now more difficult, and they knew they should head for shore. William and Joseph knew the signs well enough. The witches were at work, worsening the conditions of the sea.

They called the guards and told them to expect inbound bandits. Somewhere out there, their male counterpoints would be striking. Joseph checked his pistol and nodded for William to do the same. The gear was packed up and the fish dumped in the sea. William sighed and Joseph agreed.

The guards were supposed to be by the dock, but they were nowhere in sight. They decided by two to carry the gear and check the boat. They worried about the guards and the car they drove down in. William surveyed the beach and the houses and did not see anyone in sight.

They decided to wait under the awning for a while. They talked about the time and the locals and wondered where the tourists were. The half hour passed when they saw Joseph's car pull out and head toward where they stood. They dropped their fishing gear and pulled their pistols.

The car turned around and backed up, so they approached from the rear on both sides. The car was empty if not for one of the guards, who was injured. He told them the other was ambushed at Wendy's. He moved over as Joseph decided to drive. William got in the back seat and rolled down his window.

They noticed a flash from the apartment up the street. As they came into range of the apartment, Joseph decided to do some defensive driving by speeding up and then slowing down. The firing pattern was off, but it was close enough to hit the car a few times.

Joseph saw William on his cell phone talking to the command post, asking them to check on the safety of staff family members.

Joseph M. Due, October 3, 2016

En Guard

The morning mist coated the car's windows with water and hung in the air and cooled the beginning of the day. With the changing of the guards, the morning paper was brought in and the grounds were walked and the neighborhood surveyed. The off-duty guard was invited to do his sitrep at the breakfast table, and if they hung around, they got a bite to eat.

Then the sitrep would be turned in by the day guard when the General reported for the morning briefings. That is, unless there was trouble noted that had to be called in. Then the guard left with the car, and the other guard stayed in the kitchen as the family prepared for the day.

At 0725 hours, the guard checked all the windows and took a look up and down the street as General Carne worked on leaving for the morning brief. The guard looked around the house and walked to the car ahead of the General and checked the car's area for danger.

Then he walked to the end of the car and looked down the road and saw a vehicle with three or four people in it. He called out to the General to return to the house. The General did so as the guard took cover behind the car. He called in the emergency as he pulled out his weapon.

General Carne told Sarita to take everyone to the hallway and returned to the door. The green Dodge moved up the road toward them, and you could now see the weapons from the car. The Guard shot out the grill of the green Dodge, and it slowed to a halt not ten feet from the General's car.

General Carne heard a kicking on the back door and returned to the kitchen and crouched by the entry way into the living room. When the invaders kicked the door in, Amanda started crying. He shot the first two that entered the house straight up and then waited to see if the others would enter the house.

He heard shots fired and wondered about the guard. The criminals got out of the car, and the guard got the driver and the passenger in the front seat. The other two entered the neighbor's yard to get behind him by coming around the front of the General's car. He crept to the front corner of the car and threw a clip behind him, and the other two rushed the car.

The guard dropped both criminals with four shots. He then crept down the side of the car to check on the other two criminals he shot. He saw the blood leaking off the door panel and saw the two feet and knew he had at least one more to get.

General Carne shot at the door post, aiming for the exterior of the house. He saw a shadow fall. He looked to the window and knew there was at least one more in the backyard. He heard another four shots from the guard's pistol and, before that, two other shots. He saw the shadow move downward in the window and knew the criminal was approaching the door.

He aimed for the right doorpost and realized it would be better if he shot from the hallway. He ran around the kitchen into the hallway as the criminal rushed through the door. The criminal was looking where he used to be, and Joseph shot him three times. As he fell, the General advanced to the window and scanned to see if he could see any others.

The guard moved slowly around the criminal's car as quietly as he could be. He saw a van coming down the street and retreated to the safety of the rear end of the General's car. The van pulled up behind the green Dodge, and two soldiers started toward the car—one from the left side and one from the right.

They secured the criminals and then they called all clear. The other four soldiers entered the neighbor's yard and were doing a sweep of the

General's yard. The Guard slowly stood to let the soldiers see him and he changed clips. He nodded at his friends and walked back toward the house. He heard three shots, so he announced himself before he entered the front door.

Joseph M. Due, October 18, 2016

Hoods

The sound of automatic weapons pierced the night air. Violent yelling permeated the silence as people hid in fear. The pain of the wounded and the sounds of the dying could be heard in reply to the violence being committed.

The sounds of sirens could be heard responding to the distress calls received from the neighbors. The darkened windows were reminiscent of areas torn by war, like Beirut. The reception committee was the empty neighborhood filled with the detritus from the fighting. The police cordoned off the block and brought in the SWAT teams to clear each building so that any perpetrators that might be left behind could be found.

The building attacked was searched directly first by the SWAT team in charge and the bodies littering the landscape then checked for life. Then paramedics and ambulance units arrived to tend to the wounded. The police investigators then entered the house to secure any evidence that they could.

The watch called Colonel Donald Carne at 0721 hours as marked on the log and gave him an update. The police had asked for use of fifty investigators for twenty-five houses they needed to check out. He gave his approval and then turned on the news to see what they said on the half hour.

The investigators were ordered to report to police headquarters main briefing room, and they would conduct the briefing at 1000 hours.

The morning brief talked about readiness postures of all the different units that might be interested in the case like ATF or FBI.

At 1000 hours, Colonel Carne told the watch that if there was an update in tasking or condition, to give him a call.

Joseph M. Due, October 4, 2016

Terror

The streets were freshly paved, and the rain lightly danced on the surface of the road. The car moved slow enough to avoid hydroplaning. The people's intent in the car for the moment was unknown. The water washed down the young man's face as he walked home from delivering the early morning news.

The car crept up on the young man, and the window rolled down. He could see Jeremy's face filled with such hate and, in surprise, saw the machine gun pointed at him, spitting flame in the predawn light. Paralyzed, he just stood there as the car rolled slowly past him. He saw his sister at the wheel, and terrified, he dropped to the ground as the bullets sliced over him and past him.

He crawled across the grass, hoping Jeremy and his sister did not see him. A little while later, he came upon the spent ammunition and picked a handful of them up. *Where could a rat like me find safety?* he thought. He wondered where they were and lay flat in the tall grass as a car cruised slowly by.

The car moved on down the road, and he got up and slowly followed. *They probably did not see him in the rain*, he rationalized. As the signal light came on, he dropped flat and peered at the car, willing the car to go away. It turned left, and he saw two people in the car but was not sure if they were the ones.

Fear coursing through him, he remembered there was a police officer that lived two blocks over. He thought he might be able to make it if God would forgive him and protect him. He repented of his sins in tears as he realized part of this was his fault. The five-minute walk felt like five hundred minutes as he expected the car to come back and find him.

The police officer was up and eating breakfast when Gregory Davis showed up at his doorstep. He asked Greg what he needed. Greg pulled out a handful of used brass from a machine gun and handed it to Sergeant Johnson. He took the brass and noted the time. He did not know the number to ATF, but he did know a couple investigators from the Fifty-Seventh CID.

Greg dried in the warm car and dozed for a little while until Sergeant Johnson pulled into a driveway on Cottonwood Street. He looked at the trees, and he said to Sergeant Johnson that he was scared. Sergeant Johnson said, "There's a young man I want you to tell your story to. He might be able to protect you."

The rain was abating when he got out of the car. He thought of running away, but he had told Jeremy of all the places he hid out. He promised God he would give up his lies, which got him in so much trouble. The house was nice and comfortable, and the man received the spent ammunition without a word. He looked at Gregory and asked him if he would sit and tell his story.

He asked his wife for three coffee cups of coffee. Then he sat down on a chair that was placed in front of the couch. He asked Gregory to start with the time he woke up this morning and tell his story.

The story went on for quite a while as they all indulged in the coffee. Sergeant Johnson called in from the kitchen and gave him a synopsis of his morning and apologized for not being there as scheduled because of the boy needing protection. He was told to report in when the boy was done being interviewed.

The process finished up for the first time, and the detective called the watch center to inform them of the facts as he seen them. They put it on the boards as an active investigation and informed Joseph of the event as it happened to date.

Lieutenant Paul Mathews asked Gregory some more questions about the road conditions, the feel of the wind, and how wet the sidewalks were. He then said he needed to hear his story one more time for the record. Greg got a Danish and a refill as he recounted his paper delivering journey.

It was time for the next step of the interview. They gave Gregory a bathroom break and waited for him to return. He asked when he returned if they were going to pull his records. He admitted they did not look good. The Lieutenant told him that was mandatory for review.

They asked if he had a cell phone, and he pulled it out of his jacket. They wrote down all the names on a piece of paper as he watched with great interest. They then asked if the first person had any criminal tendencies and what they might be. Then they asked the same question about the next person. Then, to get a better picture, they asked Gregory whom each person hung out with one by one.

The questioning lasted an hour, and like the first part of the interview, they told him they had to do it again. The recounting brought out more memories and facts to check out, and the Lieutenant's wife also typed up the synopsis and the notes for her husband.

CID assigned ten investigators to the case and awaited Gregory's statement as they pulled the juvenile records of his sister and the boy named Jeremy.

Joseph M. Due, October 7, 2016

Alcohol, Tobacco, and Firearms

The dirt roads in and around Houston numbered in the hundreds. There were some people that preferred the dirt roads versus the paved roads of the city. Country life was fine for those that did not mind a lot of dings and dents on their autos while driving those back roads.

Generals Terrance and Joseph Carne found, to their surprise, they sometimes led to nice rivers or lakes where they could fish if they got permission. The healthy condition of some of the land was a surprise as well. They liked driving the back roads now and then themselves. That is, even with dings to their nice cars.

It began one day when a representative from the ATF showed up at their door looking for a little help. They called Colonel Donald Carne and Colonels Dennis and William Smith in because they had to volunteer their vehicles, and in Donald's case, it was a learning experience.

They had a major production of alcohol, which was supporting the purchase of pistols and rifles. The criminal element out in the sticks was armed, dangerous, and growing. The ATF said that Smith Carne Industry owed them one or two debts of help along the way, and they were calling that debt in.

Security helped set up the ATF in the master briefing room, and delegates from all the sections were called in for the ATF briefing. The briefing was a great series of sitreps from the back roads to the west of Houston to the branching of the network, which trafficked in the illegal whiskey.

Donald Carne smiled at the idea that he could be involved in such an endeavor. He enjoyed watching the movies that talked about this type of venture. Planning and Operations was where everyone moved next with the maps provided by the ATF. Colonel Donald Carne said he could produce thirty-three teams with a call-up from Fort Houston.

The ATF wanted twenty-eight teams extra for the farms and facilities, and they pointed out where they would like them to approach from and what buildings and facilities they were to take and keep. Donald Carne decided to call up the extra soldiers anyway to cover Houston if necessary. He also asked if, midweek, they could do the attacks so that it would not be too big a burden on Houston or the Fifty-Seventh CID.

The Colonel Smiths thought they could free up all their vehicles if the operation were on a Wednesday or Thursday and concurred with Colonel Carne's request.

The ATF, later that week, agreed on the scheduling. Their buses weren't due in from Washington until then.

Joseph M. Due, October 23, 2016

CID Convoy

The moon seemed to hang low in the night sky. They were racing the moon across the vista of the landscape, wanting to be in position before the moon went down. Recon this night would have a new experience in land navigation. It would not be pitch dark, but it would be close. Fears and trepidations flowed across the emotional landscape of the minds of the soldiers as they prepared for battle.

The whisky runners numbered over two hundred, spread out over ten square miles of forest and swamp. The women were also reputed to be armed and dangerous. When the women got to thinking twenty years to life, the ATF briefed they would not surrender gently. The women liked the men were prone to shoot back, and they, as the soldiers, were reminded know the terrain better than the infantry, who just studied maps before they showed up.

Donald, in the lead vehicle, thought, *How desperate am I to do this with the ATF?* He knew desperation bred stupidity. He thought about the needs that might drive him to do something foolish. Desiring the adventure, he submitted even that to God in prayer for his troops. Thinking about navigation, they were ten minutes from their turn off to dirt roads. He looked out the window and hoped the moonlight would hold until they all hit their departure points.

Then he thought about the desperation of the enemy. How many would not be taken alive? He thought it imperative to remind his troops that some of the men and women that were conspiring would be desperate indeed and do desperate things. He asked for the radio and the Captain's net to tell the soldiers to be prepared.

The driver slowed down at the right turn off and turned left to go south a mile. Then a turn to the right in two miles and a mile to reach the third turn, and this one was to the right as they paralleled the river frontage, which was twenty acres by five hundred acres. The groups would sweep to the river and then all move south to surround the houses and other facilities. The Sheriff's were given vehicle ID and were to stop everybody after the Fifty-Seventh CID hit that first checkpoint.

The Major said in the radio the different checkpoints as they passed them, and the rear vehicles were to park and prep to leave the departure points. The ATF command post was up on the left, and there were agents on the road signaling where there command vehicles and response force would park for the night.

Joseph M. Due, October 19, 2016

ATF Assault

The berm on the road led downward into a bumpy, swampy type of ground that, in the dark, was difficult to watch. The walk to provide a cordon that would move south took fifteen minutes from point of departure. There were two teams to each section between the farms. Each team was walking south by the time they got used to the ground, some of which was dry.

The planted crops were in small lots here and there ahead of the teams. For the most part, there were lights on where the collection sites were. They walked straight ahead while the Sergeant and the Lieutenant formulated a plan to take out security and then arrest the workers. The low crawling was difficult in the brush, weeds, and scummy water.

The takedowns were fairly easy to do in the dark. The actual arrests of the workers were difficult because they had a tendency to run even after they were handcuffed. Some managed to make it back to the houses and warn those that were there that the feds were coming. Lights were coming on all up and down the dirt roads.

Each soldier had to keep a sharp eye on their prisoners while they were being escorted to the road for pickup by ATF. The ground being difficult to see made the arrests that much harder to maintain. The buses were toiling up the road, and the teams had to wait to load up the buses that were there.

The teams would then reestablish the cordons and continue walking down security and the workers. A half hour passed without incident until security here and there discovered the feds were walking down the fields. Then open firefights became common as the living security for the whiskey runners made it to the houses. That left a team of soldiers and agents on each side of the houses being taken down.

The CID teams reformed and deployed around the houses as well as the ATF teams did. When they all reported in that they were ready, the OIC for the ATF gave the order for all troop units to commence the assault on the houses.

Joseph M. Due, October 23, 2016

House

The corn was waist-high, and the pumpkins and squash were growing quite nicely. Sarita had added gardening to her repertoire of skills and things she liked to do.

Joseph knew she was industrious enough, but she wanted to provide homegrown vegetables to the children once in a while. She asked him to add shelves to the garage for the long-term storage of the pumpkin, squash, and watermelon.

The night-light in the back of the house, she worried about. It might affect the vegetables' growth. He said the light was for advance warning of violent criminals with intent. She asked if the lights could be mounted on the house instead and be further away from the garden.

He said they could go shopping Monday to see if the lights could be picked up.

The shadows falling in the backyard left room for those that might come up to harm his children. He told Sarita he would turn the backyard light off, but it had to stay up in case it was needed.

The shelves were built, and the garden produce was in the garage. He put in a thermostat-controlled space heater to keep the garage warm as long as they had fresh vegetables.

He tested the backyard light and it was off. There did not seem to be anything wrong from the garage. He checked down the alley both ways and through the yards as much as he could. He went and looked at the light, and it was shot out. The denizens of the criminal mindset were at work. He was probably going to get a visit from them anytime soon.

He locked the garage doors and then went into the kitchen. He told the guard that the light in the backyard was shot out. The guard said he would do his rounds internally and warn the next guard there might be violence happening on his shift.

Joseph called the watch and told her his suspicions. They said they would bring team 3 to standby status in their vehicles.

He then ensured the rest of the windows were locked and the doors wide open in the hallway. Tonight they would read books to their children.

Joseph M. Due, October 22, 2016

Sarita

A whisper in the air seemed like it permeated the house. It was a call of desire and longing. He heard his love speak, and now he could respond with the care for her he had in his heart. His desire built as he walked toward her voice. He knew she was in the bedroom, and his anticipation grew.

As he entered the room, he noticed the lights were on low and she was wearing her wedding dress again. He reached for her, and she hugged him as he kissed her neck and ear. They touched each other tenderly as their lips met.

Amanda woke her up at 0530hours, and she woke up as she went to tend Amanda. She straightened the wedding dress and started to comfort Amanda. She told her that in nine months, she would have a baby brother or sister. Amanda said she would like a sister.

Amanda told her dad she had a dream about a boy at school, and she thought she saw murder in his eyes. Joseph asked her what the boy's name was and she said Ken. He sat off to the left of her. He knew investigations would want to look into the boy and his family and see what could be done.

Sarita did not want to take Amanda to day care, and Joseph agreed. They would call Mums and see if she would help out until a new babysitter could be found. Joseph called his mom, and she said she could be available. He told her Sarita would fill her in when Amanda was dropped off.

Investigations found plenty to say about the boy and his parents, so they assigned case managers to follow the family and recon went in with audio and video that night. The boy was being asked to lure Amanda to a place the parents could grab her.

All told they found fifty members of the conspiracy.

<u>Joseph M. Due,</u> October 3, 2016

Le Uhr

The hour in life is important for you and for me. Le uhr un vie es importante por vouse et por mua. The determinant will of each person may look at this truth differently—even act in consideration of this truth differently.

However, truth is truth. Joseph, at the advent of the birth of his son, determined to be better if he could so that his son would have the opportunities in life his parents gave him.

A renewal of commitment and dedication was to be seen by the men and women of the Fifty-Seventh CID, including his wife and Amanda and Dana, his two children to date.

He talked about his giving his energy for this purpose to his wife and the local preacher before God first. Then after he made his promise to God directly, his parents saw and heard it, and then it filtered down to the rest of the families.

Amore' cai vrai or "The idea of the love one has is the truth one lives by" became his guide and mentor in God's will. The days were marked, and the energy was given to teach the families how to shield their lives and safeguard their hearts in life.

The months passed by, and as the process was blessed, the abilities of his troops in extra sensory perception grew to the knowing of life's danger, and the troop loss and injury percentages started to significantly drop.

His first Meritorious Service Medal given by the President was entered into his records with the stable percentages and ratios noted, and he and Sarita accepted the President's commendation on the White House lawn.

Joseph M. Due, October 25, 2016

Compassion

The coughing of Amanda and Dana was frustrating to Sarita. Chicken soup did not seem to help. The Doctor told her they just had the flu and they would get over it. Meanwhile, she fed them orange juice and whatever they asked to eat. She had them sleep on the couch so they could rest and listen to the radio or watch children's videos.

Joseph was patient with them as they went from hot to cold. He even took two days off so the children could stay at home. She was planning on taking off Monday and Tuesday if they did not feel better by then.

The summer was warm and not too humid, and they were not being poisoned. She did her best and had to pray about the issue. So she prayed fervently periodically because she loved her children so much.

Saturday went by, and both Amanda and Dana were down to a slight fever, runny noses, and an occasional cough. She told them she would sit on the porch with them to get some fresh air and sun. They wore long-sleeve shirts, and she carried warming blankets for them.

The day passed. Their fevers broke and they both fell asleep, so Joseph and Sarita held Dana and Amanda and talked of the years they had and the years to come.

Joseph M. Due, October 7, 2016

ATF

The difference between a good man and a bad man is the heart. Sometimes, their actions are the same. Mark was turning four, and Joseph took great care to teach his children. He prayed for them frequently and worked on listening to his children the best he could.

The video was clear. The dope dealer smacked his two-year-old child across the face for picking up one of the bags he was trying to sell to raise money for buying guns for the local neighborhood gang. If their endeavor would only be the drugs, the tape would already be on the way to the police.

However, the gun dealers had to be tracked down and their weapons seized to avoid murders and assassinations. He was their first solid lead, so he had to wait to see what the person said, what he did, and where he went.

The next day in the watch center, they showed he made gun purchases from two people CID was tracking down. He made another fifty sales with his buddies, and now they had wire interception; another house was put under investigation.

CID was running the license plate numbers by courier through the FBI and ATF databanks, looking for further connections. The ATF sent twenty investigators with the list of fifteen names, and they identified eighty-five more suspects they were looking for with past associations.

The pictograph identification by CID revealed four more houses they could put under audio and video monitoring. CID wanted the arms warehouse, and ATF said, "We may find the warehouse if we bust the houses now." Since it was an ATF case at that point, teams 1 to 8 were called up for night raids against the six houses already known. ATF would lead, and the Fifty-Seventh would provide backup support.

Joseph M. Due, October 7, 2016

Children

The slow motion of the car lulled the senses. As he pulled into the drive, his guard got out to check out the surroundings and then the house. He was trained to see even how his friends hid in the dark on operations. The house lit up as Joseph and Sarita carried their babies into the house.

The day at the museum and the zoo was wearing even on Amanda, who headed for her bed. The guards gathered in the kitchen as Joseph put Mark in the crib and Sarita tucked in Dana and they met in the hallway and kissed.

They looked in on Amanda half-asleep already. Joseph picked her up gently as Sarita rolled the covers back and took off her shoes. Done, they each kissed her on the forehead and left the room and her to slumber.

They walked to the kitchen hand in hand. She got out the coffee cups, and he poured two cups. They both nodded to the guards and went into the living room. They relaxed for a while on the couch and then they talked about their children and their day.

The late evening was upon them when the talk turned into desire, and they moved to the bedroom. She whispered to him what she would like to do with him, and Joseph agreed. The vista of their passion turned into a dream as they danced slowly into the night.

Joseph M. Due, October 4, 2016

266

Poem

There is time for some things in life, and sometimes, you have to make time for those things that are important. The day's calendar looked full, but if he applied himself and things worked out in his way, he might have time to write a little note.

Hence, I thought and err do I do,
Think of how to make sweet love to you.
The day beckons, I must be about
But my love returns to you, I have no doubt.

The warning sirens went off in the distance, and Joseph called the command post to see what the alarm was about. There were children who were in the parking deck who were trying to access the elevator, and when they gathered together, the guard sounded the alarm and locked them out.

He asked if security had been dispatched to round them up or chase them off. They said, "Five minutes ago, and they are handcuffing them as they spoke." He said, "Have the police been called?" They said they would ask the police to pick them up.

He told them to check the parking deck when it was cleared and to call him with the results.

Then Joseph tucked the little poem in his shirt pocket and returned to going through the administrative paperwork for the day. He was working on an awards package when Sarita arrived for lunch.

They talked a while, and then he gave her the poem and told her to keep it a secret. She looked at the dining cart being wheeled in and laughed. She thought, *A secret—really?* She read the poem and said, "I love you."

Dinner was boiled shrimp on rice with a light sauce, beans, and carrots. The conversation revolved around games she wanted to buy the children for Christmas. He told her that he thought her list was just fine and he would learn some of the games they would buy that he did not know.

Joseph M. Due, October 14, 2016

Rome

"Rome wasn't built in a day." The idea is that Rome is a person. Before you can give shelter and serve a good dinner table, one has to build oneself up to do so. This sometimes takes a lifetime.

Dana asked Joseph about growth, and he pointed to Mark toddling around the living room. He said, "Growth is endeavor in learning new things just like Mark endeavors to learn how to walk. You commit energy to learning and endeavor well, you will learn well."

Dana thought about what her dad said, and she decided she would learn how to shop like Mom did. She prayed about the learning, and she went into the kitchen to tell her mom what she resolved to do. Her mom told her she had to learn what roast beef was like if she was going to go grocery shopping and buy roast beef. Dana nodded, and Mom said, "We will get the roast beef out of the refrigerator."

Learning to prepare dinner was difficult, but if it led to shopping, Dana was willing to learn it. The stretching of the mind left her asleep on the couch while the family watched the latest movie about the Sackets, a favorite series of Mark's.

The next day, Sarita called Dana early into the kitchen and showed her how to make another meal. Step by step, she procured and measured each ingredient for the family dinner. This time, she was awake enough for popcorn and soda before they put the warming blanket on her.

Joseph M. Due, October 8, 2016

Witches

Witches, you could say take your pick. In this day and age, there are many kinds. The first ones are the type that wear down the body and spirit being physically and verbally offensive. The second type is one that metaphysically attacks a person with the energy from their virtue as their virtue leaves them.

The men of the Fifty-Seventh CID had met a few witches here and there. Most of the witches in life were taken care of by being one with the body and saying no. The varied attacks of the witches with practice or experience can be set aside.

The art of war includes fighting all types of criminals, including witches. Joseph knew troops long past review to find the memories to build the body's integrity was an important part of learning the art of war. Thinking through one's defenses is an important way the body learns to defend itself.

Joseph knew that telling the truths of training was important. Second to that was utilizing the word to motivate the soldiers to practice their lessons on their own and to learn from their experiences.

He looked at the training tables and looked at his watch. He had half an hour to motivate by setting the example.

Joseph M. Due, October 15, 2016

Growing Love

Amanda, Dana, and Mark were sitting in the living room watching *Robin Hood and his Merry Men* when the phone rang. Mark picked up the phone and answered, "Carne residence." It was Grandpa and Grandma wondering if they could have permission to come on over. Mark asked Joseph and Sarita if they could. They nodded and, he told them it was OK but they were watching the movies.

He hung up the phone while Joseph was frowning at him. He looked at his dad and then his mom. She said, "Guests come to talk and eat dinner. We have to plan to tend to our invited guests."

He looked at his dad, and his dad said, "Your mother is right. What do you want to serve them?" He brightened and said, "Macaroni and hot dogs." "Is that what Grandpa and Grandma like?" Sarita asked. He said he did not know.

Sarita told Mark that since he did not know, that would be all right once but he should make a point to ask and know what they like. He nodded. Joseph asked him, "What kind of games do you think they might like to play?" He did not know that either. Mark just shrugged his shoulders.

Sarita said, "Pick a couple games out, and when they get here, be sure to ask."

Joseph M. Due, October 6, 2016

Terminal

The filament was frayed, and you could hear the light burn. The smell was a dank odor that mixed with the rest of the hovel to make a totally disgusting ambiance that drove away everybody that had somewhere else to go.

Only the most determined to live in the filth of the rooms of the house stuck around. From these conditions, conspiracy of the damned was derived as an act that, in their delusion, appeared at times noble to them.

Tomorrow had no meaning to some as a word of promise or hope. The pride of the damned would not let them die without one last malignant act. Some ideas came and went as some passed away, but the place was a collecting point for those determined to hurt others.

This particular group was invested in drive-by shootings to terrorize the base populace. The weapons were stolen from homes of people that thought the denizens of the group were friends with anyone. They knew the ATF was after them for the amount of weapons recovered from their activities.

They dreamed of using military hardware, which was much more reliable. They had been window peeping for years to find a cache left behind by others. On Thursday, a window peeper found a closed-down warehouse on the northeast side of town, and they drove their cars back and forth in the midnight hours to secure their haul. Little did they know the police were monitoring their activities and informed CID of their suspicions.

Their local now knew they would not have another midnight after the police report was forwarded to CID by the night shift Captain. Those that elevated the murder charges to conspiracy to commit and violations of other federal laws made it certain they would now all do twenty years to life without parole.

Joseph M. Due, October 8, 2016

Fire Starters

Some say "Cold feet, cold heart." The plea before the bench, from a couple that was caught starting fires in the community by investigators from the Fifty-Seventh CID was one of innocence. The evaluation and the collection of the data being done on Gen. Joseph Carne's shift he was tasked as an expert witness by the prosecution.

He waited in the hallway for his turn to be called. He was talking to the senior watch office when they signaled for him to enter and take the witness stand. After he had been duly sworn in, the questions began. The questions started with his background and his training. His qualifications as an investigator and data collector were keenly challenged by the defense.

The prosecution painted a nice picture of him, and he smiled at the jury. Then the defense attacked him about his motivations since his kidnapping. Then they talked about the people that did not like him and tried to kill him and kidnap his children trying to insinuate he had personal problems of his own.

The prosecution then asked him if any of those issues resolved from any questionable dealing he had done either personally or professionally. He replied nicely no. The defense could not produce a reason to the contrary so he was dismissed. His part of the case was now closed.

Joseph M. Due, October 6, 2016

The Dance

The country music was nice and the dance songs were great. The subject matter of the songs was just right for the conversation. Joseph and Sarita danced the evening away, knowing Grandpa and Grandma and their guards were keeping the children safe.

The dinner at Perkins was nice, and the customers were quiet and friendly.

The mood was light and started with plans they both dreamed about and then turned to guessing which College which child would like to go to.

The children had slept a while, so getting them to the car was fairly easy as the night progressed. Sunday was upon the Carne family, and they knew God would not mind too much if they slept in once to reenergize.

The children were agreeable to the sleeping in part but wanted to watch a movie. Sarita looked at Joseph, and he nodded. She said the children would have to reach a compromise before they reached home. The discussion was quiet but emotionally wrought. It came down to whose turn it was to choose so Amanda chose *The Quiet Man* and Dana and Mark agreed.

Mom got the popcorn out as the children settled in and dad made coffee for all and got out Styrofoam cups for the children. Amanda got the CD out and set up the DVD player and turned on the television. Joseph while the coffee was brewing got warming blankets out of the hall closet.

The children settled in to enjoy the movie together as Mom and Dad served coffee and popcorn. Everyone knew the movie, so they had light conversation throughout the movie. Each Carne cleaned up after themselves and made their way to their rooms.

The dawn drew nigh as Joseph was turning in with Sarita. She said she would like to show him one last dance.

<u>Joseph M. Due</u> 8 October 2016

Dreams

Today was fine, really. Mark did not like the remark from his sister, who was asking for help. He thought tomorrow would be good. He wanted to read *Architectural Digest* and relax. He thought about her request and decided it was something he would do. The need to see Mums about it dwindled as he thought it through.

Dana needed a helper shopping; he guessed after lunch would be just fine. He walked back to her bedroom and knocked on her door. She said, "Yes, come in." He opened the door and apologized and told her 1300 hours would be fine. He would bring his book and maybe get some reading done there and back.

The dinner was macaroni, cheese, hotdogs, and soda from the Dollar Store. After they cleaned up, she asked him if he would not mind going early. They told Sarita, their mom, where they were off to and borrowed Mom's car.

The shopping was fine to Mark, though people stared at what they must have thought was a really young couple. She bought sundries like plate sets and kitchen utensils. Mark asked her why. She said someday her husband would come along, and she wanted to be able to set up a nice house.

Mark asked her, "If you marry someone set up like Dad, won't you need less than normal?" She thought about it and said, "Dad is one in a thousand. If I were so blessed, that would be nice."

Joseph M. Due 17 October 2016

Desire

He who hesitates is lost. The sound of the day was a small thing in comparison to amore'. The desire led the hands and the mouth through the exploration of the physical. The passion and desire mounted, so Joseph and Sarita could only see through the emotions pouring forth from each other.

Tired when done but filled with the spectrum of each other's love, they found hesitations diminish with the knowledge of consideration and care. The ease at which they could now find that sea of love awed their children, and at times, they saw the beauty of that love and were embarrassed.

The evenings, the children were babysat—at times more for their protection than for the need inherent in watching children for other issues of safety. They rested in the late evening and then were picked up and laid down again around 0200 hours. This sometimes ran concurrently with Joseph's and Sarita's love affair in life.

The expression of their love was addressed by all three children when the parents were asked to consider the whereabouts of their children when passion over took them in the living room.

Joseph M. Due, October 8, 2016

Cribbage

Cribbage games are very fun to play. That is, even for those that make or use bombs. The good thing about cribbage is, you have to pay attention to the game while playing. That is true even more so when you are playing against criminals.

Gen. Donald Carne was watching investigations put up some video surveillance on a house that criminals were collecting at, and he was praying they did not notice. The Lieutenant in charge did not seem to worry too much, and he wondered if he should talk to the young women about taking the job more seriously.

Joseph walked in to the command post for an update and saw General Carne's thoughts cross his face. He told him that Lt. Nicole Anderson told him that they had been playing all day, and for all intents and purposes, the people in the house were effectively blind.

The video feed came up, and he could finally see what Joseph had told him was true. The audio came in next, and they listened in for a while before they decided to go to the dining room for coffee. They left the controller with instructions to call them if she saw or heard anything

Joseph M. Due, October 6, 2016

Lieutenant A. Carne

The mats looked a nice blue, she noticed lying there. It took her a moment to realize her friend was not kidding around about learning unarmed combat. Her jaw hurt as she thought about the skin on her face being a little scraped. *It must be from the mats,* she thought.

Lt. Amanda Carne decided to take a new look at her friend, Lt. Michelle Thomas. She put her knees up under her and got back up. Turning to face Michelle, she saw the care and worry in her eyes. The time was upon her, and she moved forward into attack and smiled back.

Michelle aimed some more blows at Amanda's face. She ducked under and stepped in close. She gave her two sharp blows to her stomach and dropped her to her knees. The instructor told them both, "Well done." They took their place around the mats, and the next two students stepped into the center of the mats.

Not to be outdone by women, the men put endeavor into sparring with their battle buddies. The exercise was a learning one of the intent to commit to judging one another. The instructor said, "This commitment reduces delay in reaction time to a physical attack."

It also shortened the chain of thoughts that were a prelude to battle, making the soldier that much quicker on the battlefield. It also helped focus in a centered manner the delivery of energy to the enemy, whether it be by fist, knife, or firearm.

They had an hour to shower and think about the lesson and take the lesson to heart.

Joseph M. Due, October 19, 2016

Passion

The companionable passions in their life filled their days as they tried to help and protect their friends and their children. The duties of Amanda were to help watch and care for Dana and Mark until she was old enough to go off to College.

She learned to be au naturel in the watching category because the children expressed themselves daily about her endeavors. The second job she had was to help out in the area of doing laundry and providing clean clothes when Dana or Mark ran out.

Dana contributed by helping cook, setting the table, and cleanup at times. She had a passion for knowing what would look good on a person and often gave help in that area as her expertise grew.

Mark helped out by keeping the rooms clean and mowing the lawn and helping out on projects when he could.

When the unit was teaching basic living skills, they were brought into work and put their hearts into learning what they could. They saw their parents' passion and committed to endeavor to build passion in their lives.

Joseph M. Due, October 8, 2016

Picnic

The baseball teams were assigned by age during the summer get-together. Mark and Dana were on separate age teams during the three-day picnic. They knew Mom would watch them play ball. They hoped their dad, Joseph, could watch them play ball as well. He was on call at work.

It was one of the major highlights of summer when all the families would bring potluck dinners and spend some downtime together. The Preacher would conduct a lesson in spiritual growth each day for twenty minutes as the families ate.

Joseph and Sarita were there for Mark's games and cheered him on as he ran the base paths. It was a good feeling all around for the family. Joseph prayed for Amanda, that she do well in California as he had done so many years before. The family took the time to say a prayer in agreement. Though Amanda was amongst friends in Los Angeles, it was still a difficult life to live there as she went to College.

Dana in the twelve-year-old bracket pitched for her team. She was used to overhand pitching from practicing in school. The game started with her team being in the outfield. She struck them out one by one, and her team congratulated her. She was doing well. The evening hours were upon the Carne family on Sunday when Mark and Dana said they were tired.

The ride home was a quiet one, both being satisfied at getting to play baseball and enjoy the food. They had seen their aunts and uncles as well as cousins and got up with the latest news. The nap_time they all mutually agreed upon, and then it was time for movie night, which featured the Fighting Sea Bees on prime time.

The midnight dance featured a serenade by Dad of Mom's favorite song, "The Blues," and sent the embarrassed children to bed, grateful not to be present for the rest.

Joseph M. Due, October 15, 2016

Meteors

The meteor was passing into the sun's gravitational field when Mark was called for dinner. He sighed and turned off the television. He already had seen the movie a couple times but wanted to see it again. He prayed about his attitude as he took his seat. He knew if it was meant to be, he would get to watch the movie again.

He sighed again when he spotted the baked salmon, vegetables, and small potatoes. He adjusted his attitude and asked Mom if she knew how to make hot dogs and macaroni and cheese. She passed him the plate Joseph filled for him and said, "Tomorrow you can do the cooking for dinner."

He brightened when he realized he wouldn't have to do the dishes either. He wondered what the Sunday matinee was and asked his dad. Joseph told him it was just a repeat movie about meteors—no big deal. Joseph promised him he would not miss much. Mark lowered his head and prayed again, and his parents looked at him.

He told them, "God is speaking to me about my attitude," and he told them he was working it out and he would be all right. The dinner progressed, and Mark said to his mom and dad, "Sorry." Joseph said for him and Sarita, "Apology accepted."

Joseph M. Due, October 7, 2016

Fiction

Lies and more lies. The gauche ideas of liars are unpleasant to deal with. Amanda looked at the clock and wondered why she woke up with that thought on her mind. Someone was lying to her, she was sure. At 0600 hours, she had to prepare. *The shower first*, she thought, and then a quick review and a liverwurst sandwich with cheddar cheese and some milk to get her on her way.

Her friends from home knocked on her door at 0730 hours every day. She wondered if her dad lived in this room while he was in Los Angeles. She thought it would be nice to think so. She heard a knock and knew she needed to be a little faster so her friends did not feel so embarrassed. The door should be open when she was ready, she thought.

Tim Smith was a year ahead of her in her studies, but he took watching out for her seriously. Her other friends were also as nice, and it was good to have someone to study with pretty much anytime.

Her bruises from practice fighting were fading. She felt that and looked at her legs. She was told she would have to come up with good reasons for future bruises and possibly worse injuries. She remembered her dad told her he got shot a couple times while training in.

Joseph M. Due, October 15, 2016

Mark

The mark of one's life starts with endeavor proven. Mark knew why he was named Mark. It was because Dad and Mom wanted him to find his destiny and make his mark. To be happy or not to be happy was part of the equation as well.

He perused the books in the library and decided to write a list of his own and ask himself why he liked this or that book. He had an hour before the next class. When he got done collecting the books he was familiar with, he pulled out a piece of paper and started writing a word about what he liked about each book.

Then he tried to relate each construct he came up with, with a career. He liked tools and production. He liked the outdoors and roads that interested him. He liked the idea of being mobile. He liked building things like porch decks and putting together schemas. He even liked eating different foods from across the states.

His next class was calculus. He enjoyed doing equations. He also wrote that down. After his class, he thought about the jobs in the area he knew about. He liked combat infantry but would like to build roads and buildings. He thought about the military again and decided if he could he would like to go to West Point.

His fears and trepidations known, he also knew his destiny awaited him.

Joseph M. Due, October 6, 2016

Eulogy

"It was a sad day in Mudville." The passing of Terrance Carne struck many as the passing of an age they did not want to finish passing through. The family knew they would see Mr. and Mrs. Terrance Carne again as the angels they were. The family gathered and remembered the past with great fondness and looked to the future with great hope.

Joseph and Donald did reception for the party after, and they insisted their kin remember the good times and the good times to come. By the time the preacher was done preaching on the resurrection, the tears were mostly put away, and as they ate their roast beef au jus and potatoes with tender carrots, the people were talking more and their spirits were lifted up.

The women tended to the cleaning of the plates, and the men did the dishes and put away the tables and chairs. Joseph and Donald bid the families good day as they left.

Joseph M. Due, October 3, 2016

Empathy

The morning passed in a haze as the day sped by. Looking for a hundred in a population of five million was like looking for a needle in a haystack. It was a big haystack. Joseph told everyone to take an hour's downtime to refresh.

He decided to get an afternoon lunch and think of the problem. Rumor had it there was conversation of hit squads to attack government officials, and governance believed the report. He ate salmon patties and small potatoes with beans cooked in onions.

The unit regrouped in the sixth floor briefing room, and he asked his team for ideas. The Investigators said that much emotional hate had to have an effect on the base populace. Joseph thought about it for a while and decided to regrid the city and have the soldiers walk each block individually. They would see if they could sense or see the difference.

Planning said they could have the units assigned and briefed within the hour. He ordered the units brought up in a half hour and briefed in the gym. He then asked his staff to go to work on the problem. Meanwhile, he ordered investigations to keep looking through normal approaches until they got a break one way or another.

The troops were dispatched by van at 1600 hours and dropped off at the beginning of each street starting on the south side; and then they would, when they were done, walk from east to west. The city grid was five miles by five miles, and they figured it would take a good portion of the night.

The evening fell away as the investigators checked off the list compiled against the houses that were already under investigation for other reasons. Twilight brought with it many things, including ten possible sites that investigations would take care of themselves.

By 0100 hours, they had a compiled list of thirty, and the teams were brought in to equip and arm to do night recon and set up audio and video monitoring. The dawn brought up the video feeds in planning, investigations, and the command post.

Needing further troops, three hundred more were tasked from Fort Houston to be online at 1600 hours. The process was to be administered by the alternate command post. The teams took a three-hour break for rest from 1000 hours to 1300 hours and were then assigned to help set up the briefing areas and the sleeping areas.

Investigations finished the monitoring setup on the first ten houses. They now had audio and video running, and the command post took the first ten houses. The conversations were slow in coming, but the command post personnel listened with patience. As they received confirmation, they marked the boards to indicate which houses had provided that confirmation.

The night approached, and the teams were awake. Equipment issue had already been made by the equipment section, with the inventory sheet on top of each bundle delivered to the gym. Investigations and planning did the first briefs, then they moved over to the operations table to receive their briefing and their maps.

The equipment pickup was last in line so the team could proceed to their assigned vans. The routes were varied, and they were tied into the command post on audio for further directions if the team leads did not know.

The night passed quietly as the teams infiltrated the neighborhoods. Being a Monday night, there were not many people about at 0300 hours. The command post wanted to know the hit team's target and the time of the intent, so the controllers were tuned in with the idea of garnering that data.

The hour whiled away as one house after another came up on video. The teams, one by one, returned to the command posts. Breakfast and sleep awaited after their sitreps were collected for planning. The day passed with no mention of their attack timing.

Robert, the police, and the FBI had representatives now in the command posts to advise within the areas of their expertise. In the daytime hours, the suspects came and went. Finally they had a break. They were set to attack at 1115 hours on Friday when most would be proceeding to one area or another for their lunch break.

The teams were told to be online for briefs at 0100s hour and attack at 0300 hours. The fifteen-man teams then proceeded to their targets, and the police lines lit up with "Shots fired" reports for the next half hour. Then the police arrested the survivors and secured each premise.

Joseph M. Due, October 3, 2016

Team Lead

The sound of the fire of pistols and rifles could be heard through the walls and windows and sometimes seen coming from the door. Listening to the open radio, Captain Carne worried a little and pushed the worry aside to be more on point. Focus and attention were her information-gathering tools.

The amount of fire from the rifles diminished, and she knew the sound of the pistols that were issued or bought by her team. It did not sound like she was losing any troops yet. Like popcorn, the last pistol shot was heard. She knew her teams were arresting those that lived and cleared the building.

The teams, by section, announced it was all clear, but they needed four more sets of handcuffs. She sent fire teams 3 and 4 in with the necessary handcuffs. As they returned to their posts, she walked toward the building to do her own recon for her sitrep. She knew command, investigations, the police, and FBI were standing by to look at the munitions, the administrative section, and the cooking section, where they made their drugs for sale.

The recon took another three minutes by her watch. She then called the command post as she put the data she saw in a logical order. The report took five minutes due to whoever in the command post wanted to lead in the investigations. She knew this was part of the drill.

The police got the response and she had the attack teams take care of the wounded. They could return to the rally point and rest. The vans were comfortable and had air conditioning. The police drove up and took over the rifle team's position first, so she had them assemble in the parking lot as the police were posted.

Joseph M. Due, October 4, 2016

Time

Time is of the essence. He wondered about time. He had two hundred families that would work in unison for God's Glory. He could do many things himself. But he did not understand fully that time was of the essence.

He thought he had an idea but was not sure. His wife was a great cook, and he thought she might understand that statement better than he did.

His phone beeped so he answered. "Joseph," he said. His elder daughter spoke. She wanted to know if she could be invited to Commander's call at Donald's house. She was very interested in that part of the family.

He laughed and told her there were consequences in time that she would be responsible for. She said, "If I accept the consequences unknown, can I be invited?" He said definitely. She was good at reading everything but her own future.

The day dawned, and man was beckoned to explore time.

Joseph called Donald and told him that he would like to add one more to his party at Commander's call on Friday. Donald said he could fit one more in at the get-together. He asked who it may be so he could have the staff prepare proper seating and plate. He said, "Lt. Amanda Carne."

Donald thought about saying something, but he just said OK. Joseph thanked him and Donald hung up. He thought about the occasion his mother was hosting. He realized she was a nice woman, and he knew she did well, but the breach of etiquette could not be allowed to just pass.

He thought of the General and knew whatever he did, he would not be insulted. He thought of her and wondered if he wanted to romance her. That seemed to be her goal. He realized he wanted someone in his life. Was it to be her? He decided to call his mother. She would have an idea.

She said, "At the end of the party, order her to the kitchen." He thought twenty hours of teaching and help would do. The unit would know that she earned everything she got. His mother said, "She will cook, serve plates, and clean up." He gave her directions for what he wanted Lieutenant Carne to know. His mother thought that would work.

Joseph talked to Sarita, and she thought about it. He said she had to learn of consequences. Sarita gave her word that she would not interfere in her lesson. She thought about it for a while and asked if she could give her daughter advice on romance. Joseph told her he did not think that would hurt.

Amanda was in her apartment, thinking of a relationship with Donald. Would it be a great love like her parents? She prayed that it would be so. Then she worked on her college studies in military law. She wanted to get a master's degree out of the way while she did not have so many responsibilities.

Sarita loved her daughter dearly. She prayed for her but knew it was her lesson she had to learn. She knew her favorite color was forest green. She thought about her achieving and prayed that she could see her wed.

Joseph hugged her and told her she knew he loved his daughter and was proud of her. So he invited her to dance to the blues with him. She found her feet and his arms, and she gave it to God. She found her passion rising in his arms, and she showed it to him with a kiss. His passion responded, and they found themselves on the couch, again experiencing their own love once more.

The night slowly faded away, and she untangled herself. Refreshed and whole, she prepared in her heart to show her daughter her love.

A good answer is what she needs, she thought. Then she moved to the kitchen to prepare breakfast. Joseph had his first briefing at 0800 hours.

The briefings were by the numbers. The teams were online, their training inordnung. Donald said that it was a fine brief as he waved to Joseph and left for home. Joseph went up to his new office and considered life's changes in relation to time.

He decided he would do a walk through starting with supply so he could see his wife at 1000 hours. He thought she would appreciate seeing him. He gathered up his radio and called the command post to tell them his planned itinerary and the fact that he was mobile. He talked to supply about the status of their requests and headed for the kitchens at 1005 hours.

She was in her office doing paperwork. He asked her what she was working on, and she said, "Organizing the unit picnic get-together."

She explained how far along she was and admitted finding the appropriate date for all concerned was difficult. Then they talked about Dana and Mark and where they were in their studies.

She worried about Dana staying at home and just working part-time. She did not seem to have found her destiny yet, though she was interested in cooking like her mom. Mark was studying engineering and would apply in two years for West Point. He wanted to attend when he was seventeen.

The day called, and Joseph said he would be down at 1200 hours for lunch. He walked through the kitchens and saw they were in fine shape as they always were, then he headed for the equipment section. They were working on the vehicles, ensuring the recent rash of bullet holes were fixed.

He looked around and asked if they had any pending issues/needs. Then he went to look at the equipment usage on the parking deck. He liked to get involved, but he had plans for the day. At 1200 hours, he tried to think of a way to help Dana find her destiny.

Talking to his wife, he confessed he did not know how to help her except to wait to find her interest in life and her passion. Sarita said that she told her that they loved her and that they prayed she find her destiny.

Investigations said they were keeping tabs on past problem children, but there was not a whisper yet of any new problems on the horizon.

Both sides of the command post were quiet. The low-level chitchat indicated that it was a fairly peaceful day. Joseph thought again of Dana and prayed she would find her destiny. After a half hour of reviewing the boards, Joseph went down to his wife's office.

She said she was going to ask if Dana would help out preparing for the meals. The women might come up with an idea, or in the flow of the conversation of the members of the unit, she might find something she was interested in. He thought about Dana's and Amanda's needs, and he thought that was a nice idea. So he said he would pray about it.

They had a training class coming up for the cooks, so she said she could not hang around long. So he went back up to his office and figured out at the moment he had nothing to do.

The evening hours saw them rushing to dress and feed their children. She told them they could eat hot dogs and potato chips. To keep busy, they could watch Netflix. They were both old enough to take care of themselves for a while.

Then they picked up Lieutenant Carne and drove over to the commander's house. Amanda was worried that her plan might not work out. Joseph asked her if she wanted to go through with her plan. She said, "No fear." Then she got out of the car and waited for them to present themselves. Donald was doing the greeting. He shook Joseph's hand and then Sarita's and nodded to Lieutenant Carne politely enough.

He told them the living room was open and they should enter. He then turned to the next set of guests. She saw Major Smith salute and shake hands. His wife he gave a brief hug. Amanda realized she had erred in military custom a great deal. She wanted to run away for the first time. Joseph saw her resolve to see it through, and he was proud of his daughter.

The evening passed pleasantly enough despite Amanda stressing. She knew everyone knew military social protocol but her. At the end of the night, as the guests were leaving, Donald said to Lieutenant Carne to report to his mother in the kitchen. It was coming, she knew, and she wanted to run again. Instead, she found herself saying, "Yes, sir." She arose and went to the kitchen.

Her Aunt was sitting at the table, and she beckoned for Lieutenant Carne to sit. She asked if she was in breach of social military protocol. She said, "Yes, ma'am." She said, "Then this is what you will do to repair that breach." She outlined her duties for the twenty hours she would work in social protocol to repair that breach. She then handed her a schedule for the next five commander's calls. She was then reminded that Donald did indeed like her.

She made her way back to her parents beet red, and the color stayed in her cheeks all the way until she was in the car. She asked her dad if these were the consequences, and he said, "Some choices have consequences all the rest of the person's days." Her mom said, "You did well, and you will see the process through because we know you will."

"Mom," Amanda said. Her mom said, "You like him well enough. You will learn to get along with him too." She then said, "We care for you very much, but do not 'oh, mom' me on this issue. This is your love. You will build it."

She decided in her house that she had to help cook, set out the plates, sit there in embarrassment, and then clean up for five dinners. She prayed it would be bearable as she marked the dates in her planner and on her kitchen calendar. She did not want it to become worse.

The night was still young, and Joseph banished the children to their rooms. She got out the music selection. Some of his and some of the music she especially liked. Tonight it would be Chateau le Blanc with almonds and such to nibble on.

Breakfast was oatmeal and bananas as well as orange juice and milk. The children were in fine form and had the day free. They were going over to friend's houses to hang out. They said they would be back by 1500 hours.

The evening meal was spare ribs and rice pilaf. He asked his wife what movie she wanted to watch, and she said, "Something new." So they reviewed new releases on Netflix and picked a comedy. Dana and Mark joined them and filled in their day's journey. They thought it humorous that their parents held hands and kissed.

Mark was going to a party on Monday for the boy's football team. His team had done fairly well, and the coach was going to supervise the function. Dana had decided to go shopping with her friends that day. On Monday night, they told their children they were going ice skating.

The night settled in, and the evening breeze turned into a gentle caress. Love doth speak.

Investigations periodically talked to CID, the police, FBI, and even the DEA. Extrapolations in collected data spit out a composite list of connections in criminal conspiracy. The proposed theory was that there were elements in ten states that were preparing through drug funding to do a series of assassinations and bombings throughout Central Texas and the surrounding states.

This went out from investigations at FBI headquarters in Washington, DC. All agencies with investigative and response capability were given the warning with a list of names at 0100 hours central standard time. The command post watch officer read the report as the message came in. She ordered the boards set up for an investigation in their area. Then she called investigations to recall their staff and pick up a copy of the message.

She then had copies made for staff dissemination. When she logged the message in, she had the controllers read it while she called the night Captain of the Watch, Major Andrew Sims, the Commander and the XO in for briefings.

The next step was to wake up team 11 and get them prepared for response. The staff was notified for unit issue and team briefs when there was more data. The command post then had many visitors as they waited for investigations to find a potential lead.

At 0200 hours, all the Watch Officers were in the building or in the command post, holding a vigil and waiting for news. By 0300 hours, the houses in criminal activities were reviewed, and investigations was busy checking data. A courier was expected inbound with more information between 0600 and 0700 hours.

The extra personnel hung around the offices or in the dining room. Coffee and doughnuts were provided. The expected wait time to determine shift work was 0830 hours.

The briefing started at 0730 hours for the staff. There were a few late arrivals. The scope of the activity was akin to their last bomb scare, but the investigation centered around Oklahoma. The primary suspect list numbered five hundred, mainly with the intent to distribute the weapons and bombs.

Fifty suspects were native Texans, with thirty-two to thirty-seven living in the greater Houston area. Their focus considering the City boundary would be thirty-seven suspects with another hundred that might help them. The investigation started two months prior with the belief that the production center made enough bombs for distribution to be used by planning IDS houses in each major city.

The facility was shut down at 1400 hours CST as well as the primary planning and fund sites. The data, when releasable, would be delivered by courier.

The purpose was to spawn terroristic processes that brought fear and incited other violent activities. The intent to focus was to bomb government buildings, especially courthouses, and assassinate social public leaders involved in that part of the governance of the people.

Donald called Robert and said he would send him team 11. He said that that would be a good idea. Then he told him he would send two-man security teams to each retired and sitting Judge in the Houston Area. When the threat is more defined, that would upgrade and turn into 24-7 security.

He then contacted The Post General, who assigned Lt. Col Dirk to mobilize three hundred troops as soon as possible. Lt. Col Dirk said, "Eight hours for full mobilization," and he said their planning team was already briefed by courier, and because of the anticipated need, the troops had begun recall at 0800 hours.

Joseph was ordered to set up the alternate command post with teams 1, 2, and 3. The training area and the gym were ordered set up, and teams 4, 5, and 6 told they were now on standby at their homes.

He told Sarita he would be at the alternate command post for his shift. She said that when day shift finished feeding the overload, she would come over. She made a note to call Mark and tell him where they would be if he needed them.

Staff took two hours for complete setup, and the teams started their briefings at 1100 hours; then they would be ready for operations by 1300 hours. Half-hour status updates were relayed to primary command post.

Site setup for the teams was set up between 1300 and 1500 hours. Then the teams were on full-time standby for the duration.

The progress reports from investigations kept coming in piece by piece. A picture of the problem was graphed and times set for team recon and then interdiction. The scale was still within recon constraints, and with augmentation by the Army, it might stay that way.

The IDS houses were tagged at 1500 hours based on the number of criminals tagged at the local. Team 12 was to do video setup and recon at 0100 hours, when it would be darkest. They still needed validation, and audio and video would provide that.

Investigations would drive by the planning house and tag more license numbers about every forty-five minutes to an hour. The police would also drive by and hopefully capture different license plate numbers so that when interdiction teams were sent out, the police could catch those on the day shift.

The armed groups of bombers was a little harder to find. So the soldiers prayed they could catch them before they could use their bombs.

The facilities for the teams was set up and the soldiers briefed. Transit was now busy ferrying troops and would be for hours. After dispatch, the remaining troops had televisions set up to give them something to do. Most decided they needed rest.

Sarita came over to visit Joseph at 1800 hours. She brought the latest news and Wendy's bacon double cheeseburgers, fries, and Frostys. He kissed her on the forehead and thanked her for her considerations. He then talked of the system setup and its status.

She then called Mark and Dana, who were out and about. She told them she and Joseph would be at home at 1930 hours and she expected to see them at 2200 hours. They knew she cared. He then walked the area with her as they talked.

The Captain of the Watch showed a half hour early and, after being briefed, said he would call if there was a need. They decided at 1900 hours to call it a day. She rested on his shoulder as he drove, humming her love song. And his love for her stirred, and he hugged with care.

Mark and Dana were home shortly after, and they had coffee in the living room together as Mark and Dana recounted their experiences for the day. She kissed them both on the cheek and bid them a good night.

They set the alarm clock for 0500 hours and decided they would pray for their children. Dana surprised them both by making waffles, eggs, and sausage for breakfast, so they had a little extra time. She told them she wanted to go to college in the fall at the local State College for Business Administration.

They asked her where she would like to work, and she said, "The Target in town." She would like to be a store supervisor or manager. They congratulated her and promised to help out with tuition.

Joseph M. Due, September 24, 2016

The Night

The haze of the streetlight as it was giving away marked the surrounding houses at night as surely as if the denizens posted signs. The utility company was hesitant to change the light in the area because of the unsavory criminal element that wandered that portion of the street during the daytime.

The lights turned down as the night progressed, and the shadows started to move up the street. Looking at the night is difficult for some for a variety of reasons stemming from Fears and Trepidations. The outline could be seen, with focus and clarity, of men and women about in the night.

The target was clear to all who could see. The brave stood by their windows. The wise looked for protection in case a bullet came their way. The dance of the night continued as the way was cleared in the approach.

The overwatch teams called in when they got in position, and they could see the windows and doors. The next step was for the teams that were assaulting the house to determine a safe approach for the rest and then take up their positions on the front and back doors.

The radio spoke and indicated the perpetrators were up and restless. The Lieutenant surveyed the situation and told the attack teams to hold with grenades. She then told the fire teams to fire on her command.

"Fire," the Lieutenant said, and four went down right away. Then they got three more that were trying to rush the windows. "Now," said the Lieutenant, and they threw in the grenades and backed up. Three seconds later, there were more down, and the attack commenced in earnest.

The wounding of one and the taking of the munitions house for the area seemed like an equitable trade. The fire teams off the alley sent their handcuffs in when the all clear was sounded. Lt. Amanda Carne surveyed the scene and notified the command post that the ATF could now be sent in.

Joseph M. Due, October 8, 2016

Amanda

The Ladies Aid Society had taught her a lot in twenty hours that she had not picked up in years of association. She now realized how important they were to a family.

Her lesson learned about military protocols in dinings-in, she decided she would not make that mistake again. The aspiration and goal of hers to meet Donald socially was his determinant choice. She just had to make her desire known. That could have been done through Mums or the Ladies Aid Society.

So now she waited for the other shoe to fall, so to say. Would he call? And if so, would she be yelled at again? A week had passed, and she waited for some sort of answer. Fears and trepidations abounded in her thoughts. Her mother had counseled her to wait, and wait she must.

Her team was up Monday at 0800 hours. The review went well, and then they tended to equipment and supply draws. The briefs were going along well when she was handed a note that UPS left her a package at the main desk on the first floor. She told her Sergeant to see to the troops and dismissed herself to see what disaster awaited her. She took the stairs to think about what the package could be and who would be sending her something from UPS to the unit.

The atrium was nice, she noted as she passed through it—another function the ladies aid society took care of well. The desk had three up, she noted. It was probably her package. She approached and greeted the soldiers and then asked to see her package.

They told her she would have to open the package here and have all the contents inspected. She colored a little and nodded. They handed her the package, and she noted its size and colored again. She thought it was flowers, and she opened the packaging. There were twelve pink roses and two cards. The guards reviewed the interior of the box and asked to see the cards.

The first card was a poem on her virtues signed by Donald. The second was a request for a date Sunday night when she was off alert. The guards handed the notes to her, and she blushed as she read them herself. She thanked the guards and gathered up the package to return to her unit. She had to show her team what she received—it was only proper. She thought of military protocols and being above board, and she blushed again.

The unit was already in the day room watching television when she returned. She showed her Sergeant the flowers and the cards as her unit looked on. She realized this was a military romance.

Joseph M. Due, October 3, 2016

Heart

Drinking coffee, he awaited his love to appear. He now knew her embrace would bring not but joy to his heart. He thought about what must be as she walks up the sidewalk to her grandparents' old house. She knocked and anticipation filled his heart.

The maid opened the door and said she could just walk in if she liked. She wondered if she had to report as ordered. It's as if he read her mind. He said, "When in uniform, you must report. When in civilian clothes, you are my date."

She checked the dress she was in to be sure and then entered the living room. He beckoned for her to take a seat. She sat on the edge of the couch properly, and he asked her to sit back and relax. The maid brought her a tall glass of orange juice and a cheese sandwich. This was one of her favorite breakfasts. He waited for her to take a bite and said, "Let us talk about the past."

They discussed in repartee the past, present, and future of the Carne family in the modern military as she struggled to adjust to a different type of social arrangement. She thought about her idea of romance and decided she did not know a thing about romance.

He said, "The protocols must be observed, but in private, before we marry, we can hold hands and kiss." He held out a hand and she took it. Then he pulled her to him, and he gave her her first kiss. She thought the holding hands and kissing was kind of nice.

He then asked her to sit with him, and the maid brought out a small table and turned the CD player on, and she heard rhythm and blues as she leaned against him. They began discussing their wedding.

Joseph M. Due, October 3, 2016

Attack

The time rolled around to 0800 hours. The thoughts of a nighttime shift were lost in the growing aches and pains felt in the daylight hour as she got into her car. She rested for a while, thinking of all the problems this world posed as it went through growing pains. A warrior like the rest of the warriors before her, she sought peace.

She said a prayer to God and looked around to back out. There was a Sergeant coming up on the backside of her car. She rolled down her window, and he said, "Captain Carne, they need you inside." General Carne wanted her to take lead on the weapons dealers and their storehouse. He was running out of troops and needed to use her teams.

She asked for an hour, and he said, "Time is important, but take two hours and have your teams ready for briefings." The two hours were up quickly, and her Sergeant woke her and said her teams would be up in five minutes. She told him to meet her in the gym.

The initial brief was nothing new, but she knew the criminals would be heavily armed. She looked at the building layout and thought she could still do the job. She nodded as the Sergeants came up and told them what she wanted each squad to do. They blinked and looked at the site pictures again, figuring out their timing.

They took their rest in the vans after they loaded. She told the drivers they would be awake when needed.

The departure points were still seeing traffic through the area. She said, "Quickly, move to the doors and take the criminals as planned."

They disembarked and strode for the doors as planned. Civilians quickly moved out of the way. As the teams hit the walls, they knew the criminals had seen them approach.

The two grenades per door did their work when they were tossed inside, killing or wounding many of the production site's security. They then attacked in echelons two by two. The shooting lasted all of five minutes, then the last ones were down.

Half an hour later, the police were allowed to enter the building.

Joseph M. Due, October 3, 2016

Doctrine

Rest to recompute and recompile is necessary for the daily operation of the body, spirit, and soul. The soldiers had a right to that rest more so than others because they went in harm's way for others and needed to be at their best.

This was some of the doctrine of the Army to the commanders that would lead effectively. Reading ideas like this one, Joseph understood from his own experience how precious rest was and why there was ten to twenty minutes between each unit activity.

He periodically worked rest into his day and the day of his troops. He asked the Sergeants what they thought of when they knew Army doctrine wholeheartedly supported their honest endeavors. The conversation turned to situations whereby the men might need more rest.

Teams 1 and 2 were searching each other out. He was waiting to see how the meeting engagement worked. The cautious walked slowly and then low-crawled. He was standing on the sideline where, all things considered, both teams should meet. The bus ride back should give them time to rest in between the nightly sitreps and then unit and individual critiques.

The night sang to the hunter as a lover to her mate.

Joseph M. Due, October 21, 2016

The Sea

The motion of the boat had some of the children like Mark and Dana a little worried. The spray building up in the base of the boat, they tried not to look at. Though to tell the truth, the hardiest child in this regard was Amanda.

She took one look at Joseph and William, and she determined to realize the boat, with a little water in it, would not actually sink. Mark and Dana looked to their life vests now and then and wondered if they could actually swim to the dock if the boat did sink.

William's children were of pretty much the same stripe. The women decided to fish a little off the dock and watch the younger ones as a burden to get out of a burden. Sarita and Theresa said they would leave Mark and Dana in charge of the younger ones tomorrow.

The fishing was fine, and the weather quite warm. The day passed by, and at 1600 hours, they told Mark and Dana they could row back in if they wanted to. Dana said she would rather use the motor, and Joseph moved up to let her work her way back to the motor.

It only took a couple pulls and a few lefts and rights before she had the boat pointed in the right direction. Mark eyed the oars and told her the oars looked just fine. William laughed and said, "You know how to row in calmer water."

With heavier waves, you would learn if you needed to. Joseph poured out coffee for each from the motor to the front. Might as well drink it up versus dumping it out.

Joseph M. Due, October 22, 2016

Life

The odor from the house was heavy and unpleasant. The couple seemed not quite right. Looking at her watch, she was expected at work at 1600 hours. She told them she might be late for work. As she rushed to the door, she got the impression they were trying to keep her there.

She realized she was getting panicky and was almost running when she got in her car. She pulled out, and there was a yellow minivan that was almost too close behind her. She got the license as she sped away. She headed for home as quick as she could, repeating the license plate so she would not forget it.

She told her mom on the phone what happened, and she was told to stay in the living room with the guard and to tell him the story just in case something happened. Her phone rang ten minutes later. It was her dad. He asked her for the whole story of how she got invited over to that house.

Dana realized she had been flattered into going, and the vanity of it brought her to tears. She told Joseph that it was two schoolchildren that had set her up. Their names were Sam and Bill. They were both eighteen like she was, and they went to the same high school. He told her he loved her and more guards were on the way.

The anxiety of the moment abated with the arrival of the guards but did not go away. There were a lot of loose ends to tie up. Though they did have a good idea of the operational arms of the kidnappers, they also had to find the body.

Dana valued the life she had and prayed she could keep it. The police identified the van and two of its occupants by 1700 hours. Dana was sitting with Sarita at the point that it was made known. The police were following the van around to see which places it stopped at. When it stopped for the night, they would send in a recon team to check it out.

The FBI was notified by courier, and an appointment was set up with Dana for 1830 hours. Meanwhile, CID did recon on the houses the van stopped at and put in audio and video monitoring. They were hoping they had caught some of the planners napping.

The interview was a rehash of all her bad decisions to date, and it almost brought her to tears. Her mom consoled her and told her that her dad would be home as soon as he could and he was doing his best to help catch the kidnappers before they could try again.

She fell asleep as the world turned; her body knew it, so she dreamed about what she should have been doing and woke at 0300 hours in tears. Her dad was coming through the door, and she knew it was him. So she rushed to greet him and get a much-needed hug.

The waiting continued for results from CID or the police. She was warned by the FBI it might take a while and even with some of the kidnappers jailed, they still might try again.

The days passed and two houses admitted to conspiracy to commit and the FBI took the visiting license plates down and rushed to identify would-be participants.

As the web of conspiracy unfolded, the teams prepared to interdict. The FBI knew CID preferred 0300 hours to attack the primary facilities, so the FBI chose Friday morning as the ideal time.

Joseph M. Due, October 3, 2016

Amore'

Sarita thought about the children she was raising. Some of the children, she raised at home, and some she raised at work. Family matters, she knew, and she prayed she was doing her best so they would not be taken away from her too soon.

The biscuits were almost done, so she called Mark and Joseph to the table. They talked about men things most of the time. However, they saved time to listen and ask questions and care about the women around them.

She admired her men and loved her man. He was intuitive and loved her very much. She thought of his expressionisms and blushed. Mark noticed and asked his mom if anything was wrong. Joseph listened with his heart to her answer.

She said she loved her men and remembered the good times and the embarrassing times that love grew. She asked Mark about his application to OCS and College funding. He erudiated for a while and then said he had a date.

He nodded to his dad and kissed his mum on the cheek as he moved on down the road in search of his destiny. Sarita had a tear in her eye, knowing he would be gone soon.

Joseph moved his chair closer and held her hand as she moved through the emotional spectrum of growth and separation. He asked her if she was all right. She said yes and asked whether he would like to know tonight the hundred kisses of love.

Joseph M. Due, October 22, 2016

West Point

The day was upon them, and the grass still contained much dew, especially under the trees. The training site was new to Mark, and he wondered if he could ask the troops to low crawl through the wet grass. It was five hundred feet to the next tree line, and the rifleman with the scope did not see the enemy yet.

Lieutenant Carne gave the orders, and his teammates looked at him; their looks told him they did not appreciate the order. But follow orders they would. The morning passed slowly as the team navigated the field. The instructors were watching on both sides.

The team made it to twenty feet of the tree line. The Lieutenant looked up and over the grass, saw the enemy thirty feet into the tree line, and they could see the grass. He talked conversationally to his troops to scan for targets while they were in the grass and open fire as they could.

The first rifleman on his right opened fire on the enemy position and sounded the person's MILES gear. The sporadic fire lit up one troop after another as both sides dug in and looked for targets. Twenty minutes later, the instructors called the exercise. The review gave both team leads high marks for good decisions made though they did not have a clear winner.

While there is breath left, there is opportunity for life.

Joseph M. Due, October 4, 2016

Fictional

He was kind of carried away at times with his speech and rhetoric. The Smith Carne families wondered about him once in a while. They prayed about Davis Smith because he bordered on the fictional in his verbal skill set. In Mark's age group, he came and went as his hits and runs earned displeasure amongst the group.

The days and years passed by as Davis grew up. He spent more time working on his verbal skills at the socials the family held throughout the year. He finally toned down his rhetoric, and the children appreciated his storytelling ability.

Mark and Davis even became good friends through the years, and he was his battle buddy through their attendance at West Point. When it was Davis's turn to select his assignment, he changed his mind about job and local when he saw Catherine Thomas at a Christmas party all grown up.

Putting down the Fifty-Seventh CID as his request was a little eutre', but he persevered, and West Point looked up a few contacts and found out there was a Fifty-Seventh CID. They disapproved a little but graduated Davis Thomas and sent him home to learn about his dream.

Joseph M. Due, October 13, 2016

Maple Lake

The end, the middle, the beginning. A Story is told. Amanda asked Sarita to tell her a story. The idea was time and "Did I want to spend the time?" Another idea was "Did I like fishing and for how long would I fish when I got there?" The next question was support of her husband and friends since they wanted her to come along.

It began on a Friday night, when Terrance told Joseph the bass were jumping on Maple Lake. He relayed the information to William at work. "Then he called me while William called Theresa. The ideas floated through my head while I thought of the need for babysitters. Sarita mentioned the need to Joseph and he told me that Jean would babysit both families."

She thought about the gear she rarely used and knew they wanted her to go fishing with them. She said yes with warming blankets and hot coffee. Then she went to the garage and got all the thermoses and proceeded to fill all of them up with two servings of cream and one sugar per cup of coffee. She then put the thermoses by the door and went to get extra warming blankets.

The drive over to Terrance and Jean's house was quite exciting for the children. They would meet their friends and have an all-nighter. There at the front door, they met their friends and started chatting so loudly that Grandpa asked everyone to be quiet until they got inside.

Meanwhile, Sarita and Theresa were repacking William's fishing gear while the men settled the children in. Then they piled in the car and drove to Maple Lake, sweaters and all.

The boat was fully ready; Joseph brought the fuel, and they loaded up. They moved out to the drop on the left side of the dock and cast anchor. Within minutes, they had their first bite. The night did not seem so bad to Sarita, and the conversation flowed freely since they were catching the bass at the right time.

Joseph sipped his creamed coffee and looked at Sarita. She said she did not know which thermos she was going to get. Joseph said that was OK and drank his coffee. William asked Theresa if she knew which thermos was which. She said no. So he sighed and picked one.

Joseph and William counted the fish to ensure they did not take over their limit for the family. When they reached their limit, they did catch-and-release until dawn. The boaters were unloading as they cleaned up the fish. Then they returned home.

Joseph M. Due, October 10, 2016

Christopher

Christopher Nidden played with Legos nonstop until his dad gave him an aircraft set he could put together under close supervision. His dad worked day shift for Smith Carne Industry and thought one day his son would follow him at work.

When he was fourteen, he met Uncle William when he was at work with his dad. William asked him and his dad how much he knew so Christopher demonstrated how he could take tools and equipment apart and put them back together. Uncle William then asked him if he would join the Army when he was older to round out his education.

He thought that would be a nice way to pay for his education. Uncle William said, "If you want to, when you're seventeen, come see me."

Joseph M. Due, October 3, 2016

Virtuous

Tomorrow is a nice word that can connote a promise. Used properly, it helps build rapport, even virtue. Tomorrow, Jean would say to one of her six children in the Carne family, meant she would do her best to see that what the children needed, the children had.

Later, when Joseph guided the families, he remembered his Mums and saw that by and large the love for the children was there and it was growing. The promise-keepers are gems in any family.

Holding onto promises, he hoped he was counted as virtuous as Mums. He knew his dad also had virtues of love and counted not the cost.

He turned to another virtuous woman and said to Sarita, "Mums, could you please get me the Eighty-Second CID training roster?" She froze and stumbled as she turned to get it off her back shelf. She realized with great joy she had wanted to hear that for a long time.

The schedule of the unit was married up to that of the Eighty-Second CID training calendar, and she helped him get ready to leave for the night. She wondered how she could love him so much for being who he was.

Joseph M. Due, October 6, 2016

Lieutenant Stevens

The sensory platform of the eyes is used for the person to see and define the environment around him/her so they can navigate safely the vista of the landscape of their life. The more experiences one has before the day of battle, the better one does in the day of battle and in the battle itself.

Lieutenant Stevens thought of the process of the eye and realized he did not have as much experience as some had. He thought about the Fifty-Seventh CID while he was cleaning his weapon. He realized if he wanted to live and be promoted, he had to pay attention, volunteer, and keep an open mind.

He brushed lightly the charging handle to keep it clean and free from being scratched. He then prayed about the three needs he had to do well in his endeavors in life. He asked God to help him and teach him so he could be acquitted well when it was all said and done.

He looked at the cleaning rod and put a piece of cloth with light oil on it to help clean the barrel. He turned to his battle buddy and asked him to describe what he knew about the steps that needed to be shown for the next exercise. He decided to be proactive and ask the questions he needed to know and remember.

Cleaning his rifle bolt, Lieutenant Daniels said the difficult thing about the exercises for him was the lay of the land in map interpretation. "The map overview in relation to visual topography, I need to practice." Lieutenant Stevens said, "The road contours, when you can see them, should tell you exactly where you are when you practice depth perception in gauging how far you are from the road."

Lieutenant Stevens took apart his bolt mechanism and started to brush down the exterior of the bolt. Looking at the firing pin so he did not lose it, he said, "The interpretation of distance in sight I have a problem with when it is time to low crawl to the attack point so I can avoid detection by hostile elements."

The day dawned, and the morning exercise beckoned. Lieutenant Stevens remembered his problem and the book solution. Because he did not hide his need inside, panic under stress let him calculate the solution admirably, and Lieutenant Daniels kept pace to the target he was assigned by remembering the interrelational process between the lay of the land and the road contours.

Joseph M. Due, October 19, 2016

Mastery

In the here and now, one finds a focus on the process of now. The definition of the motif is then derived properly, and one can feel the essence of what is extant. Another way to see the condition in which one lives is to be mortally afraid for your life.

Those that honorably die for others have perceptions sharpened, and they can see, for example, and shoot at accurately the center mass of a target. Those that live then naturally become better at interdiction, some even becoming masters of their craft.

Joseph saw in review his dad's mastery of the arts of war and later in his nephew the same thing. Even Amanda had achieved the mastery under Donald Carne's teachings. The generations were getting even better.

Joseph M. Due, October 6, 2016

Technical Advisory Service (TAS)

The evening breeze filtered through the living room as Robert sipped coffee. He had his mission before him, and he knew that Joseph would take it. It just might take a little time convincing him he was the man for the job, and Sarita was needed as well to address women's issues in regards to their role in MWR.

He could order General Joseph Carne, but convincing him would work out better for the mission he had in mind. Now that Houston could help out its neighboring cities, Houston would very well help out. The time and energy in stabilizing Houston as a city on the go was well worth the effort.

The mission of the Third Army Training Division as imagined would provide sooner or later every unit with two weeks of intense training like the train-ups of the Fifty-Seventh CID. The money for the Training Division was now available, and the personnel could be drawn and promoted from units like the Fifty-Seventh CID.

The rank structure would make Joseph of equal rank with Robert, and he knew Joseph would do the Army proud in his new rank.

Sarita was not pleased by the idea of living out of hotels or borrowed houses for eleven months out of the year. She knew Joseph did not like that much travel nor would Donald like losing some of his most experienced troops.

She also knew the Army did what it pleased at times, and assigning Joseph would be, even against his will, what they might do.

She thought it better to negotiate and work out what could be done. He looked at her, and she nodded. She would help him out.

He said to Robert, "What is the overall budget?" Robert pulled the handbook of the idea out of his briefcase and handed it to Joseph and said, "The biggest cost is travel and employee funds. The authorizations for staff are one per unit with administrative help to do the paperwork."

"The reporting process is outlined in section II. You will receive a second star, and you are authorized to hire your wife as an aide." He thought of her changing posts and smiled at her. This might not be too bad after all, he thought.

"What about internal training and further recruiting?" he asked. Robert said, "You will be able to recruit from any unit out there as long as they're qualified trainers or soon to be. Internal training is two weeks a year, and you can all attend Advanced Infantry Training—AIT." "Can the AIT school add more urban assault courses?" "Right now, I believe they only have one."

Robert thought about AIT and realized Joseph was right. He told Joseph he would work on the issue of more Urban Assault courses. Joseph said they needed enough room on each course to simulate the departure and approach to a site to be assaulted in a modern city.

"What about leave when people need it?" he asked. "You can supplement your schedule when troops are on leave. Try to schedule their leave time for Christmas or something," Robert said.

The day draweth nigh when all give an accounting!

"When do we start?" Sarita asked. Robert said, "January 1. This will give you time to organize and prepare. Christmas is only three months away, and the Third Army Training Division expects you on the first of January."

Joseph looked at the borrowed buildings and asked about remodeling funds and new buildings to be put up. Robert said, "Those numbers are under the construction section, but I am sure you will stay within your budget."

Joseph M. Due, October 23, 2016

Visitors

The strumming of a guitar could be heard in the bedroom. He wondered if it was from the CD player, but he did not recognize the tune. Putting on his robe, he grabbed his handgun and went and checked. The sound meandered down the hallway, and he followed it to the living room.

Mark was there, serenading his wife. He checked the safety and put the handgun in his pocket on the robe. He greeted Mark and then went into the kitchen for coffee. He poured the rest out and figured his wife and guests might want some more, so he put on a new pot.

He heard her in the hallway greeting her son and daughter-in-law, so he waited for the coffee to be done and poured a second cup for her. He listened to the update of their lives as he brought the coffee in. She kissed him as he put the coffee on the little stand for her.

He then sat in the easy chair to hear the repartee. The drive had been long, and they were not sure they had the time to stop on the way to her mother's house. Since they had another ten hours they had not planned for, they thought an hour's roundabout with a little rest would work out just fine.

Senior Captain Carne said the presents were under the tree, and they did not want to wake anyone. Dana came out and greeted Mark and his wife. She looked a little tired but went in the kitchen for some coffee. When Dana returned, she took Sarita's place, and Sarita sat on Joseph's lap.

The morning light broke through the curtains when Joseph said, "The third bedroom is open and the bed made. Why don't you two get some sleep before you continue your journey?" Mark and his wife agreed it would be a great idea.

Joseph M. Due, October 7, 2016

Grounds

The fairgrounds were filled to packing with people. The city had renegotiated the contract and built the fairgrounds on two plats of acreage behind Fort Houston to the southwest. Some of the acreage were baseball and softball fields to the south of the fairgrounds, and the fences were taken down for the event.

The roads were congested, but they had the sheriffs out all day to regulate traffic. The rides were partially funded by the city and county of Houston. The music was playing a little too loud for some. The picnic areas were larger, and there was no music at the table areas; so it was like an oasis that was relatively sound-free.

Security was following two couples that seemed suspicious, and others were on the way. They were not buying the food and/or the rides. The couples did note where security seemed to be stationed as they walked around.

The sheriff's department did a walkthrough, and the deputies tweaked on the two couples as well. The hour passed by as they meandered through the fairgrounds. One of the men grabbed a ten-year-old boy, and the other pulled a cloth and put it over his face. As security stepped up, the two women walked into the foremost security guards to provide a distraction.

They were quickly arrested, and the other two-man team went after the men kidnappers. The gates were a hundred yards away, and they knew the kidnappers would make for them. The security pulled close as the two perpetrators walked off the fairgrounds with the unconscious boy.

The sheriffs let them get to their car and then closed in around them and arrested a total of four would-be kidnappers at the car, and the two in the fairgrounds were taken in custody. The sheriff's department called up ten more deputies and sent them to help at the gates just in case there were more kidnapping attempts.

The Fifty-Seventh CID asked for and got the background investigative report to start their own investigation and now made the two-hour volunteer positions require four-hour stints of duty.

Joseph M. Due, October 16, 2016

Thirtieth

The dream continued through the years. Sarita saw in her joy. She had wondered if it would. Three children and many grandchildren—some yet to come—and a man she loved dearly as well as a job that challenged her here and there. She looked in the mirror and realized again she was aging, but not too bad, she thought.

Joseph waited patiently for her to speak out of her reverie. It was Sarita's day, and she could take a little more time before the natives grew restless. Amanda, Dana, and Mark were there to help escort her to her thirtieth Wedding Anniversary party at the Fifty-Seventh CID dining hall. A lot of people wanted to attend, and even though there was a lot of room, the celebration was to be posted on the hour for three hours.

She sniffed happily and said, "I am almost ready." He smiled and told her patiently that the children and he were waiting.

She knew she had to start, so she gently put on her makeup. When she was through, she kissed Joseph and went to greet her children. She asked Amanda and Dana how she looked. They both thought she looked nice, so the party proceeded to the car and thence to the dining room.

The dining room area was decorated in white and blue with lilies at every table. The lilies were Amanda's choice; she thought her mom might like them.

The greetings and testimonials were to be kept short since the major ones would be repeated on the hour.

The morning passed by with much ado and many well wishes from people, some of which knew her all her life. Joseph and Sarita left the gifts to be delivered and thanked everybody for their love. Then they returned to the house for a well-needed rest.

The afternoon saw a gentle dreamy day, and the coffee and the kiss were something to celebrate as well. Joseph slipped off the shoulder strap on her dress.

<u>Joseph M. Due,</u> October 11, 2016

Johnny

Amanda bustled about in the kitchen. She was comfortable with the pots and pans because she had cooked there before. The steak was sizzling a little, so she turned it down. The eggs were on the sideboard, waiting to be cooked. She smiled happily because she knew she was loved and she had found her home.

The quiet romance she did not expect, but she liked it well enough. At 0600 hours, she heard him moving about. The steak would be ready about just in time. She dreamt of children, six in all. She wondered how many children he would like. Arms enfold her as she came out of her reverie, and he said to her as he kissed her, "Five or six children will do."

Startled, she told him to have a seat and she would get the eggs over easy, steak, hash browns, and orange juice out. Sitting with Donald, she realized comfort and happiness with him. This was her man. He drank some orange juice and told her he appreciated their having breakfast together.

The 0800 hours staff briefs were important to him. It let him know the readiness state of each section. He told her that he must go to them every day to keep on top of things, but they could go shopping later at 1000 hours if she wanted to.

She kissed him goodbye and turned to the shower. She was dreaming as she went. Her silent reverie was broken by the moving of her stomach area, and she touched her stomach and wondered if that was number 1.

If it was, she knew she was moving out of the Captain's position to Operations in a month anyway. She turned on the shower and warmed the water as she returned from the land of dreams to the land of the living. Her teams knew she was on call and would be in at 1600 hours for the evening training day.

The Target store Dana worked at was up the road about ten minutes. She figured she could wave to her sister—maybe even talk a minute or two if she was free to do so. She was looking for looser-fitting clothes.

Joseph M. Due, October 3, 2016

Nemesis

The alarms sounded as the teams put on their gear and prepared their weapons for action. They had no brief scheduled, so they believed it was inbound. Team 1 cleared the kitchen and set up behind the serving lines. Teams 2 and 3 held in the day rooms until they were called.

Security had orders to shut down the elevators but had not done so yet. They waited for a further announcement for five minutes, then a team lead called the command post for orders. Communications on the radios was out, and some of the video was out. They were waiting for security to respond to landline, so they were to hold the elevators and the steps where they were.

Security called back ten minutes later saying about twenty armed criminals cut the ground wire communications that were external to the building and tried to raid the garage and atrium. The firefight did not last that long, but they were unsure if they accessed the building from the parking deck.

The building took two hours to clear and then three days to sweep for electronic eavesdropping. The failure to penetrate left the investigators without a clue as to goal or motive.

The days that passed gave them time to identify the criminal bodies and begin a large investigation to see if there were other conspirators and what connections in the criminal arenas of thought they had.

The lists were compiled and the locals reviewed for those that had a common thread of data. The next step was to review the houses and the areas under investigation. As the trail became clearer, the houses were put under electronic surveillance.

Joseph M. Due, October 10, 2016

Captain Stevens

Few people go the distance the first time in life. Going the distance takes a commitment. The delusional say is obsessional. The endeavor for life is a total commitment to endeavor to persevere. Captain Stevens learned this truth in his life a little bit at a time when he looked at the obstacles to success like AIT, College, Command School, and the OJT requirements for each job he sought.

The days passed in a blur at times to Captain Stevens working through one problem's solution after another. Making friends at the Fifty-Seventh CID enabled him to step back from what he was doing once in a while and relax. He thought about knowing that he should enable his friends, and he then learned that one of the greatest gifts he could give his friends was the training and learning he learned how to do.

The next lesson was in learning how to take care of a larger number of soldiers to help them all learn to overcome the obstacles in their life so that they can live and succeed as well.

The proof of his ability came on this wise. The shopping was a strain on him like many men. He had to learn to get over the idea and shop sooner than when he normally did. He decided after he went shopping to go into work and see what was going on.

The boards were posted in the command post, and they were investigating potential criminal sites suspected in bombing activities. The review was on a slow burner, so he volunteered to do some drive-bys for investigations. The recon was an excellent challenge to hone his skills, so he decided he would take his time and spend the afternoon doing as well as he could.

The report he turned in was very useful in targeting the low-budget production site that was guarded by four people at the front door and several at the back door. When it came time to raid the site, they gave him two teams to assault the facility. This was because he was familiar with the production site and had an idea or two on how to take the house.

Joseph M. Due, October 17, 2016

Commitment

The class listened to the ideas about training, but Joseph realized they were skeptical. So he took out a summary list out of his briefcase and wrote it on the rotating chalkboard and waited for them to return. He then asked them to make up a list of training ideas for Company A.

When they did, he asked a few brave souls to read their lists aloud. After they did, he asked them to discuss some of the ideas he wrote on the chalkboard as he turned it over. The class realized they had not taken the lessons to heart.

He asked them to list applications in their training endeavor, where his ideas would come in hand. The discussions were lively and the applications accurately stated. He knew he made inroads into the unit's thinking.

Joseph M. Due, October 6, 2016

Lt. S. Williams

The buttresses of the mind are virtue. The system of thought the delusional people use. Lies deny the person the full connecting points to virtue within and without a person. This hinders the abilities to do well and can even cost a person their life in battle.

Witches use energy to force lies on other people and, in God's and man's judgement, deserve the sentence of death they receive for the sins they commit.

He knew he had to write these lessons down. He had been affected by so many lies that he despaired at times in the regard to ever purging them all from his body. He prayed to God and knew he improved and survived. He just knew there were a lot of lies out there that affect the way people think.

He remembered the first time he fought in unarmed combat. He remembered waking up on a cot with a medic in attendance. He had come a long way since that first fight but desired to stand with the great warriors of the day.

Joseph M. Due, October 19, 2016

Eighteenth CEB

The temporary buildings on the post would do. Joseph thought of his and called up Robert's successor, Charles Richards, and asked him if the Eighteenth Combat Engineering Battalion (CEB) could put up the buildings. Charles thought about it and asked why. Major Mark Carne could help put up the permanent buildings since the schemas are already done.

Charles said he would talk to the Eighteenth CEB and see what he could do.

The load out was due Sunday at 1200 hours for the long ride to the Seventy-Eighth CID. The operations and daily training would be reviewed, and they were similar to the Fifty-Seventh CID. Ensuring everything was packed, the soldiers came in on Sunday at 1000 hours to assist, and then they would convoy to the Seventy-Eighth.

At 1200 hours, the last loaded van pulled into line. Sarita was finally done, and the vehicles took off to their destination. Sarita wanted to drive, so the guard rode in the back. She asked him when the engineers would be tasked. He told her he knew it was the Eighteenth that would put up the buildings, but he could not guarantee Mark would be there.

Joseph M. Due, October 6, 2016

Curiosity

The morning was warm and dry, and the fairgrounds were empty. The cleanup details found all kinds of illegal substances—even knives—and, once in a while, a handgun. This year, one of the workers found a legible notepad and decided to read the notepad before throwing it away.

Halfway through, she told her boss to get security on the phone before they left for the year. There were diagrams for the courthouse and for the social aid buildings in downtown Houston in the notes along with notes on access points and the times to access each section of the below-ground part of the facilities.

Security recorded the call and received the notepad with the name of the person that picked it up and where she did so. The Sheriff's detectives wanted to talk to Laura Bryant and agreed to compensate her for her time. The investigators asked her about how she found it and why she even looked inside the notepad and figured out the intent of the papers.

They then couriered the paperwork over to the FBI, who took the case and called Robert in and sent another copy of the book to Washington and prepared one for Robert's use if he thought it necessary. The days passed, and nothing was recorded happening around the two sites.

The police that patrolled the area were to check the areas at the times given and on the hour. Meanwhile, the Fifty-Seventh CID was tasked with finding the network until the FBI could get up and running. Col. Amanda Carne would be the point of contact for the Fifty-Seventh CID. She would field the investigators in larger numbers if it were warranted.

Joseph M. Due, October 16, 2016

Aide de Camp

Running the administration center for the two-week reviews of the units was demanding. The loading and unloading needed more organization. She knew she could cut out an hour or two on both the loading and unloading.

The system analysis teams met every morning at 0700 hours, and Sarita had to pay more attention to providing administrative supplies. She sat down and outlined a different load-packing schema and made a mental note that the supply requisition list for each load out needed updating based on consumption of supplies.

The base schema setups were fine, she noted. There was plenty of space, and the units provided the necessary tables and chairs.

Her day, except being on call, almost done, she decided to see what the General was up to.

Joseph M. Due, October 6, 2016

Amore Cai Vrai

The process of life by God's divine will is to be fruitful and multiply. That is growth within and without. Practiced living is a concept of taking training to a new level. We should practice skills and tasks as well as virtues in our daily lives on a daily basis.

To perfect the idea, we have to commit to it with a zeal in our daily endeavors to aim at perfecting what is not yet perfect in our lives. Since we began the endeavor, we should continue in it with a deeper and deeper commitment.

General Carne thought about what he wrote to his nephew about and prayed for him with fervor that he do well in his endeavors. He then looked at Sarita and decided that he needed to feel her desire and passion once again.

He warmed her feet with his hands and let his love pour forth and fill her. She turned over and smiled at him and beckoned with her hands to show him her desire with a kiss and a hug.

Joseph M. Due, October 6, 2016

Nightlife

The moon would be up in the sky by 0100 hours. What could be done must be done between 2300 hours to 0100 hours. The time has many that wander through the landscape of darkened shadows. Concern—even fear—abounds in those hours that discovery might be by an innocent or a fool.

The consideration comes with a need for the experience, learning, and then knowing, as sometimes shadows bump into each other in the night. The determinant view must consider reasons for that shadow to be there—another learned knowing.

Avoidance with the knowing leaves the innocent to wander through the days of their lives while leaving the warrior with the awareness to neutralize the shadows that bear the guilt of their sins.

Lieutenant Stevens looked at the truths of the matter and considered where his team was. Almost online and a few shadows to the fore that he can discount unless they change their minds and decide to participate in the larger group conspiracy of sins that from Humanity and God himself demand an answer.

He pointed out the shadows to his riflemen and asked if they could track the shadow's movements. They acknowledged the truth of his comment, and the soldiers awaited their fellow warriors as the net around the house was set in place.

The reports indicated his team was ready and it was time. He tasked the attack teams to take out two of the shadows that were between him and the target. They moved as ghosts, and one by one, the guards fell with minor noise in the stillness of the dark night.

Then the attack teams moved into position around the doors. The shadows behind him moved away, and the tension mounted. The assault teams were ready at the doors. They were ordered in without grenades to clear the silent, darkened house.

The soldiers flew through the doors and began to clear each room.

Joseph M. Due, October 16, 2016

Gifts

The first snow was on the ground, and there was a little bite to the cold air. It looked like the snow would be there for a while. The family was gathering for Christmas at Donald's house. The children were already hoping for more than an inch before it melted. Amanda was pregnant with her second child and as intense as ever.

Joseph and Sarita pulled up behind Mark's pickup truck and parked. They had brought the gifts early so they did not have to mail them. The children crowded around, and Sarita asked if they would take the gifts inside.

The luggage came next. She took the small one and both portable laptop computers. He picked up the three larger bags, and he followed Sarita to the door. The maid greeted them at the door, and they were ushered to the bedroom they would be staying in.

Dana and Mark greeted them in their new bedroom. They sat and talked like old times. The first of Dana's children was two and in the living room sleeping. Mark's wife was contemplating having a child but wanted him to reach the rank of Major first. Joseph and Sarita knew from the Eighteenth Combat Engineering Battalion (CEB) that it would be soon. His promotion points were very good.

Donald was in the living room, telling stories and scaring the little children. Amanda was in the kitchen with the wives, cooking and at times giving out a taste or two to the children that asked. Joseph kissed his daughter and greeted her with a hug and said there were safer scary stories being told in the living room. One of the ladies smiled at him and gave him a cup of coffee. He told Sarita he would be in the living room if needed.

Sarita hugged Amanda and congratulated her as the women gathered around. They also liked to hear stories. Sarita wanted to hear stories herself, so she asked the ladies what she could do to help out.

The men took turns listening to the stories and keeping the younger children entertained as dinner was being prepared.

The families came and went through the evening hour so people could visit and have a bite to eat in their turn.

At 2200 hours, the kitchen was shut down, and the babies were in the nursery. So Donald and Joseph went outside and talked over where their respective units were in respect to preparedness and mission profiles.

Joseph M. Due, October 3, 2016

Ode to Joy

Dana wept for joy when Lt. Col. Brian Stevens finally asked her to marry him. She thought at times she might be outside God's will and his love had passed her by. She met him at Target while she was on the floor supervising.

Brian was looking for a wedding gift that someone like Dana would like. The store had gone upscale as a supercenter since she had been hired as a cashier. There were a few gifts a woman would like from Target, she had assured him.

She took him around the store and talked to him about his friends getting married. He said it was a commitment thing—some soldiers waited so long to get married. They did not want to see a woman cry over a broken relationship if they died. She thought he was very thoughtful and told him she wouldn't mind seeing him again.

Joseph M. Due, October 6, 2016

Lieutenant Nidden

Lieutenant Nidden did not at times know the beginning of a thing. Low-crawling into the darkened underbrush, he knew he belonged where he was. His rifleman was next to him, and the spotter was on the other side of the bush, whatever variety it was.

He looked to the house to see if there was any activity. He was grateful for the bush but was mindful of the scratches he was getting. Not a person up and walking about, but the cars of the criminals were still parked in the street and the driveway.

He spoke, and he received six sitreps. When he said, "On three," the attack teams got into position. When the front and back door were covered, he told his team to wake them up.

The house was small, and the number of criminals low. He wanted them a little disorientated, so the sniper teams broke the windows, firing warning shots into the ceiling as the attack teams entered the building.

The scurry of bandits in response and the sound of return fire sporadically sounded. A minute later, both teams said they were safe and clear. He called the command post and said, "Criminals will be ready for transport in five minutes."

He then went to meet his destiny.

Joseph M. Due, October 6, 2016

Tactical Planning

Tactical planning is interesting to many people. How do you use preexisting resources to gain the advantage when the enemy knows the ground better than you do because they are living or working on the grounds the battle will take place?

The slightest changes in a building's construction can slow down or give hesitation to those on the assault teams that fight over that building. This could be fatal for the soldier. They were taught to follow orders but keep their minds open to changes in the conditions they labored in.

Col. William Smith, though in charge of Smith Carne Industry, still peeked in now and then to see what the new generation came up with. He remembers his day in planning and enjoyed finding the odd solution here and there.

Thinking about planning, he looked at the new schema model for the proposed addition to the building. He liked the upgrades; they will help the soldiers train and even sleep better. He thought about the hallway; he wanted it to be ten feet wide. Command insisted eight feet would do for traffic.

He signed the paperwork and decided he will walk it over to planning himself. This would give him a reason to be over there so the workers would not be too stressed.

Joseph M. Due, October 13, 2016

Capt. Scott Williams

His Majority was what he sought in life at this time. He knew he needed his Master's degree in Criminal Justice finished before he went to Operations. He also was praying for a good woman to help him in his days. Scott Williams looked out the Supply third floor window. Life was good and precious, and he had ideas of future operational forms he thought were of value.

His teams were avant-garde and highly effective in breaking down into three four-man teams and then into two two-man teams. He figured with a third departure point, they would be less seen and be able to apply rapid response even better.

The vans were ideally suited for the idea, and the drivers could be taught to drop off the troops and then park and wait for the troops to reach their attack points. Then they would use the vans to block the traffic flow even further out to make it safer for the teams providing security.

Turning back to business, he handed the lieutenant his supply orders for the month for his teams. He walked out of supply and headed for his office.

Joseph M. Due, October 6, 2016

Major Stevens

The glad tidings of peace were oft misplaced in the heat of battle. The process of growth and development could sometimes obscure the times one should just smell the roses. Sarita called up Major Stevens and had some small talk about contributions to the morale of the unit. She then asked him if he was interested in Elizabeth Roberts's phone number; she thought he looked nice.

It was not that he did not have dates. It was not even that he would not date. From time to time, one had to be reminded that social contact was a good thing. He called her up and asked her out. He thought it was time to think of at least the social needs he had.

He decided to pick her up on Saturday at 0800 hours. The date consisted of a football game and food at One Potato Two. The date seemed to go well enough, but she had weekend work and he had to bring her back home.

He dated her for a year but knew it would just be social dating. There was no grand love, great desire, or deep passion. They were both looking for something else.

Joseph M. Due, October 19, 2016

Schema Design

Maj. Scott Williams found his mark and made his point in operational flexibility. The extra vans were parked over at their warehouse, and the laborers for Smith Carne Industry were using the new ones there as primary issue instead of being parked below in the parking deck.

The training considerations called for an expansion on the west side of the building to at least the third floor training area. The debate was whether an upgrade in the offices like investigation was actually needed as well.

Gen. Charles Richards liked Major William's idea, but each addition needed to be justified, like an investigative control center with fifty audio/video control stations, which he could see was periodically needed. He appreciated the growth as his bosses did, but he wanted the proposed upgrade to be totally justified to avoid arguments in the Corps itself.

Gen. Donald Carne knew an upgrade to even the command post capability would be nice, and Colonel Carne thought more room in the gym might make it easier for expanded training during alert response events,

Joseph M. Due, October 6, 2016

Michael Gregory

The qualifications for life are love, passion, and desire as well as appreciation, et cetera. The Sunday morning service by Preacher Michael Gregory was thought-provoking to one of the newer members, Brenda Carne. She even preached to her brother John on the way home the different applications she had discovered by God's grace.

Her mom and dad, Donald and Amanda, saw the next generation growing in the exchange of truths both shared. They remembered their grandparents with a little sadness. They thought of their parents and where they were today. They even thought of themselves and what they accomplished.

Looking at their children, they wonder what Brenda and John would do, but considering their innocence, they were satisfied they would do well.

Joseph M. Due, October 19, 2016

Teams

The ice-cold breath of wind left him desiring to be inside. It would be another hour or so. He flexed his hands to return some warmth to them in the thin gloves issued for rifle teams. He looked to the left and right and noticed the Lieutenant and the Sergeant were even colder-looking than he was in his Thinsulate undergarments. He scanned the two-story production site lit up by the company sign and wondered where their security was.

The hour ticked by, and the Lieutenant gave the order for everyone to be up. As they reorientate their call in their readiness status, he warned the fire teams about the armed security and said, "On three." He counted down to three, and the attack teams moved into position. They were also worried about the guard's whereabouts.

The lead turned the knob on the door, and it was locked. So he backed up and let his battle buddy place the explosives to knock the door off its hinges and break the lock. She then ignited the explosives and backed away herself. The explosions were not deafening, but they were clearly heard for what they were.

A light came on in an upper left room, and the private sighted in as one of the guard's moves to the window. A double shot, and the guard fell into the window. They saw other lights in the building coming on, and the Lieutenant counted them off into his radio so the attack teams were ready for any response.

He wondered how Col. Amanda Carne would take it if the other guard was busy destroying the evidence the investigators need.

Then the teams secured their areas, and he went to see what command would say.

<u>Joseph M. Due,</u> October 4, 2016

Lovers

The moonlight was warm and beckoning, and the shadows were light and comforting. Peace reigned in the kingdom, and she knew her love was coming to the Gardens of her desire. She had waited so long for his embrace and tender kisses that sometimes she almost fainted with the passion of each tender moment.

She saw the young lovers pass to and fro while she patiently waited for his tender call. From the edge of the garden, she saw his frame. Even in the moonlight, she knew his passing. Slowly, the form took shape, and she saw him with a smile of delight that was only for her.

They walked towards each other with a passionate purpose to consummate their love. They reached out hand to hand and then slowly embraced, desire fanning into a flame of love and passion.

She asked Donald if he liked the scenario in the romance novel. The scenario was on page 58. He replied with a question, "Do I have to dress in tights or anything?" She thought about it and told him his dress uniform would do. He then said, "Of course! I like it enough to try it."

She read on as he put on his uniform. He calls her from the bedroom and told her to stand ready. She put the book down, marking the page. She waited on her love, knowing he would be there.

Joseph M. Due, October 13, 2016

Captain Nidden

The development of plans and procedures is one of the key enablers of the Army. As plans and procedures are perfected in each soldier, it shortens their response time in times of crisis. This enables a soldier/responder to overcome a murderer's intent that much more quickly.

Interdiction talks about commitment and intent to become better at what each soldier does. As the person commits and practices the procedures as outlined by Army doctrine, the proficiency of that soldier and the unit goes up.

When the team moves as one, it confuses and delays the enemy's response times, and this minimizes casualties to the soldiers of the unit and any nearby innocent person.

The soldiers are for anything that cuts down on casualties. Sometimes they need to see the idea in action before they commit their energy to the idea though.

Lieutenant Nidden knew this was a truth he could learn and learn to live with. He read the training manuals with this truth in mind and worked on perfecting his abilities with this truth in mind. He found that he learned easier and faster with his avant-garde attitude.

The learning brought opportunities to show fellow soldiers how to do things. This made him a better teacher as a Lieutenant and then Captain. The Training Section wanted him as a junior officer. And he did two years in the training department, but his forte was built around plans and procedures. So he opted when a position to transfer to planning came open to do so.

Joseph M. Due, October 21, 2016

Generations

"Some people tell me that sacrifice is vanity. <u>Sacrifice is one of the noblest virtues.</u> When I am tired and need to be refreshed, the Good Lord shows me at times the sacrifice of others across the generations, and He shows me what they have actually achieved."

Joseph kept up with the truths he knew warriors collected as well as anyone. He knew these truths quoted were true by personal experience and by the testimonials of those warriors that come before.

The upgrade of his unit to three-star status and the doubling of the teams so their impact could be felt better required fresh eyes. He knew the governance people wanted Gen. Donald Carne to be his successor, but General Carne did not want to leave his post partially unattended.

Nor did he want to leave Amanda behind for three years. His successor to the helm was ten years away. His love, he would not forsake. Joseph had need and sympathy, and he might make it another ten years. He prayed it would be so.

<u>Joseph M. Due,</u> October 6, 2016

Caravans

The winter snow was being driven by a heavy wind. The vans slowed to see the road better. As the miles went by, they went from blacktop to following the tracks in the snow of the vehicle before them. They slowed even more. The road before them could not be seen, but it could be felt as slippery as the road was becoming. All the vans slowed down to fifteen miles per hour.

The rest stop was an hour away at the top speed they were driving. The flashing lights behind them indicated it was a local sheriff's department car. They pulled over a little, and the sheriff sped by and out of sight.

The car in front slid to the side of the road and disappeared. The tracks ahead filled up, and they, too, disappeared. Panic-stricken, one van followed another into the roadside ditch. There, they slid into each other, and the two turned over.

They decided to find the road and walk to the nearest gas station. By the time they arrived, the police had found and searched the vans. When they heard about the disaster waiting to unfold, they walked to the door and started walking in the snow to the highway on ramp to attempt to disappear themselves.

Meanwhile, the sheriff's department called the FBI local office and asked them if they were interested in a caravan of vans loaded with bombs. The sheriff's department was asked to secure the vans and the bombs until they could get there. The FBI then called the Fifty-Seventh

CID and asked if they could back up security on the vans and their cargo.

Teams 9 and 10 were dispatched to find the sheriff's car and help out on securing the bombs until the weather broke. Col. Amanda Carne ordered two more teams to report in and investigations to find the vans and see what they could figure out. She looked out her window and prayed her troops would be all right.

The APB for the vans owners turned up nothing as to the van drivers and their whereabouts. The cashier was getting off shift and did not know he knew the identification of the suspected bombers. The sheriffs converged and then started doing a drive through the highway to the Houston exit. They expected the suspects were armed and dangerous.

Teams 9 and 10 set up recon on the edge of the highway in both directions then posted guards in the snow to both sides of the vehicles in the ditch. There were posted four two-man teams with pistols and rifles. The team leads decided they could spell the troops on the half hour.

The weather lessened in the morning, and the FBI was arriving in force. They requested the Fifty-Seventh provide coverage until they could get enough tow trucks at one time to haul all the vans out of the ditch.

The cars went by, and the troops wondered about the criminals trying to take the bombs back. They wondered what the bombs were intended for. They also prayed they bought the time to track the rest of the conspirators down.

Investigations looked for shipping manifests, false or otherwise. The FBI was bringing in a team to do fingerprinting when the vans were recovered.

At 0800 hours, the FBI team tracked down the people that were on shift up the road and learned the approximate transit time the criminals did when they abandoned the vehicles. They pulled the video and compared the pictures against their database and DMV records.

The local tow trucks were arranged in order of 1 through 6, and the teams from CID helped turn the vans right side up as they were towed out of the ditch. This took two careful hours to accomplish, and then the local Ford dealership provided keys to turn the vehicles on after they were inspected for damage.

The police impound lot was augmented by Houston police and FBI teams that waited for EOD to look at the bombs and their accompanying materials like detonators and attachment mechanisms to determine intent of use.

The comparison revealed the owner and four out of five of the drivers, and the APB was upgraded to conspiracy to transport bombs and associated materials. The names and picture IDs were faxed to every police department up and down the highway.

The search was coordinated, and the POVs with license plates were also forwarded to all police departments in case the criminals were picked up and still in the local area. The reports from each police department tasked to do drive-throughs of their jurisdictions would take the day.

The CID was ordered by Colonel Carne to do periodic drive-bys of the local known transit sites and hot spots. Video surveillance teams were organized, and suspected sites were then monitored on a 24-7 basis until further notice.

The news was dramatic to the point some thought it might be terrorizing and lurid. Some news reports barely skirted good manners. This irritated law enforcement in the footprint of the pathway the bombers were known to have taken.

The EOD teams arrived by plane and reached the impound lot by 1400 hours. They were called in at 2300 hours the night before by the FBI. They carefully disassembled the boxes and set up tables to examine material found.

Meanwhile, the police dragnet netted two who had returned home to Corpus Christi. They were going to go through an all-day interview once they were processed at 1530 hours.

Transit house 2 had activity at 0300 hours that morning, but the perpetrators were gone from that local. The investigations revealed that there was a production facility in Corpus Christi, and the address was known by local law enforcement and the FBI.

The investigative teams targeted ten houses by causal associations, and drive-bys and video monitoring was set up for a closer look at those sights that had many cars and people at the addresses.

The video was monitored 24-7, and in the days that followed in Houston, investigative agencies compiled enough evidence for search and seizure rules to apply. In the footpath of the criminals and later seizure of their production facility, the investigation by the FBI was widened to five states and their criminal networks.

Joseph M. Due, October 13, 2016

Excellence

The fire teams were in place outside the house of ill repute. The attack force was ready to advance when a couple walked out of the house and walked to the car. They did not look up. Lt. Sharon Tress waited until they got in the car, and she said to the fire team, "Shoot out the tires." As they did, she said, "Team 1, take the car. Teams 2, 3, and 4, advance on the house."

As soon as she heard the teams in the back were ready, she ordered the teams to take the house. The fire teams dropped four, and the attack teams got another five, all told. She received the all clear calls in three minutes and the proof of the kidnapping.

The eight-year-old boy was bruised up and frightened but calmed down when the Lieutenant told the boy his parents would be here right after the FBI. She called into the command post, and they told her ETA was ten minutes out.

The boy was hungry, so they looked in the refrigerator and found the makings for a peanut butter sandwich. Then she waited until the FBI was there and sent the attack teams to the rally point. Then when the street was cordoned off, she told the rifle teams to meet at the rally point as well.

No casualties, quick response, and the boy rescued, they all thought it was a good day. On the ride back, she could see how tired her troops were from the stress, but they were still up, so she told them to do their sitreps so they could hand them in sooner.

The morning found them asleep until 1000 hours. They woke to a commendation from their Commander and an all-around good evaluation on their review. The Lieutenant received a special commendation for quick thinking and the good training that was seen.

Joseph M. Due, October 10, 2016

Hit and Run

The wedding was scheduled for months, and the young couple looked forward to a long, healthy relationship together, enabling each other's life endeavors. The block was filled with well-wishers, and there were parked cars on both sides of the street. The trees were laced with colored paper to celebrate the occasion.

The outdoors on the side of the house held a small stage, a podium, and chairs to fifteen feet to the sidewalk. The well-wishers filled the chairs and then stood in the back to the streets. The wedding started at 1000 hours and was accompanied by a short sermon on fidelity to the crowd.

As the couple went down the aisle, they entered the street and walked south to their car. A gunman sitting in a car pulled alongside the couple and emptied a military pistol into the young couple. Both were hit three or four times. The gunman drove off south and disappeared.

The police recovered several rounds, a description of the perpetrator, and the handgun. The description of the car did not come with a license, but an APB was put out on the suspect anyway. The Fifty-Seventh CID was called in to investigate by the police because of the use of the military pistol.

The chief investigator began with the families and suspected ex-boyfriends and girlfriends. They asked if any relative had been in the military and if they knew of anyone that drove a brown Ford sedan. The neighborhood was canvassed, and the guests that left their names with the police were also interviewed.

They had to find the gunman to find out where he got the pistol. The teams were called in to do their stints, augmenting investigations as they looked for that gunman. Each team took a section of the city and walked the grid down. Two days later, they had eleven suspects that fit the description.

The teams were redeployed by Maj. Amanda Carne to focus in on the suspect list and monitor their whereabouts. General Carne ordered investigations to assign all available detectives to the case and get histories on the suspects so the search could be narrowed down to one or two.

A week later, the compiled history and the recon of the suspects left two on the suspect list that had the networking resources to do the crime and the motive to do so. Major Carne asked if their dwellings could be put under surveillance at that point. The General authorized investigations to do so.

Major Carne then gave the teams not on alert two days off to recuperate and be ready for the next stage of the case. The next stage would be urban assault if they proved the perpetrator committed the crime or the local of where the weapon was procured from was found.

The two days of surveillance showed a lot of cars at both homes coming and going. Investigations was getting license plate numbers and looking for connections. Teams 3 and 4 were asked to drive by and help out on procuring the license plate numbers of the visitors.

The days slid by as different houses became known to CID. The plan of the organization was still unknown. General Carne called Robert and asked if he would stop by. He laid out the data for Robert to see, but the perpetrators were keeping silent. Robert said his inquiry had to be silent—so it would take a day or two.

The investigators found a connection to a house that sported pistols, and they put it under surveillance like the rest. The next morning, they heard conversations relating to an idea on the sixteenth to do mass shootings at the public facilities like stores. According to the criminals, this would disrupt the social life of everyone in Houston.

Robert was back at 1000 hours with the Regional OIC officer in charge for the FBI. They went over the current lists and their plans as well as the data from out-of-state sites the FBI was willing to share. They validated the Fifty-Seventh CID's findings and recommended the night of the fifteenth, the CID round up as many of them as they can.

The planning staff went over the lists by groups and projected what houses would have the most suspects as they attempted to interdict their operation. The police would drive off the vehicles, and Fort Houston could donate three hundred people or twenty-three teams prepared for urban assault. Many of the houses could be taken and kept so stragglers would be picked up.

Major Carne took the plan and did the schedule for the assault teams that would be assigned. The alternate command post would have to be set up, and many of the teams would have to use their own privately owned vehicle for transport.

Joseph M. Due, October 17, 2016

War

The concourse was full, and the people milled about. The jets were all parked in a row. The cargo had to be off-loaded on some of the jets. Some of the jets had arms and munitions to be off-loaded, so the people were not allowed on their jets for another half hour. The guards were wearing army utility uniforms, and when this was noted, it drew a larger and larger crowd.

Suddenly, there was a dull thud of a noise, which perplexed some of the airport customers. Some shouted because some of the troops were down. The airport customers that saw the explosion pointed to the open runway where other troops wearing BDUs were inbound, and they were trying to kill those that were guarding the munitions.

As the troops died, the airport customers started to panic because they thought they might be the next target of the ones in BDUs. The concourse was filled with people now struggling in four different directions.

Then they heard the sound of an M-50 machine gun from the response force, and the attacking forces were quickly shot down as the troops from the facility fought back. The gun battle lasted another fifteen minutes while the defending troops cleared the area from those that sought to cease the munitions and arms.

The troops from the Forty-Third CID called in for troop replenishment, cleaned up the area, and arrested the wounded. Army CID Criminal Investigations was called in and the dead bodies searched. Meanwhile, the defending force established a perimeter defense around the airport runway and locked down the airport until fresh troops could arrive and the munitions could be loaded on the trucks and moved out to their destinations.

The military units receiving like Fort Houston were put on alert, and they donned BDUs and doubled their guard force just in case they attacked the armories themselves.

The addresses of the criminals were found, and the nearby Combat Infantry Divisions were sent copies of the findings to start investigations in their areas.

Joseph M. Due, October 21, 2016

Prayers

William Wallace in the movie was, to the people of Scotland, a man that was a saint that would introduce them to their new King. Col. William Smith had fine sons that would help out, but they were like-minded.

They did not want to lead Smith Carne Industry, but they would pitch in here and there, helping until a Smith successor was found amongst one of his grandchildren.

His direct children, for various and sundry reasons, realized it was not in them to do so. Dad, and later, Grandpa, would have to wait until one of the grandchildren could be raised to the post and the leadership of the family.

Joseph had to wait for a wife but not a successor. William had his wife early, but he had to wait for his successor to be found amongst his many grandchildren.

The two, William and Joseph, indeed had many things in common, including the lesson inherently learned as they worked out their destinies.

The days went by, and the people of Smith Carne Industry flourished under the flag of the business and the Fifty-Seventh CID. Many people cared and prayed for both Joseph and William that God would bless them and hence the families.

Joseph M. Due, October 26, 2016

Jubilation

The celebrations were many and for many reasons. Colonel Stevens and Lieutenant Colonel Nidden were newly promoted, and justifiably early. The family was growing. The new addition to the building was complete with all six floors. Two floors were funded by Smith Carne Industry itself.

The greatest boon was the increase in proficiency of all the troops and, because of that, the loss ratio had dropped 10 percent that year. The children felt better about what their parents did, knowing it was not in vain. Colonel Stevens even said his children were doing so good they might all join the Army.

The girls looked at him and said they liked the Army enough, but they had not made up their mind. The boys, when asked, were almost as unwilling to commit, but they believed in Army training. The festivities on the premises also included paintball scenarios for those ten years and up.

The jubilation was catchy, and the in-house orientation went from showing or, in some cases, learning to wear the equipment to hand-to-hand training in the mats on the gym's floors. The open house lasted three days during Christmas and was a great success.

Joseph M. Due, October 7, 2016

Lies Believed

She wonders with a great wonder how she made it in a so-called man's world. The women already knew they are affected by the lies of the day. This gave them something to think about and pray about. They wept over that which was lost.

She thought about Mums, who made her mark in life despite the lies and thanked God she had a dad who believed all men and women should find their destiny. The advent of the day was upon her. She dressed and kissed her husband, thanking him for being so understanding like Joseph, her dad. She moved into the kitchen and prepared the coffee and decided to make egg, cheese, and tomato sandwiches for breakfast. Donald would like two, she thought so she turned on the mini warmer on the counter and set to work.

The shower turned off, and then the door was heard. So she set out a plate of sandwiches to find it was not Donald that entered the kitchen but her firstborn son, John. She rescued one sandwich, to the sadness of John, and put it on her plate to give to Donald. Then she made another sandwich for him. John said he might eat two sandwiches if he could, and Amanda said he could ask the cook when she arrived. He thought about it and said OK. Donald asked her about her day, and she said she was going to spend the day in planning to see what they were up to.

She knew she should buy the Lieutenant Colonel insignia soon. Her promotion date was September 1—not too far away from July.

Joseph M. Due, October 6, 2016

Major Nidden

Machinery equipment he liked well enough, and he did not mind the pay. He also knew he would be frocked soon enough, and after his stint of running the contracts, he would be moved over to Operations and slotted in to the command structure, where he wanted to be for his dream.

The days went by with contracts to maintain and contracts to bid. And the management aspects of a small business were nice enough. He knew the experience would do him good.

The people were nice, but they knew he was not a Smith nor a Carne. He thought about marrying one, but he knew it would be for the wrong reasons. Besides, he thought, he wanted to be promoted to operations as promised.

Major Nidden thought about his desires and dreams and realized that they were proper and right, but he prayed about the direction of his life anyway.

The best part was when everyone needed to lend a hand on delivering and setting up equipment. That was the best job of the business that he liked.

Joseph M. Due, October 21, 2016

Lieutenant Colonel Stevens

The frost was on the ground. Lieutenant Colonel Stevens knew and appreciated it. His wife, Dana, liked ice skating when it was this cold. He knew Major Williams would be ready for his Colonelcy and the Operations position in a few months. Lieutenant Colonel Stevens would then be frocked and take over the XO position of the Fifty-Seventh CID. The pride and joy of Texas and, some dare say, the States as well.

Amanda Carne commanded the Fifty-Seventh CID, and Donald Carne was frocked and took over the Third Army Training Department, and then Sarita and Joseph would return home for the rest of their tenure. His wife Dana, he knew, would like to see her Mums more often. *The Families were looking forward to the transitions as well as the completion of the new wing being added*, he thought as he got into his car.

ATF and CID were looking for a group of criminals that were hitting the munitions convoys. The daily updates reminded him that almost heaven was not heaven and peace in one's days had to be fought for.

Joseph M. Due, October 20, 2016

Fleur due Vie

At midnight, the lilies were flowering, and the fragrance wafted on the breeze from outside the post hotel. The mobilization of Company A's platoon was underway. They were to provide interdiction support for the Sixty-Sixth CID. As they passed by, he reminded his wife of the times he had to go out to protect the innocent.

They explored the post for an hour, knowing it was a safe area to be about in at that time of night. The diner was open for troop support, and they went there to get a meal. Sausages, hash browns, and eggs were what was being cooked. She chose two tuna sandwiches out of the sandwich cart.

Sarita told him she liked the nice order to all the posts they had been on. He said they're as functional as the tending family can make them. She said she appreciated the lilies outside the hotel. She liked the fragrance when they were in bloom. He said he loved her and wanted her to know he knew she had been in bloom for decades.

She smiled and put her hand out, and he took it. She said she had some training for him if he had the energy.

Joseph M. Due, October 6, 2016

Shadows

The morning came as he and Dana knew it would. He was promoted to Colonel with plenty of time to earn his star. His happiness was tempered by the knowing of the sacrifice he and Dana agreed to, the lessons he learned along the way, and the cost in lives to make the day the way it was.

He washed and was pleased. He sang "Cai la vie la Amore" as he entered the kitchen. Dana had put on bacon and eggs and was feeding Lois Stevens, their second born, and James Stevens was eating Cheerios and eggs. He grabbed some coffee and kissed Dana with his love. She blushed and said that it felt like number 3 coming along if he persisted.

He smiled and asked James if he was up to another girl in the family. James frowned and asked why it could not be a boy. She blushed again and said, "All in all, God decides." She suggested he eat his bacon, and he decided to do some praying and put a piece of bacon in his mouth.

The morning fare was par excellence, and everyone enjoyed themselves. Mums was quite the cook. The babysitters in this case were Grandpa and Grandma on the dad's side of the family. The dawning of the day pictographed the neighborhood, and Mom and Dad had to encourage the children to get in the car for the drive.

The morning briefing had gunrunners and assassins under investigation but nothing immediate for the day, so he called the Team

Captains up and asked the heads of the sections to a meeting on how to perfect the idea of shadows in the teams by training, as he worked out how he learned those lessons himself.

Joseph M. Due, October 16, 2016

The Mist

The mist was everywhere in the cool morning air, and the guards walked out to the street to see if it were safe around the house. Joseph could almost see the prayers they were saying because of their uncertainty. He turned around and walked up the path and gestured for the first guard to check the house.

When he moved up to the door, a figure came out of the dark. Joseph slapped the person as hard as he could and then the rest of the criminals tried to get in close to try grabbing Joseph. The silence filled the air, and he saw that the one guard by the back of the car had been stabbed.

He rushed over and picked him up, and the other guard joined them in the house. He laid the guard out in the first bedroom down the hall, and Sarita tended to him. He called the Fifty-Seventh CID to send relief and get the problem to investigations. They would send a team, they said.

The other guard had Sarita stay in the living room, and he got the first aid kit out of the closet. He then did rounds in the house to ensure there was no one in the rooms. Then he closed each room window and locked each window as well.

Then he swept the kitchen, checked the lock on the front door, and made some more coffee. Help would be there in twenty minutes, and all knew it would be a long twenty minutes because of the mist. You could barely see twenty feet through as shadows, and to know the person's face, you had to get within five feet.

Joseph M. Due, October 6, 2016

Forgiveness

To err is human and to forgive is divine. Joseph's dad and mom taught him that a long time ago, and he taught it to his children, who, no doubt, would teach it to their children. A truth so powerful that everyone he knew spoke of the quote now and then.

Joseph remembered now and then some of his errors and mistakes in training that sometimes cost lives. He prayed about them and asked forgiveness when he was reminded. He knew there were hundreds of people that had come and gone in his life, and he knew very few of them. He asked God for forgiveness for this too.

Donald spreckens zie langage in vie. He thought of some of his own errors and mistakes and thanked God that He forgave.

The troops they talked about for a while as they let the day pass away.

The evening hours brought about the notes of the day, and Joseph shared with Sarita another part of a soldier's life. She fixed some more coffee and sat in lap. His arm went around her as he sipped his coffee.

The music was on a dance mix, and he asks her if she was in the mood. She smiled and got up. He put the coffee cup down. They serenaded each other while passion called and desire rose in the night to hunt.

Joseph M. Due, October 10, 2016

Eli Brown

<u>Bespeak good tidings and do well.</u> This quote is part of some of the reminders of life of even the passing of the generations. The quote was part of the preaching messages of Eli Brown, son of Samuel Brown, to effect the understanding that God is in control and guides people through their dreams.

The evenings were filled with the news of the day and the spiritual applications one found for the messages preached. The continuity and growth of ideas of the spiritual nature gave comfort from the days that could be a bit distressing.

The trials and tears as well as the triumph accompanied by tears of joy should be remembered.

<u>Joseph M. Due,</u> October 13, 2016

Review

Twenty-two houses, thirty-four deaths, and at last count, fifteen injured. The bombers put up a fight after they disbursed the bombs to seventeen of the houses for use against governance facilities throughout the city. The command structure knew the price was worth getting that many bombs off the streets.

Gen. Donald Carne had thirty-four letters to write and over two hundred commendations to sign. He knew there would be days he would weep. For his troops, he wept indeed. He looked out the window at a city that was at least safe from those bombs. He sighed and returned to the files and letters he had to write.

The day went on, and Col. Amanda Carne brought his children in, a not-so-subtle reminder not to get too wrapped up in what he was doing and a reminder that the sacrifice his people made was well worth it.

Joseph M. Due, October 13, 2016

Colonel A. Carne

The afternoon paper, Donald Carne saw, was filled with the nonsense of the day. Idle gossip was sometimes more accurate. Sometimes, he and Amanda went with the children to the coffee shops here and there around town. The gossip was rarely true, and the conversations that went with the gossip was fairly putrid. He put the paper down and picked up a letter of commendation for one of the team lieutenants.

He liked the awards side of his job very much. Reading how commendable people can be was refreshing for him. The team lieutenant was worthy as testimonials and sitreps reported. He might even make his Majority early based on good conduct on the field of battle. He thought of others who, to be promoted, had accepted transfers to other units. "Sad thing," he said, "but such is the Army."

Col. Amanda Carne said as she walked in, "What sad thing?" He said, "As the troops are trained, we lose quite a few to other units." She asked, "Is anyone new leaving?" He replied, "The next roster will be here Tuesday. I was just thinking of Captain Mirone, who is being commended and might be on the promotion roster."

He continued, "If he does not make it this time, the commendation, time in service, and time in grade will give him eight points. He will probably make it next time." Colonel Carne said, "What about me? Will I be frocked three months early?" He said, "The General's favor this time or the next. You are another fellow warrior they would like to invite to the table."

"Meanwhile, that means two years at post, and I will be transferred soon to the Third Army Training Division."

Joseph M. Due, October 17, 2016

Unison

The endeavor of two in unison can become one.

The days passed as people decided to visit as they could. But they needed a project to keep them on track, so he asked his wife why she did not tell him she liked lilies that much. She said it rarely came to her mind, and it seemed always at the wrong time.

He told her he was saddened that he did not ask. She hugged him and kissed him, and from her heart, she forgave him. He told her he wanted to do something nice like redecorate the lawn. He said it was time.

She asked him what his favorite flower was, and he said to Sarita, "Roses would be nice." She thought about it and started to design a schema for the front and backyard. They counted the flowers needed and went shopping to order the necessary supplies and buy the necessary equipment. The days passed in planning and preparation as it looked like they dug up a large portion of their yard.

The flowers took in the spring rains, and they hosted backyard parties for all to see.

Joseph M. Due, October 7, 2016

Motivation

Myriad amounts of people go through Basic Training and/or AIT and do not readily see the possibilities to grow and develop in the Army. Colonel Stevens thought about how fortunate he was to have a unit where the soldiers were already motivated. The counsel of the elder soldiers taught him how to motivate troops wanting to be motivated. They also wanted focus and direction.

How does one motivate those that do not want to be motivated? Without focus and direction, the soldier settles for just obeying orders and then does not realize their potential. He sighed in regret that some did not see, let alone go the distance they could.

The lessons learned saved lives, and he went out to prove it once in a while. His job was to challenge his troops to think and act better—to be their best.

He decided to ask the troops in the gym during the 1800 hours' briefing what their plan of improvement is. He asked supply to make sure the notepads and pens were on the tables, and there were plenty available.

The day's events were filled with internal challenges. All he had to do was find ways to maintain the momentum of his ideas.

Joseph M. Due, October 21, 2016

General A. Carne

The mall was 140 stores and anchored by Target and Daytons. The child screamed twice, and then the mother, Sophia Andrews, started crying. Her baby was gone. She was within twenty feet of the back door of Daytons. The assumption was the child was put to sleep or taken through the door. Her child was gone, and she did not know where he was.

Security pulled the store tapes and called the FBI. The FBI called CID to request manpower assistance under the mutual support agreements (MSA) that were signed. The lead investigators went over to the Houston FBI field office to meet Sophia Andrews and her family.

Gen. Amanda Carne recalled all Fifty-Seventh CID people and told the Planning Department to grid out the city by the number of personnel assigned that could be freed to do a walk-down of the city for the young boy, Johnny Andrews. The staff was then ordered to bring up the alternate command post and to set up the gym for briefings.

Meanwhile, a picture of the suspects was being picked up from the police and would be mass distributed when the unit personnel were ready to be briefed. Hopefully, names and vehicle IDs would be forthcoming.

At 1000 hours, the unit briefings were underway and the command post was listening and watching to see if the criminals would use houses known for criminal activities that were being monitored.

By 1100 hours, the teams of two were briefed and sent out to walk the neighborhood to feel or see anything that might bring about the return of the child. The day was warm, and the hopes that the boy could be returned was high.

The police staked out the parent's house of the two men that were last seen with the child. They had hopes they would at least arrest the abductors.

Joseph M. Due, October 19, 2016

Deliverance

The freeze on the roads drove the young couple with the sleeping ten-year-old into the roadside ditch as the car hydroplaned out of control. As the car slid into the ditch, they forgot they were transporting a kidnapped child across the state lines.

The sheriff's department slowed traffic up and down the interstate for the duration of the black ice that was affixed to the roads because of the sudden change in temperature. They were helping the young couple through the distress of getting their car towed out of the ditch when the child rolled down the window and started screaming for help.

The Sheriff that was helping knew there was something wrong with the parents' reaction, so he signaled to his partner and called the parents to the back of the patrol car, where they were promptly handcuffed. When the two were ensconced in the back of the Sheriff's car, they went to talk to the young woman that was still locked in the car.

The young lady said she was Margaret Renoir, and she was kidnapped out of New Orleans. The Sheriff's department was called to see if there was a flyer out on the kidnapping. Their control center gave a brief description to the officers on the scene. Confirming it was her, the control center contacted the local FBI liaison and informed the FBI of their finding.

The child, Margaret, was born of parents in the military, and she was taken off a federal reservation. So the Fifty-Seventh CID was called, and they_were told the child would be taken to the Sheriff's department for interviews and then returned as quickly to her parents as she could be.

The Sheriff of the watch asked a patrolman to go out for doughnuts and juice. They figured Margaret might need something to settle her stomach. The Deputies found needles in the glove box, and the wrappings that tied Margaret also went into evidence.

CID was pulling into the drive. As the deputies parked to let Margaret out of the car, the CID brought four agents. Two agents were females and two agents were males. This was just in case Margaret would not be comfortable around one or the other.

They walked down the hall, and the Sheriff directed the party to the break room. The interviews would be done as informally as possible. The FBI liaison showed up while they were getting settled in.

The doughnuts, coffee, and juice were offered to Margaret, and she took one of each with three napkins. When she settled in the chair, they asked her if she remembered the actual kidnapping and where she actually was. She said she was sitting on a bench of the first floor of the building her parents worked in when a man and a woman, not the same as in the car, grabbed her and choked her with a rag.

Joseph M. Due, October 21, 2016

Transit

The Fifty-Seventh CID investigators continued their investigations long after Margaret Renoir was returned to her parents. On the back burners at times, but they were looking for end use of the kidnapped children, as were the FBI. As cases came and went, the reasons for criminal transit at the houses on the hot list became more defined.

The child alerts were compared, when they could, in time to the houses that were known or suspected transit sites. They looked for positive evidence of the kidnappings, bombs or bomb-making materials, or weaponry and ammunition.

Sometimes, they could capture a conversation between criminals that signified intent. In the case of the kidnappers, when they saw a bound body, they immediately responded with an interdiction team and put out an APB for all cars using the house just in case they left before the assault teams cordoned off the house in question.

In May, the weather was cloudy, rainy, and muddy. The removal of a bound child from an SUV that was stuck in the mud triggered an all-hands alert, and the assault team was sent to the site where the criminals were last seen. The SUV was still being worked on when the assault team parked a Smith Carne Industry van right behind it to the surprise of the kidnappers. The first team on the front of the house had to run down all the kidnappers while the second team stormed the house from the backyard.

The FBI was pleased with all the live criminals and their unerased phone records that would lead to a major break in the kidnapping ring.

The phone records extended to five states on their distribution route, and they picked up another twenty-three children that were being beat, raped, and were going to be sold.

The transit corridor from New Orleans to California took a heavy blow as the FBI raided just about every house in the phone logs they picked up. The transit sites were shut down, and the properties sold in all five states.

Joseph M. Due, October 21, 2016

Transmit

The intent in communications should be crystal clear no matter what the order, report, or conversation. This is to ensure things like the commander's intent is understood and, in the case of sitreps, acted on well.

The recovery of children has been a much-debated road of considerations, and books have been and will be written about the latest tactic or tool used in recovery or deliverance of that child to the parents that care and love them. All said and done, the issue is about what is best for the child by all agencies and agents that work on child abduction cases.

General A. Carne and her staff listened to the FBI lecturers and thought that this class was insightful and helped people understand the leadership challenge in relation to child abductions. She applauded their endeavors and thanked them for the brief and the training materials for her teachers and student soldiers.

As they left, they asked if the Fifty-Seventh CID was still looking. They admitted the FBI probably only got one part of the network in each state. General Carne assured them the investigators poked at the problem here and there and kept an open mind as to the doings of ick de' mons.

The girl had already been raped, and the kidnappers had promised she would be raped again until she accepted her new destiny. She sobbed in the dark where they kept her, and she prayed to God for help and guidance, repenting of all her sins. She prayed that her voice would be heard, and she did not have to live in such misery.

The dead body was dragged inside for later disposal. The neighbors called the police and reported their suspicions. Their investigators realized there were a lot of quasicriminals holding weapons and drugs transiting the house hourly. They brought up their SWAT team and raided the place at 1800 hours. The girl was found padlocked in a room in the basement with ten rapists sitting in chairs watching porno movies in the basement.

Emily Roberts was returned to her parent, Captain Roberts, in Houston. The CID investigation for the child abductors kidnapping children of soldiers began anew.

Joseph M. Due, October 21, 2016

Enticement

The morning sun was warm over Kansas and the sound of mosquitoes droned on in the grass as the day warmed and the people started to gather for work. The construction workers were out in numbers everyone could see as traffic almost slowed to a stop.

The guards were uneasy as the mile-long traffic crept along. The 0800 hours had come and gone, and nearly everyone was late for post. The night watch and security started to worry.

General Davis and his wife were chatting when the four gunmen in work uniforms surrounded their car. They knew it was not totally bulletproof, so the guard locked the doors. The General and his wife held hands, knowing their end was near.

Up and down the line, cars were targeted for the military personnel that were going to work. The sound of screams could be heard a mile, and the effect traumatized the City.

The afternoon toll was three hundred injured, dead or dying. Joseph and his wife and Charles watched the unfolding drama that brought people from nearby cities to help handle the crisis.

Joseph told Charles, "I grieve for the people of Kansas City, but I am old with many obligations before me. You need to help choose another with younger blood that will see more than I can see."

Joseph M. Due, October 7, 2016

Histoire in Vie

The material in the packing was plastic bubble wrap. The box was UPS standard. The papers had a title, *A Love Story*. It was from Joseph. Sarita liked packages. They were mysteries to be explored. She did not know why he sent her a partially formed book though.

Taking it into the living room from the kitchen, she put it on the end table and decided coffee—maybe yet, Chateau le Blanc. It began with the story of her grandparents, she noted. She liked his writing but did not know how true some of the stories were.

She liked the honest appraisal of his and her parents. She surmised some of the stories were about her. He did ask emotionally driven questions of her now and then. She started reading about William's family and knew the comments, based on perspective, had to be true.

She sipped her wine and looked at the clock. She had enough time to read epiphany she thought. The time slowly went by as she digested each word, knowing how painful it must have been to write it and bare his true emotions.

She thought about the kidnapping and how long it took for him to recover. Her heart went out to him, and she wept for him again. She decided to leave the stories there and fix dinner. The fare was half-inch steak, baked potatoes, and red beans with sautéed onions and Chateau le Rouge.

Joseph arrived home from talking to Donald about long-term planning for both units. He smelled the food cooking and knew she had great timing. He walked into the kitchen to grab some coffee, and she said, "Uh, no. The wine is in the refrigerator."

She asks him if her parents really yelled at each other periodically at times. He said, "Three or four times as they learned to keep themselves clean from the machination of others." He realized she was reading his stories, and they spent the evening talking about them.

Joseph M. Due, October 11, 2016

Judgements

The day in the federal courthouse for General Stevens representing his unit's activities was a new one to him. Others had represented in times past. The kidnapping and Bombing cases were large, and the reputation of the division itself would be questioned by the prosecution and attacked by the defense for the offenders caught in the act.

His ability to order warrants would be questioned in the court trials. If he did badly, he might get a rebuke to even as far as the judge stripping him of his ability to order federal warrants. He prayed for the necessity of his people and the needs of the Corps that he do well.

He studied military law and applied himself to knowing what CID investigations can or cannot do. He had prayed for his troops and trained them the best he could do. He had even prayed over the orders he gave that were in question today. He prayed again and found the peace he needed amidst stressful times.

The time passed from 0800 hours to 1300 hours. The court's deliberations were slower than usual, and he worried a little. When they finally called him, he emotionally girded up his loins to do battle and give the best answer he could give.

Joseph M. Due, October 20, 2016

Practiced Living

Tabula Rasa, the blank page of a person's life to be written on, comes with the new birth of a soul or salvation. Decisions are yet to be made like commitment, diligence, et cetera. The ideal soldier is one who has a blank page that can be written on. That is a soldier willing to learn.

The Sergeants and Captains looked for those who would listen, endeavor, and learn from the military experiences they went through. Practiced living was the optimal attitude they would like to see. Lieutenant Colonel Stevens remembered the instruction he received from the Army as a young man.

He remembered his first firefight with a rifle and how he had to think through each step to hit the mark when the order to fire was given. He remembered having to add endeavor and commitment to his daily work just to keep up with the team.

He remembered an arsonist throwing a gas bomb at him as he entered with an assault team, and then and now, he knew his hesitation could have cost lives. He saw the arsonist reaching presumably for another and shot him twice through the gas vapors.

The final phase of the assault, when they straightened out the arsonist, revealed a shotgun he was more than likely reaching for. In the critique, there was no time for guessing he should have shot him two or three seconds before, and he would never have hit the team with the gas bomb.

He remembered hesitations and unnecessary stress due to a lack of practice and preparation on his part. The timing delays he repented of including lack of self-motivation. Since those days, he knew from critiques he was a whole lot better.

Sitting at the helm of the Fifty-Seventh CID, he realized he grew and now it was time to help others coming up behind him to grow.

Joseph M. Due, October 13, 2016

Lieutenant B. Carne

The instructors at AIT saw the registration for the class and rejoiced. They had seen the Carne and Smith families for four generations. This would make the fifth generation and the families seemed to be established in the Army as a tradition.

The Carne and Smith families both found their way through the traditions of the school's teachings. There were a few families with such a fine heritage. Adding to that roll call of families dedicated to God and Country brought happiness indeed.

Brenda Carne was a lot like her mother, some did say. Intense and dedicated and like the rest, trained by good instructors at home, they knew she would do well. Debra Smith was supposed to be like her grandfather—patient and methodical.

The day before class, Lieutenant Carne showed up with her battle buddy, Lieutenant Smith. They found the billeting area and received their barracks assignment. After unpacking, they toured the whole post, including the training grounds. They were showing good common sense in navigating the post with a clear head and a desire to learn.

She parked her car and ensured it was locked in authorized parking and left it behind for the two-week course. The evening discourse between the two was land-navigating the site map against the class schedule. Very few students had taken the time to prepare so well.

Joseph M. Due, October 19, 2016

John Carne

The advent of a new age began with John, Amanda told him when he was fifteen. She told him he was mature, equitable, and fair about listening to his sister as he reached manhood. She told him she appreciated and loved him very much. She also said his dad was already proud of him.

He said, embarrassed, "Thank you, mom." She hugged him and he colored. She said, "Maybe you need a little more maturing, but you are doing fine."

He asked her what AIT was like because he was training up for going. She asked him what his minor would be, and he said he, like his friends, Robert and David Smith, liked the family business well enough, and he would like to know what College and the Eighty-Third CID was like.

She told him to keep an open mind. "Everyone learns something different. But some of the common things about College were studying, access to entertainment, and social dating. And overall, you feel tired."

"The Eighty-Third will teach you military studies so you can see what you need to learn and grow from the experiences. The exercises are real and dangerous. You will learn unarmed combat and will get many bruises. The live fire exercises means you have to bear down and take great care because you can get hurt."

He thought about the expression "He who hesitates is lost." He asked his mom if that applied. She said, "In the combat endeavors, hesitations give the enemy the advantage. The Eighty-Third will teach you how not to hesitate."

Joseph M. Due, October 20, 2016

Smiths

The Smiths, having a rich history amongst the people, were a happy sort. When their children started producing good children, they knew God blessed them amidst the generations. There were Dennis and Tammy, and William and Theresa, and now Robert Smith and David Smith were upcoming representatives of the family interests, including the family Heritage.

The losses along the way were saddening at times, but God took care of his family.

Of the share in Smith Carne Industry, the boys were interested in the Army and the production side of the business, but everyone thought Robert was the more sober-minded of the two young men. As they readied themselves for AIT and College, the Smith family prayed they would both do well.

Joseph M. Due, October 21, 2016

Recon

The pleasing of the day, when found, is borne in the truth of God's love. It is a simple, unadorned beautiful thing that one sees then. In recon, it is imperative that one finds this truth to know and record what is and at times what is not.

Lt. Brenda Carne was learning this anew at times, and it sometimes seemed like a daily set of lessons. The sitreps she wrote at times seemed to be constantly critiqued. She knew she missed the import at times, and she also knew her eye definition set needed to grow more.

The challenges of the day would see to it, and she did endeavor to take in the proper definitions so she could communicate what she saw more effectively. She prayed about the issue, knowing that in the heat of the day, the truest report guides leadership the best in their decision making.

She wondered about where her second great love could be. Both her grandma and ma had found their great love. To her embarrassment, she saw both loves upfront and personally embarrassing. She remembered some of their personal tender and passionate moments and blushed profusely. She hoped, after she learned all her lessons, her Romeo would love her that well.

She returned to the class today on learning to accept the truth of what is and is there for good or bad as she surveyed the landscape she was to navigate. The objective was to report on what is all there at the location she was to recon.

Tonight, the soldiers would practice in the northern woods' night land navigation and include a sitrep of what was all seen there and along the way.

Joseph M. Due, October 20, 2016

Missed

"The pompous are delusional and work to deceive whoever they can."
Joseph heard his dad say that many times in his life. He knew the
statement was true. Joseph had a great appreciation for his dad's love
and, here and there, missed him dearly.

Terrance was missed greatly. This was true. People reflected here
and there where the truths came from in life, and Terrance lived many.

Jean was a Mums of the first order. She helped Terrance set many
a fine table and taught the ladies in the family well. Her love was a
true maternal love for her children long after they were grown. Dying
in peace as she did three months before Terrance died in his sleep
was saddening to the heart and everyone knew how much Terrance
missed her.

Joseph M. Due, October 5, 2016

Peace

"The evil that pervaded the land at times struck William and Theresa a mighty blow." Joseph prayed about what to say.

"The fishing day is over and the harvest delivered to the market for my friends, William and Theresa Smith. The days of labor have turned into days of rest as they now enjoy the bounty of Heaven's riches."

These are the words Joseph spoke at their funerals for he knew they deserved the best. The preacher said he could say no kinder words. The families suffered their days of grief over their loss. It was time to turn their minds to the good things of God, give thanks for life, and appreciate the good things in their time.

The dinner was four different types of fish that reminded the families of William and Theresa's hobbies and the joys they found in life.

The preaching service was on the bounty of God's love.

The process started with the funeral and ended with the preaching service. It was an all-day affair, and all were welcome.

Joseph M. Due, October 7, 2016

Treasures

The day dawned and the hour beckoned and the two lovers raced to meet their destiny. "La Familia un Vie" is the desire of the heart for some. In this case, it is both for a spouse and children. Joseph said to Sarita, "Is it time?" She said almost. He sighed and told her he was a little impatient; he was not used to waiting in such a manner. She smiled at him and said, "The time will come soon enough."

The car was packed, and everything was ready for showtime. She walked back and forth, slowly waiting for that special feeling. Joseph sat on the couch and worried a little though he knew his wife and child were very healthy.

It was September 25, and they both thought the day would be auspicious if the child would cooperate. After all, she thought, the nursery was painted pink, the little mobile was hung, and the clothes were bought in anticipation.

She turned to Joseph and said, "Now it is time." He got up and walked with her to their car. The ride was slow and gentle; he did not want to jar the baby. Intake was simple, and he got to go through the process with her. While she waited, he held her hands and helped her be calm and focused. The waiting began again.

The hours slipped by, and 2330 hours was upon them when her contractions began in earnest. The delivery room was only three doors away; the nurse was ready, and the doctor was paged. The labor became more intense as the doctor entered the room. He laughed and said, "I think I better hurry up." He checked her abdomen and said to her, "Breathe easy." She nodded and started taking deeper breaths.

The baby started emerging, and Joseph could see their child. He thought it was one of the miracles of life and he said so. The doctor agreed and helped the little girl emerge. The slower delivery meant no tearing, and the baby was freed from the umbilical cord and cleaned up. It was 2347 hours. The mother was strong enough to hold the baby right away, so the doctor nodded approval to the nurse.

She was wheeled back to her room as they set up a crib. She wanted to have her child with her, and Joseph insisted with her that she was healthy enough. When she and the baby were together, he went to the car to get the rest of the bags. On the way, he called the command post and told them the baby arrived.

He was ready for the all-night shift, and security stood by the door. Eight to ten hours' bed rest, and they would bring her and the child home. He had a few bad memories of medical facilities and preferred she be taken care of at home. He had already arranged for a week of in-home health care. The nurse would arrive in the morning.

The night passed quietly enough. The doctor knew of the in-home health care and signed off on her leaving early with the baby since both were healthy. He tried to talk them out of leaving early but had no good reason that they had to stay.

The nursery was ready, and Joseph had bought a rocking chair just in case the baby needed company while she slept. Amanda Theresa Carne was introduced to her new home. She stared at the walls for a little while and fell asleep.

They held each other until Sarita decided to sit. She said she would like to rock for a while and appreciate and enjoy. He brought her a turkey and cheddar cheese sandwich with mayonnaise, tomato, and lettuce on wheat and a cup of coffee with one cream and two sugar. She thanked him and started to eat. She said she was grateful she did not lose her appetite. He brought in a folding chair as she finished the sandwich.

The talk turned to her mother's experience as Amanda dreamt. She said she was grateful to be living her dream. They waited another twenty minutes and moved to the bedroom. He held her as she rested and then fell asleep. He held her and thanked God for him being allowed to live his dream.

The movement woke him, and he noted the time. She kissed him and headed for the nursery. She prepped the changing table as Amanda stirred. He watched to see how awake she was as she began to hum the blues. He went into the kitchen and put on some more coffee. He asked her if she wanted a bite, and she opened the refrigerator.

She said she was slightly hungry and stood there for a moment and thought about it. "Cornflakes," she said as she pulled out the milk. He rose and she looked at him and he sat back down. She did not want to be coddled to that degree. Capt. Johnson's Sister, Carol, the nurse, came into the kitchen and asked her if she needed any help. She pulled the cornflakes box down and firmly said no.

Joseph asked Carol to sit with them, and he asked her, "Cornflakes or raisin bran?" She said raisin bran. He got out two bowls and asked security to join him.

He opened the curtains and got another bowl and three spoons. The sunlight brightened the sky and filled the room more fully. The talk was about needs for the day starting with the baby and then her. She talked about the organization of the nursery and decided she would rearrange it.

He finished his coffee and asked her if she would like to watch television, listen to the radio, or read. She thought about washing the dishes but knew that the dishes by and large were the nurse's to do. She thought about only being able to do light prep in cooking and having to wait four to six hours before she had anything to do.

She prayed about the problem of the expectations that confined her to inactivity. She found she had to find some way to prove she was healthy and improving by the minute. Checking on the baby at this stage of the game was five or ten minutes for a change or a feeding.

The morning passed slowly by as everyone watched her. She then decided she wanted to visit Mums. Her campaigning began not with a whine but by a determined process of endeavor. She would read recipes and have the mothers of the unit demonstrate tasks in preparation. She broached the subject that with care and a lot of sitting, she should be allowed to visit Mums.

Joseph let her call Mums to see if she would be in. Sarita said she wanted to introduce the baby around. The prep time did not take any time at all. The nurse insisted on going there with security. She found her thinking was returning to normal with things to do.

The afternoon at Mums went by far quicker as the women talked over health, babies, recipes, and men. Joseph excused himself for two hours and went into work to do paperwork. He came back to pick her up a little after 1600 hours. She now had things to talk about at home that were new, and the nurse was off at 1630 hours.

Arriving at home, the nurse left, and they laid the baby down in the bassinet Joseph brought into the kitchen. She then talked him through making one of Mums's recipes. She said this made her much happier, and she ate the meal with much vigor.

She then told him that he helped her heal a little bit when he put baby oil on her lower back and rubbed it in. She then said she was wondering if he would do that again. He reassured her that he would when she wanted to do that. She asked him if 2000 hours would be a good time for him. He promised he would rub her down then.

The evening passed on the couch with them talking about the day's events, the baby's needs, and recipes. She then said she would like him to rub her down in the bed so he went and got a towel as she walked to the bedroom. He got the oil from the bathroom. She had already pulled the blankets off the bed. She looked at him with love as she stripped for the rub.

She helped put the towels on the bed from head to foot and then lay on her stomach and told him she was ready. She told him she loved him as he sat astride her lower back and began the ministrations. The hour passed by as he worked down to her feet. She then turned over and said, "Now this side." He looked at her, and she said, "I am sure."

She noted that the rubdown and she were getting him excited. She was counting on the fact that the touching would ignite passion and desire. The second hour passed by as he gently started at her neck and touched the personal areas of her body. When he got to the legs, she spread her legs so he could rub them down easier.

As he backed up to the end of the bed to do her feet, she said with desire, "Gently make love to me." He looked into her eyes, and he let his desire build. The passion—a strong, gentle thing—took them through the night.

The baby cried, and they were both awake. She turned to him and said, "My turn." He watched her get her robe and walk to the nursery. He then followed to see if she needed help. She turned on_the night-light and set up the changing table and gently changed Amanda. He marveled at her efficiency and noted her health after making love. She decided to feed the baby, so he asked her if she would like some coffee.

He turned on the coffeepot, waited, and then made two cups. She met him in the hall and said quietly, "Living room." They sat on the couch and talked about how she was feeling, and then they turned the conversation to work. He talked about the latest doings and said her shift team inquired after her and the baby and wanted to know when the baby shower would be.

Desire and passion still moved them through the night as they gently kissed.

He asked her to not set the alarm clock as he held her but to allow them to wake up by their desire to be about. She laid her head on his chest while she was enfolded by his arms. They gently moved from one dream to the next.

At 0550 hours, he watched as he tried to remember when he last held her. He stretched out his senses and heard the faint sounds of pots and pans as they were moved about. He knew she took care and was healthy enough. Maybe it was time to schedule the baby shower and take her shopping. He got up to shower and dress. Singing the blues, he began his day properly.

Refreshed and invigorated, he looked at her with fresh eyes. *Happy she is*, he thought. He asked her how she was feeling, and since she had already done a systemic review, she told him by the numbers. He kissed her and told her he was content and happy at how well she was doing. He looked at the breakfast: egg casserole, fried mashed potatoes, sausages, and biscuits. And he sat down and waited for the plates to be made up.

The morning air permeated the house as the nurse was let in by the security guard. She saw the dishes, and worry blossomed in her eyes, but there was no pain in Sarita's eyes. So she asked for a plate and decided to go talk to the security guard. She thought he might need a nurse.

The morning sky lightened, and they could now see from the window the outer edge of the sun. It was going to be a beautiful day.

Sarita felt her energy and decided to check on Amanda. The afternoon would be fine for a visit to her mom's house. The baby was fine sleeping with a selection of country music and rhythm and blues. She went and sat on her bed. Joseph asked her if she was all right. She said, "There is no pain. I just am a little tired." He suggested she nap for a while, and he would fix dinner.

She hugged him and moved up the bed to lay down, and as he watched her, she drifted off. He reported she was just getting some more rest—nothing to worry about. He went into the kitchen and looked through the groceries for something to make. He decided he had the ingredients to make Norwegian Meatball Stew.

He pulled the ingredients out and put them on the table. The guard said he would do the breakfast dishes. Carol said she would prep some of the vegetables. That left him with the roast beef and making the white sauce that made up the stew. The time passed as the meat and vegetables cooked. Sarita came into the kitchen to see what was cooking and took over making the white sauce.

Joseph set the table since Carol and the guard were done with their tasks. Sarita then had him cut the meat and put it in the pot with the white sauce and cooked vegetables. It would be an early dinner, but Sarita did not mind. She could spend more time at her mom's.

The Command Post wanted to sack an IDS/IDC site, so Joseph told them to bring the unit up to speed and prepare the unit for action. He said he would be in at approximately 1400 to 1500 hours.

The time passed quietly as everyone ate the stew. The guard told Carol it was her turn to do the dishes, making sure Sarita would not just up and do them herself. Joseph agreed, so the guard got a little look. She put herself on it though, so she would be ready to accompany her when she upped and decided to leave because Joseph would let Sarita do so.

She prepared in leisure to give Carol time to do the dishes. Joseph brought the bassinet out and put it in the car. He then decided to put the diaper bag in the car, but Carol insisted on carrying it with her. The drive over was unhurried, and traffic was light. Sarita told the group that the women had to be left alone while they talked of babies.

Her mom had definite ideas of what a healthy woman could do, so when she greeted her daughter, she grilled her about her health and her activities. She thought of how she determined she was strong enough and, when the ladies were in the kitchen, told her mom about the baby oil.

Her mom heartily agreed then that she was strong enough to have a cooking lesson and share in the making for the experience. The day passed quickly as the ladies chatted about the unit and its needs. Christy came up, and her mom called Mums and mentioned that she might need a wedding planner and if she was busy. Sarita's mom volunteered herself.

Joseph met with the unit in the briefing room. They were rested and ready for duty. The cause was propagation of urban violence. The investigators learned select families were encouraging their children to do violence and terrorize people in the neighborhood around the ice skating rink. They had pictures of the perpetrators, recorded conversations, and eyewitness affidavits from recon witnessing the carrying out of planned activities as well as illegal drug sales and use as incentives to commit crimes.

Joseph authorized two teams with two-man buddy teams to target all those in direct long-term conspiracy. The teams would be ready to go at 0200 hours and should be done and back in standby mode by 0400 hours. Hopefully, this would discourage the children before they got into rebellion any deeper by scaring them enough they might quit.

The status boards were recording the counting of the numbers of violent ick de' mons; and some of those, for various reasons of active acts of violence, were coming to a threshold of thought where interdiction might be necessary.

He ordered investigations to pinpoint meeting points so they could be monitored more effectively, the criminal elements. He then reorganized his to-do list at his desk so that he could take care of issues in a timely manner. He then did the most urgent and left some to do when he and William were in the next day.

He then called the command post and said he was on his way to pick up his wife.

The retrieval was difficult because they let her walk around and cook. She looked at him, and they both knew she now had to be at home and rest up again.

Carol did a new set of measurements on the baby and determined the baby scored well on all scales. She then gave Sarita a physical in the nursery to ascertain her health, which was quite embarrassing. She then called it in to the hospital to get the administrative review process for her early release closed out.

Sarita was mortified that everyone heard and it was reported over the phone. Carol told her it was part of the job, but she apologized for her feeling mortified about the idea.

Joseph would commiserate with her when the nurse left. He knew she needed a hug. So he asked her since the baby was sleeping, whether she would rest for a while. She agreed. He talked with her while she was resting until she fell asleep. Carol was gone by the time she awoke.

He stopped her in the hallway and held her. He asked if she was all right. She thought about agreeing with the doctor to the intrusive physical, and she adjusted to the doing of it. She hugged him back and said she was all right.

They had a couple hours, so they took over their couch. She filled him in about Christy and the latest developments, and he told her about interdiction to date. They then talked about light shopping for music the next day. They discussed the latest band while the guard sat in the kitchen.

At 2000 hours, they ate popcorn and watched *My Fair Lady*. The process was entertaining and sometimes humorous. They then went to bed at 2200 hours. She decided to give him a back rub with baby oil, and they decided they were not so tired after all.

She awoke at 0530 refreshed and energized. She struggled out of bed and then kissed him. She realized she had the kitchen to herself again, so she happily cooked oatmeal and omelets and sausages for her man. She collected the eggs and other ingredients for four. Then she had some coffee and waited for her man to awaken.

He was getting used to her leaving him when he was dreaming. The experiences augmented his understanding to help him develop his love for her. He talked of his angst until she finally understood his inner conflict. She kissed him and told him that for the sharing, she had learned another lesson and now had another reason to love him more.

"Ze crem de la crem in dinea." Breakfast was another feast to satisfy the heart and soul of a man. It was another egg concoction that his mother made. She was developing as a woman and a chef. His mother, studious as she was, took years in developing the recipe and the taste. He told her he was pleased, and she smiled with strength. She knew he was truthful and honest, and she also knew she deserved the praise.

Amanda was showing she was a happy child and enjoyed her family. She adjusted well to rest and play. Both parents took time to touch and talk to her. It is important that parents do, so the child learns to interpret language and learn to speak as early as possible. Joseph tried to get her interested in listening to stories about fishing.

Sarita pointed out Amanda had a tendency to fall asleep when he talked of fishing. She then spent a half an hour talking to Amanda about cooking. She struggled noticeably to stay awake. Joseph decided he would save the fish stories for when she needed them, and they needed her to have a nap.

Instead, he told her stories about the unit and interdiction. This seemed to keep her attention. Sarita noted that for her future training endeavors. She would train her as an operations agent, she decided.

The nurse was watching the demonstration, and she realized this was something she could do for her children. She thanked Sarita for the lesson. Sarita seemed to be more at ease around the nurse. The shopping trip was outlined, and the nurse agreed she could be escorted by the security guard while they were in the music store in the mall.

Carol told the security guard she wanted seven children. He looked at her and said six. She said, "Deal, and by the way, what is your name?" He told her, and she told him her name and address and told him not to be shy about showing up. Sarita and Joseph smiled.

Another love would blossom, and peace would expand its boundaries.

The music selection was three aisles of different music. They found their sections and reviewed the latest releases. Then they picked out what they liked and got together to exchange the CDs. They then listened to each other's music and picked the music they could listen to on a long-term basis. Carol noted the process and asked Romeo if he would be so considerate. He said he could work on it when the time came.

She seemed to come alive with the respect and consideration Joseph gave her. She seemed to be able to walk around longer without being tired. Carol would put that in her report.

The afternoon was scheduled, so they stopped at One Potato Two. And she told Joseph she was hungry, so he told the cashier he wanted four. She chose her toppings, and then he did. They found a chair and waited for the guard and Carol to finish their order. The meal conversation centered around Amanda. Sarita crushed up part cream and part potato and blew on it. She then wiped Amanda's lips with the mixture.

Carol asked her why she did that. She said, "My mom told me it helps children to learn to digest regular foods and helps them be not so finicky during the baby food times of their life." Amanda had made a face and proceeded to digest the cream mixture while Carol and the guard took a mental note to remember the lesson.

William and his wife were waiting on the couch in his office, so they took the chairs. The nurse was with the guard meeting his unit. The kitchen staff brought up Turkey and Cheese sandwiches for William and his wife and coffee for four.

William opened up Donald's OJT records of skills and tasks he was being introduced to. The conversation started to wane around 1700 hours, and the men started to talk about the proposed three-day fishing trip they were going to take in the fall. The women were going to come along, but they did not want to linger on the details too long, so at 1730 hours, they asked their men to call each other to finish out the details.

The air was warm, so Sarita and the rest rolled down the windows to take in the fresh air on the way home. September turned out to be a fine month.

Dinner was pork chops and mashed potatoes. The pork was tender, and Sarita mashed some and mixed it with the mashed potatoes she had made. Amanda decided she liked the taste. So Sarita tried beans. The beans did not go over too well.

The conversation after dinner revolved around Donald's training as Sarita nursed Amanda. The issue was when to start a child's education. Joseph addressed Amanda and asked her if she liked being educated. She gurgled happily, and Sarita marked that down in her heart.

At 2000 hours, they put Amanda in her crib and turned on the CD player. Amanda stared at the mobile happily enough, so they quietly left her to her listening environment. They made coffee and decided to talk on the couch.

He told her that games were important to play with the child. He also said talking to them about their needs helped them define a language in which they can profitably speak of their needs. She thought about the truths he learned from his parents, and she thanked God for his parents' love. She leaned on him, and he held her as they listened to the same music Amanda listened to.

They looked in on Amanda from the hallway. Children sense when parents are in their room. She looked at her daughter and thought to her their love. She stirred in her sleep, and so they moved into the bedroom.

Sarita told him she had a romance novel that talked about things she would like to do. She read to him until he decided to turn out the light and kiss her. They moved in sync through the evening.

When they were done, they decided to get some ham and cheese sandwiches. On the way to the kitchen, she asked him if he liked liverwurst and cheddar cheese as a combination. He said yes. She made a mental note to get some next time they went shopping.

The television was playing Errol Flynn sailor movies through the night. She said she would like to see a couple of the movies. He got two blankets while she went to the kitchen and got some cans of Mountain Dew. They would stay up as late as possible.

On Friday, two guards showed up at 0600 hours instead of one. The nurse showed up at 0800 hours and said she recommended they only go skating for an hour. The rink was fully open and playing country music as they skated. She had to admit after an hour and a half that she was getting tired, so Joseph took her home and she went to bed.

Carol was worried about Sarita. Joseph reassured her she only needed rest, and then she would cook dinner. Carol went into the kitchen and got out the ingredients to make spaghetti. She did not want her charge overdoing it.

Amanda was in fine fettle, and they put her on a blanket in the living room as they talked. She was working on turning over. Joseph told Amanda as he put the toys down, "It might be a while before you can turn over, but the toys are yours." She followed the toys with her eyes, then they disappeared as he placed them on the blanket.

Sitting with his wife, they watched Amanda's endeavor. The time passed peacefully until Amanda got hungry. She fussed a little then started crying. Sarita asked him to put up with Amanda's crying so she would learn to wait. So he waited a minute or two, and then Sarita told him he could calm Amanda.

After Amanda's dinner, she slept for a little while, so they did likewise on the couch. When she was up, Sarita wanted to be up. When she was sleeping, Sarita wanted a nap as well if possible. She told Joseph that when Amanda was trained in, it would be in four-hour blocks of time first. He filed that away in his mind so he would not interfere in Amanda's training.

Dinner was hot dogs and potato chips. Amanda did not like creamed potato chips, but the bread and then the hotdog went down well. The nurse took a bite of her hot dog and looked in the bassinet to see Amanda's response. She seemed to be happy with the taste of food she was getting.

She noted Sarita's health and realized she was good to go. Her shift would end at 1630 hours; and Steve Bargo, the guard, was going to take her out negotiating while they went skating. She knew he was interested in her. He kept saying nice things to her about her, and he tried to help her here and there.

Games were on their list to buy, and Joseph thought Saturday would be fine. They would also go to the command post and see what his dad and the unit had accomplished. The day was filled with the sounds of new music, and Sarita was separating the new songs onto an additional playlist. He got to be the critic and find out later what the playlist sounded like.

Amanda was another critic, and she would cry a little if she did not like the song. Sarita talked to her about the music. The child was being taught well, and he told Sarita so. After a while, Sarita said she was through playing CDs for a while, so she said everyone needed a nap. The music was even too much for Joseph, and he knew his head was nodding a little.

The bedroom beckoned. "Comfort and peace," it said.

Another day done and gone, she thought as she laid Amanda down for a nap. She prayed she had done well. Her husband waited to show his appreciation by hugging her as he drifted off to sleep. In his arms, she reviewed what she would like to teach Amanda. She thought about it for a while before she drifted off to sleep.

The CD stopped playing, and the silence filled the house. Amanda amused herself for a while but missed the music that kept her company. She started to cry, knowing that that would bring Mom and then usually Dad.

Mom heard her and waited two minutes to see if she would adjust. She then got up and went to check on Amanda. It was not time for a feeding, so she checked her diaper. The diaper was dry so she tried comforting her, and she was only partially comforted.

Joseph, trying to help out, turned on the CD player, and like magic, Amanda quieted down. They figured in short order the music comforted Amanda and she relied on it. They went into the kitchen and talked about it for a while.

Since they were both up, he told her of the latest things the unit was doing like who was on leave. They even talked about promotions and decorations. The standards for promotions and decorations were also discussed.

At 2300 hours, they decided to get some more sleep. Amanda would be up in an hour. The night slipped away as they dreamed their dreams. At 0012 hours, Amanda was up and wanted to be played with. Sarita, tired as she was, did not mind. A half hour later, she was fed and back in bed. Amanda reset the CD and returned to the land of dreams with her husband. Her tired mind noted he had not worried about her enough to get up after her. That made her feel glad.

Rested, she wondered why she awoke. She felt perfectly fine. She turned to the clock and realized it was five minutes to 0600 hours. She then realized it was Saturday, her turn to sleep in. She knew she still had some adjustments to make. As she thought about Saturday, she discovered she had woken a hungry man.

His ministrations were nice, so she reached out and shut the alarm clock and decided to go with the tide. It was pleasant enough. His desire became palpable as he came more fully awake; her passion stirred and she gave it wings.

The time disappeared in the desire of his hands, and they gave in to their desires in the dark of the morn. Sated, the passion was still there, and they kept kissing tenderly.

She wanted to write the book about their love. It was passion and desire at times. At others, respect and consideration reigned in their emotions. The ideal almost-heaven life gave her profound joy.

Satisfying one of her loves, she felt the other start to call. She waited two minutes and then told Amanda it was Saturday—she should sleep in. She fed Amanda after cleaning her. She then checked to see how much time was left on the CD and went to get another. She thought the one on love songs would give her daughter something to think about.

She went to the kitchen for some coffee and said hi to the new guard. She wondered if they had been overheard. The coffee was on, so she decided to bring Joseph a cup. He would appreciate being woken to the smell.

He was sitting up in the bed when she came into the bedroom. She said she was disappointed she could not wake him up. He smiled and said that was a nice thought. He then said, "I am living in a very nice dream." She smiled and said she thought the same way.

Sarita asked him what time they were going in. The briefing was scheduled for 0900 hours. "If we get there early, we can go up to my office and let Amanda experience the ambience of the unit." She thought the idea was a nice one. He said, "We need to buy another bassinet for the office." She agreed and said, "I will shower first."

Breakfast was raisin bran and oranges. The guards did not mind eating twice. Amanda took to the raisin bran but not the taste of the orange. Sarita encouraged her daughter to reconsider because oranges were a part of a healthy diet.

They left an hour early because they were ready. The drive was a little cold, but Joseph had left the warming blanket in the back seat, so that worked out. They pulled into the parking lot; Sarita grabbed Amanda, and Joseph carried the warming blanket as they proceeded to his office.

Amanda and her toys were placed in front of the desk, and Sarita took one of the closer chairs. Joseph talked over the supply requisitions. The unit needed at times more bullets and new chairs. She asked, "How often did he replace the chairs?" He replied, "A little after the expected life span of the chair, which was five years for some."

He said, "The people here treat the place with respect. Sometimes there are mishaps though, and then we deal with those on a case-by-case basis." She then asked about the bullets. He said, "We project the possible usage three months out and buy the bullets ahead of time to ensure we have enough ammunition."

He went on to say that procurement of weapons and ammunition takes about two to three months. "The weapons are sometimes lost in a firefight, and they disappear for a variety of reasons. We fill out a lost equipment report and use the storage weapons in the meantime until we get a replacement." She looked at him. He continued, "Storage weapons are used for extra troops that we need to issue hand weapons to."

Then they rested for a while because he was out of reports and requisitions and she was out of questions. Both were temporary conditions. At 0850 hours, they walked over to the briefing room. Amanda, a quiet baby, was even quieter.

She thought Amanda would start crying after a while, especially with all the briefers coming and going, but instead she listened until she fell asleep again. It seemed this was the ideal arena of thought for her. Even her busy husband looked at Amanda once in a while and wondered why she listened so intently.

The units only got in a few scuffles, all told. He was relieved. The teams found every one where recon and investigations said they would be. They only suffered a few embarrassing bruises. Ammunition expenditures were nominal as expected, and equipment recovery was almost 100 percent.

The net effect would be monitored over the next month to see if the older teens would give up their terroristic activities. The drug dealers were noted for their houses, and Operations wanted to hit them Tuesday if possible.

The civil side was not affected during the unit's actions. There were enough vehicles to go around. Then the brief slowly finished up with no status changes for equipment and supply. They returned to his office after the brief.

Joseph said to Sarita, "Why don't you leave the blanket and the toys here on a shelf for future visits? We can go shopping for more when we leave." She agreed it was a good idea when she folded the warming blanket. She found a fairly empty shelf and put the toys up. She asked him if she could leave some changing clothes. He said, "Yes, there is a closet in the little room."

He thought his wife deserved to have the perk. Having clothes here would make it easier on her mind. He thought of the change to his life again, and he realized he did not mind. The day was upon him, and he prayed he make the right decisions.

The store was just fifteen minutes away, and they decided to buy some stock in diapers and such for the office. She told him what was not used could be used by the next. He agreed and paid for the perk out of his own funds.

They put the bassinet and supplies in the trunk and headed home. It was a little cool, so the extra half blankets came in handy. While driving, they talked about Amanda's reaction to the office and to the briefing room. He said she could have a copy of his own OJT records so she would know what to brief Amanda on.

She was tired, so Sarita talked to her to keep her up so they all could have a nap. They wondered when she would be able to crawl and then speak. They discussed their ideas based on the thinking of the pace she was developing. Sarita then told Joseph of some of her ideas on introducing the child to the babysitting environment.

He told her he had already talked to his dad and mom, and they said they would think about babysitting in part. Maybe Hope could babysit until 2200 hours. She thought it a safer idea to keep the babysitting in the family.

The morning nap was realized in part because they could not keep Amanda up the whole way home. She was up again a half hour after they had laid down. So they took her to the living room and Sarita Ordered some Errol Flynn movies from Netflix.

The conversation was sporadic as they laid down to rest while watching the movies. She talked to him about her sister's marriages and her brothers who were still single. He asked her questions for a while until he drifted off. She snuggled into him and enjoyed the movie.

This one was about hunting down privateers who were also accused of piracy. She thought about her mother, who might like some of the recipes she picked up. She had grandchildren but not from her sons. She prayed about the idea and drifted off. When Joseph awoke, he had to go to the bathroom, and as he passed Amanda, he noticed she was on her stomach.

He realized he missed her endeavor and told her he was sorry he missed that endeavor. A little sad, he continued on the way to the bathroom. Sarita stirred and noticed and turned her daughter over so she could breathe better.

The next movie was on, so she got two cups of coffee and prepared to settle in again. He came from the bathroom, and she waited until he sat and then she gave him a cup of coffee and then sat close to him. He adjusted and noticed Amanda trying to turn over again and smiled.

Sarita noticed what he was looking at and said, "She will achieve again." He sipped his coffee and nodded in agreement. He looked at the television and said to Sarita, "Where are we in relation to the movie?" She explained the scenes up to the present one. He realized Amanda might not have gotten some of her interests from him.

He told Sarita, "You like action movies once in a while. Your daughter is just like you in that way. When she becomes a Colonel, you can be proud of her." She thought about her remembering all the Errol Flynn movie scenes she knew and realized she liked a little action with her romance. She was just worried that her daughter liked action a lot and would be romantic once in a while. She told Joseph so.

He said a little reminder once in a while to have a little romance in her life would help her a lot. Sarita thought about Amanda's need and decided to talk to her about it from time to time.

They watched the rest of the movie in silence. When she was done with her coffee cup, she moved closer to Joseph and leaned on him. Her touch was nice, and he put his arm around her as he drank his coffee.

The afternoon was whiled away as they watched old movies. Amanda was on her stomach again when they noticed her. She seemed content, so Sarita gave her five minutes to see if she would try moving. Then she told her it was changing time. Joseph went for coffee for two. She decided to feed her daughter in the living room.

Joseph took some of his coffee and put it on her lips. She seemed happy enough, so Sarita told Joseph later. She wanted to feed the baby first before Amanda started asking for more coffee.

The command post called and said the investigators were on their way to the suspect's area and they would do recon. He told them to take care. He told Sarita and she nodded. She did not like those that dealt in drugs too much. She had to deal with some in high school that were spastic, violent snots.

He said, "Tell me a story." She talked about a character named Bill that proffered her some drugs. She would not accept the free drugs, so he went from persuasion to being violently minded and back again for quite a while until her friends came up to her and then he got mad. After that, he acted like a petulant snot. Joseph asked her if she knew what happened to him. She said she did not know.

He told her they usually net with conspiracy, end up in jail, or some of them quit. There were a few here and there in his life, and there were some that sold drugs while he went to College. Then there were quite a few on the beach and in the parking lot. They were always a danger.

The morning passed by, and they remembered they missed church. Sarita felt like Joseph, so they planned on attending the late service at 1900 hours. They even talked to Amanda and told her it was not her fault.

Dinner was hamburgers and baked potatoes like One Potato Two. They both spent time in the kitchen, filling with the toppings little bowls with lids Sarita had. Amanda seemed to be focusing better, and that gladdened their hearts. They filled the bowls while the potatoes baked. They then spent the time waiting talking to Amanda about what they thought was important to know. She got an earful about back rubs with baby oil. Sarita said she bought some baby oil for her.

At dinnertime, they creamed some more potatoes and both spent a little time feeding her the mixture. She was taking to it really well. She asked him if he needed to go in when they interdicted the drug dealers. He said if there were only one or two people no. The command post would tell him if there was a need.

The next four hours of the day were spent reading. Sarita read her book to Amanda. Joseph told her he admired how she had trained her voice. He picked up a new biography as the time drifted away.

An hour before church, she changed and fed Amanda. Then they changed for church. They decided to arrive early. She decided to spend time with the ladies in the nursery, and he spent time talking to the ushers until the 1800 hours service was over.

The service was on the Judgement proper and what to expect for both saved and lost souls. The ideas were organized very well and compelling. They talked about the service on the way home.

Sarita put Amanda to bed and said they had to finish the playlist review for her so she had new ideas to think about now and then. He got some coffee, and she got out the CDs they had not gone through yet. The hours passed by, and they finally finished the last playlist.

She said she now had a desire to read to him. She smiled and said she might grow hungry but was not sure. She read from the romance novels while he rubbed her feet. On page 151, she read the action sequence twice and asked him if he was hungry.

The morning brought Sarita awake with a strong, compelling voice. Her daughter was calling her. She turned off the alarm clock and went to see her daughter. She was fine. Sarita chided Amanda for calling her for nothing. She then told her should call if was in danger, was wet, was or hungry. She then told her she could call Dad if she needed something.

Returning to bed, she figured she had fifteen minutes for a light rest. Moving closer, she put her arms around her husband and closed her eyes. The alarm clock said 0600 hours. She had to be about, so she kissed him and went and took care of Amanda.

He showered and dressed and met him in the kitchen. She asked him what he wanted for breakfast. He said two egg and cheese sandwiches. She made him two and one for herself. He then asked her if he needed any shopping done. She said she had enough for the commander's call that night.

He thought about the setup and thought he could remember the design for tables and chairs. He then asked her if she had enough help. She said William's wife and two daughters and Hope and her mother would help out on this one. He thought of twenty-five to thirty guests and figured they could handle it.

The morning passed in chitchat as they talked to Amanda about not bragging about her abilities. Some people, when they hear about a child, want to abuse the gift, the child, or both. Sarita looked at her fear when they explained that to Amanda. She thought about Amanda's birth in a new light. She had wanted to leave the hospital before they could typify her daughter. Now she knew part of the reason why.

She reminded him of how uncomfortable the hospital was; they just did not know why. He called the command post and said, "Remind me when I get in the application of the specialty of Amanda." They said they would write down in the log and remind him next Monday when he got in. He thought some dangers were more innocuous than others. Some dangers were difficult to see.

He told her he had to see operational labor hours for contracts and said it would take a while. He asked her if she wanted to come into the unit with him. She looked in his eyes and agreed. They moved slowly but surely to the door and then to the car. The drive in was silent as Amanda fussed.

They called investigations to meet them in his office when he was in the building. The ride up the elevator was tense, but he told her now she could talk. She asked how good the building's shielding was. He said the very best. He explained about electronic, passive, and energy shielding that was designed into the building.

She listened as they entered the office. She got out the baby blanket and Amanda's toys and watched her eyes and body follow the toys as she put them down. He turned the CD player on low for her. The time was taken to think about the latent danger he was going to put investigations onto finding.

They appeared with an open mind. When they were seated, he asked Sarita to explain. The time moved on as she recounted her story from arrival to departure. Then the questions began for a better view of the problem. They were used to such investigations. When they were satisfied they knew all they could, they asked their commander to define the scope of their investigation.

They said it would be an hour before the house was cleared and they should sit tight until the investigators returned.

He then had the Captain of Security phoned to come to his office. He wanted the house watched and an eye kept on the child for the next month. Sarita realized the extra security was necessary but realized her heating budget would be surpassed by all the people coming and going.

The wicked mind, she knew, was noxious. She asked Joseph if they could read the hospital personnel. He said, "Over the next month, it will be done. The general review will be started with those you met in the course of your stay then expand to the rest of the personnel in the hospital including temporary hires."

She asked if she could get some coffee and said she could call down for two hearty meals as well. He then asked for a courier and wrote up his request for the file of hospital personnel for investigations. Then he called down to the command post and asked the Captain to come upstairs.

That done, he greeted the courier and sent him off to Robert's house with the package. He then greeted the command post watch officer and explained his initial call. He wanted a status board set up to monitor investigations. "Call it Maternity." Then he released the officer to proceed with the mission.

Security sent up a female named Sarah. He introduced Sarah Estes to his wife. She would babysit the child for the duration. Sarita and Sarah then started negotiating over turf while Joseph relieved himself. He looked at her with sympathy, and Sarah took her place against the wall, scanning for threats like their other security guard.

The hour stretched to two as investigations found one problem after another. There was a multitude of taps in the area they had to look at. As they identified the sender and monitored the house, they realized they had more than one problem.

He recommended Sarita put Amanda in the bassinet in the ready room so she could sleep. Sarah went first to establish protocol and then Sarita with the baby. The command post was to bring team 3 up on alert for when they fixed the house local for where the intercepts were going to.

Following communications lines was difficult but not impossible. The investigators that were dispatched to the house quietly labeled the sites that were bugged and then they made sure they identified each signal. The monitoring team finally pinpointed the house and went in at 0300 hours to take a look at the building. They were due back at 0400 hours and their report submitted by 0430 hours.

The investigations team at the house was notified by communications to one of their vans at the house as to when they were to seize the bugs. This would be in conjunction with the taking of the house the criminals were using.

Sarita started to doze, and Joseph told her he would wake her at 0530 hours if she wanted to rest. The bed seemed nice, so she went into his ready room and lay down.

He talked to the Captain of the watch over operational issues. He said the unit was ready, and he recommended calling up team 4 and 5 with a warning order that return fire from their houses was more than possible. Joseph gave his authorization as Robert entered the room.

The Captain left and Robert took his chair. He said, "What have you got?" Joseph told him what investigations came up with and the dispatch of team 3 to their departure point. They were sure the sight was only communications for illegal wire taps. The communication sites directions would give a fuller intent picture as to what they plan to do with the information.

Robert said to Joseph, "When do you want the FBI notified?" He said, "When the capture team or teams are neutralized." "What about hiring and planning?" "The FBI can get them once they're notified." Robert agreed and asked if he could see the baby. Joseph said, "Amanda is in the bassinet in the ready room."

Robert said, "Amanda is already a blessing to the State and to the Country, so I will give her my blessing in turn." Joseph knew Robert had a great love for his children, so he accompanied Robert to his ready room. Sarah opened the door for Robert. He walked in and apologized to Sarita for waking her then he talked to Amanda about debts, duties, and obligations. He said he has a gift for her and blessed her with a touch to her forehead. Amanda quieted down, but you could see she was thinking about the gift.

Robert then bid all a good night and a good day.

At 0500 hours, team 3 received their final briefing and headed out to their departure point. They were to hit the house as fast as they could at 0530 hours. They were to terminate all with extreme prejudice. Investigations would depart at 0530 hours, arrive at the site, and begin their review of material found.

Teams 4 and 5 began their final briefings for their mission. When the site was found for the teams that did the kidnapping, they were to execute with extreme prejudice as well.

Sarita refreshed herself in the bathroom and took a seat next to Joseph's desk. He did not seem to be bent on returning to their home yet. She asked him, "How much longer?" and he said, "About 0700 hours should tell the outcome on the grab teams, and then Robert will notify the FBI." She asked him if he wanted breakfast, and he said 0600 hours.

She looked at the clock and decided she was not yet hungry enough either. He asked her if she was hungry. She said no. The teams were in motion, and there was nothing to do but wait. He told her she was very talented in the department of perceptions, and he appreciated her for it because it saved many people physical emotional loss. She smiled and thanked him.

She knew her baby was one of those lives she saved. This helped her get over the temporary loss of her and her husband's home as well as the knowing the house now needed repairs where the electronic wires were.

She asked him, "Who will repair the damage to the house?" He smiled and said, "We do." She smiled back and thinks repairing the damage will be educational, if not fun. She told him she was willing to learn.

Breakfast was brought up for five. Investigations had their brief to do. She decided to feed Amanda in the ready room and then smush some eggs for her. The investigators waited while she fed Amanda. The houses were discovered in short order, and the Watch Commander had ordered teams 4 and 5 in to execute the kidnappers.

The list of names and copies of the evidence was sent to the local FBI field office. Robert had called Washington, and the wheels were rolling. They response force was briefed to stand to post, and all additional duties were cancelled just in case the planners or hiring people wanted to retaliate.

Joseph determined he did all he could do, and with four security guards, his family was probably safe enough. He decided that shopping today would be out of the question just in case one of the criminals decided they had an opportunity. He explained this to Sarita, who stood, and then said, "We can go now then?" He closed his planner and said yes.

The sky had plenty of light, and the day was warming.

Joseph M. Due, September 24, 2016

Crime Spree

The whine from the jail cell was in several parts; part a saying the burden they would now bear in the way of prison term earned was too much, and part b saying they were betrayed by their buddies and did not know what their buddies were actually up to. There were so many categories that the sheriffs wished the police had not brought them in.

Across town police donned civilian garb and took to five houses. They would do 12 on and 12 hours off for the duration. As long as one was up they could rest in turn. They were on their lunch breaks outside for site time to let the people know they were still open for business.

For three days they waited for criminals who had not known to come on by. The police got about another 20 criminals all told before they put up the yellow crime scene tape on the houses.

The ATF were conducting full interviews for those that would accept an interview. All they had to do was tell the truth about the crimes they committed to include illegal weapons and drugs.

As the newly caught came in they were double billed with the other criminals. The net was spreading its manpower to get as many of the criminals as it could.

Joseph M. Due 8 October 2016

Lieutenant D. Smith

Precious are the times when love manifests in desire and passion. Lt. Debra Smith thought she might at times be a wishy-washy warrior. She loved reading statements like this and imagining how they would work for her in her love life.

She believed her first great love was God and Country and put endeavor into showing and proving what her first great love is. On the other hand, book comments like "Her bosom beat to the desire of her man and the passion flared" occupied a part of her time to the point of total embarrassment.

Her friend and she would do night land navigation, and she was perusing the Army makeup used to break up a person's facial outline. She bought one set for Brenda and one for herself. She knew her friend would pay her back and, better yet, look out for her needs when she was at a store.

She then looked at the different types of combat boots to see if she found a pair that would help her feet out better. She thought about the webbed ones that allowed air and water in and out, and she tried on a pair. She would give them a trial run, she thought.

Then she looked at notepads and minipens for her and Brenda's improved note-taking ability. She bought six pens and notepads—one for each uniform so they would not forget. Then she purchased colored lenses for their flashlights and four sets of batteries.

Joseph M. Due, October 19, 2016

Loves Beginning

The lilies reminded her of the beauty of life—how precious that life can be. It also provided a fragrance that was pleasing to her. She thought about writing her memoirs, but that was not her yet. Sarita believed someday she might write of her love in depth, but for now, she could not bring herself to do so.

Joseph did not write memoirs exactly. He wrote stories about those people and things that he loved. She knew the children would remember her through association and because of those beautiful stories of her that Joseph had written, and he said he would write more because he had a great love for her.

She knew not what their love would turn into when they parted the veil. She did know he would always love and care for her. She also knew she would always love him. She thought of all her loves, including her children, and thanked God as she numbered each love He had provided for her.

She rested, and heaven called her name.

Joseph M. Due, October 13, 2016

Memories

The memories of love are strong in those that love.

Amanda was cognitive of many things in her childhood, and all of them were complimentary to her mission purpose in life. Her intent was grown, refined, and honed so that she could equitably stand with the best of the best.

Dana Carne, now Dana Stevens, grew her love as well—just in a different manner. She also learned what it took to be a Mums like her mother. Her contributions in her family equitably shone forth.

Mark, though not born to do interdiction, was part of the family and the greater family of the Army. He learned his mission purpose well. He had done well for his people.

Joseph said and wrote these things above in reflections on the love of God given to mankind in their days.

Joseph M. Due, October 6, 2016

440

Combat Engineering Battalion

For when there seemed to be no hope, there was thought and then prayer. For when the tidal waves seemed to preclude anyone hanging ten, there was the moment when the energy of the storm passed and opportunities abounded if one was prepared.

So it is with every interdiction of violent waves of malignant hate. Mums told these ideas in thought and deed every step of the way. She hanged ten with her man to her children and grandchildren.

Mark's confidence navigating the seas of disappointment in part was sustained by the knowing of such things. Though he did not surf, he learned to hang ten.

His hopes for honor graduate at West Point faded away in the light of the morning as well as his hopes to be posted closer to home with the Thirty-Third Combat Engineering Battalion (CEB). God rewards love with love though, and Alice Delores Franks married him in formal ceremony and in heart.

Joseph ruminated about his children in the closing of his life, grateful they all joined the greater family, enabling each individual freedom of choice and times of peace to choose wisely. He thanked God for each one and asked God to bless the family as he was wont.

Joseph M. Due, October 5, 2016

Pause

The rhythm of the day can stop when God is willing for a short time. Gen. Donald Carne thought about the construct in which man's will can affect time. He remembered conversations in which he needed a pause to collect his thoughts, and to his surprise, the time was there for him. Then sometimes he knew he needed the time, and time felt his will and paused for a while.

After a while, there were key times in battle in which the rhythm of the battle needed to change, and as he prayed and stretched forth his will, he could, to a little degree, affect the flow of time for his people's sake.

He turned to the training schedule for the Fifteenth CID and thought about the flow of training. For the unit, he pulled out a piece of paper and a pen and started to write down a flow of training that might be better suited for their training needs than that which they already had.

He called in Gen. Amanda Carne to discuss the key ideas because she had a different type of insight into the training issues than he did. She reported as ordered and then took her seat. The advent of the training she could imagine in her sleep. They worked out a recommendation for training, and then he gave it to her to send out.

Lunch was steak au jus, rice pilaf, and assorted vegetables. They then turned their considerable talent to helping the Eighteenth CID.

Joseph M. Due, October 15, 2016

Memorial

Lilies adorned her hair and were placed around the coffin. The backdrop had lily plants in great abundance. One was given to each family as a memory of her and the hope they would remember her contributions to the family.

Joseph and family took turns for being in attendance the three days as she was shown in estate with the story lines written by the children and those who knew her best. The diner was festooned with lilies as well, and they served all her favorite foods for the three days they allowed her to be seen.

The memorial service was on the hope of the resurrection, and testimonials were given after the service. The people came from all over the States to say their goodbyes. The afternoon and supper meals at the diner were roast beef au jus, carrots, and mashed potatoes.

Joseph M. Due, October 6, 2016

Made in the USA
Middletown, DE
07 December 2022

17489113R00274